CARNAL WEAPON

D1738597

PETER HOFFMANN

First published by Dog Ear Publishing
4010 W. 86th Street, Ste H
Indianapolis, IN 46268
www.dogearpublishing.net

ISBN: 978-160844-059-7

This book is printed on acid-free paper.

Printed in the United States of America

For
Kathy and Pearse

Acknowledgements

Special thanks to Stephen A. Davies, Molly E.K. McGrath, Susan Brean, Alice Rosengard, Jonny Podell, Izabelle Miko and Charles Salzberg. Your honest critiques helped make the manuscript shine.

PROLOGUE

1942

The squadron of Zeros passed low, and the battalion greeted their pitch plummeting drone with a hearty "Banzai." Major Hiroshi Nishimura mounted the steps of the sacred terrace and reached for the handle of his sword. When he turned to review his soldiers standing in rigid formation before a metropolis of temples spread across the Bagan plain, emotion relaxed his stern gaze and froze his tongue. This victory belonged to the Emperor and his divine ancestors. Was a soldier nothing more than their servant? Yes he was, and it was his privilege to die for them. Let nothing more be said about it.

To the west of Bagan lay India with her innumerable riches, but to get there, the Imperial Army would first have to conquer the Burmese jungle before engaging the British on soil well known to their generals. That would be tomorrow's battle. Let the soldiers rest for now for they had earned it.

Major Nishimura raised his sword. "Victory!" he shouted.

"Victory!" they returned in one voice.

"Soldiers… You are dismissed," he ordered lowering his sword.

The formation dissolved into a stampede of humanity scattering to the four winds, where so many temples beckoned, and from out of this surge, a communications officer raced up the steps. He held a dispatch embellished with the seal of the High Command.

"There is no need to rush, Lieutenant Takahashi," greeted Major Nishimura returning salutes. "We have secured our positions. I presume your message can await a moment's reflection in a lofty sanctuary."

The lieutenant bowed in submission and pointed to a terraced temple nestled on a knoll, where its majestic height over the others made it stand out as the sentry over the plain. "From the cockpit, I admired that

structure foremost above the others," he said. "Could I beg your indulgence?"

"Say no more, lieutenant. You have chosen well."

Already, a mob of soldiers had broken through the entrance and
had crowded into the lower chamber, where they had laid claim to the
choicest objects of veneration bedecking the walls and niches. Yet despite
the undisciplined frenzy, each soldier snapped to attention as the major and
his escort passed.

"If I may be so bold to comment, sir," said Lieutenant Takahashi,
"This temple is confused. I see Buddhist architecture housing Hindu arti-
facts."

"And could not a man have both a Buddhist father and a Hindu
mother and still remain a man?"

"My apologies sir. I have not chosen so well after all."

The two wandered into a dim passageway, where a line of soldiers
heaved a rope fastened in intricate patterns around a honey colored trunk
large enough to hold five men inside. And as hard as the men strained—
oblivious to the officers in their presence—their booty refused to budge.

The major stooped alongside the trunk and stroked the taut webbing. "Who tied these knots?" he asked.

Suddenly recognizing their commander's presence, the soldiers
dropped the rope and bowed deep. "It is I, Sergeant Taki," one of the men
admitted raising himself up to standing position and then bowing lower.

"Did you not know that this trunk is made from teak wood? You
would need a team of yak to move it. Such a waste of beautiful ties,
sergeant."

"Yes sir!"

Major Nishimura gazed deeper into the passageway and spotted
two larger than life statues of the Buddha squatting side by side. "Lieutenant Takahashi," he called pointing to the statues.

"Sir!"

"Those painted Buddhas cause us to reconsider this temple's confusion. We should rub their bellies for enlightenment."

"At once, sir!"

Each officer claimed his own personal Buddha, but as the major
stooped to stroke its rounded abdomen, his eyes drifted sideways to a knee
high teak chest lying on the floor between the two statues. In a single movement, his hand swept across the Buddha and continued onto the chest,
where he caressed a series of ivory inlays festooning the chest in bas-relief.

"Exquisite!" he exclaimed, "Our soldiers do not recognize superior
spoils when they see them. I would have claimed this box first."

Lieutenant Takahashi then too placed his hand on the prize. "I picture the trunk containing ingots of tarnished silver, yet within this box, I envision a single pearl."

"But it is a perfect pearl. Is it not lieutenant?"

"Anything less would defile the spirit of this dwelling."

Major Nishimura closed his eyes, and after a deep breath, he slowly exhaled. "Please read me the nature of your dispatch, Lieutenant, and you may omit the flowery prose and other such formalities."

With a flick of the finger, Lieutenant Takahashi broke the seal on the dispatch and ran his finger past the lengthy salutation. "You are to return with me to Hanoi today. Permit me to be the first to congratulate you on your promotion—Colonel."

Expressing a grimace bordering on disgust, Colonel Nishimura braced his hand against the lieutenant's shoulder. "Do not bow to me again. I find this news disturbing. Does the High Command believe that we cannot reach India before the monsoon begins? Will Burma be the extent of our advance this season?"

"India will always be there for the taking. For now, partisan activity in Indochina has become a threat to our Pacific campaign."

The colonel spit on the floor and crushed it with his boot. "Those damn French! I detest them for their arrogance."

"I agree, sir, but in a different way. It is the Indochinese natives who test us while the French colonists sit back and make all the money. We could learn much about western commerce from those omelet makers."

"Then let us use displays of painful bondage to strike fear into the hearts of the real troublemakers. Would not a master of rope and knot contribute to that goal?"

"My plane holds four. I shall reserve a rear seat for Sergeant Taki."

Colonel Nishimura glanced at the teak chest. "And I shall require a small case for my personal effects to occupy seat number four. I shall trust your good taste in this matter... Now please excuse me; I must pack."

Lieutenant Takahashi bowed, and as the colonel hurried off, he sized up the chest. To his surprise, he found that he could lift it with only a minimum of strain. Closer inspection revealed that the generous amount of ivory in place of teak within each of the panels yielded less weight. This reassured him, for as a pilot, he knew that an overloaded aircraft could fly no better than a Burmese elephant.

CHAPTER 1

The Up and Comer

Jack Preston pushed his tailored suit against the revolving door that led into the lobby of Twenty-Four Broadway and adjusted his tie in the reflecting glass. He tugged on his lapel and swaggered past the newsstand, where the headlines ho-hummed domestic tranquility. The front page of *The Daily News* featured a wide shot of President Eisenhower making the putt on the eighteenth hole at Burning Tree. Ike's spacious smile signaled triumph, and all must have been right in the world—newshounds be damned.

The shoeshine chair sat just beyond the newsstand. Chester Brown, the lone bootblack, called out, "Mornin' Mr. Preston. How about those Dodgers?" Chester, a colored gentleman with untold years of courteous service notched into graying temples, flashed his handsome ivories.

Jack raced to the open elevator. "How about those Yankees!" he replied.

We're gonna get you this year," Chester said. The sliding doors swallowed Jack whole.

Waiting inside the elevator was one Nora Kincaid, an eighteen-year-old receptionist fresh out of commercial school. The grid of a fresh crossword puzzle held the rapt attention of her mascara and shadow-silhouetted eyes.

"Watch out for the little guys. They can break you," Jack said pinching the brim of his fedora.

"Oh Mr. Preston, what's three letters for snake?" she asked, her East Flatbush Brooklynese jamming every syllable into a single word.

"Try asp," he suggested.

Nora scribbled the word in her puzzle book and then quickly filled in all three interlocking words. "You're a lifesaver, Mr. P," she said with nasal abandon.

Jack brushed his collar and preened his hair. The doors slid wide, and the duo hustled through a winding corridor. Jack held the office door for Nora and glanced at the title stained on the window.

DUNSTON, HARGRAVE
AND THORPE
ATTORNEYS AT LAW

A double space intruded between the proper names and the professional title. Obviously, this left an opening for the name of a future senior partner. Jack rubbed the space for good luck.

Nora headed straight to her desk. For Jack's reception, the office manager, Thelma Kane, handed him a sheet of names and more names. "Your appointments for the day," she said, sounding motherly yet business-like. "I did manage a ten-minute lunch break at the end of your Amalgamated Steel consultation."

"And what did I do to deserve such benevolence?"

"Just keep to the schedule, and we'll call it even. Mr. Hargrave will see you now."

Jack snapped a crooked salute and answered this directive with a beeline to the corner office, where Winston Hargrave III, the supreme power and partner-in-chief of the firm, transformed corporate America's most vexing legal hurdles into stepping stones. Jack saw that the door had been left open for the purpose of this visitation, and so he invited himself in with a humble rap on the wood.

Mr. Hargrave sat trance-like in his swivel chair and stared out the window as if he had stepped into the canvas of a Hopper painting. Without looking back, he pointed to the door. Jack gently closed it and then approached him but stopped short of any greetings. He knew better than to interrupt the man's meditations—all the better to take the time to admire the trappings of success.

Somewhere up on the walls were diplomas and plaques, but they were buried in a labyrinth of black and white photos displaying the life of a man, whose legal acumen remained always ready to serve the specialized needs of the powerful and the connected. On the far wall hung a string of pictures featuring Mr. Hargrave with Governor Harriman, Senator Wagner, President Roosevelt, Sir Winston Churchill and of course the venerable legend of Wall Street and the founding director of the Securities and Exchange Commission (SEC), Ambassador Joseph P. Kennedy. Jack hadn't seen Mr. Kennedy since sandlot days, but there was no mistaking those teeth that jumped right out of their roots. That was Mr. Kennedy all right.

"Jack, Jack, my boy," Mr. Hargrave said spinning around in his chair and pumping him with a two-handed shake, "the SEC just approved the Westinghouse-GHK merger you headed. None of us believed it would fly, but you—you pulled it off with over a dozen citations that no veterans in the firm ever heard of. Who trained you? Houdini?"

"I do what you pay me to do, Mr. Hargrave," Jack replied, his voice flat, but then it broke into a more melodious tone, "however, it's this kind of accomplishment which gives me the greatest reward."

Mr. Hargrave rose up and squeezed Jack's shoulder. "It seems like we don't pay you enough. Perhaps—and this is just perhaps—a partnership contract might land on your blotter if you keep on track."

"That's what I'm aiming for," Jack returned, his enthusiasm tempered by the knowledge that in this firm, partnerships dangled from the bouyant praise of every commendation, but they almost always came attached to the word, "perhaps." To join the select few, Mr. Hargrave would have to commend you in full view of your colleagues. Otherwise, these private tributes served strictly for motivation.

Mr. Hargrave sunk back into his chair. "Of course you realize that the senior partners would have to unanimously approve my proposal; however, I don't foresee any lasting objections. You may be a bit short in the age department, but you are a scholar. What is it, two publications in the law reviews this past year?"

"Three actually, but—if I may be so bold—who outside of our opposing counsels reads them?"

"Don't be mistaken, son. Publication brings prestige, and prestige brings in clients. In this firm, you have become an asset."

The intercom buzzed, and Thelma Kane's voice cut in. "Mr. Hargrave, the Acme Hydraulics party awaits Mr. Preston outside his office."

"Offer them coffee and a cruller. I have some unexpected business at hand."

Mr. Hargrave opened a safe and pulled out a manila envelope. He leaned forward and lowered his voice to a hush. "What I have here is the business merger to end all mergers. Now I do not know the principals, nor do I wish to. All I can say is that this envelope contains the names of two blue chips who have secretly declared their intentions to enter into the state of corporate matrimony with you administering the ceremonial vows."

He handed Jack the envelope and continued. "I can't overemphasize the need for secrecy on this one, Jack. One leak could set off a dozen inside trades that ripple the market and scuttle the deal. You must lock this envelope in your safe and share the contents with no one inside or outside of this firm, or the SEC will come knocking on your door. Is that understood?"

"As always, I understand this standard declaration."

"It pains me to call your impeccable ethics into question each and every time, but the law is the law."

Again, the intercom buzzed, "Mr. Hargrave—," came the harried voice.

"Patience, Mrs. Kane. He's on his way."

Jack tucked the envelope under his arm and nodded a silent *adieu*. Starting off the day with a high profile merger made him want to shout out his fortune from the balcony of the trading floor, but alas. All the attendant secrecy worthy of a Masonic lodge would delay such satisfaction until at least the summer. Such was Ambassador Kennedy's first law of the Street, which with its capital S could only mean Wall Street.

Jack arrived at his office's reception area, where he found two middle-aged businessmen, presumably from the Acme Hydraulics Company, patiently sipping on Thelma Kane's coffee. Jack attempted to extend his hand for a shake but was cut off by a blind-sided block from young Paul Jeffrey on his morning rounds.

"Just a moment of your time, Mr. Preston, I need three signatures here," said Paul slapping a short stack of papers onto Jack's open palm. Paul followed Jack into his office, and Jack placed the manila envelope from Mr. Hargrave on the desk. Paul's eyes trained in on it for a moment but then darted back to Jack.

"So, you'll be my office assistant for the next month. What crime did you commit to deserve this punishment?" Jack said. He signed the first paper.

"I start my senior year in September. Mr. Hargrave said your name would glow like neon on a recommendation to law school."

Jack slashed his signature across the second paper. "Hmmm, why is it that I have to sign all the escrow accounts?" He wondered out loud. "Neon, eh? Are you sure he didn't say Freon? Say, what's this transaction?"

SECURITY PACIFIC BANK, APPLICATION FOR SAVINGS ACCOUNT stated the third piece of paper in bold lettering. This was something new in the daily routine—something totally out of the blue. "Has the firm adopted procedures for private savings funds that I don't know about?" he asked.

"It's not my privilege to inquire into financial records. Would you authorize me to run over to the accountants?" Paul replied.

Jack stared into space and then focused, spotting Thelma tapping her foot outside his office. She pointed to her watch and glared back at him.

"Let's let this one go through," Jack said, signing the application anyway. "Who's got time to ask a bean counter about his beans?"

Paul grabbed the papers and made tracks past Thelma, who ushered the Acme Hydraulics party into Jack's office. The meeting would last exactly one hour. The chiming grandfather clock in the neighboring conference room would see to that. An ensuing meeting would snare exactly sixty minutes of clock time after which another hour meant another meeting.

At noon, Jack locked his door and retrieved the manila envelope from his safe. After two bites of a pastrami on rye, he picked up the phone.

"United States Securities and Exchange Commission, Corporation Finance, Steven Pickering, counselor for mergers and acquisitions," came the telegraphic greeting from the other end.

"Steve.... It's Jack Preston at DH and T," he returned, "I'm making an application for corporate consolidation of the Humble Oil Company and Scully Petroleum and will serve as broker for their corporation counsels."

An extended silence at the other end of the line segued into a gagging sound. "Holy smokes Jack! How come you get to dance with all the pretty girls?"

Jack curled his fingers and blew on his nails. "I've been batting a thousand for the last year. The word gets out you know."

"A word to the not so wise," Steve cautioned. "A colleague, Fred Haskins, down at GD and P optioned both stocks in a merger dossier. He took in over one million dollars in inside trades."

Jack flinched. He would have expected such illegal dealings from a floor trader or a board member from one of the merging corporations but never from an attorney handling the transaction. "Did you collar him?" he asked.

"Effortlessly. Our compliance trackers spotted his vapor trail right after the ticker prices jumped. Haskins was smart enough to take instant redemption in cash but stupid enough to count sheep on a fat mattress when the FBI came calling."

Jack felt his tongue sticking to his palate. He took a sip of ginger ale. "The man should have booked a flight."

"It wouldn't have mattered. Our trackers always set up shop at the clearance houses within hours after the press announces a merger or acquisition deal to the trading floor. A nimble trader would have had to have cashed out and cleared the runway before the sun hung low."

Jack looked at his watch. Already, five minutes of his lunch break had passed. To make up for lost time, he took a double bite from his sandwich. "So what happens now?" he inquired, his mouth spraying an errant crumb.

"Pursuant to the conventional plea bargain, the U.S. attorney has dropped all the charges in return for complete restitution of the tainted money and lifetime disbarment. Haskins is now free to flip burgers for a living."

How could such a trained mind be so stupid? When Jack hung up the phone, he stared dumbfounded at his sandwich. A fleeting tinge of sympathy passed through him, and he checked his watch again only to discover that his ten-minute recess had expired. He tried to extend it to eleven, but Thelma—bless her heart—put him back on track and would keep him there for hour after hour and meeting after meeting until the clock struck six.

"I pronounce you free," Thelma said to the fading chimes of the grandfather clock.

"I don't know the meaning of the word, warden," he sighed. "What kind of day have you cooked up for me tomorrow?"

"I've spotted you the afternoon to work on your new account. Feel free to lock the door and turn on the game, but give me the full list of players for next week's rituals."

Jack batted his eyes. "I could so easily fall in love with you," he gushed.

"Back off, Romeo. You'll be keeping your lovely fiancée waiting."

Jack snapped to attention. He tightened his tie and slung his jacket over his back. "Judy, Judy, I'm coming for you, my lark!" he exclaimed.

And then Jack thought about what kind of dish Thelma must have been back in the days of cloches and raccoon coats. He retouched her black-Irish face with a dash of youth and draped a flapper's dress over her trim figure as if to beautify for further safe flirtations this corporate model of efficiency clad in a matching gray ensemble. But then he recalled that she knew too well how to throw the monkey wrench on a counsel's unproductive musings even if they didn't chip away the time on the firm's clock. Jack grabbed his hat and bolted for the evening train.

CHAPTER 2

Elevator Love

When the elevator dial hit forty, Chester Brown crossed his fingers and prayed that the car would return directly to ground level without any intervening stops at a so-called floor of exclusion. This unusual appeal to Providence came about because some time around noon, he had spotted one G. Randolph Smythe, the president of the General Stores Corporation, enter the elevator with three other visitors, and after two intervening stops, the car ascended to the top floor, whose sole occupant, Patterson and Stern, merited the distinction of being the largest bankruptcy law practice on the Street. Still, Mr. Smythe could have been one of the passengers disembarking at floors seven or thirty-two, and so Chester needed confirmation from the return ride to tell him that this captain of retailing had indeed journeyed to a "Grave Dancer's" floor.

The car stopped at twenty-two, and Chester knew that either Jack Preston or Thelma Kane had called it a day. Then the doors opened, and Chester sighed. The rider from the fortieth floor was a secretary pulling overtime. Perhaps Mr. Smythe had already jumped out the window.

"Have a pleasant ride home, Mr. Preston," he called out to Jack, who on this end of the day always traveled like he had wings on his shoes.

But this time, Jack turned on his heels. "Hey Chester, how about spiffing up my oxfords?"

"Yes sir," Chester called back accenting his raspy voice with a tuneful flourish. "A man has got to look sharp for the ladies."

"Oh yes the ladies," came Jack's awkward reply.

As Jack climbed into the shoeshine chair, Chester figured that he had better change the subject. Jack might have hit the big time in the law league, but one look at the soft curves and peach fuzz on his creamy skin made Chester think of a choir boy's face—not to say that with a little more education the man wouldn't have had women swooning in his arms—but heck, they didn't give those kinds of classes in the fancy schools he went to.

Chester stepped to the side of the chair to fetch the Shinola, and he glanced at the elevators. "Yes sir, Mr. Preston," he said. "My pastor and all the Crow Hill baseball coaches want to thank you for your kindness. That money you donated will put new uniforms on every boy in the league. Bless you."

"Baseball makes people happy," Jack said beaming, but then the corners of his mouth dropped. "I just wish I could donate money to my own church for the purchase of an organ, but a majority of the elders still believe that music leads to sin."

"Then I guess you were never sang in any choir," Chester chuckled wondering how else he could picture such a sweet face with the big kind of cheeks that every aunt loved to pinch. Were it not for the gobs of slickum plastering down Jack's sandy locks, he suspected a massive cowlick might unfurl from its roots and become the crush of every girl in seventh grade.

Chester dabbed on the Shinola and gently worked his horse bristles over the paste until the leather took on a rich gleam. But a gleam wasn't good enough; Chester wanted those shoes to sparkle. Meanwhile, the elevators whipsawed high and low like rigged stocks, but none of them went anywhere near the top. Chester's eyes darted back and forth so as not to miss a peak destination on the dials or a bare spot on Jack's shoes.

"How is it that on some days those elevators have you mesmerized?" Jack said.

"Well Mr. Preston, it's sort of like the ladies. Sometimes you love them, and sometimes you don't. Today, I've got nothing but love for those elevators."

"Yes, I see."

But did the man really see? Chester knew that he could always throw Jack off his mark with the mere mention of women, and he couldn't figure out why they could give such a clean-looking guy the jitters when he should have had them falling at his feet. Perhaps it had something to do with the man belonging to a congregation that wouldn't allow music in its midst, but then again Chester didn't want to speak ill of any church, especially Jack's denomination with its history of preaching freedom and equality for everybody.

The far elevator rocketed skywards as if it would blow off the roof, and when it hit the big four-oh, Chester wrapped a buffing cloth around his forefingers and blew on it. Then he slapped it and snapped in four–quarter beat to a rhyme that only he could hear.

"Elevator down... Coming to the ground...
Skip the other floors... Then open up your doors...
I'm polishing the shoes... And paying all my dues...
Three two one... Run baby run!"

And run the elevator did—all the way to the lobby, where with upturned collar, cocked fedora and shifty eyes, Mr. Smythe advertised his departure to Chester's twinkling eyes. "I can't charge you this time Mr. Preston," he said. "You've been a giving man, and I've got to show some generosity myself."

"Only this once," Jack replied. "Save your money for Ebbets Field."

Ebbets Field—Bless the man again! Chester planned to take his grandson to Saturday's game against Cincinnati, and he promised himself that after Jackie Robinson's first hit, he would raise a beer to Mr. Preston's sinless honor.

CHAPTER 3

Of Sirens and Mutts

Jack pushed his stride into a gallop and made the six twenty-nine out of Grand Central Station by a nose. He knew the drill all too well; the last man on the train got the last available seat. He queued up behind the rest of his fellow caboose chasers, and—always the last in line—followed them toward the front of the train. For four cars, not a seat was to be had. Number five provided the initial openings, and in deference to the ladies in the group, the gentlemen at the head of the line marched straight past them. It wasn't until car number seven, a non-smoker, that Jack found his spot. A foursome playing cribbage had reversed one of the seats so that the participants faced each other as they knocked pegs on the board. Jack spotted naked fabric facing him, and he claimed his place looking back at a stunning brunette with heartbreak curves. Sometimes life was just too darn good.

They made glancing eye contact and flashed each other courtesy smiles. Jack knew that this encounter would go no further in the physical sense, and so he opened up his evening paper while she sank her eyes back into a potboiler, which she held—title kept discretely hidden away—on her lap. Let the real journey begin.

She wore the kind of tight sweater favored by screen sirens Jane Russell and Marilyn Monroe, which meant she must have worked in the garment trade either as an apparel buyer for Macys or Gimbels or as a floor model for a fashion house. She certainly had the legs for a model. And that sweater! Any business cultivating public respect insisted that all its female employees wear blouses with their skirts. Tight sweaters betrayed lax moral standards, not that Jack had any problem with them.

Jack held the *Evening Star* edition of the *Journal American* up to eye level and read the headline.

VIET MINH ENCIRCLES FRENCH TROOPS AT DIENBIENPHU

His eyes then retreated below the bottom edge of the newspaper, where he could admire—sight unseen—those luscious legs without raising the suspicion of their proprietor. The lass had angled her legs to the side and crossed them daintily at the ankles. A patent leather pump dangled from the tip of her right foot, which she fidgeted up and down. Would she allow him to rub his cheek along the softness of her calf and ravish it with kisses? Jack bit into his bottom lip just enough to cause slight pain. He knew all too well that if he admired long enough at the struts of this siren, he would awaken "the Mutt."

Sirens tempted not just the foolhardy. So said Homer's epic, *The Odyssey,* back when Jack studied the classics in his undergrad days at Cornell. He pictured gorgeous women lounging about on the exposed crests of shoals requiring precise navigation by passing sailors and wondered how any good man could resist shifting course straight into the rocks. Meanwhile back on Mount Olympus, the gods settled accounts between those wagering on safe passage verses those betting for a shipwreck.

If only we mortals were privy to their musings, Jack reasoned, then life would be free from all danger. But the gods had to have their sport. Jack pictured Aphrodite, the goddess of beauty, gloating over how she had created perfect women to lure the doomed sailors. Eros, the god of pleasure, would beg to differ. "It is I, who gave the sailors the desire. What is more important? The object of desire or the desire itself?"

"Enough of this bickering!" scorned Zeus. Then the sight of a god's best friend wriggling on his back in the meadow would make the mighty one's face light up.

"Priapus! Come here boy!"

Jack never could find a picture of the original Priapus. For all of those other gods, you had a starting point in the form of an idol, which gave you an idea of the work delegated to them. Zeus was the chief god, so he had a muscle man's physique to convey power and a beard to indicate wisdom. Both Aphrodite and Eros had most flattering images as befit their mythic occupations.

But Priapus... Who was he? And what did he look like?

Actually, he was the god of the erect penis. And to answer the obvious question—a flaccid phallus did not make the grade. Was it any surprise then that given this information, the Romans, who had borrowed their gods from the Greeks, figured him to be an average Joe with a flagpole jutting from his loins? But what kind of god was that! All the other gods had either superhuman or animal form. Why not Priapus?

Jack had him figured all right. He knew the Greek Priapus all too well. Whenever the unspeakable urge struck, Jack derived instant pleasure from his expanding organ; however, after the initial thrill, his manly craving became an intolerable diversion, which obliterated any rational thinking until he stroked himself into a state of satisfaction. Once relieved, the whole horny episode seemed like a momentary lapse into insanity, which reminded him of his boyhood dog, Rascal, a terrier and spaniel mix with a penchant to hump the leg of a table, a chair or proper company—much to mother's mortification.

When the teenage years arrived in all their testosterone surging glory, Jack realized the biological truth in Rascal's proclivities by coming to grips with hormonally induced cravings all his own. A magazine shot of Jane Russell vamping in her push up brassiere in the movie, *The Outlaw*, could drive him to unburden himself in the middle of breakfast, lunch or an economics assignment…

…And then one lonely evening in the college dorm as he fondled himself to that well-worn picture of Jane, he unintentionally reflected upon his boner, Priapus and Rascal so that the three united into a pagan trinity.

"Priapus is a dog… a mixed terrier and spaniel mutt!" an inner voice proclaimed. "How could all the great minds of civilizations past and present miss it?"

Jack lowered the newspaper to get a glimpse of the brunette's bosom. The train wheels screeched.

"Bronxville… Bronxville," called the conductor.

Jack folded his paper. This was his stop.

CHAPTER 4

Cutie Pie

Spring had sprung for this splendid evening, and the milder weather and lingering daylight had finally convinced the foliage to dress up. Jack walked along under a canopy of blooming oaks and sucked in the perfumes of the topiary. Activity filled the air. The train whistle blew a distant farewell, and Jack strolled past the baseball field where he spotted two boys playing catch. In the adjoining playground, a father pushed his boy on a swing while the child's mother fluttered her hand in front of her rosy cheeks, causing the little one to giggle.

"Push me higher, Daddy!" The boy squealed with delight.

Jack wanted to slap himself hard. Here he was, a master facilitator in the making, and in all his twenty-seven years of living with his parents he had never marched a woman into the bedroom to give Priapus his due. What stung the deepest was that every one of his local classmates had married, most when they had graduated from college. They could enjoy this wonderful evening and cap it off with a night of ravishing treats. It was not so with Jack. Three years of intense study at law school, followed by another three chained to Thelma Kane's clock had put him on a dating quarantine.

Jack rounded a street corner onto a block of oversized Tudors and Georgians on one-acre lots; there was nothing fancy in this neck of the woods, just understated prosperity. Jack's house, or rather his parents' house, where he lived, stood halfway down an impeccably maintained boulevard lined by an abundance of curbside Hudsons and Cadillacs, each one sporting a fresh wash and a new coat of wax. Not an aberrant tree bloom or a speck of bird dropping was to be seen. The affluent citizens of this enclave had declared that Mother Nature must be conquered, and conquered she was at whatever price deemed necessary.

"Jack, Jack! Are you coming to Saturday's game?"

Jack looked behind him. His neighbor, Roy Tucker, resplendent in his Bronxville home baseball uniform, raced up to greet him. Roy was two years Jack's junior but was a kindred spirit in the sense that too many hours working in his father's architectural firm and too many broken dates had kept him from fulfilling his manhood.

"I'll need a rain check for Saturday. Judy wants to go to the city and shop for a stone," Jack replied. The two mates pushed through the gate to the Preston residence, a fifteen-room monster with clubhouse-size gables.

"All the good places are closed Saturdays. If you want a deal, you'll have to sacrifice a lunch break," Roy said.

"Yeah, all ten minutes of it. Looks like I'll have to pay retail."

"Don't let life pass you by, good friend."

Roy turned to leave, but then Jack's mother, Emily, poked her lean figure out the screen door. "And who says that life gives you the right of way, Roy Tucker? We're setting an extra place at the table. It's not polite to refuse."

"Your poodle cut becomes you, Mrs. Preston," Roy returned.

Emily folded her arms across her button-down dress and put on a scowl. "Needless flattery," she remarked. Then her lips relaxed into the shape of a cupid's bow. "And for that, you get a double serving of dessert."

The threesome retired to the living room, where Jack's dad, Oliver, slouched in his cozy chair. The picture of comfort, he held a glass of sherry under his gray mustache, and with his eyelids on display, he savored the bouquet.

"Oliv-errrrrr," Emily intoned with a gentle trill.

Oliver grabbed onto his bowtie as if to keep it from spinning, and as his hazel eyes opened to the evening light, Jack's baby blues caught a flashing glimpse of his fiancée, Judy Faraday, who came alongside him and placed her hands over his peepers. "I have a surprise," she said with a schoolgirl giggle. Her hands still in place, she guided Jack forward.

The aroma of sautéed vegetables stimulated a gush of saliva, lubricating Jack's tongue and gums. "You must be taking me to the kitchen," he remarked.

"Don't ruin the fun, Mr. Preston."

Judy momentarily uncovered one eye just in time to prevent Jack from crashing into a crystal-laden breakfront in front of an archway. Blinded once again, he heard a solid tapping under his feet, signaling a transition from broadloom to linoleum. The light returned as Judy dropped both hands from his eyes. On the far wall, the slit-like pupils of a Kit-Cat clock shifted back and forth over tray upon tray of glazed ham, tossed salad and garnished vegetables resting upon an arsenal of boomerangs imprinted into the Formica countertops. Jack told himself that he had to stop checking the time; he was home now.

"Isn't Judy something? She made this all by herself," Emily said.

Ah, Judy! She certainly was *something*, but something of what, Jack thought. How could he not adore those gleaming eyes, that pert nose and those luscious dimples? They positively beamed at him. And there she was, all fancied up in her ruffled blouse, her tartan skirt, her bobby socks and her penny loafers with a Mercury dime in each slot. Judy could have been twenty-three going on twelve. But what could one expect of a kindergarten teacher? A checkered apron covered up her otherwise womanly figure, and a horseshoe clip tamed the locks of her blond Toni. Not a speck of eyeliner or nail polish was to be seen.

On the other hand, Judy could be a quick study. Barely two months of cooking lessons at the church hall had produced this meal. Even without the tasting, Jack would give it three and a half stars. But what did they say about the proof of the pudding?

Judy dipped a ladle into a pot of soup and held it to Jack's lips. "Do you like it Jack? It's *vichyssoise*." She batted her eyes as if she had caught a cinder in them.

Damn! Jack thought. She's perky. She's chirpy, and she's as wholesome as a stack of buttermilk pancakes. Oh so true…and, she's got the looks…and all the right equipment…so what's wrong with this picture?

Jack looked to the distant rocks, where he heard the sirens calling out to a wayward vessel. He could see their faces, all sultry vixens with their bosoms crammed into tight sweaters. This evening an entire school of sirens lolled along the shore, but try as he might and try as he had many times before, Jack could not find his Judy among them.

"Jack… Jack… Are you alright?" she called.

The perfect balance of leek and potato cascaded across his taste buds. A crispy grain tweaked the palate, and a subtle hint of onion wafted along the back alleys of his nasal passages, where it caressed only the most sophisticated of his olfactory receptors. What was missing?

Jack knew. "Now I know it's supposed to be cold, but couldn't you just—"

Judy had already dipped the ladle into a second pot and had brought it to his lips. As he tasted it, Judy finished his sentence. "—Heat it? What do you think?"

"A veritable masterpiece! You outdid yourself today, sweets."

"Wait until you see what she's cooked up for desert," Oliver chortled.

"Oliv-errrrr!!! Don't give away the ending," Emily sang poking him in the side.

The family retired to the dining room, where Jack's younger sister, Denise, and his brother, Will, the baby of the family, joined them at the table. Judy and Emily carried in loaded platters and placed them on serving trams. Jack observed Judy's finishing school touches in her bearing and mannerisms. She held the tray with her left hand and served with her right. She stood ramrod straight, never stooping or bending, and she never touched or brushed against a single soul as she dispensed just the appropriate portion.

Roy raised his glass. "Let us toast Jack and Judy," he said.

"How can you hoist mere apple juice? Let me put a snort in it," Oliver offered grandly.

Emily poked him in the side again. "Apple juice will do just fine, thank you," she said adding, "Denise, how are you fixed for film?"

"Half a roll, maybe less." Denise pulled a camera from her handbag, and after licking the contact end of a flashbulb, she inserted it into the flash bonnet. The gathering raised high the glasses of apple juice.

"To Jack and Judy," Roy said.

"To Jack and Judy," they all chorused to the pop of the flashbulb.

The scent of burnt magnesium emanated from the bonnet, and Will and Oliver rubbed the flashbulb ghosts out of their eyes. With the obligatory pose now disposed of, the feast commenced. For dessert, Judy brought out an apple cobbler still warm from the oven, and she apologized for not using fresh apples, even though they were a rarity in the middle of spring.

At dinner's end, Emily and Denise commenced rounding up the dishes and silverware. Judy reached for a serving tray, but Emily took it right out of her hands. "You've toiled more than your share this evening. Why don't you and Jack catch some fresh air?" she suggested.

Roy slowly made his way toward the front door. "Thanks for the invite, Mrs. Preston. You can cook for me anytime, Judy," he said.

Jack, meanwhile, slipped out the back door and onto a porch, where the conversations carried through the screens. "Say Dad, let's catch game two of the Dodgers-Cubs double-header on the TV while we can," Will said.

"Only until nine, Will. We don't want to miss *Dinah Shore*," Emily cut in.

Judy followed Jack onto the porch, where he already sat to one side of a love seat. A witch's moon cast a faint glow across his pompadour.

"Uh-oh... I know what you have in mind," she said, coyly.

Jack sprang out of the love seat and embraced the small of her waist. "Why should I wait for you to sit when I can take you for myself this very second?" he asked.

Damn that checkered apron! Underneath the squares was the ruffled blouse. Now if only Judy's apron had ruffles just like the French maids in the fancy hotels, then things could heat up a little. But why stop there? Judy could wear one of those cheeky black uniforms and a pair of black stockings with the seam up the back. *Oo-là-là!* He could be a traveling businessman, who after a long day of successful negotiations had found himself road weary. He would draw a hot bath and slowly lower his tired body into the soothing waters...

Knock-knock!

"Who's there?"

"Maid Service, sir. I have come to turn down your bed... Please excuse the intrusion. And what is this? Your muscles are all in knots. May I lather them?"

Jack kissed Judy, but her tightly pursed lips caused his mouth to bounce back as if it had hit a trampoline. She giggled, and he went back for a second try. Her lips must have had stitches holding them together!

Of course. She was saving herself. Perhaps a squeeze play might stir things up. As the sound of the ball game from the TV set provided background chatter, Jack unlocked his embrace.

"Erskine delivers a fast ball down the middle... (crack of the bat) ...and it's a bloop to shallow center for Ernie Banks..."

Jack's right hand gravitated upward to just under Judy's armpit, and then it slid forward, ever so gently, to cop a feel.

"...Snider is rushing in, but the ball's going to drop, and I don't believe this... Banks is going for two...."

Jack's hand reached the base of Judy's bosom. One corner of his mouth slowly ascended toward heaven; however, before his hand could rub against soft flesh, Judy's hand swept his arm back onto her waist.

"Not until you say, 'I do,' you naughty boy. Then you can pet both my cupcakes."

"...Reese takes the throw, and Banks is... out! The Dodgers win the game."

Cupcakes? Cupcakes!!! Judy could never be a siren. She was too damn cute. And where was a Greek chorus when you needed them?

It took almost a minute for the Cubs fans to stop booing.

CHAPTER 5

A Morning Break

Friday mornings in the city always put an extra bounce in Jack's step. He pushed past the revolving doors, and Chester, the bootblack, offered insightful commentary into the previous night. "Hmmm... Ernie Banks wantin' more than his share? Maybe the Duke or Pee Wee could give him a talkin' to on entitlement. Right, Mr. Preston?"

"It's the price of greed, Chester. When the bat says 'one', that's all a man's entitled to."

The Dodgers must have been on a three-game streak because Chester carried the team cap proudly on his head, and there it would stay until some upstart team bested them. Of greater note were the three bottles of single malt scotch sticking out of a shoe polish crate.

"I see the Ambassador paid you a visit this morning," Jack said.

"I don't know any ambassador. He's always been Mr. Kennedy to me. He was asking for you."

"He's always asking for me, and I always seem to miss him."

"You missed him by minutes today. You've got to catch an earlier train."

"No thank you; I need my sleep."

Jack found it odd that Joseph P. Kennedy would tip Chester three bottles of a premium brand of scotch that most lords with peerage could not obtain. Chester was certainly a master of his trade, but the Ambassador tipped appropriately not generously. Jack knew this from back in the days of the Great Depression when every Sunday the Kennedy family traveled in three separate limousines to Bronxville's Roman church. To help raise money for his own church, Jack rode his bike to deliver *The Wall Street Journal* and charged his customers ten cents a week for a subscription. Mr. Kennedy used to tip him two cents, and for that, Jack was satisfied—not elated, mind you, just satisfied. So how did Chester merit three bottles of the pride of Scotland? And as rumors go, why had this ritual gone on for over twenty years? When pushed for an answer, Chester would explain that Mr. Kennedy had rewarded him for profitable investment advice. Come again?

Jack stepped into the elevator for the flight back to reality. With her crossword puzzle book in hand, Nora Kincaid hit him with the daily clue.

"Do you have any four-letter words for sole-mate, Mr. P? Sole is spelled S-O-L-E."

Jack marveled at Nora's diction. Four-letter words became "Fawled-dawoyds." He figured that she might be better suited for a job as a secretary rather than as the one and only receptionist, but that's how secretaries started out in the firm these days. They answered the telephone. Regardless, if Thelma Kane and the partners were happy with such elocution, it wasn't any of his business. "Try heel. H double E then L," Jack suggested.

Nora jotted down the answer, and in seconds flat, she had filled in all four interlocking words. "Wow! You college guys don't miss out on much, do you?" she exclaimed.

The two entered the reception area just in time for World War III to erupt between Thelma and Paul. "A four fifty-five cancellation gives me *plenty* of time to fill the slot. I have a *three-page* waiting list. You should have come to me at four fifty-*six*," Thelma said, her face scarlet.

"The papers just kept piling up on my desk. That cancellation was an interruption of an interruption," came Paul's watery retort followed by, "Oh, good morning, Mr. Preston."

Jack hung up his hat. "I take it that some counselor has a hole in his schedule. Who, pray tell, is this lucky soul?"

"It's you. Your morning appointment with Corning walked into August. You can push papers until ten—that is if I had any prepared!" Thelma sounded on the verge of tears.

"It was unintentional, Mr. Preston, I, I..." Paul stuttered.

"I could hug you, Paul," Jack said. He retrieved his hat.

"That's so thoughtful of you, Jack. What do I tell Mr. Hargrave?" Thelma asked.

Jack waxed philosophical. "Mr. Hargrave is an understanding man. Just tell him that Paul is a rookie, and that he will make the cut. Meanwhile, I shall proceed to the corner drugstore to pick up three rolls of film for my sister."

"I could run that errand for you, Mr. Preston," Paul said.

"What, and rob me of fresh air? If anybody calls, tell him I'm wasting company time at the apothecary."

As Jack made an abrupt about face toward the hallway and temporary freedom, Thelma made tracks to Mr. Hargrave's office. Paul, meanwhile, headed over to the reception, where Nora kept her tidy shop, and he grabbed her phone.

Nora glared at him. "So nice of you to say 'please', Paul!" she scolded, but he paid her no mind. He just dialed his party as if the phone was his for the taking.

CHAPTER 6

A Black Bag Operation

Treasury Agent Michael T. Malone placed the retirement paper between the towers of dossiers piled upon his desk, and after filling in the blanks, his hand hovered over the signature line. With his eyelids pressed into slits, doubts remained. While the grinding of his stomach and the creaking of his joints told him to hang it all up, some primeval force kept the stylus from touching the paper. But then he opened his sunken eyes and realized that the resistance to his signature came courtesy of Regional Director Carlton B. Tanner's grip on the tip of the pen.

Tanner placed an open folder over the retirement form and fingered through various glossies of two men grappling each other's naked torsos over satin sheets. "I always maintained that Hoover couldn't find a wife because he was too busy running the FBI," he remarked with icy indifference. "Who's the buck hosing him with his back to the camera in every frame?"

Rather than reply, Malone pulled a spare photograph out of his top drawer and handed it to Tanner. In this shot, the mystery man's face appeared front-and-center, and Malone wondered how long Tanner's professional demeanor would keep his emotions in check.

"Damn you Mike! It's Roy Cohn!" Tanner gasped to the point of making a gagging sound. "Senator McCarthy charged him with rounding up the commie writers infecting our society."

"That's crap, and you know it!" Malone shot back. "Those two goons are hurting hundreds of innocent people. They've got to be stopped."

Tanner cupped his hands over his ears as if he wanted to hear no evil. "And by whom?" he returned. "You and your spy friends down at the NSA! This is America, my friend. What judge gave you the okay to run espionage-style surveillance on the only two officials who could shoot us down on the front pages of every rag from here to Frisco?"

Malone laughed, but then he realized that his involuntary response smacked of insubordination. "It just occurred to me," he said in a low monotone, " that after seeing the almighty J. Edgar Hoover take it in the tailpipe, the notion of him putting me on his enemies list doesn't scare me one smidgen as much as the sight of a Jap Zero diving for my rudder. You were in the Pacific; you know what I mean."

Tanner threw up his hands. "I put those days out of my head, and so should you."

Malone's eyes shifted to the piles of dossiers on his desk. "Then give me some adventure, Carl. I'm sick of chasing after tax cheats while the Bureau filches our SEC referrals. Use those photos to persuade Mr. Hoover to hand us back our authority over the Street, and I'll pledge to you another year of service."

Tanner placed the revealing snapshot into the folder with the various other glossies. "I'll put a call in to Washington, but your war buddies at the NSA will have to classify these photographs first." After wiping his brow, he closed the folder and moved on with a second request. "Today is graduation day at the Academy. I'd like you to show a rookie the ropes."

Malone placed each of his hands on a pile of tax dossiers. "I'm a generous man," he said. "What's mine is his.

CHAPTER 7

The Drugstore Incident

With almost an hour to burn, Jack ambled past the sundries and cosmetics sections of the William Street Dispensary and inhaled the sulfurous vapors emanating from some unpronounceable nostrum getting compounded in the druggist's mortar. In roundabout fashion, he arrived at the magazine racks, and his eyes trained in on the detective periodicals, where he found to his enchantment a bound and gagged blonde gracing the cover of *True Crime* magazine.

The picture was merely an illustration and not a photograph, but the artistic realism of it amazed Jack. Then again, the picture was more artistic than real because it showed this damsel in distress to have too much rope covering too little clothing. Extra twirls of hemp locked her hands behind her back and held her abdomen tightly against a cheap chair, thus causing her bosom to jut out in a most provocative manner. Intricate knots bound her legs to the forelegs of the chair, but interestingly enough did not run her stockings. In a similar vein, the gag left ample room for both her ruby lips to ride over and under them so that nothing of substance prevented her from screaming at the top of her lungs and being heard. What's more, not a trace of lipstick stained the gag. Very curious... the whole picture was a pose and nothing more, yet similar depictions had become the stock and trade of the entire pulp detective genre.

Jack glanced across the magazine rack, where *Baseball Digest* and *The Sporting News* caught his eye. At the far end of the rack, Archie Moore with boxing gloves in hand struck a pugilistic pose for *Ring* magazine. Wow! The Moore-Whitehurst bout was tomorrow night. This issue was a keeper. Jack reached into the rack, and while his left eye kept its focus on Archie Moore, his right eye moseyed past the end of the rack and into the next aisle to zero in on a creature more perilous than the middleweight champion of the world.

She was breathtaking, this siren, browsing through the aisle and wearing the requisite tight sweater and clinging skirt. How many ships had she sunk in her lifetime? How many sailors had she doomed? Jack rubbed his eyes and almost expected an alto sax to break in with a squishy nocturne.

She stooped slightly so that her almond shaped eyes might compare the brands of shampoo. Then she pressed a finger against the fullness of her bottom lip, and Jack almost hit himself in the chest with his jaw. Oh the roundness of her rump! Mercy! A mere ribbon of belt cinched her waist upon which the tight sweater commenced. But it wasn't any run-of-the-mill tight sweater that this vixen chose to lure the sailor boys. No... this was a ribbed sweater, the most deadly of all.

Jack followed the knit ribs on their northward journey and into the realm of her bosom, which after becoming snared and sheathed in these playful cords, also became magnified and glorified by the light and shadow playing off them. The impulse for Jack to get on his knees and worship them had to be avoided or else the pagan mutt would demand his due. Jack closed his eyes briefly and counted to three in his head. Then he opened his eyes, and—poof—she was gone. Magic!

Jack tucked the magazine in his arm and headed down to the film section, where he grabbed three rolls of color film and three packs of flash bulbs, all of which proved to be more than a snug fit between his two hands. As he twisted his fingers to get a better grip on the merchandise, the magazine started to slip down his arm, so he pulled his arm in closer to his chest, which stopped the magazine in its tracks but then caused a pack of bulbs to slip from the rest. He lifted up his leg and used his thigh to steady the errant bulbs, and holding his breath, he proceeded steady and stable to the cashier when—*boom*—he got knocked to the side, and everything fell from his hands.

"Oh, I'm so sorry! I didn't see you. Here, let me help you," said the siren in the ribbed sweater.

Jack looked down at his dropped merchandise on the floor and got to take in a pair of most graceful legs and a bottle of egg shampoo. He wanted to say something suave, something witty to impress this beauty, but his mind went blank from the sweetness of jasmine emanating from the recesses of her neck. Is this what happened to all the sailors before they hit the rocks?

"You dropped your shampoo, Miss... Miss..."

She offered her hand. "Mercer... Alice Mercer," she said, her voice as soft as a breathy kitten.

Jack accepted her hand with nary a hesitation. "Jack Preston at your service. It serves me right. I should have grabbed a shopping cart."

The two squatted down to retrieve their goods. For the benefit of Jack's scrambled mind, Alice's skirt rode up to the garter line in her stockings. He tried hard not to look, but he sure made it obvious when he did. With great despair, he turned his head away from the metal and rubber clamp that held up her stocking. If he stared at it any longer, he was certain he would go blind.

"I'm not very keen on carts either," Alice said. " I always get the one with the broken wheel." She reached for the *Ring* magazine on the floor and spun it around so that it faced her.

"Archie Moore, eh? I bet Whitehurst doesn't last six rounds against him," she opined.

As the magazine cover claimed her full attention, Jack found himself at the perfect vantage point to peek into the low cut of her sweater, where the channel between two dangerous boulders threatened to swamp him.

But what was that she said? Jack couldn't believe his ears. "Do you follow boxing?" he asked.

Obviously, the garter clamp had overloaded his circuits. She was, after all, a woman, and everybody knew that fisticuffs were about as alien to the fairer half of humanity as were cigars and seven-card stud. He regretted asking such a stupid question.

Alice shadowboxed. "Nothing beats a jab hook combination to get the adrenaline pumping, but that's my second love," she admitted. Then she swung an air bat. "Now baseball, that ranks with religion!"

Who was this woman, Jack wondered? She spoke of baseball and religion in the same breath! Was she the goddess of sports whom the ancients worshipped? And where did one find the candles and incense in this store so that he too might pay homage?

Elation turned to depression. Jack realized that he didn't stand a chance with Miss Alice Mercer. High cheek-boned gals like her went out with guys named Mantle or Sinatra. Let her crash their boats. She was out of his league in spades.

"I wish I had three hours for that great church in the Bronx," Jack said, his lower lip hanging wistfully. He meant it, too. He hadn't seen the inside of Yankee Stadium in three years, roughly the same time he had started with the firm.

Alice placed the packs of flashbulbs in his hand and let her fingers momentarily linger on top of his—as if on purpose. He imagined himself gently ravishing the palm of that perfect hand with the tip of his tongue.

"Oh Jack," she returned in a painful moan, "I rarely miss a series opener against Boston. Why should you?"

Jack. She called me, *Jack.* Alice the ribbed-sweater-adorned-goddess-of-sport remembered my name. How do I ask thee for a date?

The wares finally sorted, Jack and Alice stood up together. After straightening her rumpled skirt, she steadied Jack's overloaded hands with a gentle grip. Her violet eyes gazed into Jack's, and he blinked.

"Nice meeting you, Jack," she said, only to rush off into the ether. Obviously, she had to wash her shiny tresses of auburn hair, which bounced when she walked, and which too begged to be ravished by something more passionate than egg shampoo.

Jack returned to his office and buried his nose back into his work, which had the therapeutic effect of pushing Alice Mercer out of his mind. Since Thelma had freed his schedule so that he could work on his latest merger, he opened his safe and removed the envelope containing the paperwork. Meanwhile, the grandfather clock in the conference room chimed an hour's passage, but as Jack lined up the papers on both sides of his blotter, all he could hear was an inner voice dictating a nonstop succession of cumbersome paragraphs, each one laden with "wherefores" and "heretofores", which he transcribed at dazzling speed onto every other line of an awaiting stack of legal pads.

When the shadows from the Venetian blinds had finally angled across his desk, he jotted down a series of names and telephone numbers onto a wrinkled napkin. The last of six chimes on the grandfather clock came accompanied by a knocking sound. Jack unlocked the door to let Thelma enter. He folded the napkin, and handed it to her.

"Is this the entire list of contacts for the merger?" she asked.

"I've omitted two tip-off names because of their close association with each company. If rumors fly on the Street, I don't want the government saying we were the ones who tattled."

"Outstanding work. I'll fill next weeks' reserve slots with these appointments. Enjoy the weekend."

The journey home provided the usual passing scenery and the "thumpetta-thumpetta" of steel wheels rolling across the track. The bold print on the back page of *The New York Post* read:

YANKS TAKE SECOND PLACE WITH LARSON SHUTOUT

But the scribbles below said:

Alice

—Over and over again with varying forms of artistic expression.

The train pulled into the Bronxville station, and Jack exited the train a somber man. He dumped his newspaper into an awaiting litter basket, and with but a bag of film and flashbulbs left to carry, he made his way toward home.

CHAPTER 8

Midtown

The morning larks sang a symphony for Jack and Judy as they strolled toward the Bronxville station, where the Saturday nine fifty-one would take them for a quick jaunt into the city. Jack dressed casually, which meant khakis and a button down shirt that wasn't white, while Judy sported her basic maiden's attire of bobby socks, tartan skirt and ruffled blouse. Only the patterns for both the skirt and the ruffles varied slightly from the day before and the day before that. The penny loafers, however, remained the same, and as always, she wore that horseshoe clip in her hair for good luck.

Arm in arm, they arrived at the station, and when the platform bell rang out the southbound train's imminent arrival, Judy leaned her head against Jack's shoulder. Jack knew that the action wouldn't get any hotter than this though his desire to push convention always remained. The train squealed to a stop, and the two betrothed boarded without incident.

Judy sat next to the window, which for Jack provided the same old scenery just as the train wheels provided the same old "thumpetta-thumpetta" that they had for the last three years. But on the romantic side, Judy took Jack's hand, and she stroked it. He cast her a sideways glance, and she went so far as to pucker her lips and kiss the air in front of him. *Scandalous!*

"Grand Central Station… Final Stop!" shouted the conductor, and Jack, Judy and barely a dozen other souls filed out the doors for the wonders of midtown Manhattan.

Lo midtown! In his short career, Jack had sampled only morsels of this glittering domain, which had served merely as a way station on his commute to and from the Street. To Jack, Midtown was magical. Take the women for instance. On Wall Street, your toothless granny would fit right in if she could pound the keys at sixty words per minute and take Pittman shorthand. Brokerage houses, law firms and insurance companies valued utility over style, so somebody like the motherly Thelma Kane merited maximum advancement because she had a sergeant major's command of order and precision. Why, even Nora Kincaid with her fractured diction could rise to Thelma's level in the chain of command if she didn't marry a cop or a fireman and have five babies first. You would never find that in midtown.

Ah yes, midtown… Here was the land of fashion houses, glamour magazines, trendy stores, Madison Avenue, modeling agencies, legitimate theater and the mass media. The midtown woman possessed a certain pizzazz not to mention some pretty jazzy looks. She might hunt and peck on the keyboard, but she had a manicure and a pedicure, and she wore real women's clothes that cuddled her frame and hugged her curves. Okay, so maybe tight sweaters were still a taboo item, but who needed that kind of distraction at the office? Would the work ever get done?

Jack and Judy walked up Madison Avenue, where female mannequins draped in the latest fashion coup kept watch from every shop window. Judy peeked into the window of a corner boutique catering to the bone girdle set, and Jack detected genuine interest on her part for a matching ensemble. The fashion might have been a bit understated, but compared to her girlish wardrobe it was Paris after dark.

"If you want it, I'll buy it for you, " Jack offered.

"Oh Jack, you are such a darling, but a young lady wouldn't wear something like that. It just wouldn't be proper," she replied.

"Forgive my presumption," Jack returned. And then he thought about the words, "young lady". In polite society, were they not synonymous with the word "virgin" and all its supposed innocence?

Jack and Judy reached Forty-Seventh Street, the Diamond District. They had window-shopped for maybe four or five storefronts when Judy said, "I see a few attractive rings, but they lack that *je ne sais quoi*. Let's try Van Cleef & Arpels or Harry Winston."

Jack gagged. Even on his comfortable salary, those pricey establishments would leave him lunching on macaroni and cheese for the next year. On the other hand, could it be that the right ring might bring out the midtown woman in Judy? "Why don't we try Tiffany's first?" he suggested.

"Yes, of course, I like that store. Mother shops there all the time."

The blood returned to Jack's brain. Tiffany's was hardly a charity store, but at least the place didn't shake you down for your firstborn. And despite Judy's prim demeanor, he told himself that he did love her. Yes, there was a lot to admire.

He squeezed her hand just to let her know that he appreciated her willingness to meet him halfway, and she reciprocated by intertwining her fingers with his. *Oh the cleanliness of her affection!* They made brief eye contact, and he realized that he wanted her cuteness now more than ever. He had heard from Roy about how she had entertained the little boys and girls in kindergarten class with tales of *Hugo the Hippo* and *Uncle Remus*. And when Hugo the Hippo talked, Judy made husky hippo sounds, and all the children giggled. The parents and school administrators loved her, and though polite company never dared to broach the topic, offhanded comments about her expertise with children had assured Jack that she would make an excellent mother. Now if only she would let her fingernails grow…

"Oh Miss Faraday, what a pleasure it is to see you again," called the sales manager at Tiffany's, his west London accent as smooth as decanted sherry, "How is your dear mother?"

Jack imagined himself as a duck in a shooting gallery. He and Judy had barely stepped past the first sales counter when they had been spotted. In his limited experience, Jack assumed that client spotting was a craft strictly confined to the financial community, but then again why shouldn't a midtown business catering to the carriage trade use a nifty trick known to put an extra million or two in a speculator's back pocket? Yes, this man had the eye and the instincts of a spotter. So why wasn't he working for the Ambassador?

"Mother is well these days, Errol," Judy answered with a curtsy. "I shall say that you were asking for her."

Errol! The man was forty years Judy's senior, yet she addressed him by his first name as if he were a domestic in an Anglican household.

"I am so pleased," Errol replied. He held up his index finger, and an entire entourage of sales personnel descended in wolf pack formation on both his flanks.

"Good morning, Miss Faraday. What will be your pleasure this morning?" greeted a junior sales clerk. Jack couldn't help but notice the taper in her calves as they plunged into her stiletto pumps.

"Oh Meredith, my fiancé, Jack Preston, wishes to present me with a ring for our engagement," Judy answered in a gush but without the curtsy. Jack wondered if this lack of gesture was intended to inform the delectable Meredith not to display her alluring bosom in front of his morally corrupt eyes. If that was the message, Meredith certainly got it because she stepped aside to let a male of the species take the lead.

"As director of sales for the entire Tiffany staff, I extend to you our congratulations on this joyous occasion," he said with genteel charisma. "My name is Bartholomew…and now if you will, please step this way."

The entourage formed a perimeter around Jack and Judy to escort them outrider-style to the back of the store. Jack expected a shakedown, which in Fifth Avenue parlance meant a salon presentation. How much would this outing cost? Jack could already taste the cheese sauce.

And sure enough, Bartholomew led the entourage to a private room. Errol and Meredith came in tow while the rest of the sales staff disbursed to their pre assigned stations. Let the show begin.

Errol pulled out an ersatz Louis XIV chair from an ersatz Louis XIV table, and—oh so properly—he seated Judy. No such chair awaited Jack. Errol positioned him so that he would stand behind Judy's right shoulder, where she wouldn't see him cringe in pain whenever she shrieked with joy at a priceless bauble with a priceless price. Of course, the net cost after two percent sales tax of said bauble would never be mentioned until Judy staked her claim on it. And let it be understood; there would be no haggling, no compromising down and no comparison-shopping. Leave that to the Philistines on Forty-Seventh Street.

"Your tea, Miss Faraday," said Meredith, pouring a sturdy, orange pekoe blend from a Tiffany teapot into a Tiffany cup. Neatly placed upon the Tiffany saucer was a thin wedge of lemon and to no great surprise, a Tiffany teaspoon.

Meredith prepared a second cup for Jack and placed it next to Judy's cup. He reached for it, but Judy gently pushed his hand to his side. Meredith then placed milk and sugar service on the table, and Jack's hand figured that it could now water his sandpaper tongue. *Not so fast*, said Judy's hand brushing Jack's hand back to his side again.

"I'll take one serving of sugar, Jack," Judy said, and, reminded of his manners, Jack placed a heaping teaspoon into Judy's cup.

"Shall I squeeze your lemon, my dear?" Jack said in his best Peter Lawford voice.

Judy gave Jack a subtle poke in the side, and he remembered that Mother used the same finger to admonish Dad for any *faux pas* emanating from his mouth. *Was this less than genteel touch a product of the same finishing school?*

"Mr. Preston," Errol said causing Meredith and Bartholomew to fall in line next to him, "before you begin your quest for a gem, I must say that you have already asked the most precious of gems to be your wife. I have known Judy since her nursery school days when her mother brought her here to select a charm bracelet with its very first charm. Do you still have that bracelet, Judy?

"I shall treasure it always."

"Then let us add to that treasure." With the grace of a ballerina, Errol extended an open palm to his side, and members of the sales entourage, each one bearing an engagement ring on a blue velvet tray, paraded before Jack and Judy.

Bartholomew acted as master of ceremonies and announced each entry vying for Judy's heart. "Here, Minerva displays a one and one-quarter Tiffany-cut stone in a platinum setting. Notice the brilliance of the stone in the ambient light…"

As Bartholomew spoke, Minerva handed the ring display to Meredith, and she in turn presented it before Judy's admiring eyes. Jack's eyes, however, gravitated toward Meredith, or to be more precise, Meredith's bosom.

Meredith displayed ring after ring to Judy, and Bartholomew droned on, "…where we use only eighteen-carat gold…notice the attention to detail…in a tradition dating back one hundred years…Veronica brings you a… first worn by the Empress of…an investment that has outpaced the Dow Jones Industrial Average…"

Suddenly, an elegant bauble made Judy's eyelids retreat into her sockets. "Oh Jack, it's… It's… May I try it on?"

Meredith set the tray on the table. As Judy splayed her fingers, Meredith slipped on the ring with a rocking twist.

"It fits perfectly. I adore it!" Judy squeaked in sonic pitch. "How about you, Jack?"

"I adore you," he replied taking hold of her hand, "and nothing in man's creation is too good for you."

"Oh Jack, I love you so much!"

Judy and Jack kissed the most innocent of kisses, and the entire sales staff beamed at the purity of this act. Meredith then whispered in Jack's ear to follow her, and he dreamed for a second that they might attempt some quick spooning in an adjoining salon. Alas, she merely ushered him to the cashier, where she presented him with an invoice for eighteen hundred dollars plus tax, roughly three months pay; not too bad a fleecing. He whipped out his Carte Blanche, and she processed the transaction.

When Jack and Judy joined up again, she was in tears. "Oh Jack, my sweet Jack, I love you so much," she stammered and then dabbed her eyes with a cotton handkerchief, which Bartholomew produced from his vest pocket.

Judy splayed her fingers during the entire ride back to Bronxville. "Do you love me, Jack?" she asked.

"I love you," he replied, and she laid her head on his shoulder.

"Do you really love me, Jack?"

"I love you so much it hurts."

"How much does it hurt?"

It hurts more than thirteen hundred dollars, and I still don't get to ravish your bosom…not even sneak a peek," he thought, and then he pondered what adventures Meredith might have embarked upon had he presented her with such a chunk of ice.

Judy stared at Jack like a forlorn waif, and he realized that along with Alice Mercer, he had to relegate Meredith into the trash bin of futile whimsy and come up with an answer to Judy's satisfaction. "It hurts… It hurts…" he stuttered to no avail.

But then the "thumpeta-thumpeta" of wheels on track called out to him for the briefest of moments, and his mouth reconnected with his brain. "Judy, I can't bear the pain of not being with you every hour of the day, and the sound of this train reminds me that it will take me from you every morning that I go to work."

"Oh Jack, it's you and me forever."

And Jack recalled the joyful chirping of the larks that morning.

And they sang *Beautiful Dreamer* all the way back to Bronxville.

CHAPTER 9

Venus in Silk

Jack held the handle to the front door of his home. "Are you ready?" he asked.

Judy gulped and nodded her assent.

Jack pushed the latch. "Are you sure your mother is here?"

"She said she was coming to prepare a D.A.R. reception with your mother and Denise; something about a salute to the descendants of General Putnam."

"Well then, let's go on in and surprise her."

Jack pushed open the door only to discover that surprises could be relative.

"Surprise!" greeted a crowded ensemble of over thirty well-wishers to a fusillade of popping bulbs. Balloons and party favors festooned the entranceway, and a hanging banner proclaimed:

CONGRATULATIONS JACK AND JUDY

Jack's face blanched to the color of Chablis while Judy's visage preferred the subtle blush of rosé. "Did you know?" he asked her.

"No. I never..."

"Let me see your ring," Denise interrupted, whereupon the entire female contingency converged around Judy to catch a glimpse of her sparkling nugget.

Jack spotted Roy in the corner. "You told me you had a baseball game today," Jack said.

"The game was just a ruse to get you to reveal your whereabouts so that we could organize this bash behind your back. The season doesn't start until next week, good friend."

"Well, you caught me looking. Touché!"

The party retired to the backyard, where a caterer had set up hot and cold buffets. A bartender served up the good stuff including a case of iced bubbly, and waitresses scampered to and fro to hand out hors d'oeuvres. While Judy held court on the back porch with ladies young and old, the men lined up behind Oliver for their shots of sunshine. Their drinks already served, Jack and Roy ambled over to a rose trellis, where each accepted a pig in the blanket from a waitress with fiery red hair. The sashay in her step was not lost on Jack.

Roy threw up his hands inadvertently spilling drink on his sleeve. "Don't you ever stop with the wandering eye? I mean what would Judy say?"

Jack knew that Judy couldn't say a word because she didn't see a thing. And since her hypothetical response was none of Roy's business anyway, why not change the subject? Jack grit his teeth. "Well, what would my dad and all his Presbyterian buddies say about you spilling their Scottish gold? "

"Tell them that we Congregationalists abhor pleasure in all its forms except when it comes to scalping Indians and burning witches."

"We? Did you say 'we'?" Jack exclaimed. He downed his scotch in one gulp and coughed out his words. "With dad's backing, I can choose the Presbyterian lifestyle once I leave this household."

"Not if you marry Judy you don't. Face it, good friend, once a Puritan, always a Puritan."

Jack's bottom lip dropped into a pout. With the scant gulp of scotch taking hold of his senses, the last thing he wanted to think about was his pastor's teachings, which condemned you to eternal fire for even contemplating illicit intercourse. He remembered lovely Alice in the drugstore aisle. For her, religion could be a bat hitting a baseball. It sounded like his idea of heaven.

Jack looked across the back lawn and spotted Will accepting an appetizer from the redhead. "Come with me, and I'll introduce you to Maureen O'Hara over there." Jack already made his move in that direction. Roy didn't follow.

By the time Jack reached Will, the redhead had already moved on to other guests. Jack glanced up at the back porch and noticed Judy and her ladies in waiting retiring to the great indoors. What could they be up to? Perhaps they might explain to her the facts of life.

Jack put his arm around his little brother's shoulder. "She's dramatic; isn't she Will... the redhead, I mean?"

"Too old for me. I'm the baby in the family. You know, the one that all the neighbors call 'the mistake'."

"Mrs. Kennedy used to call you the bonus baby."

"That was easy for her to say, because she had so many of them. Besides, I don't remember the Kennedys too well. They packed up for the Cape before I could walk."

"Actually, they moved to London."

"That's right…when Mr. Kennedy became the Ambassador. Dad told me that mother was upset about the appointment. Why would it matter?"

"She thought it provocative for FDR to name a Boston Irish envoy to St. James Court. Still, she was very fond of Mrs. Kennedy, especially after she designated you the bonus baby."

"Then get me a drink, and we'll toast Mrs. Kennedy."

Even though Will still had the summer to go before he hit the legal eighteen, Jack considered it ill mannered to refuse a toast. He reflected upon the negatives incurred in plying his baby brother with booze when suddenly it occurred to him that with the exception of the redhead and her clan, some mysterious force had sucked all the women inside the house. Break out the poker chips!

With Will by his side, Jack strutted over to the bartender and ordered up two scotch neat. The bartender took one look at Will, winked, and then served up doubles.

"Remember little one," Jack said, "if Mother or anybody of the feminine persuasion comes out the back door, it's bottoms up into the grass."

"To Mrs. Kennedy," said Will, holding up his glass proudly.

"And to the great Joseph P.," added Jack.

As Jack took a measured sip, he watched with delight as his brother took a grand quaff, which sent his throat into spasm. Jack attempted to slap him on the back so that he could get a good cough out of his system; however, Will backed away and returned a slow breath of satisfaction. Jack reciprocated with a nod.

But then the wide shoulders of Will's lips transformed into a big zero, and he spilled his drink onto the grass. Upon seeing this wasted treasure, the bartender almost rent his garment.

"Bogies at three o'clock!" Will said stuffing the shot glass in his pocket. Jack spun around to behold Denise bearing down.

"Pour a pitcher of water where you dropped your drink before it makes a brown spot on the lawn," she advised Will.

She then turned to Jack. "Judy has a surprise for you."

A surprise! Denise's rising inflection on the word of the day gave Jack cause to think of Judy sitting erect in a bathtub laden with bubble bath. Copious suds adorned her bosom.

He followed Denise through the kitchen, where an awaiting tea service of gilded china told him that he had entered a woman's world. She led the way up the stairway, where he could hear women's chatter in the distance, and he followed her into his parents' perfume-laden bedroom, where a coterie of women attended to Judy as if she were the Queen of the Nile.

Except she wasn't Judy anymore…

She was a vision in a contoured blouse and a clinging skirt. Lipstick painted her lips, and shadow and liner highlighted her eyes while silk stockings and patent leather pumps sung *Hosannas* to her legs. Verily, Jack wanted to drop to his knees, and with hands outstretched over his head, bow to the floor.

He knew he was not worthy of this divine creature. Would she allow him to grovel at her pumps and caress the sheerness of silk upon velvety flesh? Prostrate before her, he would ravish her legs with a thousand nibbles and kisses, and thence he would rub his cheek in the crook of her leg and run his hands along her garter straps only to ravish her thighs and ravish her hips and ravish the bend that commenced…from…her hips…and…and…

"Aren't you going to kiss me?" she asked.

Kiss her? Jack wanted to rip the clothes from her skin and devour her. Then again he looked around at all the proper ladies, each holding her countenance so properly still, and he suspected a setup. He had to come up with something quick.

"Do you mean that we should give a public display of affection?" he returned.

"Bravo, Jack!" Mrs. Faraday applauded. "You are a true gentleman."

"I try my best everyday, especially with our beloved Judy."

The ladies all sighed in unison. Such gallantry, such chivalry and such gentility… Was not this man an exemplar of righteousness and a guardian of virtue?

"I'm so proud of you, Jack!" Judy cooed. "I want to shout it out from the top of the Chrysler building."

"Will you come outside with me?" he asked.

But Mrs. Faraday answered in her stead. "We've all had our fun today prettying my baby up, but we don't want to let appearances spawn any scandal among the men. So enjoy the afternoon with your friends while we slip Judy out of these borrowed clothes."

Well, Mrs. Faraday was definitely onto something when she told him to enjoy the companionship of the fellows. Tonight they would reconfirm their male bonds by screaming for blood in front of a television set presenting the rumble between the Ole Mongoose, Archie Moore, and Bert Whitehurst. Did life ever get better than that?

Jack returned to the male fold outside, where he whiled away the afternoon in energetic conversation about baseball statistics with family and neighbors. As evening drew near, the ladies rejoined the backyard party to offer Jack and Judy a champagne toast. Judy may have returned in her maiden's outfit, but to Jack the memory of her dressed as a midtown woman remained, and although she had smeared off her lipstick, the eye shadow and eyeliner remained, which in the evening light gave her eyes an oriental guise.

Jack imagined himself as a pilot shot down by the Japanese over China, and Judy was a Chinese artisan in a *cheongsam*, who had pulled his wounded body from the wreckage. Despite the peril imposed by hostile troops, who could break down her door without a moment's notice, she bravely hid him in her studio, where during the day he would pose in the nude for her. At night she would let down her black pigtail and would nurse him back to health with her bosom. Yes, yes, yes…after he married Judy, he would buy her the finest silk from Hong Kong, and he must not forget the black wig either.

"Let us have a toast," Oliver announced. He led Jack and Judy over to the rose trellis, where the shutterbugs in the group took snapshots of Judy standing demurely behind Jack, who sat straight-legged in a dining room chair. Meanwhile, the rest of the party gathered around them, and the waitresses handed out the champagne. Finally, with all the glasses elevated to the heavens, Jack nodded to his dad.

"To Jack and Judy, the perfect couple," Oliver said, and the assembly echoed his words in perfect unison.

The ladies sipped; the men gulped, and Will slugged down the bubbly. Thus, the party had come to its conclusion, but not before Will reminded Jack, Oliver and Roy about dessert. "Hey guys, it's almost time for the Moore–Whitehurst showdown. I claim the easy chair," he called.

"Ha! The rented bridge chairs will claim the ringside view tonight," Oliver said.

Meanwhile, Emily, who had been conversing with Judy and Denise, put in her two cents. "You men may watch that boxing match if you must, but not here," she said.

"*Mother*!" Jack whined. "Boxing is a noble art. I don't understand your objection."

"If you don't understand that your noble art is a violent remnant of Roman hedonism, then understand this: the ladies of the house have reserved Saturday nights for *Your Hit Parade*. That's the way it's been, and that's the way it stays."

The very idea of watching a musical revue on this night of all nights made Jack want to run on over to Sears Roebuck and bring home the latest in television technology, namely a portable unit with a handle on the top. Fortunately, Roy had a better idea.

"You can come over to my place. We've got a second TV in the basement. The place may be a little dingy, but..."

"Say no more, Roy. We're coming," Jack said.

"*Jaa-ack*, you can't leave me tonight," Judy whimpered with a wounded expression that befit a poster of a starving child holding out an empty bowl in war-ravaged Europe.

Emily and Denise glared daggers at Jack, and so he looked to the guys for sympathy, but sympathy he would not see; Roy turned his head away; Oliver shook his head no, and Will just threw up his hands. And with minutes to go before the main event, the three of them trotted off with five other men to leave Jack in the proper company of proper ladies.

True to Roy's word, his unfinished basement with its concrete floor and exposed pipes was indeed dingy, but add to that the smoke of four cigars and a live boxing broadcast, and one might call it ambiance. "...And White-hurst jabs again but doesn't find his mark," called the announcer with luke-warm enthusiasm.

Will pointed ringside. "Look, Dad. You can actually recognize the faces beyond the ropes. There's Jack Dempsey and Joe Louis," he said.

"That's only a taste of what you can see with this twenty-four-inch screen," Roy bragged. "I bought this model yesterday as a Saturday night companion."

"Whitehurst hooks with his left, but Archie Moore answers with a punishing combination..." This time the announcer's voice climbed an octave, and Will shadowboxed in reply.

Back at the Preston residence, the ladies devoted their fond attention to *Your Hit Parade* cast singers, Dorothy Collins and Gisele MacKenzie, war-bling the Rosemary Clooney super hit about pipedream love, *Hey There*. For eight weeks running, this song sat unchallenged at the top of the *Bill-board* charts, and according to formula, this represented the eighth time that it closed the show. Jack believed that such success merited retiring this monster ditty with a gold watch, and yet cash registers the world over still gulped down record-breaking amounts of legal tender from women of every age and ethnicity. But Jack was a man—a real man—and not a sissy. Wouldn't the ladies let him have a quick peak at the boxing match? Pretty please?

The ladies stared at the TV set as if it had taken possession of their souls. The song built into a crescendo, and Judy put her arm around Jack in a public display of affection.

Jack smirked. Her hand felt so soft. What did the rest of her feel like?

CHAPTER 10

In the Bag

Jack pushed through the revolving door and rushed past the newsstand, where the Moore v. Whitehurst showdown had merited front-page status on every newspaper stack. Wasn't it enough that every commuter from Bronxville to the Battery had remarked that this fight was the greatest he had ever seen? Now Chester Brown would take his turn throwing salt and pepper in his wound.

"Put me in a cage with a tiger. Chain me to a bear. But please, Lord, please hide me from the likes of Archie Moore!" Chester jabbed and feinted, then jabbed and hooked.

From the suburbs to downtown, Jack had witnessed this new dance infecting the male populace in every train car and on every corner. But did those happy souls know the words to *Hey There*? "I heard it was the fight of the century," Jack mumbled, his head hung low.

"What do you mean, 'heard'? Can't a rich man like you afford a TV set?"

Jack shrugged his shoulders. How could he ever explain? Fortunately, a new workweek and an empty elevator beckoned. After a moment's meditation on the futility of women's television entertainment, Jack slipped into the back of the conference room, where the partners and counsels of the firm gathered to kick off the week.

The grandfather clock chimed out nine bells, and Mr. Hargrave scooted through the door and went directly to the head of the mahogany table. He nodded to all present, which was his way of saying a general "Hello... How are you?" without sacrificing the time to do so. Time was money, and nowhere was it more the case than at a white-shoe firm, where time translated into billable hours. This meeting, however, didn't punch the clock. It would be brief.

Mr. Hargrave took his place at the table, and the counsels and remaining partners followed in unison. Thelma Kane sat to his side at a transcription desk.

"Tell me, Mrs. Kane, did we meet our target for the previous week?" he asked.

"Even with the subtraction of one lost appointment in mergers and acquisitions, we exceeded our goal by sixteen billable hours."

"Excellent! Speaking of mergers and acquisitions, could you give us a report, Jack?"

"Including Thursday's add on, we now have six pending mergers and eighteen pending acquisitions, which is not only a record for the firm but one for the Street as well."

Considering the lost billable hour came from his department, Jack expected a polite nod from Mr. Hargrave at most, but what he got was a nod and applause. Then, the partners voted aye with the palms of their hands followed in turn by the counsels. It could have turned into a standing ovation, but hey, this was Wall Street not midtown.

Mr. Hargrave beamed. "Counselor, it's time you knew that our top clients now ask for you by name."

And with the ovation rising to a crescendo, Thelma flashed the thumbs up sign to Jack. At long last, Mr. Hargrave had rendered him commendation among his colleagues. And so the process would begin.

Jack would pick up an occasional assignment that was usually relegated to a partner. After six months or so, the partners would meet to formulate a buy-in deal for Jack, and if all went well, they would unanimously vote for him to fork over two years worth of current salary to become a junior partner. Of course they would allow him to sign his name to a promissory note so he could pay his way in on the layaway plan, but it didn't matter. Partnership was equity, and if he ever decided to leave the firm, the firm would pay him that money plus appreciation back. Furthermore, partnership made him bulletproof, and short of killing another partner, he could never receive the pink slip. Ah yes, this ovation meant more than just being in the running for the brass ring. Partnership was now in the bag; let the generals of the Street speak his name with awe.

The meeting concluded, and after some pats on the back, Jack headed into his office to seize the day. As he leaned back in his swivel chair, Thelma popped in waving a requisition form in her right hand. Jack smiled at her and nodded his head up and down. Thelma reciprocated with barely raised lips and shook her head back and forth.

"No applause... Thank you very much," Jack said holding out his hands to wave off any further accolades.

"A word of warning," Thelma deadpanned. "Don't let today's tribute go to your head. If you don't make the grade tomorrow, that head will roll."

Jack dropped his hands to his side. Joviality and wise cracks didn't impress Thelma, especially when she came to issue motherly advice. Jack put on his lawyerly face. Something was eating her. He could just tell from the way her hand crumpled the requisition to turn it into wastebasket fodder.

"I like you, Jack," she said. "You're talented, and you have a good attitude. That said, you lack a certain—how shall I say it—sophistication. Be aware that sharks lurk in friendly waters."

Jack couldn't resist the opening. "Hey, I'm a lawyer. I trained to be a shark."

Thelma placed the requisition on Jack's desk. "Go ahead and joke, but you can forget about charging the firm for a luncheon with tomorrow's noon appointment. Given your present rank of associate, it may strike the partners as—let us say—presumptuous."

"The luncheon was Paul's idea."

"Was the oyster bar at Oscar's Delmonico's his idea too?"

"As a matter of fact, it was."

"Oh for crying out loud!" Thelma bit into her lip. "Look, Jack," she said, "I'll finagle an hour and a half window in your schedule tomorrow, but you'll have to make up the time at the end of the day. Go to Delmonico's by yourself on your own time and your own money. Since Paul is such an expert on this matter, let him set up the reservation."

Thelma had no sooner marched out of the office than Jack folded the requisition into a paper airplane. With a flick of the wrist, he tossed it toward the doorway, where it banked into Paul's incoming chest.

"She went for it, didn't she?" said Paul, making the catch.

"Not quite... There's no company support on this one. She's humoring me by letting me fly solo into this eatery so I can pretend I'm one of the big shots."

Paul pumped his fist. "Yes! That's even better."

"How so? I've got no client to impress."

"Uhh... wha..." Paul stuttered. After a moment's hesitation, he found his words. "What I mean is that you can spend your time watching whatever it is that makes the big shots so big.... You won't have any business dealings to get in the way of your research."

"How astute!" Jack remarked. "I'll be conducting research."

Paul handed Jack the paper airplane, and Jack glanced out the window. How far would this aerodynamic wonder fly from the twenty-second floor?

CHAPTER 11

Oysters on the Half Shell

Jack's shoulders slumped, and he abruptly straightened them. Delmonico's was not the place to look like an intimidated kid. He followed the maitre d' past the tables of scions, captains and pillars of high finance, who in their tailored suits and polished shoes could have ground him into filler for their hand-rolled Havanas.

Waiters scurried back and forth, filling pitchers and lighting cigars. Some even carried trays of food, but food had the air of side attraction for those in the know with the money and the power. No, these guys didn't come here to fill their bellies; they came here to conquer the world. Jack knew that within a year, he would be their peer. Following his honeymoon with Judy, he would return to the Street a fulfilled man, and Mr. Hargrave would escort him here to introduce him to this crowd of top feeders as one of their equals. But for now, he could only look at them like the kid he was; a ragamuffin with his nose pushed up against the glass. All things would come in time.

The waiter pulled out a chair from a table for two over by the oyster bar. "Enjoy your meal, Mr. Preston," he said handing Jack a menu and seating him properly. Jack gazed at the entrees, and, what was this? A hand waved to him over the top of the menu. Who could he possibly know in a place like this? But this hand belonged to a woman, the only woman in a sea of lapels and neckties, and what a woman she was!

Two tables down, that siren of the ribbed sweater, Miss Alice Mercer, entertained a distinguished looking gent with Wall Street all but stamped on his elegantly coiffed, steel gray hair. Jack politely nodded to her, and Mr. Wall Street never noticed. And why should he? Jack knew he was out of his league with the both of them; so let them enjoy each other's company.

A waiter approached. "May I make some suggestions, sir?" he asked.

"That's all right. I'll go with a dozen oysters and the house white."

"Very well, sir."

The waiter retrieved the menu and headed toward the oyster chef. Jack watched him go, but then his eyes darted back to Alice's table, and—

poof—two vacant seats meant that she had once again pulled her disappearing act.

Jack sighed at the cruelty of his desire. What prized possessions would he have given to spend a night with her? If she asked him to abandon his family, his career and his Judy for her womanly favor, would he acquiesce? Would he allow himself to crash upon her rocks?

Jack sensed a presence behind him and glanced over his shoulder to behold, as if by some sleight of hand, his siren. Jack tried to say something clever, but he just gawked.

"What's the matter, Jack? Don't you know how to say hello to a girl?" Alice asked in a voice light and feathery.

Remembering his manners, Jack snapped to upright attention and extended his hand. "Alice! So good to see you again! Where are you rushing off to today?"

"Actually nowhere. Aren't you going to invite me to your table, or are you expecting someone?"

"No, ...uh, I mean yes... Uh, what I mean is, yes, please have a seat, and no, I'm not expecting anybody."

Alice laughed at his response and brushed his hand as if to tell him that her delight expressed amusement and not ridicule. He pulled out the chair facing him and attempted to seat her there, but defying convention, she moved her chair alongside his as if to imply a desire for intimacy. *Let the gods make their wagers*, he thought before settling into his seat.

"What about your lunch date?" Jack inquired.

"My what? Oh, you mean Dudley. I'm just his escort... his beard."

"His what?"

"His beard... I hide the fact that he's queer. You know... He likes men."

"But he's such a good-looking guy."

Alice giggled. "You're a good-looking guy, too. Shall I introduce you to him?"

Jack pulled on his collar. "I'd much rather get to know you."

For a moment, Jack regretted saying those words. Had he been too forward with her? How could he explain to her that she gave him no choice? Of course he preferred women to men. How could a man want otherwise? Fortunately, her leg rubbing against his leg within the confines of an extra long tablecloth raised the level of forwardness. And what was that she had said about his good looks?

Alice reached into her purse and pulled out two tickets. "Perhaps these might interest you," she said. "I have two box seats for tomorrow's game against Boston. Would you be my date?"

"As long as you don't pinch me… I don't want to wake up."

The waiter delivered a platter of shimmering oysters on the half shell as well as a bottle of Chablis with two glasses. "Forgive me, sir, but when I noticed present company had joined you, I presumed that you may wish to share a bottle," he said.

Damn, these waiters knew how to troll for tips, Jack thought. He nodded his affirmative to the waiter, and after the obligatory uncorking and tasting ceremony, two glasses received their just due.

"To the Yankees," Alice said hoisting her glass. Jack touched his glass to hers, and with the ice certainly broken, he picked up a forkful of raw oyster and dangled it in front of her mouth. She grabbed his hand and directed the slimy gob past her teeth. Then she gave his hand a pinch, and he knew that this dream of his hosted living flesh.

And, oh, what desirable flesh it was!

CHAPTER 12

Burning the Oil

When Jack returned from lunch, Thelma greeted him at the reception with a steady tapping on her watch. Had she no faith in him? After all, he had completed this successful outing before the gears on the grandfather clock clicked into chiming mode, and he could already feel the primitive urge to impress his first group of afternoon clients who had journeyed from the furthest reaches of Minnesota to stake a claim on a Pennsylvania foundry. At the moment, the names and the particulars of this deal escaped him, but why clutter one's brain with such detail? All Jack needed was for one of the clients to produce a business card, and the file cabinet inside his head would spit out the requisite dossier. And if that wasn't enough, Jack could rest assured that Thelma had already placed the physical dossier for this transaction front and center upon his blotter.

Jack loved this part of the deal. Hundred of hours in solitude could be spent chasing paper on just one acquisition, but then came the time to shake hands. *Mr. Henry Robertson, executive vice-president and agent for the 3M Company wishes to conclude the purchase of Bethlehem Foundries. Let it be known that a trustee from the 3M Board of Directors and a company counsel accompany him.* Ah yes.

"Welcome to New York, Mr. Robertson… Jack Preston at your service."

"Please, Jack… You can call me Hank."

"Good news, Hank, the SEC has waived intervention for your purchase. You can handle it as if you were buying a car."

"But this is a seven-figure deal, Jack. How could the feds possibly issue a waiver?"

"3M is purchasing only six figures of equity. The rest of the sum pays off promissory notes. Utilizing an appellate ruling from a Chicago case last year, I convinced the feds to scale back their purview. Reluctantly, they bought the argument."

"You're the tops, Jack. What's left to do?"

"Sign the papers; then pop the cork."

And so went the day. Serious clients entered Jack's office; happy clients exited. The grandfather clock struck six, but this only meant payback time for Jack's extended lunch break. Was it worth it? Jack rubbed the ticket to the Yankees-Red Sox game that Alice had given him. Gladly, he would have worked beyond midnight for the privilege of this date.

Jack settled into his desk and rolled up his sleeves. A pad of blank paper stared him in the face. With a dossier and stack of case reviews by his side, he picked up his pen and commenced writing his signature wherefores, heretofores and whereases.

And so on... And so forth...

Jack immersed himself in his lawyerly prose and tapped into a rhythmic train of cogitation that made the clock jump ahead in beats until a thousand sparkling lights flickered across the downtown skyline. Only the phone ringing in the reception could break him from his rhythm, for only he among the many remained on post at this nightly hour. On the fourth ring, he picked up his receiver and punched the illuminated line button.

"Good Evening... Dunston, Hargrave and Thorpe... Oh hello, Judy... Yes, I'm burning the oil here... Yes, I'll be leaving shortly... Sure, I can stop by... Of course we'll make an appointment to see Reverend Holmes... I love you, too."

At times like these, one needed a Checker Cab to deposit oneself at one's destination, and with briefcase in hand, Jack arrived just so at Judy's doorsteps. Mrs. Faraday answered the door.

"I hope they're paying you for the hours you put in, Jack. Judy has taken over the kitchen," Mrs. Faraday said.

Jack tipped his hat and made a left turn past the foyer, where he wended his way past the drawing room, the game room and the study, thence through a back hallway, which lead to the informal dining room, which adjoined the kitchen. Jack couldn't conceive of a Congregationalist family living in such an abode. Regardless of a family's fortune, church edict had forbid the hiring of servile labor, which meant that Mrs. Faraday had to clean and maintain each room by herself. It must have come as an endless undertaking. Then again, Jack loved how Judy would regale him with childhood stories of playing hide-and-seek with over thirty well-appointed rooms to explore. One round of play could literally last an hour.

Jack didn't know what to find in the kitchen's light. Would it be Chef Judy laying out an assortment of tantalizing dishes? No, at this witching hour, the saucepans and cutlery surely lay sleeping in the cupboards. Or would it be ingénue Judy holding a sipping cup to a Teddy bear?

Perish the thought!

Jack entered the cavernous kitchen, where jumbles of swatches, sewing patterns and bridal magazines had invaded and taken over the tables, the chairs and the counter tops. At the carving table, Judy sat with pencil and pad. Veritably, she had become General Judy planning not a mere wedding, but a full-scale assault on the church. What would her Puritan ancestors say?

Upon seeing Jack, her face radiated sunshine, and she jumped up to tap an innocent kiss on his lips. "You should have called me. They have no right to keep you there so late," she said pouting prettily.

"I don't punch a clock. I finish when the work is done, sweets. You know that."

Judy picked up a swatch. "I was looking at fabric for the bridesmaids. This is my absolute favorite."

She handed the swatch to Jack and pointed to a pattern in a magazine. "The fabric and the pattern match perfectly. What do you think?"

Jack rubbed the swatch between his fingers. It was printed silk, probably the finest weave that money could buy. It felt so cool and slippery, almost as if the silkworms spinning it had subsisted on a diet of saddle soap and linseed oil. What in the name of Cain had planted the impulse in his beloved to go out and accumulate all this paraphernalia?

"Judy, the wedding is a year away. Isn't all this preparation a bit premature?" he asked.

"You have to plan these things almost a year in advance. As we speak, Father is looking into a banquet facility. The one we want is almost completely reserved for June. They want a twenty percent deposit by Friday."

"Oh, good grief!"

Judy stroked Jack's face. "Don't worry, sweetheart. They guaranteed us the date. Now, the next thing we have to do is meet with Reverend Holmes."

"And when would be the most opportune time call on him for this chitchat?"

"What about tomorrow evening?"

Jack rubbed the silk swatch again, and with his other hand, he patted the Yankee ticket in his pocket. Certainly the silk would have its day, but that was a long day off. Tonight, the ticket would win his affection. "I'd hate to leave the good Reverend hanging out to dry tomorrow evening, sweets, but I'm currently working on seven mergers and twenty-eight acquisitions. I may not get home until midnight." Jack had rehearsed those exaggerated numbers many times over during his ride in the Checker Cab, and with a little help from a straight face and a smooth delivery, the words sped flawlessly past his lips.

Judy sighed and shook her head. "Oh, you poor baby! I'll think of you tomorrow night when you're locked away in that cruel, cruel office."

CHAPTER 13

Extra Bases

The crack of the bat was electric. The ball shot in a straight line deep into right field, and Mickey Mantle ripped around first base on a quest for a little something extra. Right fielder Jackie Jensen dug in after the ball, and after taking the ricochet off the bullpen fence, he hurled it smack into Ted Lepcio's glove. But the fleet-footed Mick slid under him with room to spare. The fans went nuts.

Tucked into their fifth row box seats behind the first base dugout sat Jack and Alice, who set the pace in the madness. Jack shouted his approval while Alice gripped her thumb and forefinger under her tongue and let out a whistle blast that must have stopped every taxi on the Grand Concourse. Around them, an expanse of animated faces tucked snugly into fedoras hollered tribute to the Mick as he slapped the dust off his knickers. Alice grabbed Jack by the forearm. "Do two bases excite you, Jack?" she asked.

"I'm always a sucker for extras. I can't thank you enough."

"Thank Dudley. It's his box."

"No, thanks. You're more my type."

Yogi Berra stepped up to the plate. If there was any lull in the excitement, it quickly vanished as all eyes focused on the pitcher winding up… All eyes that is except for Jack's… He couldn't take his baby blues off Alice. For this outing, she wore a loose sweater to disguise the treasures that lurked within, but Jack already knew what bounty said sweater contained. Besides, there were those violet eyes, that auburn hair and those full lips, which no sweater could hide. To hell with the game! Jack just wanted to nibble those lips, then ravish that face and preen that hair, all the while gazing into those eyes.

Priapus might announce his intentions, but Jack was ready for the Mutt. On the way to his seat, he purchased a scorecard so that he could rest it on his lap to disguise any accident. Let the Mutt bark and whine all he wants. Jack had him locked in the basement with a leash around his neck. But even with that base covered, Jack figured he better show some semblance of propriety, lest he scare this magnificent woman into permanent hiding. He pointed his head at the catcher's glove as the first pitch curved low.

His eyes, however, strayed in another direction. *I've got to make my move... How do I make my move?*

Hey stupid, she was the one who invited you to this ballpark. There must be some kind of mutual attraction.

But you're blowing it, you moron. Say something clever. Get her to laugh. Do something—anything—before she runs off with a real man out there on the ball field.

"Red hots... Get your red hots," shouted a passing vendor.

Jack looked back to Alice and raised two fingers. She grabbed his fingers and said, "Yes, and with plenty of mustard."

Jack signaled to the vendor and made the transaction for two hot dogs and extra mustard if you please, and thank you very much indeed. With trembling hand, he passed one of the dogs to Alice.

"Don't be nervous, Mr. Preston. It's the frankfurter I want to bite, not you," she teased.

"I feel like I'm on a first date back in high school, except that you address me as if I were the teacher."

"Then in that case, teach me something about yourself. I don't mean your work. Tell me about you."

Alice brushed Jack's hand, which he regarded as a signal to either relax or stop thinking so hard or probably do both. *You don't need to impress me Jack. Just talk to me as if you were conversing with a dear friend*, she conveyed with her touch.

"I'm close with my dad," he began. "He taught my brother and me to love baseball. When the trees started to bud, the three of us would be out on the field... throwing and hitting."

"Is he a lawyer too?"

"No. He's a partner in an advertising research firm. When he's not teaching psychology at Columbia, he sits in a concealed booth and watches people look at test merchandise. Sometimes he scares me. He can follow a customer into a store and tell you what items they plan to buy with astounding accuracy. It's like he can read their minds. How about you?"

Alice took a bite of her hot dog. Rivulets of mustard dripping onto her fingers made her look more approachable. With a reptilian stab of the tongue, she obliterated a cascading yellow stripe off her index finger. Jack blinked. Had he done so a half second earlier, he knew he would have missed this feat.

"I'm a model," Alice replied.

"I should have known."

"But it's not what you think. My proportions are too full for fashion modeling, so I do cheesecake shots in front of racing cars and motorcycles for auto parts distributors."

"I bet you could teach those machines a thing or two about beauty."

Alice placed her hand on Jack's thigh. "That's easy for you to say. Yesterday, I posed against the hood of this new model for Ford called a Thunderbird. It has 427 cubic inches topped by a four-barrel carburetor. A positraction differential splits the torque so that—"

She took a breath. "I hope I'm not boring you with all this technical minutia."

"On the contrary... fascinating is the word." Jack looked out the corner of his eyes toward home plate. The pitch sailed low and inside, and Yogi hammered a line drive, which according to Jack's reckoning didn't move in space; it only expanded in size from a bullet to a missile. Instinctively, he stuck out his hand.

"Alice, duck!" he shouted, and before she could blink, he snatched the ball out of the air just inches short of those full lips and those very breakable teeth.

"You're late on the ball again, Yogi," he cracked, wincing from the kind of sting that only a hot souvenir could deliver.

Alice grabbed Jack by both cheeks and squished her face against his. Her tongue darted under his top lip, then over his bottom lip and then straight across his tongue in less time than it took her to slurp the errant mustard from her finger. With the fire in his hand now doused by more primitive sensations, Jack wrapped his arms around the small of her back, and she gyrated in motions that allowed his embrace to sample the side-to-side whiplash of her bosom.

Arise, Sir Priapus!

A Yankee victory put a nice finishing touch on the evening. Being of gentlemanly stock, Jack escorted Alice to her third floor walkup down in Greenwich Village. As she placed the key in the lock to apartment 4C, he could still taste that torrid kiss. His only lip workouts to date had been with Judy and with perhaps a handful of coeds in college, all of whom likewise vied for the title of "Young Lady." If there were any sirens out there, they hadn't discovered Cornell University by the Finger Lakes or Princeton Law School in the New Jersey farm belt.

With the door unlocked and opened, Jack made his move. "Nobody ever kissed me like that before. Too bad I can't ask you for a first one now."

"Second kisses are better!" Alice said yanking him by the tie into her apartment. Before Jack knew what hit him, her lips bore down on his kisser to the sound of the door slamming behind them. Jack attempted to place his arms around her, but her elbows got in the way as she grabbed his hair with clutched fingers before running them down his chest and torso, all the while fluttering her tongue along the side of his neck. With his arms now merely dangling in space, Alice guided an idle hand to her breast, and Jack popped a boner so large, it almost split his zipper down the middle.

Jack's mind raced so fast that he lost all sense of reason in this liaison. Was he the ravisher or the ravishee? He gasped for air, and her lush lips zeroed in for the kill. What was it about her kiss? The lips moved and they sucked. The teeth nibbled sometimes synchronously with the sucking, sometimes not. Her tongue jabbed and it wagged, but then came a nibble and a suck or a synchronous nibble with a suck after which her tongue trapped his upper lip against her upper lip or his bottom lip against her bottom lip, thence painting their underbellies with dainty brushstrokes worthy of a Flemish master....

Jack stopped thinking about it. Indeed, the siren had lured him onto the rocks, where resistance was futile. She began to unfasten the buttons of his shirt, all the while directing him backward past the kitchen and then through a doorway. Suddenly, the backs of his legs buckled against an unseen object, and he fell. Panic overtook him, but it came to naught when he realized that he had tripped on a bed frame only to make a cushioned landing on its mattress. Still on her feet, Alice towered above him and sneered as if to say she had him in her power. And who was Jack to argue against a point so incredibly moot?

Alice grabbed the foul ball from her pocketbook and pressed it against Jack's lips. Then she seconded the kiss and left a clean print in cherry lipstick. "Now you will always have my lips," she said placing the ball on a night table.

The sneer transformed into a leer, and Alice unfastened the top two buttons of her blouse to expose nature's bounty, not to mention the fine latticework of a black brassiere. *Oh, how could such a precious object exist?* Jack knew his brassieres from the collection of clinical whites that his mother and sister threw into the laundry basket. But black! It looked so naughty... so wicked. What manner of woman would wear such a diabolical treat?

Alice licked her upper lip and then moistened her lower lip off the top one. Gone was the whip action, and in its place came a creeping movement that stirred both excitement and fear.

Oh, the fear! *Thrilling!* Alice was not a siren. She was Calypso, the sea nymph, who had held brave Odysseus in her clutches for seven years while he tried in vain to return home to his wife and son. But how hard did Odysseus really try? Every day, Calypso seduced him anew, and he had become a prisoner of his own desire.

Alice unbuttoned the remaining buttons on her blouse, and with a deft flick of the wrist, she tossed the blouse onto a floor chest at the far side of the bed. Jack spotted the chest out of the corner of one eye. On its teak exterior, twisted figures carved out of ivory inlays provided a momentary distraction from the goodies-packed brassiere staring him straight in the face?

Still flat on his back, Jack wanted to make some kind of suave commentary that marked him as an urban sophisticate, but the boy in him couldn't stop gawking. This was Alice's show, and as she undid her brassiere, he awaited the coming revelation.

Jack realized that Alice hadn't completely unbuttoned his shirt, and so he raced to finish the job before she could unhook her brassiere. He had the advantage; her hands had to reach behind her; but she also had the speed, and before he could unfasten button number two, her brassiere landed—cups up—on the floor chest.

And behold!

Alice's magnificence had so overtaken Jack that he completely forgot about the rest of the buttons on his lipstick-stained shirt. As he reached upward to clasp her womanhood, she undid the last of his buttons and lowered herself on top of him so that her womanly flesh rubbed against his torso. Jack moaned. His carnal needs demanded relief, but he would not permit the raging eagerness inside him to spill his juices as if they were mere excretions. No! This night was a special night with a special woman, and he must be a man.

Alice's hands groped and petted their way around his chest, and when they found a ticklish spot, the reptilian tongue attacked it. Jack clutched the bedspread; the pleasure was unbearable. He attempted to reciprocate by stroking her sides and back, but his movements felt so awkward compared to her artistry.

She pushed up off of him partially, and still holding his hands down in a sort of schoolboy pin, she arched her back so that her breasts loomed over him in power and majesty. One by one, she ran her pinkies along the sides of her tongue and then drew little circles on her nipples. "Do you see anything you like, Mr. Preston?" she asked.

"Let me pay homage to all of you," Jack blurted out.

Alice giggled. "Do you mean homage as in worship?"

Jack felt a gush of sanguineous warmth fill his cheeks. Perhaps he had laid it on a little thick, but he couldn't back down now. He meant what he said, and then some. "And why shouldn't I worship you?" he asked. "You are more beautiful than Aphrodite. You are more pleasing than Hebe. Cast those pretenders down from Olympus."

Now came Alice's turn to blush. She ran her fingers across his lips and manually puckered them for impact from her diving mouth, but at the last moment, she pulled up. "Promise me you won't get me into trouble," she said.

Jack's eyes rolled back. Had he counted on an evening such as this one, he would have come prepared with a packet of rubbers, but how could one anticipate such outright fortune? "I would never hurt you, Alice... I would never... uh... never..." Jack groped for the right words, but kept tripping on his tongue.

Fortunately, Alice came to his rescue by squeezing his lips together again, this time to hush him. "Let me tell you something wonderful," she said. "Scientists have invented these pills that will prevent an accident, but you have to say the three magic words for me to take them."

"I love you, Alice."

Alice's lips locked onto Jack's cheek, and she kissed it with a sucking-slurping sound. "That's four words, but I'll give you credit for the first three," she said.

Jack stroked the sides of her bosom. *Rapture!* "And w... where do you find these p... pills?" he stuttered. He had heard in many a locker room that using a rubber took the zing out of the sensation. Using the wonders of science to stop an unthinkable complication intrigued him.

"A gynecology professor up in Boston runs a clinical study; however, I have to take them for ten days before we go soaring into the clouds. In the meantime, come back tomorrow, and we'll give each other some more flying lessons."

Uh oh, Judy had booked that time slot...

"Any night but tomorrow night is good."

"Then pay homage to my breasts tonight. They long to be worshipped."

Being ever the gentleman, Jack could not refuse the lady's request. And though his technique needed some development before it could ever approach Alice's finesse, Jack ravished her bosom with soft nibbles and tender kisses that raised goose bumps and left the taste of fire in his mouth.

CHAPTER 14

Detective School

Midnight had come and gone with many minutes to spare when Jack hopped into a taxi for the ride home. Rather than invoke Greek lore or wax poetic about the evening, he realized that he had to do some quick thinking and come up with a plan to cover his tracks for what could be a prolonged affair—at least ten days, anyway—with Alice. As the taxi climbed the median ramp onto the West Side Highway, Jack opened his briefcase and pulled out a yellow legal pad. He remembered the telling words of a homicide detective, who once gave a guest lecture in his first year course in criminal law. *When the perpetrator commits murder, he will make a dozen mistakes, and if he's exceptionally smart, he will recall only three of them.*

Okay, so having a tryst with Alice didn't quite belong in the same league as murder one, but it would certainly send his engagement with Judy to the chair. He loved Judy, but Judy could never understand that his affair with Alice could benefit her, too. Already he had learned that kissing involved much more than thrusting one's tongue like a battering ram. Jack held his hand to his mouth and recapitulated Alice's kissing movements against his skin. The nibbling part was an easy hit, ditto with the sucking part and sucking/nibbling combination. Now came the challenge. Jack tried to flutter his tongue à la Alice and found his effort laughably wanting.

Words from the homicide detective came back to haunt him. *The perpetrator has guilt written over his face, his words and his body. Whereas the victim's innocent friends and relatives succumb to grief, the perpetrator emanates anxiety. A journeyman detective can pick him out of a room of twenty.*

Jack realized that the kissing exercises would have to wait, and so he put pen to paper and drew a line from the top to the bottom of the leaf. On the left side, he wrote the heading, "Problems", and on the right side, he scribbled the word "Solutions." A red mark on his shirtsleeve reminded him of a telltale bloodstain from his criminology lecture, which caused him to write, "Lipstick on shirt" on the left side of the pad, followed by "Chinese laundry" on the right. For the next problem, he wrote, "Coming home late," which he solved by writing "Extra work at the office on Tuesdays and Thursdays might require overnight stays." He especially liked the Tuesdays and Thursdays part. A regular schedule like this would facilitate the ruse and keep his separate worlds from colliding.

Jack remembered another inside tip from the detective. *Unless the victim's body is discovered, the possibility of proving homicide in a court of law is slim at best.* Jack then realized that other than his dad, who worked in midtown, nobody else in his circle of family and friends traveled to the city, much less downtown. Alice would forever remain a mystery to them, so he need not list any serendipitous discovery as a problem.

Finally, he wrote on the left side of the page, "Feelings of anxiety and guilt," which made him write this dissertation on the right side: "You love Judy. Judy refuses any further advances. Let Alice be your safety valve. Alice will eventually leave you for some matinee idol. No harm done!"

Other problems might crop up, but Jack felt confident he could handle any unexpected developments on the fly. For now, however, contentment seized him as he removed the foul ball from his briefcase and kissed it. He attempted to flutter his tongue on it but his primitive movements only succeeded in smudging the lipstick mark. Perchance the back of the hand might serve as a superior recipient in this exercise.

After arriving home, he stuffed his shirt into his briefcase. Since his office was within walking distance of Chinatown, he knew he would have his choice of laundry service in the morning. Things were going to work out just fine; he would just have to take an earlier train to work.

CHAPTER 15

The Spotter

"I have to charge you ten cents for same day service, Mister," the laundry-man said handing Jack his ticket. The laundryman didn't seem to notice the lipstick marks on Jack's shirt, but the customer behind him sure did. This Wall Street Joe had the worn heels and hungry look of a floor trader, whose beady eyes couldn't resist a wink as Jack hurried out the door.

No sooner had Jack swung through the revolving doors to the lobby, than Chester gave him a face-splitting grin. "Who shot that foul ball at you? Cupid? That kiss could have melted a snowman!"

"You were at a Yankee game?" Jack returned. He wondered how many other people, who he knew, might have seen that spectacle.

"Hell, no! I saw you on my TV set."

"How's that possible? I can barely see the ball on the TV."

"When my number came in, the woman told me to get us a twenty-four-inch. Heck, I can read the time on Art Linkletter's watch."

Jack's mind slipped into panic mode. First, Joe Floor Trader at the laundry spotted him for a womanizer, and then Chester got into the act. Okay, so Joe with the gaunt face didn't count, but what if Chester told a couple of customers, and they told their coworkers, who in turn told the jan-itor, the window washer and so forth? In a day's time, the story could get back to his office. Jack had to close the barn door on this horse. "Uh, Chester... could you keep this between us... uh... man-to-man?" he mumbled.

"I see what you mean," Chester chuckled. "Heck, I won't even tell my dog."

Jack headed toward the elevator. He thought about his mother pos-sibly folding his laundry a day earlier and noticing one of his shirts missing from the count. In this event, he would have to make up a story and tell her that when he came home last night, he was so exhausted that he forgot to put his shirt in the hamper. Next, he realized that if his mother waited to do the usual Friday load, she would definitely spot a freshly laundered shirt in a linen basket, so he had to intentionally sully and wrinkle it to make it look like it had been worn for a day. Would she notice a difference in the press-ing pattern or in the texture and the fragrance to the starch? Probably...

Jack began to hyperventilate. He had made a dozen mistakes with his liaison with Alice, and he had only identified a few of them.

I'm just paranoid, he told himself. *Mother only thinks nice things about me.*

The elevator doors opened, and Jack stepped in; but then he stepped back out. "Oh, Chesterrrr," he cooed walking back to the bootblack stand. Chester put his teeth back on display.

Jack returned the smile. "I wanted to ask you. How was Boston last night?"

Suddenly Chester's teeth retreated behind a frown. "Why are you talking crazy, Mr. Preston?" he asked. "You saw me here yesterday. Now how do I get to Boston and back in one night, and on what account?"

"Excellent questions, my friend… You have the makings of a trial lawyer. By the way, do you ever watch the Dodgers play at home?"

"You know I do. I never miss a game."

"But you don't ever watch the Yankees. Do you?"

"That's a fact; you got me there, sir. But like I said, I saw you on TV last night."

"Of course you did, but you watched the game on the Ambassador's TV set in Boston. I know you did because unlike the Dodgers, the Yankees never broadcast their home games in New York. The only city that you could have watched that game in is Boston. Now why would Mr. Kennedy fly you to Boston?"

Chester slapped his knee and chuckled. "Yes sir, Mr. Preston. You sure are a smart lawyer. You got me there. That's right, sir. But I have to tell you that there sure are a lot of shoes to shine in that Kennedy house. I kind of lost track of all those feet walking around."

Jack took due note of Chester's sudden descent into minstrel show locutions. It might have been a quirk with colored people straight from the briar patch, but Chester always conjugated his verbs correctly, and he never used a double negative. Sure, he could chuckle with the best of them, but he had never crossed the line into knee slapping territory, like he had just done. And all those silly compliments… Jack recognized them for what they were. They bought Chester a few extra seconds to make up a story that a first year law student could poke holes through. *What was Chester hiding?* Jack believed he already knew.

"But the Kennedy family doesn't live near Boston anymore," Jack said. "According to my dad, they now call Hyannis Port their home. The Ambassador had you flown to Boston to talk to you personally. Didn't he?"

"If he wanted to talk to me, wouldn't the phone be a whole lot easier?"

"Good point, but he can't show you any pictures of company executives over the phone. Can he? I'm onto you, Chester... you are Mr. Kennedy's spotter, and from your bootblack empire here, you spot faces from the pictures he shows you, and you observe them enter the elevator after which time you note what floor the elevator stops at. Shall I tell you why?"

Chester looked down at the floor. "Please, Mr. Preston, don't say anymore. Mr. Kennedy has been good to me," he begged, his eyes then turning back to Jack.

"I will keep your secret, just like you will keep my secret, but you've got to tell me one thing. Do you report on anybody visiting my floor?"

"The man doesn't care about what your company does with its lawyerly time. He takes a special liking to the grave dancers on floors eleven, nineteen and forty."

"Grave dancers!" This time Jack slapped his knee. "The man is supernatural."

"If you say so, Mr. Preston, but it always sounded crazy all these years. How could the man make his money off somebody going to a bankruptcy lawyer? What does the man get if the company is already broke?"

"He can make wheelbarrows full of money, my friend, and one day I will tell you how."

Jack headed back to the elevator. What Chester did not know was that you could sell a stock that you didn't own by a method called selling short. Rather than buy and sell, you sold and then bought, and if the stock dropped in value, you made money. In practice, you were betting to lose on the stock just like the guy who takes money from a friend to put down on a horse but then skips the pari-mutuel window to pocket the cash. And on the Street, who could find a bigger loser than a company preparing bankruptcy proceedings? Jack marveled at the multidimensional talent of the Ambassador and how he gleaned his information. How many other spies worked in his employ on the Street?

Jack stepped into the empty elevator, and after the doors closed behind him, he fluttered his tongue against his wrist. According to his watch, he had averaged three jabs per second, which meant a fifty percent improvement from last night. Not bad, but Alice's trilling vibrato could bury him in the dust. Still, with persistent practice, he figured he could match her stroke for stroke—all the better to ravish her into a frenzied state.

CHAPTER 16

Rendez-Vous

Alice checked her watch and kicked the ground. Meeting in alleyways made her feel dirty especially when it involved pigs. And speaking of pigs, why did the pigs keep her waiting? But then a black Crestliner driven by Bernard the pig crawled to a stop, and André the pig stepped out. Instead of a courtesy touch to the brim of his fedora, he held a photograph in front of his lips and spit on it. Alice detested those disdainful lips, which curved down on each side like a sea bass, and from which emanated foul words and shrill clatter.

"Your pictures are garbage, Alice," came his greeting in colonial French. "Hasn't taking off your clothes for pornographers taught you anything about photography?"

Alice wanted to bore André's baggy eyes with an ice pick for spouting such lies. In the first place, she had never disrobed completely, and for seconds, professional photographers used professional equipment. She opened her pocketbook and pulled out a camera the size of a cigarette lighter. "Take this fake Minox with the warped lens," she returned. "As I told you twice before, the fine print on the spec sheets requires a thirty-five millimeter single lens reflex model as well as a tripod and a light meter."

André waved to Bernard, who stepped out of the car and retrieved a leather bag from the back seat. "Here young Alice," he said opening the bag to reveal everything on her wish list. "The camera is fully loaded."

Alice traded cameras and noted the brand mark, *Asahiflex*. "Asahi," she remarked, "Isn't that a Japanese name?"

"I believe it's Italian," André replied.

Alice examined the lens, and shook her head. "I once knew a Captain Asahi, but then a patriot's bullet pierced his chest," she said poking herself in an imagined entry wound. Then her articulation took on the teasing melody of a bratty child. "Tell me André… Do you not believe that those patriots were real men like my Papa?"

André raised his hand as if to slap her cheek, but he drew back when she flinched and almost dropped the camera. "Stupid girl!" he growled snatching the camera from her hand, "Unless you bring us back clear photographs, you will remain unpaid, and your father will answer for his deeds. Now stop wasting time, and go back to work."

And gladly Alice went. When she reached West Street, she waved to the Crestliner crawling behind her, and the car U-turned in the opposite direction. *Stupid pigs! Did they not realize that she could spot their clumsy surveillance without looking?* Alice rounded the corner and arrived at a loading dock just as Dudley stepped out of a taxi. A wall sign next to the landing signaled the end of her lunch break.

BELL LABORATORIES
DIRECT DISTANCE DIALING RESEARCH UNIT
EMPLOYEES ONLY

"How was last night's date with Baby Face?" Dudley greeted her. His eyes made a rebounding roll in the direction of her photography bag.

"He's a gentleman, and he likes me."

Dudley clicked his tongue. "No my dear... he likes baseball, and he likes boxing. Let us hope that his feelings for you rise up to flights of fantasy."

"I don't know what you're talking about."

"Then spare me five minutes, and I shall teach you about the male imagination."

Intrigued, Alice followed Dudley inside to his office and recalled that in the days of training her womanhood, her tutor, the great Madame Tran never discussed such a topic. *Surely, a man's desires demanded more than skilled motion—as pleasurable as that might be.* Alice wanted to know more.

CHAPTER 17

The Rookie

Malone opened the dossier and pondered how the new man would fit in. According to his background check, he was one Thomas Byron Sparks, a farm boy from Huntington, Long Island, who along with his brother and a yard load of ducks, was reared by devout Episcopalians, who wore orange on St. Patrick's Day.

But Tommy—as the report further stated—never had any religious chip on his shoulder, and he got along well with his Irish, Italian and Jewish teammates on the rugby team at Hofstra University, where he earned a B.A. in business plus a C.P.A certificate. A stint at a clearinghouse on the Street must have given him a taste for the big time, but in that arena, there was no surer ticket to a dead end than becoming an accountant who had signed off on yesterday's transactions. And after two years of counting other people's money, only a simpleton wouldn't have wised up to the fact that he would never strike it rich. So why not join the exalted ranks of Uncle Sam's cops?

Malone glanced up at a youthful face that had finally grown into its ears. The evaluations from the academy spared no praise... *highly motivated... a crack shot... outstanding initiative... best in his class for problem solving skills.* The list went on, but Malone needed to judge for himself.

"It says here that the FBI declined your application. Do you know why?" he inquired.

"The rejection letter stated that the Bureau accepted only a handful of applicants from a pool of thousands. It didn't go into any detail."

"If I were Hoover, I would have taken you on the spot. On the other hand, you never would have fit into his mold. You're not Irish enough."

Sparks recoiled at the comment but resumed his composure. "How is that, sir?" he asked.

"The Bureau looks for recruits, who will conform to its code of uniformity no questions asked. Had you attended Catholic school, the nuns would have beaten every ounce of individuality out of your fiber."

"I don't see what that has to do with law enforcement, sir."

Malone glanced down at the dossier and circled the comment, "outstanding initiative." From his perspective, this trait came in short supply and was one that required nurture and not banishment. "Look Thomas..."

"I'd prefer that you call me Tom or Tommy," Sparks interrupted.

Malone twiddled his pen. "Look Tom, at Treasury, we're all part of a team, and yet each of us has to pull his weight as an individual. For its part, when the Bureau runs one of its cookie cutter investigations, no agent—attired in suit, white shirt and short brim fedora—ever flies solo, which makes for some lousy surveillance. Wouldn't you conclude that a professional criminal could spot the black Crestliner with the two-way antenna through a narcotic-induced haze? Sure he could, but the newspapers never reveal the Bureau's deficiencies. Hoover sees to that. He's an out-and-out prima donna."

"I presume with an emphasis on the word, 'prima'," Sparks joked.

"No, try 'donna'," Malone returned.

Sparks did a double take. "Doesn't that translate to 'lady' in English, sir?" he inquired.

"Sharp!" Malone replied, penning the exact word in Sparks' dossier.

"I beg your pardon, sir."

"Save all your 'sirs' for the House of Lords, Tommy. You've earned the right to call me Mike."

CHAPTER 18

Spiritual Advice

For this special evening, Judy had chosen a dress in basic black with a white yoke, which resembled more a doily than a collar. Black knee socks matched her orthopedic-inspired shoes, and white gloves provided a semblance of coordination with her yolk. *All she needed was a black shawl, and she could have passed for somebody's grandmother at a hundred paces,* Jack thought fleetingly.

She walked hand in hand with Jack past the white clapboard church, but when they reached the adjoining parsonage, she unclasped her hand and placed it by her side in a ladylike manner.

Jack gulped. What kind of moralizing would Reverend Holmes dish out on this occasion? He knew from previous sermons that this proper man of the cloth never mentioned any sort of romantic contact by name, not even a kiss. For out and out canoodling, he had a special moniker; he called it "The Act."

Jack knocked on the parsonage door and anticipated the fire and brimstone to follow. *On the night of your marriage, you may engage in The Act solely for the purpose of procreation. Hark, my children; The Act is evil, The Act is wicked, and The Act is dirty. After you have brought forth two children into this realm of darkness, refrain from The Act forevermore, and sleep in separate beds so that you may avoid all sin and temptation.*

The door opened, and the good Reverend showed them into a bare living room unadorned by pictures, statues or other graven images. "We don't have to be formal here," he said motioning for Jack and Judy to sit in two plain seats that kept a respectful distance from each other. "I am pleased that you have come for this visit."

"Thank you for seeing us on such short notice," said Judy.

Jack positioned himself behind her chair and held it as she quite properly took her place. After she folded her hands across her lap, he waited for the Reverend to take his seat before taking his own. Regardless of the Reverend's view on informality, Jack knew he had to bow to convention.

Convention also required that Jack and Judy would speak when spoken to, so they waited for the Reverend to issue forth. "Let me just say that June weddings disturb me," he began. "I presume that five bridesmaids will lead the procession, and that you'll pay peak rates for banquet facilities that overcharge anyway. Wouldn't that money be better spent as a down payment on a home?"

Jack nodded his head in agreement, causing Judy to stiffen her lips. *Uh oh*, he thought, *maybe the Reverend isn't so bad after all, but Judy thinks I'm gloating over the fact that I too disapprove of Roman-style receptions.*

Undeterred, Judy countered the Reverend's question with a question of her own as if he were a rabbi. "But what if we could afford both the wedding and the down payment?" she asked.

"I'll be frank. This kind of monetary outlay may compel you to make your vows long before you exchange rings. You may begin to have doubts about your relationship, but the contracts and the cash will hold sway over your thinking and will lock you into a wedding that never should have occurred in the first place. I've seen this tragedy take place more times than I care to mention."

"I assure you that our love is real. Isn't it, Jack?" Judy said. The Reverend looked into her eyes, which showered the room with a stream of valentines.

"Oh, it's very real. It's so real you wouldn't believe it," Jack replied.

The Reverend reached for his appointment book. "Very well," he said, dipping a quill into an inkwell, "you have my blessing for June 12th, but please... please... if either one of you has a hint of a doubt don't hesitate to talk to me in private."

"Of course," Jack agreed with a sigh of relief. He couldn't believe how easily this whole affair had transpired without any passing allusions to sinfulness. Had the Reverend gone soft?

But then the good man raised his finger to the heavens. "One other item," he said, "I know engaged couples sometimes like to take extra liberties with their affections if you know what I mean. The two of you may wish to stray beyond the bounds of wholesome love, but I urge you to avoid such temptation."

As the Reverend paused to take a breath, Jack turned to Judy and beheld a chaste radiance. He wondered what Alice would have said to this man. *With all due respect, Reverend, lovemaking is beautiful. It inspires great art and poetry. How dare you belittle such grandeur?*

Meanwhile, the Reverend continued his sermon. "You don't want to open your presents before Christmas. Let the wedding night be a night to remember. Is that understood?"

"I promise you, Reverend. We'll be good," Judy agreed. "Right, Jack?"

But Jack's mind had already wandered into a secret realm some-where between Alice's ribbed sweater and her gourmet breasts. He heard Judy's question but had to think about how to answer it.

"Jack?" said Judy, the pitch in her voice now ascending half an octave.

"Oh, we'll be good... so good you won't believe it," he said causing the Reverend to drop his book before he could blot the entry dry.

The meeting ended, and Jack escorted Judy to her threshold. "Are you going to continue your cooking lessons at the church hall this Satur-day?" he asked.

"Don't make small talk, Jack Preston. You were bad tonight... so bad you wouldn't believe it. Oh, how I want to spank you!"

It was an enticing proposition, but Jack held his tongue.

CHAPTER 19

A Perfect Treat

Jack was frantic. Judy had informed him that since she had missed the previous cooking lesson when they had shopped for her ring, she would make up the lost time on Saturday with an all-day session. This presented the perfect opportunity for him to slip into the city to play footsy with Alice. But how could he get in touch with her from his office? She had a nonfunctioning telephone, and she lived in Greenwich Village. With a mere twenty-minute allocation for lunchtime, he jumped in the elevator and darted through the lobby to almost throw himself bodily in front of a cab cruising down Broadway.

"Here's a fin for the roundtrip to Barrow and Eighth," he told the cabbie handing him a five dollar bill.

As the cab zipped around to Church Street for the race uptown, Jack pulled a pen from his jacket and printed on his legal pad:

Alice:
Let's play baseball. I'll bring the equipment, and you bring your pretty self. Meet me under the arch in Washington Square Park tomorrow morning at ten.

Love,
Jack

The cab screeched to a halt in front of Alice's building, and Jack raced into the foyer. He rang her bell, but the door buzzer never replied, and so he stuffed the note into her mailbox. Would she respond to the invitation? It might be a long shot, but Jack knew he would kick himself if he didn't at least try.

At home after a most pleasant evening of lemonade-sipping with Judy on the back porch, he dug a bat and a hardball out of his closet, but on second look, he realized that the Spaldine sitting on the shoe rack might make a safer projectile. Not to be overlooked was the foul ball with Alice's lip print on it. Jack took it to bed with him and snuggled up to it for good luck.

And it must have worked because as the bells on Grace Church struck ten, Alice strolled up from behind him to plant a fresh set of lip marks on his cheek. "Play ball!" she announced appearing in her ribbed sweater and Yankees cap, and the two of them retired onto the grass to play that great American pastime.

With Alice assuming batting stance over an imaginary plate, Jack lobbed her a meatball, and she chopped a grounder up the middle. The fact that a woman could actually make contact with the ball caught Jack by surprise, and so he had to hustle to make what should have been an easy catch. Alice, meanwhile, trotted in the direction of a park bench, which in her mind must have represented first base. Without a first baseman to cover, she could have easily gone for two, but she slowed her pace, which gave Jack a chance at the play. He cut in front of her just before the bench, and she plowed right into him. Jack dropped the ball to catch her, and she tripped sideways, causing the two of them to roll into the grass, where they lay, side by side, each one staring up at the Fifth Avenue apartments looming above them.

"Who says I only talk baseball? What a hit!" Alice boasted.

"But I tagged you," Jack said noticing that she must have been counting the floors of the nearest building, an activity not uncommon to out-of-towners.

"No, you didn't. You dropped the ball."

"But that was only so I could catch you."

"So you find me better sport than baseball."

Such an understatement! If it weren't a public space, Jack would have smothered her with kisses starting with her little toe and covering every inch of her all the way up. Instead, he brushed her hair. "Alice, I would give up every sport known to man if the choice were between them and you."

The reptilian tongue danced between Jack's lips causing a surge of blood to swell his bony netherworld. He reciprocated with several stabs of his own and garnished it with a flutter, which made Alice throw back her head to expose the bottom of her chin. And Jack would have nibbled her neck from ear to ear had she not directed his mouth back to her awaiting lips first for a simple kiss and then to hear her say, "Fortunately, you won't have to give up boxing. I have two tickets to the Rocky Marciano, Ezzard Charles fight a week from Thursday. Would it please you to come?"

"Please me? Please me!!!" Jack exclaimed, not completely sure that he had heard her correctly, "That's a heavyweight championship fight. If I fall into a coma, promise me you'll carry me to my seat! Dare I ask, did Dudley have anything to do with this?"

"I think he likes you, Jack."

"If he wants to kiss me, here I am. Hey... maybe I want to kiss him."

Alice grimaced. "No, you don't," she said. "Besides, you belong to me... and... and... I have an idea..."

She tickled the rim of his ear with her tongue until he cracked a grin and then whispered, "I can't take it anymore. I want to rip all your clothes off right here."

Jack whispered back, "You are so gorgeous; I could just eat you."

Alice furrowed her brow. "What are you saying, Jack?" she asked, her gravitas taking Jack by surprise.

"It's just an expression. You are the prettiest meal that I have ever feasted my eyes upon. I could swallow you like butter."

"Oh... Now I understand," she giggled. "And do you believe I would taste better with mustard or catsup?"

"Neither! With a wee bit of mayonnaise, you would become culinary perfection."

"Then let's go."

"Where are we going?"

"My bedroom—but first we're stopping off at the store to pick up a jar of mayonnaise. I want to serve you the perfect meal."

CHAPTER 20

Coming Clean

What was this all about? In the back of Jack's mind, he had planned this date like Ike had planned D-Day. He had intended to bid Alice adieu at 4:30, take a cab to the Commodore Hotel, retrieve his briefcase from the checkroom, drop into the men's room, change into the clean shirt from within his briefcase and then head across the street to catch the five-twenty-two back to Bronxville to make a timely arrival as Judy unveiled her latest epicurean delights. Yet here he was, at ten to six, sitting on Alice's bed, where he shared with her a pickle, a knish and a sliced chicken on rye—hold the mayo, please. *How did it come to this?*

"How's the knish?" asked Alice, clad in only panties. The remainder of her clothing lay in a disarticulated pile on top of her curious floor chest while Jack's outerwear lay strewn across the floor.

"It's sticky, just like my fingers, just like my armpits, and…and…"

"Just like me," Alice quipped.

"A shower would be nice."

"Would you settle for a bath?"

"Ladies first."

"In the interest of efficiency, I believe we should share the bath."

"Ah yes, the efficiency," Jack agreed.

Alice retreated to the bathroom, where she drew the water. Jack, meanwhile, admired the décor of her bedroom. Above her dresser was a mirror, of course, but in an unconventional twist, corkboards containing various photos of her posing over high-end sports cars and motorcycles framed both sides. Jack especially liked the way she accentuated her cleavage by sandwiching her bosom between outstretched arms, or how she kicked her leg back so that the heel in her pump almost spiked her bottom.

Alice must have had a penchant for oriental art because he recognized an *ukiyo-e* landscape sharing the far wall with an impressionist painting of a street market, which upon closer inspection bore the caption, "Le Vieux Carré—Hanoi, Indochine." Two macramé veils hung from the near wall. Jack marveled at the geometric precision of the knots within the veils. *Had a giant spider knit a web to catch human prey? And what about that teak floor chest with ivory inlays of intertwined human figures?* Jack would have liked to study those figures further, but an abrupt silence meant that the bathtub was full enough to receive two occupants. Alice returned to the bedroom.

"Let's send all that mayonnaise down the drain where it belongs," she said.

"Of course you realize that we will have to take off our remaining attire for this high seas adventure."

"But certain mysteries will still remain between us."

Jack took her to mean that he would not behold her downtown privates, and sure enough one look at the volcanic gush of suds in the bathtub told him that he would barely see anything uptown either. Alice reached for her panties.

"Turn around, and I'll tell you when to look," she said.

Jack stared at the topside of the toilet lid.

"Come on in; the water is fine," she then called.

Jack dropped his underpants and turned around to behold her covering her eyes with a washcloth. Gingerly, he stepped into the opposite side of the tub and slipped beneath the bubbles. "You can look now," he said, and Alice uncovered her eyes.

She commenced rubbing his shoulders with the washcloth. "Did the mayonnaise teach you anything today," she asked.

With the warm sponge soothing his deltoids, Jack let out a gasp, which segued into a moan. "I loved the way you spread the mayonnaise on your skin with a butter knife. For me, you became a food that I had hungered for my entire life but had never tasted. I noticed that when I nuzzled certain spots, like your nipples, your navel and the sides of your neck, you squirmed and twisted. Were these places the most pleasurable for you?"

"Yes."

Alice grabbed Jack's arm and scrubbed it in a manner so as to convey that she meant to clean it rather than arouse any sensual cravings. Methodically, she worked the washcloth across his chest and other arm.

But Jack could not let the dog sleep. He closed his eyes and imagined himself to be the road-weary businessman for whom the French maid dispenses favor. As his manhood snapped to attention, he realized that Alice might consider this state a childish violation of a more mature intimacy. He covered his member with his free hand to prevent her from accidentally rubbing up against it.

"I wish I could kiss better. Compared to you, my efforts are feeble," he said.

"You kiss gently and with care. You never rush, and you never try to impress. I feel that you draw your pleasure from giving pleasure. I would be foolish to ask for more."

"I would like to please you to the loftiest heights of Olympus if only I knew how."

"If I had spread the mayonnaise within me, would you have tasted it?" Alice grabbed a bar of soap.

"I would have kissed your womanhood a hundred times on my knees and licked it clean."

The soap shot out of Alice's hand and ricocheted off the wall before plopping into a peak of bubbles. "But what if you had found my taste disagreeable?" she asked.

"Then I would acquire the taste in order to serve you in whatever manner you desired." The soap touched down upon Jack's thighs, and he handed it back to Alice

Instead of taking the soap, Alice guided Jack's hand to her puckered lips, and she kissed it without any nibbling, sucking or flutter. The soap fell back into the water, and Jack realized that here was a woman to whom he could reveal all those silly fantasies that had stimulated him since the onset of puberty.

Perhaps they weren't so silly after all.

CHAPTER 21

A Defender of Honor

Jack expected the scowl. After all, Judy had spent the entire day sweating over the most trivial of details to create this opus magnus of braised lamb with béarnaise sauce, coq au vin and pineapple soufflé, and here was Jack—two hours late—and the lamb sat cold and chewy alongside a gelatinous blob of yellow glue and a collapsed soufflé. Yet somehow, the chicken had survived the ravages of time and looked downright appetizing in its wine sauce, which must have acted as a kind of preservative. Jack reached for the tongs to grab a piece, but Judy pushed her arm in front of his and grabbed them first.

"No chicken for you…bad, bad, bad!" she scolded.

"You won't let it go to waste! That would be sinful," Jack replied.

"And what do you know about sin, Mr. Preston?"

"Let me show you."

Jack moved in for a kiss, but Judy raised the tongs in front of her lips. "And no dessert for you, either," she said, her eyes ablaze.

Jack engaged her stare for stare, and he waited for her to blink. Had Judy been Alice, he knew his own eyelids would have surrendered at first grimace, but Judy might need a few years of seasoning before she could play in Alice's league. That was not to say that he preferred to spend the rest of his life with Alice—not at all.

Now that he had experienced the touch of a woman's bosom, he could undress Judy in his mind and know the treasures that lurked within. Yes, beneath the fathomless cuteness, the homemaker's apron and all the ruffles and the curlicues lurked a real woman. Sure, Alice was the siren, Alice was the teacher, and Alice might have been the horse on which he would learn how to ride, but in that metaphorical vein, Judy was the horse that he would possess. He foresaw himself training her as Alice had trained him, and he reminded himself that Judy's fragility required special handling. Yes, he must be gentle with her and unlock her womanhood in a stepwise fashion, so that bit by bit, she would free herself of the inhibitions that had plagued all young ladies since witch trials and chastity belts.

But first, he had to break down that scowl with an off-white lie.

"The only reason I returned to my office today was to catch up with the paperwork," he explained. "It's more of a bore than a chore. When I put my head down on the desk, I nodded off into dreamland… but I dreamed about you."

"And what did you dream about? What was I doing?" Judy asked batting her eyes.

"We were on our honeymoon, and you had smothered your body in mayonnaise, and…"

"Don't tell me those kind of things," Judy interrupted. "I'm not a turkey sandwich."

Jack pointed to the coq au vin. "Judy, my sweets, can't we just make up and have dinner together even if it's a trite old and rusty?"

"You may eat the salad, and only the salad."

"Do you think it would go well with mayonnaise?"

"Ha-ha, Mr. Preston. Don't push your luck."

As Jack dug into his greens, he remembered words from *The Oath of Chivalry*, "…with courage and strength, I will protect the weak and defend the honor of ladies."

Inspired, he took Judy by the hand and kissed it. "To your honor," he quoted.

Judy blushed. She returned the kiss to Jack's hand, and he noted that was the second time this evening that his hand had received such gratitude from a lady's lips. Were not Judy and Alice as close to each other in heart as they were different in desire? Jack pondered this question after he had kissed Judy goodnight and fished out his baseball bat, the Spaldine, two fielders' gloves and a lipstick-stained shirt from beneath the hedges next to her driveway. As he stuffed the shirt back into his briefcase, he realized that he would have to take an early train to work on Monday. Perhaps he might sample some dim sum for breakfast.

CHAPTER 22

The Juggling Act

Jack never had much interest in criminal law, but he respected the practitioners of it, especially the cream of the trial lawyers, who could take a minute discrepancy in evidence or testimony and use it to poke hole after hole in an airtight case until a jury could do nothing but affirm the innocence of their homicidal clients. Jack tapped his pen against his blotter and then pointed it at a legal pad on which he had written the heading, "Monday, Day 1." The phone rang, and he picked it up in mid-jingle.

"Jack, I'm calling from the drugstore. Are you feeling lonely this evening?" came Alice's breathy voice.

Jack panted like a dog gaping at a carved roast. "I'm always available to serve your fondest desires," he replied pulling the baseball from his desk and rubbing the lipstick mark on it against his cheek. "I just finished my last brief."

"Then please hurry over. I'm scared to be alone."

Jack could hardly believe that last part. After hanging up, he called Judy, "I'm coming home late, sweets," he said and crossed his fingers. "The partners have me entertaining a client at Mamma Leone's."

"I'll miss you," Judy said, and though Jack could envision her pouting, he pressed two fingers against his lips, and he feigned a kiss from Alice.

Jack scribbled on the legal pad, "This evening I accompanied a GE executive to Leone's where I washed down a chicken cacciatore with the house Chianti. The client feasted on lasagna."

Jack knew that Judy would quiz him about the evening and would focus obsessively upon the food. "Did you order an antipasto? How many pieces were there? How did they arrange it on the plate?"

Fortunately, the partners in the firm entertained their clients lavishly, and so they kept a stockpile of menus and restaurant reviews in a drawer next to the grandfather clock in the conference room. Jack flipped the pages to a glowing endorsement of Leone's in a 1952 issue of *Diners Club Magazine* and noted on the legal pad, "Tremendous portions. Most dishes are accompanied by spaghetti. Espresso comes in large cups with a lemon rind on the saucer. Wandering troubadours with lutes and accordions serenade the patrons."

Jack dwelled upon the wandering troubadours part and hummed "O solo mio" to himself all during the taxi ride up to Barrow Street. Finally, when Alice buzzed him through the foyer, he burst into song as he danced up the staircase, where along the way, he pictured himself as Gene Kelly or Fred Astaire in a Technicolor musical.

Gus Andersen, the elderly super, didn't know what to make of this spectacle when Jack slid backward across the freshly mopped fourth floor landing. This could have had a slapstick outcome; however, Gus stuck out the handle of his mop, and Jack grabbed hold to brake himself merely inches before a potential encounter with a bucket of sudsy ammonia.

"Isn't it kind of late to be working?" Jack asked.

"It serves me right for taking the day off," Gus replied in a singsong accent. "Somebody must have danced in a puddle of mayonnaise this weekend and dragged it out on the bottoms of his feet. The floor had the texture of flypaper."

"Well, thanks for the emergency brake."

Puffing his cheeks, Jack headed straight to 4C, and with a single knock, the door flew open. Alice dragged him by the tie into her bedroom, where she stripped him to his skivvies while her blouse and brassiere flew onto the floor chest. With erect nipples pressed against his chest, he felt his own fullness poking through the slot in his boxers.

But he would ignore the beast.

Instead, Jack concentrated on Alice's needs, and as she whip-stroked him with her tongue, he set out to ravish her bosom with a thousand strokes of his own. His mouth descended to her navel, and she squirmed with ticklish delight. Then, he grabbed hold of her thigh and ravished its supple posterior with nibbles and broad licking strokes.

Getting warmer...

Jack's mouth drifted inward on her thigh, and he nibbled his way toward her womanly orifice draped in but the flimsiest of black panties. A womanly scent of lavender lured him forward, and as his nibbles and lashes approached the fold in her thigh, he realized that this flowery essence was but a perfume to disguise a muskier aroma lurking beneath the surface. Jack needed to take a whiff, but in that moment, Alice's hand guided his chin toward hers.

"I was only joking, Jack," she said, looking directly into his eyes. "You shouldn't have taken our bathtub conversation so seriously."

"But what if I have? My intention is to please you. May I proceed?"

"You might find the results unsanitary. The answer is no."

It wasn't the answer Jack wanted to hear.

The following evening, he escorted Judy to the park, and he wondered if her orifice emanated the same earthy aroma. Just the memory of that scent aroused him, but if Alice had already rendered it taboo, he knew that the mere mention of it to Judy would trigger a seismic outburst. Still, it amused him that these two very different ladies shared a common discharge. *So Alice used lavender to ward off her womanly spirits…what might Judy utilize? Jasmine? Lilac? Peanut butter?*

Jack laughed.

"Do you care to share the joke?" Judy inquired.

"Being by your side brings me such happiness that sometimes I burst out laughing."

"Oh, Jack." Judy snuggled up to him and rubbed her cheek against his shoulder.

"Unfortunately, I won't be able to be by your side for the next two nights. Duty calls, and I will have to work late."

"But you'll think of me every night. Won't you?"

"Every night."

Jack kissed her on the forehead. Damn it, she was cute; eat your heart out Doris Day!

CHAPTER 23

Painting the Town

Jack wanted to take Alice out on the town, but he didn't want to get sighted by any friends, family or coworkers. True, New York City was a town of eight million souls, but on any given evening, he might pass a couple of thousand people just on the streets, which put the odds of running into somebody he knew into a playable range. In spite of that, he reasoned those odds could climb back up into the stratosphere if he avoided certain midtown spots like Fifth Avenue, where the ladies of his fair village shopped, or the Theater District, where he might bump into an entire Bronxville family.

Looking back to his childhood, he remembered sighting the Ambassador at the stage door of the Shubert Theater. He would have waved to him, except that his father told him that Mr. Kennedy had some very private business at hand and could not be disturbed. *One more thing,* Jack remembered, *Dad made me promise not to talk about this sighting to anybody else. How strange!*

But as they say in the courtroom, the whole point was moot because Alice lived in Greenwich Village, and the citizens of the northern suburbs avoided this viper's nest of bohemians, crackpots and communists as if crab lice crawled across every toilet seat from Houston Street to Union Square. Such a pity because the Village boasted dozens of unique restaurants that could go head to head against their midtown counterparts at half the fare...

On Wednesday evening, Jack treated Alice to Chez Brigitte not more than two blocks away from her walkup. This made for an easy escort back to her apartment, where they grappled and groped until midnight. On the ride home in the taxi, Jack made note of their selections on the menu and remarked that he had taken a client to Chez Beatrice in midtown.

On Thursday, however, Alice glared at him from her doorway, and rubbing her belly, she remarked, "Are you fattening me for the kill? No restaurant!"

So instead, they ventured off by subway to Coney Island, where Alice worked off her extra pound on the Parachute Jump, the Steeplechase ponies and the batting cages, where Jack nailed the "Flagpole Duck" with a pulled heater off the sweet spot. As the painted disk flipped head over heels, an overhead squawk box emanated a succession of duck calls. Several quacks later, the attendant handed Alice a Louisville Slugger with Carl Furillo's signature stamped into the grain, and after a spontaneous jump for joy, she lead Jack to a photography booth, where they posed with their trophy, and—quicker than a timed egg—a fully developed picture popped out of the machine.

Back in the bedroom, Alice posted the photo next to her cheesecake shots before pushing Jack backward onto her bed. "Keep your beak out of my panties," she said tapping him on the nose.

"Tasting you never crossed my mind until you divulged that desire in the bathtub," Jack replied.

"Is it my desire or yours?" she teased.

"Then place my lips where it pleases you most, and I will worship you there."

Alice licked her lips. "Allow me to do the worshipping tonight. Pleasure is a two-way street, and I find your body sacred."

Jack swallowed hard. No woman had ever said anything like that to him before. As she descended to embrace him, he vowed to banish all thoughts from his mind. He would surrender to her passion, and in the fire of the moment, there would be bliss.

But what was bliss without sorrow to act as its counterweight? "Tomorrow, I have to go to Boston for a modeling shoot, but I'll be back for next Thursday's fight," she said when she kissed him goodbye.

Oh the bitter agony! Jack trudged over to Seventh Avenue, and after hailing a cab, he commented on his pad that he would make up for lost time with Judy. He had much to teach her.

CHAPTER 24

Working the Ticker

With Friday's arrival, Jack got down to the business of chasing paper. By the hundredth "wherefore" somewhere on page sixty-five of a three hundred-page contract, the intercom buzzed. Jack welcomed the break in the tedium with a stretch and a vertebrae cracking twist. "Tell me something good, Nora," he said.

"Mr. Lawson from the SEC is on line six," she replied.

Jack's heart raced into syncopated time as he pressed in. "Mr. Lawson, how go things in Washington?" came Jack's melodic greeting.

"Securities Exchange has approved merger H-16. You may inform the press no earlier than noon today," came the brusque reply.

The terseness in his voice didn't matter; all these bureaucrats had a terminal case of it. Jack punched the air in a victory salute. "That's less than an hour from now. Did you pick up any irregular movement of the pertinent stocks?" he inquired.

"None at all. You guys at DH and T are pros."

"Always happy to hear that."

Happy might have been an overstated understatement. When Jack hung up the phone, he launched into a jitterbug around his desk and punctuated his steps with so many victory salutes that a casual onlooker might have gathered that he had learned his craft from heathens dancing around a missionary in a stew pot. Such joy needed company. Jack hit the intercom button.

"Yes, Mr. Preston," Nora answered.

Jack reached for a fountain pen and doodled "Alice" on a pad. "Nora, assuming it's a thirty-second coffee break, what is the crossword clue of the day?" he asked.

"I have 'femme spy.' It's eight letters ending in 'I'."

"That's easy. Try 'Mata Hari'."

"You're the best, Mr. Preston. Is there anything else?"

"Yes, please tell Mr. Thorpe that I have a brown envelope for him." Jack embellished each letter in "Alice" with assorted swirls and curlicues.

"Sorry, Mr. Preston... Mr. Thorpe is attending a tax code conference in Philadelphia. He delegated merger announcements to you today."

"Then call in the press. Let's start the show."

Announcing a corporate merger to the press was a first for Jack, and he realized that with this assignment, his elevation to partnership in the firm was as certain as a Yankee pennant in September. With brown envelope in hand, he strutted into the conference room and adjusted the rostrum. Paul Jeffrey ambled in behind him.

"Nora tells me that you're a temporary senior partner for the next hour. How may I assist?" Paul asked.

Jack handed Paul the brown envelope. "When I point to you, hand me this merger announcement," Jack replied while, unbeknownst to the two of them, Thelma Kane slipped in the back door and took a seat next to the grandfather clock.

"But you worked on this case. You already know the company names."

"Of course, but the press doesn't know that. They'll see me as a rising star with a personal assistant."

"It'll be more like a pack of wolves that see you holding an unpicked bone," Thelma cut in.

Jack thrust his head back. "You don't approve?" he said.

Thelma rubbed the side of the clock. "I'm sorry we had you locked away in your office during all these years of press conferences, but here are the facts of life. At the twelfth chime just throw them the bone."

Jack took note of the clock face. "It's ten to twelve. Where are they?"

Paul, meanwhile, held the brown envelope up to the light.

"Give them nine minutes," Thelma said adding, "and no peeking through that envelope, Paul!"

As the minute hand on the clock moseyed forward, Jack realized that he would have to make up this wasted time on the back end of the day. What if the members of the press were late? Fortunately as the clock's chiming mechanism clicked into its melodic prelude, a crew of eight disheveled characters, each one carrying an army surplus walkie-talkie, filed into the room.

Jack's lips pursed at the sight of this parade of threadbare suits slung beneath gaunt faces, each with a day-old shadow framing a set of nicotine-lacquered teeth that chattered incoherently. Forget manners; hats remained securely planted upon heads. As the ink-stained fingers of one member of the pack loosened his tie so it hung down to his zipper, his colleague lit up a cigarette, which dangled from his lower lip as if glued there. Simultaneously, three other reporters reached for their smokes just in time to get them all lit on the first man's match. Such efficiency!

The clock began chiming out the hour. At the twelfth chime, Jack tapped the rostrum. "Good afternoon, gentlemen, my name is Jack Preston, and…"

"Pleased to meet you! Who's the lucky couple getting hitched?" greeted a smoke- and whisky-cured throat.

"Yes, I was leading up to that," Jack replied.

"Great lead, kid! Just give us the names," a second voice with barbed wire for tonsils returned.

Thelma pointed to the grandfather clock as if to imply that too much of the firm's time had been squandered already, and she pushed Paul toward Jack. Paul then handed Jack the brown envelope, but Jack merely stared into space as if he were waiting for a hypnotist to snap his fingers.

"Speak up, kid. I've got moss growing under my feet," a third voice blurted out.

Jack ripped open the envelope with such awkward force that he tore the paper inside. Holding it upside down, he announced, "Merging today are Alcoa Aluminum and Great Lakes Mining and Shipping."

Suddenly, a flock of walkie-talkies flew skyward, and each reporter radioed in a report in his own telegraphic style.

"The merge is Alcoa and Great Lakes..."

"No!!! Alcoa... not Anaconda..."

"Yeah... Send the messenger to Clancy's and pay my tab with the vigorish."

Jack nodded to Thelma. "They're talking this up like it's a front-page banner," he said grinning out of one corner of his mouth.

Thelma rolled her eyes. "Don't kid yourself," she said. "That's not the copy desks they're calling; it's the trading pits."

"You mean they're working the ticker?"

And sure enough, Jack saw the reporters encircling a tickertape machine in the far corner of the room, where one of them grabbed hold of its elongating ribbon. A dozen ticks later, his voice assumed the booming treble of a guy announcing the feature race at Jamaica. "They're off and running. Alcoa is up three-quarters... Waiting on Great Lakes... It's up two and a quarter, no two and a half. Waiting... Waiting... Egad—It's three! Hey, early birds, it looks like we caught ourselves the whole can of worms."

"You wanna blow this joint?" a falsetto voice called out.

"Yeah, let's see if Mr. And Mrs. DiMaggio have checked into the Plaza. I've got dibs on the little lady," a second voice returned.

"Little! You must be blind!" said a third.

The herd of reporters deserted the premises en masse, and with his eyes bolted shut, Jack sank into a chair and hung his head. Obviously nobody in that rogue army was going to print the story. They played him for an inside tip, and worse than that, he knew that Thelma knew that he had been played.

Jack opened his eyes to behold Thelma standing over him with an I-told-you-so smirk on her face. Okay, he thought, maybe he deserved a serving of crow with a little humble pie on the side, but Thelma beamed at him like she meant to feed him the entire platter.

But then Thelma's look softened. Perhaps it had been soft all along. "Jack, I want you to meet somebody special," she said.

And there standing beside her was a lone gentleman of more refined bearing, who in his three-piece suit, could have passed for a member of a blue chip board—were it not for the reporter's pad clutched in his left hand. Jack admired the weave of the man's vest, and the symmetry of the Windsor knot fastening his tie. Surely one of the riffraff had dropped his pad, and this good fellow had retrieved it in the hope of returning it to its rightful owner. The gentleman held out his hand for a correct handshake.

"Good morning, counselor, I'm Pat Considine from *The Wall Street Journal*. I believe you have a story of interest to the financial community," he said opening up his pad. "Do I have the correct spelling of your name?"

Jack sighed with contentment. Nobody ever misspelled his name.

CHAPTER 25

Passionate Kisses

The Preston family gathered around Oliver in his cozy chair. Denise handed him his reading glasses, and he unfolded the Weekend Edition of *The Wall Street Journal*. By special invitation, Judy shared the sofa with Jack. Oliver licked his thumb and turned the page.

"Here it is," he announced. "SEC approves Alcoa merger."

"Skip to paragraph eight, Dad," Will suggested. "Most of the story is financial gobbledygook."

"No fair, you peeked," Denise protested.

"Will is right," Jack said. "The story evokes the taste of dry cereal. It assumes you can talk the talk."

"So you peeked too," Judy teased.

"Only five times," Jack said, and everybody laughed.

Oliver's finger slid down the copy to the bottom of the page. "Here, in paragraph eight," he said arching his eyebrows at Jack, "it states, and I quote, 'A point of contention arose when the proffering counsel, Mr. Jack Preston, briefed the government that synergies of complementary operation would offset any merger-induced loss of competition. Since enactment of the Clayton Antitrust Act in 1914, such arguments rarely held sway with government counsel, but Mr. Preston convinced them that imminent entry of three Canadian rivals into the American market would maintain price equilibrium.' Did everybody get that?"

Judy threw her arms around Jack. "I'm so proud of you!" she gushed.

Denise shook her head. "What are synergies?" she asked.

"Think of it as bad arithmetic," Jack explained, "kind of like one plus one equals three. Let's say we're both hungry and thirsty, and I have a donut while you have a soda. We can share the donut and the soda, and that way, we'll both get satisfied."

"It sounds like the two of you will satisfy only half your hunger and half your thirst," Will said.

"Which is precisely the government's argument," Oliver added.

"So your job is to fib to the government using phony numbers," Denise said.

"Fibbing to Uncle Sam is illegal. My job is to plead my clients' case," Jack replied.

"Enough of this!" Emily said rising from her chair, "I'm clipping this article and saving it. Now if you'll please excuse me, I'm going upstairs to find the scissors and some glue."

Emily kissed Jack on the temple, and then Denise followed her up the stairs. Oliver and Will, meanwhile, departed for the family room, leaving Jack and Judy alone together on the sofa. Was this simultaneous exit meticulously planned or was it merely a coincidence? Jack could only speculate.

Jack guided Judy's hand to his shoulder and she pecked his lips. He reciprocated by kissing her on the neck beneath her ear. This marked a spot that drove Alice into near frenzy, but Judy simply giggled. Let her beware; he was just warming up. First came a nibble and then a suck, and then Jack fluttered his tongue at an amazing twelve beats a second down the side of the neck, *at reptilian speed*, he thought proudly. Judy moaned, but in the next instant, she pushed him away.

"What in the name of propriety gives you the right!" she squealed, her face contorted as if he had passed bad air.

"I wasn't going for your privates—scouts' honors, my sweets."

"But you used your tongue on me. How vulgar!"

"But I heard you moan. You felt pleasure. Didn't you?"

"Stop it, Jack! Please stop it right now!"

Judy's voice had broken as if she were on the verge of tears. Jack threw back his arm to punch a pillow, but then he scratched his side instead. Meanwhile, Oliver had unexpectedly returned to retrieve his reading glasses. After establishing eye contact with a lampshade, he scooted back to the family room.

"Such an advance was improper…and…and…unacceptable," Judy said choking on her own breath.

But Jack had had enough of her frigidity. "And what will you call my advances after you throw the bridal bouquet?" he asked.

"I will promise to love, honor and obey. Does that answer your question?"

Judy's face was red, not blushing red but alarm box red. Jack knew he had to back off. "Judy, I love you, and I'm sorry I upset you. Listen, would it be an inconvenience for you to come with me to the park today? I promised Roy that I would take in one of his games?"

"Alright," she agreed, "but let's not stay for the whole game. You know how much I dislike baseball."

CHAPTER 26

Deluxe Accommodations

After filling the coffee cup, the waitress moved on to the next table, and Alice pulled a vial from her pocketbook. The pills inside the smoky glass looked innocent enough, but the label carried enough caveats to merit a skull and crossbones.

> *Experimental Progesterone Compound*
> *This is not an FDA approved medication.*
> *Do not take while pregnant.*
> *May cause nausea, vomiting or irregular menses.*
> *Discontinue if prolonged vaginal bleeding occurs.*
> *JOHN ROCK, M.D.*

Alice washed down a pill with a sip of coffee and paged through the morning edition of the *Boston Post*. An item on page thirty caught her attention.

JAPANESE TRADE DELEGATION TO VISIT HARVARD AND MIT

However, the three-paragraph article offered no indication on the makeup of this group. Alice closed the newspaper and noticed her hand twitching. She refused to believe that a pill could make her jittery in such short order. Maybe it was just a case of nerves.

But as Alice strode past the central tower of Trinity Church, a bead of cold sweat dribbled down her cheek. She would have preferred to linger on the steps and bask in the June sun, but she had business to attend to, and the sooner she attended to it, the sooner she could leave it behind her. She put some mustard in her gait, and when she arrived at the Copley Square Hotel, she bounded three flights up the stairwell to her appointment.

Oh those pigs! Had they no shame when they decided to prop open the door to their room utilizing the Gideon's Bible as a door jam? Alice drummed her nails on the door and entered, whereupon André and Bernard greeted her with a round of applause.

"Your photographs and other booty are spectacular," Bernard said toasting her with an imaginary glass of wine.

"And this is for your troubles," said André. He slapped her palm with two hundred dollars in crisp twenties.

Alice surveyed the cavernous quarters with matching wings, each one leading to a separate bedroom. "So you get to sleep in the grand suite while I share my shower with the entire YWCA," she remarked.

"This is our place of work. Here we represent the Republic," Bernard explained.

"I see that the Japanese are in town. Why don't you represent them?" Alice returned.

"Enough of your insolence!" André barked. "We try to be civil with you, yet you insist upon opening imaginary wounds. Since our business this time requires a minimum of your expertise, I ask you—why are you staying in Boston for an entire week?"

"My gynecologist requires my attendance for an experimental protocol. Would you like to hear about my womanly functions?"

"Please spare us!" André replied crumpling his nose.

"Look Alice," Bernard interjected. He reached for the contents of an attaché case, which lay open on an adjacent table. "This is a microphone," he said holding up a metal cylinder the size of the eraser end of a pencil. "And this is a radio transmitter," he added pointing to a device the size of his hand. These miniature products owe their existence to the transistors you brought us from Bell Laboratories. The Republic is grateful for your service."

"Yes, and the Republic still owes me a promise to release Papa, not to mention an outstanding balance for two years of unpaid service."

Bernard headed over to the door and peeked through the crack caused by the Bible lying on the floor. There he remained as if standing sentry. Alice, meanwhile, placed the fresh money into her purse. "What you paid me covers half the bill for my disconnected phone," she said.

"But you work for the phone company," André replied. "Why don't you go to bed with one of the accountants in the billing department, and he'll fix your bill? It's as simple as that."

"Goodbye André!" Alice huffed backpedaling toward the door. "I draw the line between opening my legs for the Republic and whoring for long distance charges."

But when she reached the door, she bumped into Bernard, whose full weight leaned against it and crushed the Bible below. "The only whoring you have done is with that lawyer you date," he said.

Alice turned and slapped him across the cheek. "Stop spying on me!" she exclaimed.

"But that is what we do, my child," André said with an affected cackle. "I'm a spy; you're a spy; Bernard's a spy… and we don't need some

Wall Street smarty-pants to figure it all out. So dump him! His professional knowledge is of no use to the Republic. From now on, you shall bed down with scientists and engineers—as originally planned."

"Drop dead, Andre!" Alice reached for the door, but Bernard still blocked it. However, this time, André flapped his wrist, and Bernard moved away.

"Remember your Papa," André called out as she pushed her way into the hallway. When she reached the street, she kicked the curb.

Bernard lifted the Bible from the floor, then closed the door and locked it. André, meanwhile, reached for the miniature transmitter and rubbed it for luck. "We've got to get Alice away from that lawyer. I believe that we should find our disgruntled child a new home in Boston," he said.

"Would you like me to plant that transmitter and the microphone in the lawyer's office? That would make one less body to watch," Bernard offered.

"Yes, and while you're at it, you should deliver more of our booty to Hiro's technicians. We may need an extra microphone or two."

Just then, a light tap on the door made Bernard spring to attention. "Bonjour mon ami!" he greeted the new guest with a slap on the shoulder, "your timely arrival has saved me a trip."

Hiroshi Nishimura doffed his hat and bowed.

CHAPTER 27

Natural Selection

Jack loved the smell of cut grass in the morning, especially the grass of a baseball diamond. As he and Judy ascended the Bronxville Park bleachers, Roy Tucker waved at them from the foul line. Jack excused himself to say hello, but Judy grabbed his hand and followed.

"Are you game for the Marciano fight on Thursday?" Roy asked.

Jack wiped the side of his face. *What if he ran into Roy at the fight? How would he explain Alice to him?* "But they're not televising it. How'd you get tickets?"

"Tickets? What tickets!" Roy chuckled. "Don't ask me how it's done, but they're broadcasting the fight to selected theaters, like the RKO in White Plains."

"I don't approve of boxing," Judy cut in.

"It won't matter anyway. I may entertain a client that evening," Jack said.

"Well, at least he won't be watching the boxing match, right, Judy?" Roy put in.

"But his restaurant duty with clients never stops," Judy whined.

"Then you should cook for the whole lot of them," Roy said.

With a tip of the cap, Roy trotted off to second base. Jack and Judy, meanwhile, returned to the bleachers, and after three scoreless innings, they set off for the Bronxville library, where Professor Grant Kingston from the Audubon Society gave a lecture on North American finches. At the end of the presentation, Judy inquired about variations in the finch's crown, and the good professor related it to the male's mating ritual. She didn't ask another question.

From the library, they headed over to Judy's home, where she treated Jack to a Danish-style *smorebrod,* featuring strips of herring on buttered bread with the crust cut off. Jack admired how skillfully she sliced the fish, and then lined the strips diagonally over the top. If she ever wanted to open a restaurant, she needed to come no further than him for financing, but then again he figured that her trust fund probably trumped his portfolio ten times over.

Following lunch, they retired to her backyard, where she recited her favorite verses from early nineteenth-century English poetry. Keats,

Coleridge, Wordsworth and Browning…she knew all the romantic poets by heart. Jack marveled at how her skin erupted into goose bumps when she recited verse upon verse about measureless caverns and unheard melodies. *Was this the key to her boudoir?*

As the afternoon wore on, Judy's mother received visits from patrons of the First International Debutante Ball, and Judy helped prepare the tea and crumpets. Jack saw this as an opportunity to slip out the door, but no such luck. These blue-haired ladies quizzed him incessantly about his work, but their interest transformed into vibrancy when Judy's mother disclosed that his mother's bloodline descended from the Mayflower Allertons. He might have mentioned to them that before the Pilgrims set sail for the New World, they temporarily sojourned in the Netherlands, where the tolerant Dutch gave refuge to all of Europe's persecuted and unwanted. Apparently even Dutch tolerance had its limits, and the Pilgrims found themselves in exile in the North American wilderness, where half of them died of starvation or exposure during the first three winters. Being first comers, however, did have its advantages, and within ten years, these crafty folk had bought, bartered or swindled the Wampanoag tribes out of the choicest real estate in Massachusetts. And so began the Social Register!

By late afternoon, Jack and Judy returned to the backyard, where they played nine-wicket croquet with her parents, who came dressed in their regulation whites. Early evening saw them ride in the family Hudson to the Siwanoy Country Club, where they rubbed elbows with the local Knickerbockers, many of whom claimed lineage going back to Peter Minuet's trinket traders. The game room offered a sanctuary of emerald-topped billiard tables in an atmosphere of manly smoke, but alas; Jack would receive no entry. Instead he and Judy received a long line of wives of distinguished members, who offered their salutations and congratulations along with suggestions for china patterns and place settings in the newly-weds' future abode.

Dinner conversation accompanied by paltry portions of pheasant and parsnips ran along the same line of domestic niceties, and when given a chance to get off the topic, Jack did offer a short critique of Professor Kingston's lecture on North American finches, but he left out the part about their crowns and attendant mating rituals. At that point, Judy let out a sigh and rested her hand on his knee beneath the tablecloth.

By late evening, the Hudson dropped him off at his front walk, and for his farewell, he kissed his betrothed on the forehead. Perhaps this good-bye was a trifle understated, but how could he dare kiss her on the cheek in front of Mommy and Daddy?

Jack lumbered toward his front door and muttered to himself, "Help me, Alice," before finally slipping inside, where, except for a wedge of light peeking around the cracked door to the family room, the place stood silent and dark. Jack flipped on the light, and as he approached the room, he began to make out the strains of Charley Parker's alto saxophone erupting into a bebop finale. *Ah yes—Dad and his never ending research!*

"How goes the society circuit, old chum?" came Oliver's lockjaw greeting in the Queen's English. With his reading glasses dangling from a neck chain, he leaned over a bridge table upon which he had laid out end-to-end photographs. The needle on the gramophone, meanwhile, played to the end and conveyed a hiss-bump pulse at seventy-eight beats per minute. Oliver switched off the player and returned to his pictures.

"Old chum? Don't be sarcastic, Dad" Jack replied. "If you're hip enough to appreciate Bird on sax, then you darn well know that I don't fit in with the blue blazer set."

Oliver shrugged. "Sarcasm aside, I had set my sights on buying you a double breasted version with a crème-colored ascot as a wedding present."

Jack smiled out one side of his mouth. "I'd prefer if you bought Judy some patterned stockings, but how can I convince her to step into them on our wedding night?"

"You can't. Judy comes as a package deal, and if you want to play under a woman's covers, then you'll have to play by the woman's rules."

Jack knew he could have rebutted this aphorism with a side story about his adventures with Alice, but he put the brakes on any account about mayonnaise soaked bed sheets. *What if Dad talked in his sleep with Mother listening to his every word?*

Oliver's fingers walked along the tabletop sequence of research photographs until they came to a halt at the last one. He handed it to Jack and said, "What you see here is a fundamental force of behavior. Did you ever read the works of Charles Darwin?"

Jack studied the photo. It showed a man standing in front of a table, where he ogled a picture of an attractive woman, whose bounty exceeded her bathing suit. Next to this picture within the picture, a platter of steak and potatoes beckoned the taste buds. "Sure, he's the naturalist who wrote that all living organisms today are the evolutionary product of survival of the fittest ancestors. What does that have to do with your advertising work?"

"Yesterday, we withheld food for twenty-four hours from a group of paid male subjects aged eighteen to thirty-five. We released them one by one into a room, where we had placed a rewarding meal alongside a color print of a nubile female. Every subject took a prolonged look at the woman before gobbling down the food. What does that tell you?"

"Uh... love conquers hunger?"

"Nice try, Jack. That's what most of the creative types at the agencies said. I had to inform them that ole Charlie D. got it twice right when he said that survival of the fittest organisms means nothing in the evolutionary process unless those same organisms reproduce as well. So does it surprise you that hanky-panky is soldered into our masculine brains with more wiring than our lust for food?"

"You got me, Dad... But I'll take traditional lust any day of the week."

"Okay... But let me just add that given half the fasting time, almost every female in a reciprocal experiment preferred beef to beefcake. I believe this means that you should turn down the heat with Judy."

The turn in the conversation caught Jack off guard, and he realized that his father's discretion during Judy's protest with him that morning had been for Judy's benefit. "I presume you took note of our misunderstanding on the couch," Jack volunteered.

"Judy's chastity shouldn't surprise you. It's the ladies who have the most to lose in a terminated courtship ritual. Like most good girls, that's the way her mother raised her to think."

"Gosh! You make it sound like she's some sort of finch. Can't we just spoon?"

"Until the big day comes, you can sow your oats but not in that field. Am I understood?"

Jack nodded yes—perhaps a little too enthusiastically. He kissed his father goodnight and departed.

Oliver gathered up the photographs and blew on them as if they were lucky dice. For over one hundred years, advertisers solicited customers by stating that they made the finest quality merchandise utilizing the finest materials and the finest craftsmanship with the finest this and the finest that. Now, his data told him that advertisers had to impart upon the male of the species an implicit imagery with an implicit message that implicitly stated that if you bought this product, you would get laid. This portended a more psychologically correct approach to advertising, and all these pictures of horny, hungry males—in that order—didn't lie.

Pleased with his results, he picked up the telephone and dialed the operator. "Long distance, please.... Hyannis Port, Massachusetts," he requested. He knew the results of the study would delight Joe Kennedy. After all, Joe had not only funded it, but he had hypothesized it too. Perhaps the man could give Professor Einstein a few pointers.

CHAPTER 28

The Main Event

Pandemonium…utter mayhem…. It couldn't have been otherwise as a tidal wave of humanity swept Jack and Alice through the turnstiles and into Yankee Stadium for the Rocky Marciano v. Ezzard Charles championship match. And what was that saying about the effect of absence on the heart? Jack couldn't take his eyes off Alice, whose black dress with the plunging neckline and the slit up the side transported his senses back to the realm of nymphs and sirens.

He placed his arm snugly around her waist, and with a swagger in each step, he escorted her past the box seats and onto the field to row C, where the swells at ringside gawked and ogled at this goddess sent down from on high.

Ah yes, Alice had returned to his life. After seven days, nineteen hours and fifty-two minutes, Jack could once again savor the delicious essence of womanhood displaying the black dress under which a black brassiere and the naughtiest of black panties surely awaited.

But all that womanhood could wait for later. For now, Yankee Stadium took on the air of the Roman Coliseum circa 120 A.D. The announcer, the boxing commissioner and the referee stepped over the ropes, and the crowd sprang out of their seats. Bodies bobbed and weaved; spectators called out for blood, and cameras put on a fireworks display though not one boxer was yet to be seen.

Amidst this clamor, the announcer grabbed the microphone. Alice rubbed Jack on the shoulder and kissed him under the chin, where she left a lipstick mark that tagged his collar. Jack didn't worry about that. He had become an expert in laundered shirt swapping. And as for the multiple broadcast cameras protruding from the press boxes in the mezzanine, he wished them luck in trying to pluck him and Alice out of this mob scene. This would not be a repeat of the Yankees-Red Sox game.

"Good evening, ladies and gentlemen," echoed the booming voice from the house speakers. *Ladies and gentlemen!* Jack's eyes meandered into the farthest reach of the bleachers and saw only suits and fedoras. Was Alice the only lady in the house?

But at these words, the crowd erupted into a deafening roar, and Jack made out scattered words here and there. "…in the light trunks… The

Cincinnati Cobra… The former heavyweight champion of the world, Ezzard Charles.…"

His arms raised in victory, Ezzard Charles emerged from the third base dugout and pranced toward the ring, all the while delivering fluid body shots to the atmosphere. Finally reaching his corner, he climbed over the ropes and held them for his manager, the cut man and the water boy.

The announcer continued, "…and wearing the dark trunks… from Brockton, Massachusetts… the undefeated heavyweight champion of the world… Rockyyyyyyyy Marciano!"

Rocky Marciano bounded out of the first base dugout, and as he skipped in time to an imaginary jump rope, he whirled around in a complete three-sixty. As Rocky approached ringside, Jack realized that he would pass right alongside his aisle seat. Alice craned her neck around Jack to get the best view, but the simultaneous discharge of hundreds of flash-bulbs in their direction rendered them both temporarily blind. Jack wondered how any man could box much less walk through this assault on the retinas when he could barely tell the difference between Alice's teeth and all those effervescent bubbles floating in front of his nose.

The referee called both fighters together to explain the taboos of illicit body contact. The fighters nodded, touched gloves and retreated to their corners. Then, with the ring of the bell, they commenced a punishing attack that lasted fifteen rounds and left them both standing.

The outcome stunned the crowd. They had come expecting a knockout but had received a mere decision. Were they disappointed? Not by the lamest of long shots!

And in the end, the judges awarded the fight to Marciano, who had clearly out pointed his rival but did not vanquish him. As testament to this, Jack, Alice and all the forty-five thousand other spectators in Yankee Stadium jumped to their feet and screamed in perfect synchrony, "Rematch…rematch…rematch!"

Once Outside the stadium, Alice whistled down a taxi, and Jack offered to escort her back to her apartment. Alice, however, put up her hand. "It's late, Jack, and you need your sleep. Go home. I'll see you on Monday."

"But that's four days from now," Jack whined. "Can't we…"

Alice pushed her forefinger against Jack's lips. "Do you remember me telling you about those magical pills that prevent mishaps?"

"How could I forget?"

"I started taking them in Boston last Saturday. That means Monday could be a very special night for us. Would it please you to bring a toothbrush and a change of clothing?"

Jack gagged. Did he hear her right? Could this mean the big event was near? His breathing went into overdrive. "Alice, my love, I'll bring flowers, candles and a pair of rock lobsters."

"Kiss me goodnight, Jack."

The fight of all fights and soon the feast of all feasts, Jack just wanted to eat her whole!

CHAPTER 29

Spotted

After Jack pushed through the revolving doors on Friday morning, he realized why the Ambassador kept Chester in his employ as a spotter. At this task, he was superhuman, almost like the eye on the top of the pyramid on the back of the dollar bill. He came; he saw, and he never missed a face.

"The man and his lady get third row seats to see Marciano dish out another whoopin'. Lord, please tell me how this is possible?" he joked slapping Jack on the back.

But Jack wasn't laughing. "Who told you that?" he gasped.

"My eyes looking at the big screen at the Fox Theater told me. Heck, I saw Graziano and LaMotta turn to see if they could get a piece of what you got."

Jack palmed his cheek. How many other fans had witnessed what Chester had attested to? Particularly, how many people known to both Judy and him had used the movie screen to crash his date with Alice?

Chester cocked his head to the side. "Now don't you worry that smart head of yours, Mr. Preston," Chester reassured him. "I spotted you and your woman for a second, maybe two seconds tops. You know me. I only tell what I see to Mr. Kennedy. But your business doesn't concern him. And since that's the case, he doesn't get to know."

"You're a good man, Chester," Jack said, relieved. "So how come you don't call me by my first name?"

"Shucks, Mr. Preston, I can't do that here. People might say that I'm acting uppity or something more, and no matter what the Supreme Court says these days, business might go bad. You understand me?"

"Sure I do, but that doesn't make it right."

Chester nodded but didn't say a word. Jack then proceeded to the elevator, where he held the doors for Nora. On the ride up, he observed clumps of mascara dangling from her upper eyelashes, which made him want to suggest that she would look a whole lot prettier if she didn't plaster on so much foundation and rouge. However, this was not the kind of subject that a gentleman dared to broach with a young lady. Instead, Jack stared straight ahead at the elevator doors and asked himself why her twitching hands were empty today.

CHAPTER 30

The Craftsman

Roy Tucker paged through the stack of newspapers under the watchful eyes of Irv Spiegel, who ran the candy store by the Bronxville train station. One by one, be it *The News*, *The Mirror* or *The Herald Tribune*, Roy opened to the sports section and perused the pictures of the fight. When he didn't find what he wanted, he moved on to *The Times* and *The Morning Telegraph* and likewise found nothing of interest. But hope was not yet lost. In roughly five minutes, the afternoon distributors would deliver bulldog editions of *The Post*, *The Journal American* and *The World Telegram and Sun*, and Roy would stand ready for them. He stepped over to the soda fountain and put down a nickel.

"I'll have a chocolate egg cream, Irv," Roy said.

Irv spritzed three splashes of chocolate syrup into a fountain glass and topped it with a splash of milk. Next, he placed the glass under the vichy tap and let the bubbly water rip, all the while holding a long spoon underneath so he could deflect the stream down the side of the glass. To the uninitiated, this presented a simple enough task, but to the *cognoscenti*, the inch-thick frothy head that emerged on top of the drink demonstrated superior crafts-manship. Irv swapped this misnamed drink, which contained neither egg nor cream, for the nickel on the counter, and he handed Roy a straw.

Roy took a sip. "Nice drink," he remarked.

"So, you don't like my newspapers," Irv returned.

"I'm looking for pictures of the fight that show the faces in the first few rows."

"But the fight was in the ring."

Roy ran his straw along the top of the drink and sucked down the head. "You don't suppose I might get lucky with the afternoon papers?" He licked the straw.

"Why don't you try the Italian dailies? The whole country has adopted Rocky Marciano as their son, and the sports editors there like to feature pictures of the rich and famous sitting ringside."

"So when's the next flight to Rome?"

Irv laughed. "Come rush hour, an Al Italia DC-6 stacked with tabloids will touch down at Idlewild to bring the local paisans enough pho-tos from the fight to paper a wall."

"I presume you know a vendor."

"Try Dateline Distributors in Times Square. Just follow the smoke rings from the Camel sign."

Roy guzzled down his egg cream and bounded out of the store as the four-fifteen to the city blew its approach whistle. He made it aboard with barely a second to spare.

CHAPTER 31

And Away We Go

Chester had a line of customers waiting for his services, and so Jack merely nodded to him as he stepped lively toward the closing elevator doors. With a flick of the wrist, he stuck his overnight suitcase into their path, and the doors rebounded open. Once inside, he tipped his hat to Nora, who gazed at the floor buttons as if she had taken on the curse of the zombie.

"What? No crossword book today?" Jack asked.

"I'm in a bad mood. My boyfriend dumped me because I spent more time with the books than with him. He told me I had a compulsion problem."

Nora's eyes shifted from the floor buttons to Jack's suitcase. "Are you going somewhere, Mr. P?"

Jack could think of nothing but Alice in her entire glory. He fantasized to what places she might take him on this special night. "I'm going to the moon," Jack cracked. "Do you know where that is?"

"Yeah, that's where Alice is going."

"Alice!?!" Jack gasped. How could Nora Kincaid from Flatbush Avenue on the far side of Brooklyn possibly know about his other life?

Nora had a ready explanation. "Sure, don't you ever watch the Jackie Gleason show?" she asked. "When he plays the bus driver, he always promises to send his wife, Alice, to the moon."

"Ah yes... Alice... Alice Kramden.... How could I be so dumb?"

"Yeah, you are lucky that wasn't a crossword clue; you might've actually missed one," Nora kidded. "Are you all right, Mr. P.? You look kind of pale."

CHAPTER 32

Special Delivery

Judy Faraday giggled with joy, and why not? On this first day of summer and the first official day of vacation from her kindergarten class, the sun cast its rays along the fringes of the puffiest of clouds, and the birds chirped sweet songs of love. Oh yes, the sweetness of love! She pictured herself exchanging vows in her bridal whites. Jack and she would seal their love with the purity of their lips meeting for the first time within the holy bond, and their affections would grow deeper every day.

Judy placed her bridal magazine on the kitchen counter and whistled through the screen to the birds in the garden. And, like her kindergarten class, they warbled back only the most gentle and heartfelt, greetings. "Yes, good morning to you…and to you…and to you," she chirped. Could life get any sweeter than this?

The doorbell rang. "I'll get it, Mom," she called up the stairway and then sashayed to the front door.

"Special delivery for Miss Judith Faraday," greeted the postman.

"That's me," she announced. The postman handed her the letter, and she cuddled it in her arms as if it were a baby blue jay.

"Is it true what they say that special delivery is bad luck?" she asked.

"No, you're thinking of telegrams. Special delivery is…uh, special," the postman explained.

"Then that makes me a special lady," Judy giggled almost to the point of giddiness. The postman tipped his cap and departed.

The postmark said, "Grand Central Station." Judy turned the letter over and found the return address on the flap smeared and illegible. Would the letter inside suffer the same fate?

There was only one way of finding out. Judy opened the flap and pulled out a newspaper clipping with a note taped to the front. She read the note first.

Jack is two-timing you.
He's got a girlfriend in the city.

The note was unsigned.

Judy bit her lip and lifted the note up from the clipping only to behold a picture of Jack sitting at the end of a crowded row of seats. A woman, who looked very much like his date for this event, craned her neck across his chest, and in the vilest of manners, her hand rested upon his lap. *This couldn't be!*

Judy looked for a caption beneath the picture but found that it had been cut off. Dazed, she turned the clipping over and encountered a fragment of reporting printed in Italian. What kind of cruel joke was this? Did Jack have a body double living somewhere in Italy? And what kind of person would take pleasure in shocking her with this obvious look-alike? Judy stuffed the note and the clipping back into the envelope and then placed the envelope in her purse.

She ran upstairs to the corner salon, where her mother busied herself writing invitations for the Saratoga Cup Ball in August. "What is it, dear?" her mother greeted her.

"Do you know anybody vacationing in Italy this week?"

"I can't say that I do. The country has been slow to recover from the war. Nobody I know would recommend a sightseeing tour there yet."

"Of course."

"Is there anything else?"

"Would you know the address of Jack's firm in the city?"

"I entered it in the black book right after your official announcement. Why don't you pay him a surprise visit? He might like that."

"Of course he will.... He loves me!"

Judy refused to let a stupid picture ruin her day.

CHAPTER 33

Gumshoe

What a day! Jack tried to banish all thoughts of the coming evening with Alice from his mind, but all that did was make him think about her more. Fortunately, he chased paper from nine to six, and so he didn't have to worry about any lapses into fantasy in the presence of clients. On the other hand, semantic booby traps accompanied every contract and agreement on his blotter, causing him to double-check every line both backward and forward to root out any million-dollar bombs hiding in plain sight. For three hundred and twenty-seven pages of proof reading, Jack deactivated fifteen such bombs, and at the end of the day, he handed his blue-penciled handiwork to Thelma, who nodded her head in admiration. At the stroke of six, Jack picked up his suitcase and headed for the elevator.

Down in the lobby, Judy with a kerchief already tied to her head, donned a pair of dark sunglasses and tucked herself in a back corner away from the flow of traffic. There, she opened a newspaper and peered over the top of it. When Jack exited the elevator, she followed him through the revolving door.

He stopped first at a grocery, where she watched him through the window as he placed a box of candles at the register. Next, he stopped off at a florist's shop and emerged with a dozen long stem roses wrapped in wax paper. From there, he headed east all the way to the river, where he arrived at the Fulton Street Fish Market to purchase—of all things—two lobsters. Judy frowned. Even in burlap bags, these were not the kind of items that one brought back home on the evening train.

Finally, Jack brought all of the merchandise to a street corner, where he looked like he would hail a cab. With no taxis in sight, Judy realized that this might mean the end of the line for her for how could she keep on his trail unless a second cab showed up seconds later? And then a cab did stop, but the driver balked at the fare. Perhaps the likelihood of two lobsters dripping on the upholstery gave him second thoughts.

Jack picked up his booty and then doubled back up Fulton Street to the Broadway-Nassau IND station, where he arrived on the platform for the uptown A-Train. After the train screeched to a halt, he entered through the front doors of the second car, and Judy stepped aboard using the rear doors of the first car. From there, she spotted him through the windows on the connecting doors, and she noted that when he took a seat, the adjacent passengers gave him wide berth. It must have been the lobsters talking!

When the train arrived at the Canal Street station, Jack gathered up his belongings, and Judy had a hunch that he might get off at the next stop. The express train bolted past Spring Street, and at the West Fourth Street stop, Jack exited the train to the left, where he passed in front of Judy's car. She buried her head in her newspaper and walked out the door in blind pursuit, only to march straight into a steel support. She wanted to shriek, but her mind could think of only one thing, "Keep following Jack."

And so she did, up the stairs and along the crooked streets of the West Village until he arrived at a nondescript apartment house on Barrow Street. As Jack entered the foyer, Judy snuck up from behind and squatted on the far side of a parked car, where she watched him set down his suitcase and push buzzer number four in column three directly above the mail boxes. Jack then spun around to push open the door with his back, and as he bent over to retrieve his suitcase, Judy ducked below the car window just before he momentarily glanced toward the street. When he disappeared into the lobby, she let out a surge of held breath.

After mumbling to herself, "It's not what you think," she entered the foyer and noted that Jack had pushed buzzer 4C next to which the name, A MERCER, stood out in block print. Was it true what that horrible note had said about her beloved? At that moment, she didn't want to think about it, and so she rushed out to the sidewalk and ran half way to the Hudson River docks.

An urge to return home came upon her in a frigid blast, but she knew she couldn't leave—at least not yet.

CHAPTER 34

Home Run

Alice's kitchen took on a ghostly glow. The shadows of roses in wine bottles and lobster husks in discard bowls danced across the checkered tablecloth in perfect synchrony to the strobe beat of flickering candles. In the living room, the television image rolled top to bottom at a turtle's pace, but the sound came through as clear as a church bell.

"Hello, everybody!" the announcer drawled, "Mel Allen here for Yankee baseball. We visit you from Comiskey Park in Chicago tonight, where a Yankee win could tie them for first place with Cleveland..."

In the bedroom, longer, that is to say more freshly lit, candles beamed their hypnotic light across a blouse and brassiere, which lay on top of the floor chest. And in quick succession, a skirt, a pair of garters, and a pair of stockings claimed the top spot on the chest, only to be supplanted by a pair of lace panties.

Jack stared at Alice in all her naked glory, and he would have gasped if he hadn't almost swallowed his tongue.

"Come inside, Jack. Take all of me," she said.

But Jack wanted to savor this moment. "Let me ravish you first. Let me smother your neck with kisses and then your..."

"I get the idea," Alice giggled. "You may kiss me everywhere you desire except in that one forbidden zone. Understood?"

Jack nodded yes, and without a second to squander, he caressed, petted, licked and fluttered homage to Alice's womanhood in all her places but that one. If he could not kiss her orifice, perhaps he could make other arrangements. "Alice, may I touch your private part with my fingers?"

"I cannot refuse such a gentlemanly request. Please be gentle with me."

Gentle! How could he not be gentle with such womanly treasure? His hand descended, and he fingered the moist flesh within as if it were a Stradivarius. Her muscles stiffened, and she moaned.

"Did I hurt you?" he asked withdrawing his hand to her hip.

But Alice's hand reached for his hand and placed it back where it had been. "You talk too much," she said. "Your lips have another purpose tonight."

And how could he argue with such wisdom? Jack stroked her loins both inside and out, and she reciprocated by licking her hand and grabbing hold of Priapus. Her fingers slithered effortlessly up and down and in reciprocal semi rotations along the girth of his erect staff and overpowered the Mutt to the point where Jack could take it no more. "Please don't make me climax now," he begged.

"Then don't make me wait any longer," she returned using her hand to guide Priapus into the forbidden chamber of pleasure, which Jack had desired ever since the days when pubic hair had first decorated his pelvic mantle. *At last, the fraternity of manhood!*

But did not the Mutt merely jump from the frying pan into the fire? Jack did not care. If his manly fluid demanded discharge, then let it flow where nature had intended. Besides, Jack knew that the faithful Mutt had two, possibly three more shots left in him, so why not let him surge? But Alice's anatomy would not be so accommodating. As her legs clamped around Jack's posterior, the silken sheath surrounding the Mutt exerted a crushing force as if it were compressed by a hydraulically powered boa constrictor. Had not Alice's legs immobilized Jack in their embrace, the Mutt would have popped out like a champagne cork, but now he remained secured inside this vise-like well, whose sheer pressure strangled his gullet and prevented him from spewing his contents.

Jack grunted, and he groaned. In all his virginal years, he had never anticipated such weaponry hidden inside this heavenly portal. The cavity had taken on its own spirit and issued forth a witches' brew of pain and pleasure upon his entrapped member, driving him beyond the brink of madness. Dare he beg for mercy!

"Oh yes, baby!!!" he bellowed as if he had swallowed a megaphone. "Oh Alice, you're the one and only. Oh! Oh!! Oh Alice!!! I love you more than anything in the whole world!!!"

And in that moment, the hydraulic boa retracted, and the Mutt spilled forth. Sanity returned to Jack, and he glanced at the bas-relief figures on the floor chest, which showed lovers in various entangled positions of lovemaking while from the TV set in the living room, Mel Allen sounded as chipper as ever. "...Here's the pitch. Skowron swings... (Crack!) ...And that ball is going... going... gone! The first major league home run for Moose Skowron... How about that!"

Outside in the hallway, Judy Faraday sat leaning against the apartment door, where she wept into her kerchief. "Can I help you with something, miss?" Gus, the super, asked, his trusty mop by his side.

But Judy shook her head before picking herself up and running toward the landing. When she reached the street, she slowed her pace and walked all the way to Grand Central station. Not once did she ever look back.

CHAPTER 35

The Day After

With a skip in his step, Jack pushed through the revolving door and whistled the climactic theme to the *1812 Overture* as Dizzy Gillespie might have interpreted it. His suitcase swung high with each step. At the newspaper stand, Nora Kincaid paged through a crossword puzzle book while next to her, Chester wiped down his bootblack's seat.

"Top of the morning to you, Nora!" Jack greeted her almost sounding like he had sucked down an entire stick of reefer. Then his face broke into a monstrous grin. "It's a spectacular day. Isn't it, Chester?" he asked before sauntering on into the elevator.

"Wow, you'd think he just won the Irish Sweepstakes," Nora said shrugging her shoulders.

"Only one thing I know puts that kind of zip in a man," Chester chuckled, his wisdom teeth on display. "Yes, indeed!"

Still whistling, Jack pranced into the law office reception, where Thelma was on hand to greet him. "My-my-my... we love coming to work, don't we?" she said.

"What's the deal for today?"

"Mr. Thorpe has volunteered you to announce all approved mergers and acquisitions to the press. I trust you know how to handle them—veteran that you are."

"Find me a bottle of Chivas and I'll have them bleating like lambs."

"You're simply marvelous!"

At the stroke of twelve with Thelma and Paul by his side, Jack kept it simple for the gaggle of reporters in the conference room. Without any fanfare, he announced, "Today, Armstrong Tires acquires Akron Chemical Works."

In turn, the reporters relayed the breaking news into their walkie-talkies before filing out the side door; however, two of them actually waved at Jack, and one even shook his hand. Thelma nodded her approval while Paul grabbed the announcement card and the white envelope from the rostrum. After a cursory look, he chucked them both into the wastebasket.

On the evening train, Jack had the fortune to sit across from a voluptuous blonde in a clinging skirt and a pullover blouse. Jack peered at her over the top of his *Journal American. She sure was a nice dish... Actually, she was a knockout, but she was no Alice!*

Page one led with a story about the imminent nationalization of rubber plantations by the revolutionary government in Indochina. Jack flipped to the financial section and noted that Akron Chemical was up six and five-eighths for the day while Armstrong Tires fell a point. Apparently, the anticipated expropriation of all those rubber plantations in Indochina had caused rubber futures to skyrocket at the expense of the industrial processors.

When Jack arrived home, he found Emily in the kitchen, where she peeled onions to the accompaniment of sniffles and tears. She kissed him and handed him a small envelope. "Judy told me to give this to you. She almost choked on her words."

Jack opened the envelope and pulled out a note. As he unfolded the note, Judy's engagement ring fell onto the kitchen table. Jack read the note.

June 22, 1954
Jack:
It wouldn't surprise me if one day a giant lobster drags you
to hell.

Judy

The note and the ring said it all, but Jack's mind raced to fill in the blanks. *So Judy knew about the lobsters; then she must have found out about Alice and last night. But how could she have possibly suspected this liaison, let alone know the details? And how do I talk my way out of this mess?* But then the note and the ring both spoke, and in a mighty voice they chorused, "Don't ever darken my doorway again!"

Emily picked up the ring. "What is this? It's over between you and Judy?" With the ring still in her hand, she wiped a tear from her cheek.

"It wasn't meant to be, Mother."

Emily pulled on her hair as if she wanted to tear it out. "Judy would have crawled on nails for you. What did you do to her?"

"She's a kid. She can't take a punch."

With an open hand, Emily landed a right hook across Jack's cheek. "That sweet girl is not one of your prizefighters! What made her come to this?"

Jack rubbed his cheek. "It's personal, Mother. Let's leave it at that."

"How dare you! How…. How…" Unable to finish her sentence, Emily broke down sobbing, and after placing the ring on the table, she scurried up to her bedroom.

As the upstairs door slammed shut, Oliver ambled into the kitchen. "So who is the bombshell that you're hooked up with, son? I'd like to meet her," he said in a cheery fashion, which could have meant either genuine interest or sarcasm.

"Yes, and Mother would like to boil her in lye," Jack replied.

And then it hit him. What infernal gossipmonger had told his father about the affair? "Does the whole town know about my private business?" he fumed.

Oliver picked up the ring and held it up to the light. "I bumped into Judy outside just after she had dropped off the envelope. She told me all about your madcap adventures in the Village and left a few watermarks on my shoulder in the telling."

"So what would you do?" brandy

Oliver waved the ring at Jack. "If it's broke, fix it. You might want to try the telephone." Oliver placed the ring back on the table and grabbed a bottle of sherry from the cupboard. He poured a healthy taste and departed.

"I've got to be a man about this," Jack mumbled to himself before clearing a lump in his throat with a string of coughs. He dialed Judy, and she picked up on the first ring.

"Hello."

"Judy, I can explain—"

But Judy cut him off. "Merry Christmas, Jack! Enjoy your presents with your new friend!" She slammed the receiver in his ear.

So that was it with Judy… over… finished… gone… *poof*! But then Jack spotted the engagement ring on the table. He held it up to the light and raised one corner of his mouth. Judy may have left his life for good, but she still had exquisite taste in jewelry.

CHAPTER 36

Ecstasy and Bliss

Jack bore roses, and on his way up to apartment 4C, he kept telling himself that his engagement to Judy had been an error all along. Had they followed through with the wedding, he supposed that she would have indulged his desires for the first few years, but would he have satisfied hers? And, he had to wonder—did Judy have any desires? Certainly she wanted children, but after dutifully bearing two of the little darlings, would she demand separate beds or even separate bedrooms?

Alice waited for Jack at the doorway and rushed to embrace him when he reached the landing. After a smoldering kiss, they retreated into her apartment, and Jack offered her the bouquet.

"No more flowers! I still have the roses from the other night," she said.

"Alice, close your eyes," Jack said, throwing the roses aside.

"What? Why?"

"Please close them, and give me your left hand."

With her eyelids pressed together, Alice held out her hand, and Jack placed Judy's former engagement ring on her fourth finger. "Voilà! A perfect fit! Will you?" he asked.

Alice stroked the diamond and wobbled. Sensing that she might faint, Jack led her to a chair and helped her sit. "Oh, Jack! Is this what I think it is?" she asked.

Jack dropped to his knees. "Alice Mercer, if you married me, every day of my life would be ecstasy and bliss. What do you say?"

Rebounding from the chair, Alice threw her arms around Jack and whipped her tongue halfway to his tonsils. With their mouths still locked, she pushed him toward the bedroom and into the bed. "If you can survive a whole night of ecstasy and bliss, then the answer is 'yes'!!!"

And asynchronous moans wailed into the night.

The following morning, Alice and Jack shared a bath, and this time she allowed him to peek at her whole package. They began the task with practical intentions; she gave him a thorough scrubbing, and he reciprocated; however, the touch and feel of her womanly flesh in the warm suds provoked him to the point where he required further samplings of ecstasy and bliss, this time to the rhythm of splashing water and flatulent gurgles emanating from the soapy film between his chest and her concavity.

Once cleansed of grime and any further desire, they headed straight to the kitchen, where Alice prepared breakfast. "So when do I meet your family?" she asked.

After placing a medium size bowl on the counter, she lined up a whisk, a grater, a spatula and three small bowls next to it. From the refrigerator, she removed a bottle of heavy cream, a stick of butter, a wedge of cheese and half a dozen eggs. Jack paid particular attention to her hands, which moved without a hint of wasted motion. Alice lit a burner with a stick match and placed a skillet with a quarter stick of the butter on the flame. On a cutting board, she placed a bundle of scallions and chopped them at an oblique angle before placing them in small bowl number one. Next she grabbed a series of spices from a wall rack and pinched a sample of each into bowl number two. Then she grated the cheese into bowl number three.

"You do have a family, don't you, Jack?" she teased, her busy hands almost placing Jack in a trance. He recalled watching Judy cut scallions at precisely the same angle, but with more labor and less panache. Then, it dawned on him that that Alice had just asked him to meet the folks, which, he had to admit, was an all too reasonable request for a woman newly betrothed.

"How about getting together with them this weekend," Jack suggested. He realized that he could not refuse Alice's request without insulting her. Then again, what noxious bombs awaited her arrival when Mother found out that she was the woman who triggered Judy's departure?

The butter in the skillet bubbled to life, and Alice emptied the bowl of scallions and the bowl of spices into it. After giving the sauté mixture a quick stir, she poured a half-cup of heavy cream into the medium bowl and whipped it with the whisk until little peaks formed.

Alice bit her lip. "The weekend is bad for me, actually. I may have to go to Boston again." Using only one hand, she cracked the eggs over the medium bowl and dumped them on top of the cream. At the same time, she stirred the sauté mixture with her other hand.

Jack couldn't believe his luck. If the coming weekend was out of the question, then that meant that seven more days would have to pass before he made proper introductions. He just might have his house in order by then. "What about your family? Do they live in Boston?"

"Oh no. Boston is just another place to work. Papa is in the military. He and Mama live overseas." Alice whipped the egg and cream ensemble until it doubled in size and then folded in the grated cheese. From sight unseen, she pulled out a bottle of sweet vermouth, and splashed a bit upon the sauté mixture to yield a sudden puff of aromatic steam. Finally, she emptied the contents of the medium bowl onto the sauté mixture and rotated the upturned bowl around the spatula to get every last drop into the skillet.

"Wow, I've seen French cooking before, but never with such skill. Where'd you take your lessons?" Jack exclaimed.

Alice stirred the contents of the pan. "Cooking lessons? *Moi*?" she said. Then she splayed her fingers to admire her ring. "Oh, my sweet love, do you know what you're getting yourself into?" A tear rolled down her cheek.

Jack kissed the tear before it could fall to the ground, and he savored the salty taste. "I've never been more sure of anything in my life," he said, bestowing a wet kiss on her palm.

"Good," she replied. And with a gentle push from the kiss mark, she added, "Now get out of my way before I burn the omelet."

Jack left for work a half hour later than his customary departure from home, yet he still had time to spare after the mile and a half walk to his office. Had he taken a taxi, he could have arrived there in mere minutes, but the day sparkled with sunshine and low humidity, and the walk gave him the opportunity to reflect upon his fortunes.

Looking in time's mirror, he remembered the sublime airiness of his omelet and the virtuosity of the hands that created it from scratch. He especially liked Alice's manner of conversation. She did ask questions; after all, she was a woman, but she didn't badger or nag, and she remained rooted in the present tense, so there were never any questions about the family tree or the interior design of any future family kitchen.

And then there was Alice the mistress, Alice the lover and Alice the goddess of sirens. Never in the deepest pit of his bawdy imagination could Jack have conjured up such delight. Certainly making love in the bathtub highlighted her willingness for spontaneous action, but the hard porcelain and the water splashing over the sides imposed its limits—even upon her womanly skills.

And what skills they were!

Forget the sucking, nibbling and fluttering action of Alice's kisses, for they bowed in awe to the mysterious workings of her orifice. But did not all women possess such a vital organ, and could not all women command it to engulf the mighty male member and subjugate it with snapping, whipping, pumping, tearing and strangling movements that could crush walnuts into shards and dust? For all the years of Jack's reverie, he had never dreamed of this power within. Truly, this heavenly den possessed both mind and reflex for which men—the so-called master sex—had paid tribute for all the ages. For now though, Jack wanted to get down on his knees before it and profess his devotion. Yes, he would worship Alice's orifice with a thousand kisses, a thousand licks, a thousand flutters and…

    …Damn! Jack could feel that infernal mutt taking a stretch. Was he ever satisfied?

CHAPTER 37

Sage Advice

As soon as Jack leaned over his desk, a kink in his back bore through him like a Milwaukee drill. Damn bathtub! Or maybe getting twisted into a pretzel for three and a half hours on Alice's bed was the culprit. Stretching relieved the spasm. Jack stepped over to the window and pulled on the frame. That did the trick!

"Hard night at the office, Jack?" greeted Thelma Kane.

"It's just a slight twinge. I'll live."

"Sorry I'm late with today's schedule, but the boys in the press will raise their glasses high in your honor tonight. The SEC approved two of your cases, merger H-19 and acquisition J-41. A brown and a white envelope in one day... Messrs. Hargrave and Thorpe send kudos."

"Neither case presented a worthy challenge."

After a momentary glare out of the corner of her eyes, Thelma departed to make further rounds and almost bumped into Paul Jeffrey coming from the other direction. She averted her gaze from Paul with sufficient exaggeration to make the gesture obvious to both him and Jack. But Paul was unflappable. "You wanted to see me, Mr. Preston?" he said, his fingers hoisting a V for victory sign in front of him.

"I'm puzzled about that savings account you had me open with Security Pacific Bank last month. I have yet to see a bankbook."

"I'm on it... Anything else?"

"Yes.... What did you ever do to get that cold shoulder from Thelma?"

"She's still stewing over that one incident when I botched up her calendar. I tell you, Mr. Preston; if you make one mistake with a woman, you wind up regretting it for the rest of your life."

"Such sage advice, my friend... such sage advice..."

Paul departed, leaving Jack to contemplate the unusual savings account that somebody in accounting had set up in his name. For what commercial purpose did it serve? Jack just couldn't figure. He looked at his watch and came to the fiscal conclusion that all this figuring had cost him two minutes of the firm's time. He had to get back on track.

Jack opened his safe and pulled out two manila folders. Today the boys in the press would love him more than a four-year-old loves Santa Claus. At twenty dollars per stock tip, each one would make enough money to keep his bartender's arm cranking for the next month.

Only in America!

CHAPTER 38

Fire and Ice

Alice ushered Jack into her apartment with a gyrating hug that pressed the fullness of her bosom ever upward until Jack could not help but stare down at her lush contours enveloped in the confines of a silk kimono glistening in the candlelight. "This is so right," he said planting but a morsel of a kiss upon her forehead. "If you desired, I would tie the knot with you tomorrow."

Alice relaxed her embrace and splayed her fingers to admire the glitter from her ring. "State law says we'd have to wait a week for the blood tests to clear."

"So you're a lawyer now. I believe we could get a waiver in Massachusetts if you let me come with you to Boston this weekend."

"Sorry, my love, but Boston is a job for me. You know what they say about mixing work and pleasure. Are you hungry?"

Jack looked across the room to the dining table, where upon its checkered tablecloth, two complete place settings, a bottle of Chablis, two half-filled wine glasses and a platter with a partially sliced baguette sat in compositional harmony as if they had become subjects in a still life. Jack hated to spoil the picture, but that baguette meant reprieve from a nagging growl in his stomach. He dabbed on a pat of butter, and before biting down he remarked, "What did you cook up for us this evening?"

"Behold the main course," Alice replied spreading open her kimono to flash her bosom at a razor's edge from his peepers.

Jack took a deep breath and inhaled a crumb of bread down his windpipe, which retaliated with coughing fits and spasms. Alice rushed to his rescue with a glass of wine. "Oh Jack, I'm sorry! I shouldn't have blindsided you like that."

Jack took a sip of wine and stretched out. "Excellent vintage! You have marvelous taste."

"I know I do. Have some more." She stabbed the side of his neck with her tongue and topped off his glass.

"What are you trying to do?" Jack knew that Alice knew that one didn't fill a wine glass to the brim. He swigged down the overflow.

"Take advantage of you, *mon cher.*"

Alice pulled on Jack's tie and led him into the bedroom, which in his eyes seemed to tilt sideways on some hidden axis. He eased back onto the bed, but Alice did not follow. Instead, her face drifted in and out of focus and settled into a soft blur.

"Feeling drowsy?" she said.

Jack rubbed his eyes. Her words weren't synchronized with her mouth. "When it comes to alcohol, I'm pretty much of a lightweight," he admitted.

"Let me make you comfortable." She loosened his tie.

Jack watched her nimble fingers unfastening the buttons on his shirt, and he counted them off to himself. "One…two…" And then a whirling vortex sucked the room into blackness, and he sank into a dreamless sleep.

Jack heard the whoosh of air ebbing and flowing through his nostrils. And what was this! Intricate patterns of rope not only bound him belly up and foursquare to the bedposts, but also wrapped around the bed boards where they doubled back around his elbows, waist and knees to weave him into the bed with a latticework of braids and hitches. A pillow propped his head at just the correct angle from where he could observe Alice securing his left leg to the bedpost.

"Alice, my love, what forbidden fruit do you feed me this time?" he asked shaking the spider webs from his mind, only to find that the web around his body would not be so yielding. He tugged on his bindings, and the only comfort he found was from the strips of moleskin that she had placed on his wrists and ankles, presumably to prevent any rope burns.

"I liberate you, Jack. Tonight you become a free man."

Jack told himself not to panic. If Alice wanted to play naughty, then let her proceed. Obviously, the pillow and moleskin indicated that she intended no harm. "Seriously, how do you intend to liberate me by tying me up?" he asked.

Alice put the finishing touch on the last knot and climbed onto the bed, where she rubbed her kimono against Jack's bound flesh. "I free you from having to prove yourself a man to me. Now that I am in control, I must prove myself a woman to you."

"I never had any doubts!"

Alice reached to the side of the bed for a steaming cup of tea, which sat on a serving table along with a bowl of ice water. She took a generous sip and swished it in her mouth. Suddenly, a searing lash whipped across Jack's belly causing him to recoil with no place to go. He looked past his chest and beheld Alice tagging his pelvis with brush strokes from her tongue, which had dropped in temperature from blistering to merely hot.

And the Mutt arose in all his glory.

"Oh! Oh!" Jack groaned biting his lip and shaking his head from side to side.

"Did I hurt you?"

"No, not at all... it feels quite good... Really, it does!"

Actually it felt A-plus superb. Jack marveled at Alice's creativity, her technique and her capacity to innovate. As he settled into his restraints, he realized that for the very near future she owned him and could do anything she wanted with him.

And he could hardly wait!

Alice loosened the sash of her kimono and took another sip of tea. With a swish and a swallow, her lips dived onto Priapus and enveloped him whole into her scorching mouth. Jack shrieked in pain but then cried out in rapture. "Oh! Oh!! Oh!!! Do it harder... faster... Oh, baby... Yes! Yes!! Yes!!!"

The Mutt had teetered on the brink of explosion, but then Alice grabbed a dishcloth from the bowl of ice water and slapped it across his muzzle. The poor beast turned tail into Jack's groin and flopped down limp and comatose. "Yeow! That's freezing! You stopped my climax. Why?" he protested.

"I have not yet proved myself a woman. I am still a girl." Alice nibbled on Jack's arm and moved toward his armpit, all the while gently plunging her nails into his skin.

"You're mad! I could be happy with *half* the woman you are."

"Don't humor me with kindness, Jack. A real woman would possess you body and soul. A real woman would get you to reveal your deepest intimacies. Without shame, you would tell me your darkest secrets."

Dark secrets? What the devil was she talking about? Jack wondered if he ever told her that being reared in the Congregationalist mode meant leading a perfect existence of straight-laced purity and boring virtue. *Dark secrets!* As far as he knew, she was the only dark secret in his life, and she wasn't that secret anymore. Maybe he could entertain her with stories about how he stimulated himself while breathing heavy over a picture of Jane Russell in her push-up brassiere. Nah, that was Little League stuff, and Alice played in the majors.

"Sorry Alice, but the last time I checked the closet, there were still no skeletons hanging from the tie rack," he joked.

Alice refilled her mouth with tea, and this time she branded Priapus with a burning hickey. Jack bucked high and low, but with all the rope work holding him fast, he barely moved the sheets. "Oh, it hurts, but please don't stop," he begged.

He knew that if he had the freedom to move, he most certainly would have jerked himself away from this glorious pain, but Alice—to her credit—made sure that he would not exercise such a cowardly option. The masterly tongue danced along the length of Priapus's soft underbelly, and Jack could feel the pressure of his manly fluid hitting the red zone. His muscles tensed, and his legs stiffened, and then—*wham*—Alice slapped the icy dishcloth on the beast.

"Stop! You're killing me," Jack howled. The beast sunk back into oblivion, and Jack considered that Alice might continue this game for hours. Indeed, what was to stop her from prolonging it until sunrise? Oh, the poor beast! Never before had he been so ravished, and never before had he been so abused.

"What dirty secrets can you tell me? If you do not tell me then I have failed you. I am just a silly girl, who licks a spiral lollypop," Alice said in goo-goo baby talk.

Confession! Jack surmised. *That was it. Alice wanted a confession…* And then it hit him; if he revealed his innermost desires to her, she would attend to them.

"Oh, Alice… touching your breasts gives me such a huge boner. Oh! I love the feel of your stockings. I want to sniff your panties. A woman wears those panties, not a little girl. Let me taste your womanly organ. Let me worship it and praise it on high."

Alice arose from the bed and slipped off her kimono, which dropped to the floor to reveal bare flesh. After retrieving her stockings and panties from the top of the teak chest, she opened the lid, then returned to the bed and hovered in a stooped position over Jack so that her bosom dangled over his face. With to and fro movements, she teased and tantalized him with her endowment, and he responded by chasing it with his mouth. At first, Alice's nimble feints kept Jack's lips at bay, but then she switched tack and gyrated her torso in ever tightening circles until Jack's tongue could flutter at will upon the walls of her cleavage and awaken the sleeping puppy.

Alice straightened up into a squat upon Jack's chest and rubbed her stockings against Jack's cheek. "How much do my stockings please you?" she asked.

"Immensely," he replied. He looked up, but could only see the midline of her face, which from his point of view appeared sandwiched between her breasts.

Alice wrapped one of the stockings around Jack's neck and pulled on the ends as if to strangle him. Jack yanked on his bindings. "Trust me," she assured him, "this heightens the sensation."

Jack's felt his eyes bulging as the blood backed up into his head from his compromised jugulars. The touch of asphyxiation excited him to the point of bone hardness. "How do you know these things?" he asked.

"The feeling excites me, too," Alice replied cautioning, "but always remember that a loop around the neck can lead to death by asphyxiation. If you ever have me in this position, you must never take your eyes off my eyes. If my eyes roll back, or if I lose consciousness, then you must let go of the loop, which must always have the freedom to loosen on its own. What I mean to say is that you must never tie a knot in the loop. Do you understand these precautions, my love?"

Jack nodded yes, and without taking her eyes off his eyes, Alice reached into the bowl and pulled out an ice cube, which she then dropped into the cup of tea.

"And do you have full confidence in what I am about to do?"

Again Jack nodded yes.

Alice dismounted from the bed and picked up the cup of ice buffered tea. Drop by drop, she poured the marginally bearable contents onto Jack's chest, abdomen and thighs and massaged the contents into his skin with Jack grimacing in ecstasy at every painful drop. Finally, she wrapped her hand around Priapus to give him his due. With the other hand, she twisted the stocking around his neck, and with the first one, she stroked, choked and stoked the dog until Jack could feel an imminent volcanic eruption complemented by a consciousness that seemed to drift and float outside his body.

"Not yet, my love," she commanded him, stroking all the harder.

"I cannot control myself. Oh, oh, oh!" Jack grunted, feeling like he had drifted into a heavenly domain somewhere over Olympus when from twelve o'clock high, the frigid dishcloth crashed into his loins in a kamikaze splatter. Alice released the tension on the noose, and jackhammer pulses of fresh blood surged though his brain, allowing him to experience frustration with crystal clarity.

Jack cried out in anguish. "I can't take this anymore! Why won't you finish the job you always start?"

"Because I am still that little girl. You do not bare your soul to me. A real woman could make you tell all. I am but a thumb-sucking child with pigtails and freckles."

"I'll tell you anything you wish. What is it you want from me?"

Alice stroked Jack's chest. "Oh my betrothed, reveal to me the sweet mysteries that you hide in your soul during the day... mysteries unknown to all but you and the mighty clients you serve. Who among them wish to join hands?"

"An attorney is sworn to secrecy... I'm... ohhhhh!!!"

Alice dusted Jack's nose with her panties. He took a deep whiff, but all he could smell was the lavender douche meant to overpower her womanly essence. It was a pleasant scent for sure, but not what he had hoped for. Even so, the naughtiness of the black lace delivered its own excitement as Alice rubbed this most intimate of undergarments back and forth under his nostrils. Slowly, the Mutt crept back to life, but Jack would not allow Alice the pleasure of yet another tease, and so he willed his canine friend back to sleep by picturing in his mind's eye that she had become his sister, Denise.

The ruse worked to a point, but then Jack's nasal passages had become used to the lavender essence and had begun to pick up cruder scents emanating from bowel and bladder function. And then came another odor, one more heady and potent, but at the same time still overwhelmed by all the others. Jack breathed deeper into the panties, which made him take his mind off Denise. And with Alice becoming Alice again, this subtle hint of womanly aroma made Priapus rise up thicker and more powerful than ever.

"What do you smell?" asked Alice.

"A woman... I swear to you, I smell a woman, not a girl!"

Alice sat back up on Jack's chest, but this time, she kneeled forward so that her orifice came to within pecking distance of his mouth. He elevated his head to pay homage, but she pushed it back with the dishcloth. Jack didn't mind the cold on his face. If felt bracing; however, he knew that at any moment Alice could turn around and slap that rag on his manly fire. Then again, Alice could also offer him the taste and smell of her essence if he played this bizarre game by her rules. But given the circumstances, what other rules were there?

Jack gazed into her crevice, and his pulse raced. He wanted it to come closer and dock with his lips, but it moved back ever so slightly out of reach, where it lorded over him with cruel disdain. "Please, Alice, please, just a mere taste," he begged.

Alice swept her loins past Jack's chin, and for the briefest of moments, his nose cut through the lavender and found hints of musk, old socks and Long Island Sound at low tide. Yet despite such raw elements, the odor roused primeval urges, which Jack could not resist. "More! Give me more!" he demanded as if he were the one in control.

But Alice would not cede. Instead, she dipped the dishcloth back into the ice bath and slowly reached back to KO the Mutt, at which point Jack panicked. "Oh, woman, not the cold! Please, not the cold!!! I'll tell you... I'll tell you!!! Ford Motors will acquire Allied Piston... Humble Oil buys out Scully Petroleum... Great Northern, Erie Lackawanna and

Burlington Freight merge lines... Bethlehem Steel and Birmingham Steel merge... Please, woman, that's all I know!!! No cold!!! No cold!!! You are all woman! Not a girl!!! Take me, woman!"

And with those revelations, Alice pressed her mighty orifice against Jack's face, and he rendered worship with flailing lips and fluttering tongue. At last, the true essence of womanhood bared itself in all its pungent glory, and as Jack inhaled the tart vapors deep into his being, his tongue danced in and around every fold and crease. The dainty nubbin crowning the peak of the crevice slipped in and out of his lips, and Jack savored it with runaway gusto, causing Alice to moan and shriek.

"Don't stop Jack; please don't stop!" Alice took hold of the bedpost side of the wrist bindings and pulled on the tail ends of rope, which had been fastened in slipknots. As the bindings came loose, the latticework of interlocking loops around his upper body unzipped. Turning left and then right, Alice unfastened Jack's ankles, and the webbing around his lower body followed suit.

Freedom at last!

Jack clutched Alice's thighs and flipped her beneath him, where he buried his face deeper into the intoxicating vapors of her pleasure dome. She in turn seized him by the cheeks and directed his mouth back to her nubbin. "Here, do it here!" she moaned.

Jack withheld his tongue. "I should punish you for what you've done to me...."

Alice was frantic. "Yes, I've been bad girl, and I deserve a severe spanking, but if you take care of me tonight, I'll prepare the best breakfast you've ever tasted! I'll satisfy your needs until dawn, and I'll give you a dozen babies if you want them! Please, Jack, please! Do not forsake me!"

Forsake her? Was even the thought of it a possibility when the taste and tang of her carnal canal drove him into a preternatural frenzy, which could find relief only by ravishing the crown of her loins with a fusillade of licks, nibbles and flutters? Alice squealed; Alice screamed and Alice hollered. And then she grappled and clawed his arms in epileptic staccato, all the while kicking her legs against the mattress as if touched by madness. Finally, her legs locked around Jack's head, smothering it in her womanhood, and she roared at the top of her lungs to heaven and earth, not to mention the neighbors in apartments 3B and 3D.

"Forever, Jack... love me forever!"

Not yet done, she grabbed Priapus and guided him into the snug and warm depths of her chamber to give him the ride of a lifetime. And somewhere beyond the Elysian Fields, the noble beast spewed his contents with an intensity that Jack had never imagined could exist within any plane of reality.

Jack stroked his freshly shaven cheek and observed Alice's nimble hands working their magic with mixing bowls and skillet in which she whipped up from scratch a double serving of banana crepes in strawberry compote; however, instead of admiring her customary flair and lack of wasted motion, he obsessed over his work-related revelations in the bedroom. True, he had divulged to her only a portion of pending mergers and acquisitions, but even that piddling amount could bite him hard if a savvy trader optioned the corresponding stocks ahead of the official announcements. Once served, he chewed his food in measured strokes and filled in the time between bites by fiddling with his knife and fork and shifting his weight from one buttock to the other.

Alice tilted her head. "You're not enjoying your breakfast. Why?" she asked.

"Alice, what were the names of the companies I revealed to you?" he returned.

"Let's see…. You said something like Scully Steel, or was it Burlington Steel?"

Jack lit up a left-sided smile; She had mixed up the names. "This is privileged information, my love. You must never again ask me the names of my clients, even in play. Understood?"

"I promise. Now eat your crepes, and after you finish, you must lick clean the remaining contents of the saucepan from a part of me that you most desire. Understood?"

"I promise."

Jack licked his lips in anticipation. Could one feast on any finer delicacy in this world than Alice *au jus*?

CHAPTER 39

An Account by the Bay

Friday moved along with paper-chasing vengeance. The safe was open; the door was locked, and strewn papers corrected with blue edit marks covered every square inch of the blotter. Then came a knock. Jack cracked open the door, and Paul handed him a folded slip of paper.

"Here's the savings account number and telephone number at Security Pacific that you inquired about. You have to request a bankbook personally. Just ask for Mrs. Garcia," Paul told him.

Jack glanced at the telephone number and scratched his head. "I don't recognize the telephone exchange. What part of the city is it?"

"It's downtown near Broadway," Paul said adding, "in San Francisco."

"Good work. I'd invite you into the office, but—"

"No need to explain, Mr. Preston. I apologize for the interruption."

Jack closed the door and relocked it. He regretted cutting Paul short; however, taking care of the firm's business, especially with the confidential agreements in plain sight, merited first priority. But that didn't belittle the fact that Paul Jeffrey was one heck of a guy. In Jack's view, this young man was discreet, efficient and very well mannered, and if the request ever came, he would say so in a sterling letter of recommendation.

Jack checked his watch, and he calculated Pacific Time at fifteen minutes after lunch break. He dialed 0.

"Numberrrrr, please?" came the friendly greeting from the Bell operator.

"Long distance... San Francisco... station to station... Telegraph 6-03..."

And just like that, the phone rang at the other end! Jack couldn't believe that such a feat was possible in an age when calling Boston required routing through the Bridgeport and Providence operators. Jack considered the possibilities. How might this development affect his way of attracting new clients?

"New accounts... Reina Garcia speaking," greeted a pleasantly accented voice.

"Jack Preston here... I'm inquiring about a savings account set up in my name."

"Oh yes, Mr. Preston. I've been expecting your call. The bank anticipates several deposits within the next month. I didn't want to send you the bankbook until final entry of these transactions."

"May I ask about the nature of this savings account?"

"According to your accountants, it's an alias. Due to interstate banking regulations, your firm would have had to open a branch office in California to set up a corporate account here. This private account will still allow your firm to initiate escrow transfers in San Francisco, but only one person, namely you, can sign off on the transactions."

Jack shook his head in confusion. "Banking law is not my strong point... in any event, I shall call you about those pending deposits. Would it inconvenience you to have that information at hand?"

"I'll make it my first order of business every day."

"Then I thank you for your time."

Jack hung up the phone and placed a train schedule on his blotter. "Why don't the partners ever take care of their own escrow accounts?" he mumbled to himself. "They're big shots; that's why... And heck... If I don't get back on track, I'm going to miss the Yankee Clipper roll out of town."

CHAPTER 40

An Interrupted Evening

With just one lingering kiss, Jack wanted to rip Alice's clothes from her body and throw them to the ground; however, Grand Central Station was not the venue for such uncontrollable behavior. Not that kissing wasn't; further down the platform, a sailor and his sweetheart embraced for a farewell smooch, and one car away, a summer student bound on the same six-twenty-six to Boston caressed his beloved while she ran her fingers through his lacquered hair, causing it to crack and fray.

Between nibbles and flutters, Jack giggled. "How dare you laugh at me?" Alice teased. "Kissing is serious business."

"A dozen babies…you promised me a dozen babies," Jack returned. With that kind of number, it occurred to him that Alice did not subscribe to the Congregationalist faith.

"And twelve you shall have, and then you'll see how funny kissing is." Alice almost sounded serious, but then her firm embrace tossed in a pinch to the buttocks, and Jack spotted a bulge in her cheek.

Alice handed him a key to her apartment. "Move in with me, Jack," she said, this time without a trace of mockery. "I feel so alone without you."

"All aboard!" shouted the conductor, and the sailor with his duffel bag, the student with his trunk and Alice with her half-valise stepped inside. Jack watched the train depart with a sense of dread, for Alice wouldn't return until Monday. *Agony—I know thee well!*

Jack traded platforms for the Bronxville-bound train to begin a journey home that he hadn't taken since the night that Judy had broken off their engagement. And then it occurred to him. Given that sudden turnaround, was he welcome there anymore? He told himself not to think about something he couldn't control, and so when he took his seat in what could have passed for a men's only car, he opened his briefcase and removed the baseball with Alice's lipstick mark on it. The outlines of the lips had smudged into a Rorschach blot from overzealous handling, but of what concern was that? If he wanted a pristine set of lip prints, all he had to do was ask the bearer of said lips, and she would have given him a hundred of them with nibbles and flutters to match.

Jack arrived home to an almost deserted house. Only the sound of bebop music coming from behind the closed door to the family room told him that scientific advancement never ceased in the world of advertising. He opened the door to discover research folders scattered across the bridge table. In the far corner, Oliver fiddled with the swinging arm of a new record player, whose modern design allowed the listener to suspend a queue of records above the turntable for successive playback.

"That's one heck of a toy!" Jack greeted him.

"Welcome back, stranger," Oliver said shutting off the player as if to state that more important issues needed address than an automated box that spun vinyl disks. "Mother, Denise and Will went to the movies. There's some overcooked chicken and boiled vegetables on a plate. All of it should be tepid by now."

"So how bad is it?" Jack asked.

"It's not quite Judy's cuisine, but…"

"You know I don't mean food, Dad. What were the repercussions from Tuesday?"

"Let's just say that the neighbors are talking, but nobody knows the real story. Mother defends your honor, albeit with some degree of mortification, and Denise and Will argue over which one of them will get your room if you keep spending your nights in quote, 'your office,' unquote."

"And you, Dad?"

"I just wish that you and Judy could have parted on better terms. Other than that if happiness is a gal named Alice, then let's make her feel welcome here."

"Maybe I could bring her along next weekend?"

"It's too soon. You don't want Mother figuring that Alice was the woman who came between you and Judy."

"But isn't that the truth?"

"Take it from an advertising man; sometimes the truth needs to be packaged."

Jack understood this to mean that in order for his mother to accept Alice, he would have to play by certain rules of hypocrisy. For appearances sake, they would have to feign a puritanical courtship without the slightest hint of hanky panky—particularly shared bubble baths and rope play. The time frame would be important, too. If he introduced Mother to Alice at the end of summer, then Alice could not conceivably appear as "the other woman".

On looking back, Jack realized that he had plotted and planned with military precision a foolproof scheme to keep Judy from discovering his double life, yet despite his best efforts to cover his tracks on pages and pages of legal pad, Judy knew how to catch him in his lie almost as if she had gone to detective school. Would not Mother also see through the cha-

rade and inquire of Alice—casually of course—as to when and where introductions—in a manner of speaking—first took place?

"Somebody snitched on me," Jack blurted out. "Judy couldn't have
known. Everything was going swell, but then she dropped in on Alice's
apartment as if somebody had given her a roadmap."

"You can't expect the unexpected; isn't that logical?"

"Well maybe I should send the fink flowers for forcing my hand
with Alice."

"Let it go, Jack. You're guilty as charged. Besides, I never figured
you and Judy to make any kind of music together." Oliver then pointed to
the record player. "Now Bird and Diz and my newfangled phonograph…
that's beautiful music!"

"It's beautiful how you use your machine to change the topic," Jack
said acquiescing with a look down his nose. "Was it expensive?"

"No, it's on unlimited loan from the manufacturer."

Oliver opened a folder and pulled out the top page, which he
handed to Jack. Jack's eyes immediately trained in on a young couple dancing cheek to cheek. The woman's bosom pressed against the man, whose
face betrayed utmost satisfaction. On a table next to them sat the newfangled phonograph, and above them boldfaced copy proclaimed:

UNINTERRUPTED PLAY FROM RCA VICTOR

"What a crummy advertisement!" Jack opined. "That's it? Just five
measly words?"

"Yes, but it's more clever than you realize. The term "uninterrupted
play" has two meanings. The phonograph plays without interruption so that
the man and woman can play without interruption. We test marketed this
advertisement in Hartford and Omaha and had to restock the shelves three
times in one week. Dare I say that Charles Darwin's theories have now tri-
umphed in the cutthroat world of marketing and promotion?"

The doorbell rang. "Are you expecting anybody?" Jack said.

"Nobody called. Maybe it's Roy in need of a spare baseball."

Jack hastened to the front door, and when he opened it, his eyes
twitched as if they had made contact with a ghost. "You're taller than I
remember, Little Jack," said the commanding figure, his steely eyes beaming through horn-rimmed glasses, "or maybe I'm getting smaller."

"Come in, Mr. Kennedy," Jack said. "Can I get you a scotch?"

"A coffee will do just fine. I'm still on business time. But business
aside for a moment—Rose and the children send you their love, and do call
me Joe."

With one hand, the Ambassador doffed his homburg, and with the other he waved two fingers to the chauffeured limousine waiting by the curb. The limousine departed for whereabouts unknown, and Jack surmised that it would return in two fingers worth of time. That's the way things worked with the Ambassador. When it came to the clock, he worked like a lawyer; only he was twice as efficient.

CHAPTER 41

Coffee Klatch

As the percolator sputtered along, and the aroma of fresh coffee filled the air, Jack took a seat at the kitchen table and waited for Oliver and Joe to conclude whatever business arrangement they were conducting in the family room. From an ethical standpoint, Jack chose not to overhear any of the particulars, lest he offhandedly make a professional comment, which could be construed as entering into legal counsel outside the environs of the firm. Yet Jack knew that Oliver's research into sexual imagery as a motivator for impulse purchasing in the marketplace had struck the mighty Ambassador as valuable ore, which with refinement would provide a revolutionary change in consumer preferences and taste. Jack wished he could have buried his head in the sand rather than gain knowledge of this scientific revelation. In his world of sirens and ribbed sweaters, women represented mythic creatures, whose lovemaking potential became fulfilled with sensuality that drew upon flowers, poetry and naughty lingerie for inspiration. Enter then Oliver with his Darwinian approach, and women descended to mere touch points in a reproductive destiny that could now be exploited to sell—of all things—phonographs!

Were the gods laughing? Indeed, did the gods really care?

Laughter, however, emanated from the family room. That was good. Jack reckoned that RCA Victor had sold many phonographs, which meant that Mr. Kennedy had already optioned the stock at the beginning of the week, and after leaking word of the hefty sales figures in the middle of the week, had subsequently redeemed his options for substantial profit as the word filtered out onto the Street.

The percolator climaxed in an effervescent hiss, and Oliver and Joe arrived just in time for Jack to pour the honors. All three settled around the kitchen table, where Joe placed the latest issue of the *Princeton Law Review* on the table and pushed it under Jack's nose.

"Your dad showed me your latest contribution to legal scholarship here," Joe said. "Do I get your current citations right? If my holding companies own significant ownership in both sides of a possible merger, federal law permits me to accumulate more stock in any of the two companies until such time that the merger is formally proposed to the Board of Directors, even if I initiate the proposal."

"That's the law," Jack said marveling at how the man could take an article written in arcane legalese and distil its essence into a single sentence.

Joe slapped his hand on the table. "Damn it, Jack!" he exclaimed. "Why do you have to blab your findings to the rest of the legal profession? I'll pay you triple what Hargrave and company put in your pocket for this kind of information."

But Jack would not be bought. "Winnie doesn't pay me for scholarly papers, and neither do you. If you require me to perform confidential studies, then ethics necessitates you to contract my service through the firm. Wouldn't you deserve the same allegiance if I served in your employ?"

"Yes," Joe agreed. Then he looked over to Oliver and added, "One can never put a price on loyalty."

For a moment, Jack fantasized about bringing the account of the mighty Ambassador into the firm. It had been almost twenty years to the day since he had become the first chairman of the SEC, and in his whirlwind debut, he rallied Congress to ban the very stock manipulations that had made him a fortune.

Gone was the inside trade, which in 1922 netted him almost a half million dollars on a single transaction! At that time, the thirty-four-year-old Kennedy had worked for the legendary speculator, Galen Stone, who had informed him that Ford Motors wished to acquire The Pond Creek Coal Company. Based on that information, Mr. Kennedy had put down ten percent of one quarter of a million dollars on Pond Creek. Commercial banks provided the balance financing in what was known at the time as a margin account. When the stock went from sixteen to forty-five on news of the acquisition, he cashed out of the stock and used the proceeds to fund his stock pool trades where the real riches awaited.

A stock pool was nothing more than a license to print money. In practice, a group of speculators would agree to buy up roughly twenty percent of a midsized company, which in the roaring twenties would have been capitalized to the tune of around twenty-five million dollars. Basic math meant that these insiders would have to scrounge up a total of five million dollars, but with the banks allowing ten percent on margin, a half million dollars would suffice.

Then the real fun began: after the insiders scooped up the necessary stock, their various holding companies would trade it back and forth to each other at predetermined prices, and the sheer volume of the stock trades would force the market to accept those choreographed moves as the going rate of exchange. But by itself, this type of price manipulation provided no monetary gain since the stocks only traveled back and forth within this closed loop of insiders. To profit off this zero sum game, the insiders then executed day trades with the general public, which almost never caught on to the fact that they were betting against loaded dice.

Jack realized that he had much to thank Mr. Kennedy for. In addition to outlawing the stock pool, his reign at the SEC forever put the legal profession in charge of all mergers and acquisitions and thus assured fiscal integrity to these transactions at the cost of billable hours. Since that time, Congress had rewritten the rules, and the courts had reinterpreted them so many times that even the Ambassador himself needed the advice of counsel to navigate these shoals. *Perchance Joe might have need for the leading expert in the field.*

"Let me have your card," said Joe as if he had read Jack's mind. "When you finish your next paper, have your people send it to me instead of a reviewer, and I'll pay the meter."

Jack's face lit up like a Broadway marquee. In that moment, he remembered his call to San Francisco, and how instead of waiting the usual fifteen minutes for all the connections to transpire, he had conversed with the party on the other end as if he had called the corner drug store. He reasoned that such instantaneous communication would have a profound effect upon local distribution networks that he could now merge into more efficient nationwide conglomerates.

"The subject of my report will be the impact of new communications technology in matching companies for takeover," Jack said. "Are you still interested?"

"I'm salivating," Joe replied. "Now if only my chauffeur would return with the number two deli sandwich that I signaled him to pick up, my saliva will not go to waste. Would you like the pickle?"

CHAPTER 42

Transient Guilt

Jack wished he could have forgotten the weekend. Aside from the Ambassador's brief appearance Friday evening, life in the Preston household had taken on an eerie quiet. Oliver closeted himself in the basement, where he now aimed his Darwinian assault upon the legions of cigarette consumers, and Emily planted herself in a vegetative state in front of the television in the family room. Only sporadic blinking across glazed eyes gave hint that she had not yet departed for the great hereafter.

Some vital life force was missing, and Jack had no problem figuring out what it was. Without Judy radiating sunshine and bubbles, Denise would not be licking any flashbulbs, and Will would not partake in any libations. Emily would not stand guard over Oliver's utterances, and Oliver would utter not.

"I'm guilty... I've betrayed Judy, and I've betrayed my family," Jack muttered to himself. But then he remembered that Judy had not only walked out on him, but she had also refused to give him a second chance.

In his mind's eye, he pictured Judy's cutie pie face and her womanly curves, and he imagined the pink flesh waiting for him beneath the frilly blouse and girly skirt. He saw himself ravishing her naked body from top to bottom and back to her middle, where the moist folds of her womanhood awaited his worship. But imagine as he might—in all the ways, from tender to lewd—nothing resembling passion stirred inside him. And verily, the Mutt remained in a comatose state awaiting Alice's imminent return.

CHAPTER 43

Hall of Fame Material

Jack leaned back in his swivel chair and closed his eyes. He hadn't yet told any of the partners that he had landed the Kennedy account. To be sure, the Ambassador had requested only legal research, but even that humble activity might present entry into a wider scope of profitable service. And following that horizon, Jack figured only a limited imagination would hold him back from becoming a legend of the Street.

The intercom buzzed. "Mr. Lawson from the SEC is on line three," greeted Nora.

Jack picked up. He expected good news. Of what other kind was there? "How can I be of service, Mr. Lawson?"

"Your breakneck pace has the boys in the legal division racing each other to clean house before summer vacations," came the official reply, "so sharpen your pencil, and copy down these file numbers. Every case more than three months old has received approval."

"And when do I make the announcement to the press?" Jack blew on his fingernails and polished his lapel.

"Hold off until noon tomorrow just in case a last minute retraction pops up. As for now, let me fire away."

One after the other, Jack jotted down the file numbers, and when he had finished at case number seven, he realized that he had broken a Wall Street record comparable to DiMaggio's streak of making at least one base hit in fifty-seven consecutive games. Indeed if the Street had its own hall of fame, Jack considered himself a shoe in on the first ballot.

The grandfather clock chimed out the noon break, and Jack dialed O for operator. "Please connect me with the service department," he requested, and in the time it took him to bite through half a bologna sandwich, he had arranged for a telephone technician to meet him at Alice's apartment that evening. The rush service had cost him a few extra bucks, but what was that compared to hearing her call to him from her den of ecstasy? Besides, he wanted to find out what kind of smoke and mirrors the American Telephone and Telegraph Company had used to connect him so swiftly to the Security Pacific Bank in San Francisco, and in that sense, he regarded the telephone activation as an extension of his research for Ambassador Joe.

Jack straightened his tie. *I make everything fall into place. One day, everybody will know my name.*

CHAPTER 44

Transistors

With his suitcase by his side, Jack removed his personal key from his pocket and unlocked Alice's door. When he swung the door open, she greeted him with outstretched arms and lips, but her kiss carried the sting of an angry hornet. "Why did you bite my tongue?" he protested.

"You should have cleared it with me before you reconnected the telephone. By the time I make three phone calls to my parents overseas, you'll have me so deep in debt that I'll be sitting on the curb alongside my belongings."

"Is the phone man still here?"

"He's working in the kitchen, but did you hear what I said?"

Alice sounded angry. Jack had never seen her in this state. "From now on, I'm paying your bills... all of them... rent, utilities, food and, dare I say, the telephone," he said, issuing the command as if he were the chairman of a Dow Jones Industrial.

"Then in that case—" Alice threw herself against Jack without finishing the thought; however, the grinding motion of her hips told him she had gratitude on her mind.

"Uh, excuse me, folks," interrupted the telephone technician placing a copy of the work order on top of the television. "Your new number is on the face plate of the dial. Any questions?"

As Jack sauntered forward to check out the work order, Alice reached for a half-consumed glass of Chablis resting on a wall shelf and took a sip. "Would you happen to know the latest technology for routing long distance phone calls?" he inquired.

"One word... transistors," said the phone man, whereupon a spasm of choking coughs delivered a wine-laden spray straight onto Alice's blouse.

Jack patted her on the back, but she brushed him off. "You take care of business, and I'll clean myself up," she said hacking out the words.

Alice retreated to the kitchen, and Jack signed the work order. "What the heck are transistors?" he asked.

"Transistors," explained the phone man, "are electrical switches comprised of solid pieces of doped silicone, which either conduct or impede the flow of electricity from their in to out leads depending upon whether they receive a positive or negative charge on a third lead called the gate. You can put thousands of them on a six-foot switchboard, and since they don't have any moving parts, they can automatically route a signal to every major city in a ninety thousandth of a second. Once your operator dials in the city code for your destination, your connection becomes almost instantaneous."

"Incredible! And here's a five for coming on such short notice," Jack said impressed by the man's know-how in addition to the prompt service.

"You are incredibly generous sir. Please allow me to pick something up for your wife from the drugstore."

Jack listened to the coughs coming from the kitchen. "I'll take care of her," he replied, "but thanks anyway."

Jack liked the sound of that...the word "wife." This fine gentleman had called Alice his wife.

CHAPTER 45

Tales of Two Cities

July came in like a steam bath, and Jack spent much of the day repositioning paperweights on his blotter so that his desk fan didn't blow any of his contracts out into the reception or, worse yet, high over Broadway. After a most productive day, he retrieved four suitcases from behind Chester's bootblack stand and hopped into a taxi for the short trip to Alice's building. At the foyer, Gus the super greeted him and helped carry the overstuffed baggage up four flights of stairs in the sweltering heat. Jack tipped him a deuce.

The evening provided little relief, especially since Jack and Alice preferred to spend the time rolling around the bed sheets and slithering across each other like two garden slugs engaged in a reproduction ritual. As twilight set in, common sense intervened, and they slipped into a bathtub filled with cool water, where between the bubbles, they shared a glass of chilled Chablis and traded sensual massage from fingers lubricated with egg shampoo. Emerging cleansed, they snuggled up on the living room couch to catch the Dodgers' game, but one thing led to another, and before the Mutt might say, "Eros, Aphrodite," or "good old Mother Nature," they found themselves back in the sack and grappling each other in a pool of sweat.

A cacophony of street sounds, ranging from children reacting to the Pavlovian bells of an ice cream cart to neighbors calling out to each other through open windows and across fire escapes, filtered through the bedroom screens. Could that mean that the grunts and groans coming from inside returned the favor much to the amusement of neighbors, children and the lone ice cream vender? The two lovers dared not share such concerns for fear that a sense of pragmatism might impel them to shut the windows on their carnal act and oblige them to perpetrate it in an atmosphere conducive to stroke and suffocation.

Exhaustion, however, tolled its witching hour, and as the rest of the city tossed and turned in sticky discomfort, Jack snuggled up to Alice, and the two of them sank into peaceful oblivion until the ring of the alarm clock introduced them to another clammy day. For breakfast, Alice put together a chilled fruit salad accompanied by partially frozen pineapple juice, which her blender ground into slush. The whole repast might not have stuck to the ribs like one of her omelets, but it certainly fit the season.

After a parting kiss, Jack leisurely strolled off to work, where he and his colleagues doffed their jackets and slackened their ties to cope with the cranky thermometer. More shocking was the fact that all the female employees had left their stockings hanging on their back window clotheslines. In the interest of health, Thelma Kane did not want a repeat of last year's episode in which one of the secretaries fainted from heat exhaustion, and so with utmost discretion, she advised all the ladies of the firm to let the hosiery dangle in the sultry air until further notice.

Out in San Francisco, a cool fog drifted past the Golden Gate and enveloped the Financial District in a fine mist. There, a streetcar clanging down Nob Hill ground to a halt at the corner of California and Battery streets. A slew of commuters bundled up their trench coats and grabbed hold of their briefcases before disembarking for the short walk to the city's investment houses, where they would spend the day clamoring on trading floors for a piece of the dream. As the crowd drifted up Battery Street, they dispersed into the various office buildings lining the route, and one gray soul—as average as the next man clothed in a fedora and a trench coat—entered the Security Pacific Bank and proceeded to the teller's window, where he handed over a deposit slip and a check for seven thousand dollars from the Easton Holding Company. The teller looked at the deposit slip, pulled out the carbon paper and stamped all three copies. "Thank you again, Mr. Jones," she said, and Mr. Average Man doffed his hat with one hand while pocketing the pink copy with the other.

All was not so quiet back in New York, where at one minute past noon the usual gang of reporters could barely keep pace with Jack's kitchen-sink announcement of approved mergers and acquisitions. "Yeah, it's Humble Oil and Scully!" screamed one reporter into his walkie-talkie. A standup fan roared full blast behind him.

"Will you shut up!" shouted another, wiping the perspiration off his face with his shirtsleeve. "Mr. Preston has got more announcements to make."

"What do you mean 'repeat again'?" hollered a third reporter into his walkie-talkie. "I can hear you perfectly."

"If I may…" Jack started again, but in all of the hullabaloo, nobody heard him.

Thelma then came to the rescue by blowing on a police whistle, and the place settled down into an uneasy calm. "At Mr. Preston's suggestion," she said, "we have mimeographed the entire roster of today's amal-gamations and consolidations. Please pick them up from Nora Kincaid at the reception on your way out."

And on that remark, a herd of cattle stampeded out the door, only to become transformed into a pack of snapping wolves, who after acquiring their piece of flesh in the form of mimeographed copy, proceeded en masse—some sniffing its fragrant ink and others howling into their army surplus gear—to leave the building. Jack, Thelma and Nora could only watch with blank expressions; neither of them had a word to say.

That evening, Jack sensed apprehension as Alice slid back on the sofa to watch the game with him. Certainly her eyes faced the TV set, but every so often they took quick aim at the far counter of the kitchen, where the telephone sat. Jack didn't consider it polite to pry into any private matter that she chose not to share, but he still wondered what kind of call was she expecting? That had to be source of her distraction.

"I told you never to worry about the phone bill," he said trying an indirect tack, but Alice responded with a grimace, which became a frown, which then transformed into a hysterical convulsion of tears. Jack attempted to comfort her with a hug, but she pushed him off, then ran into the bedroom and slammed the door behind her.

With his hand to his chin, Jack attempted to figure out what had just transpired, but all he could reason was that the answer could only come from Alice. He glanced at the telephone and concluded that any impending phone call, no matter how grave its nature, was her business and her business only. Whatever flaws or secrets she had kept to herself could not concern him.

When the bedroom door opened, Alice emerged fresh as a daisy. She carried a headmaster's paddle in her hand. "I've been a bad girl and deserve punishment," she said handing Jack the paddle.

Although the request would have seemed out of the ordinary in an ordinary relationship, Jack knew that he didn't have to second-guess Alice. If she requested a spanking, then that's what she wanted, and—damn it—that's what she would get.

"Well, Miss Mercer," he said slapping the paddle against his palm, "tell me how bad you've been. Bad is ten whacks; very bad is twenty, and very, very bad is... well... you tell me."

Alice flipped up her skirt and dropped her panties. Holding up her skirt again, she draped herself across Jack's knee. Dumbfounded, he stared into a full moon of flesh. Her buttocks were so round and juicy. Jack only wanted to stroke them and caress them or perhaps rub a few drops of oil on them to make them shiny, but now Alice compelled him to discipline them with a wooden paddle that displayed rows of holes drilled into the striking end to cut down on air resistance. Had she lost her mind?

"You will give me forty hard swats, and do not stop no matter how much I beg you," Alice demanded. "Tomorrow, I want to be reminded of my punishment every time I sit."

Jack stretched out his hand for hit number one, but then the phone rang. Alice jumped to her feet and almost tripped over the panties caught between her ankles. She raced to the phone.

"Hello!" she blurted out, greeting the caller with a mixture of exuberance and anxiety. "Yes, I'm Alice.... Yes, I look forward to meeting you, too. Let me put him on."

Alice held out the phone for Jack. Her long face told him that this was not the call she had expected. Jack took hold of the receiver and exchanged salutations.

"Hi Dad...of course.... I will have finished Mr. Kennedy's research by next Friday. We'll send it out special delivery. ...Well, tell Mother that city living agrees with me.... Bye."

After hanging up, Jack again slapped the paddle against his palm. "I'm not sure this is the answer," he said.

"And what is the problem?" Alice returned.

"I'm guessing it's the telephone."

Alice fingered Jack's cheek. "I'll be okay. Mama and Papa have moved, and I get nervous whenever I don't hear from them for weeks on end. We usually communicate by mail because the phones don't work very well where they live."

"So why punish yourself? It's not your fault they can't call."

Alice flipped up her skirt again. "Oh but that's not the reason why I deserve pain. Now give me forty whacks, and make me beg you to stop."

"Alice, I..."

"Do it!"

As distasteful as Jack found this wish for pain, he positioned her straight across his knee and smacked her butt cheeks with all the force he could muster. "Talk dirty to me. Call me filthy names," Alice begged between whacks.

"Take this, you pig... I should throw you out into the gutter where you belong, you tramp," Jack snarled in the baritone of a B-movie hood.

"I'm sorry, I'm so sorry," she replied. By the fifteenth or so whack, her cheeks had taken on a red glow. Jack wanted to stop, but Alice had other ideas. "Slap my face. Make it hurt, too."

"That's where I draw the line! Would you ask me to deface a Rembrandt?"

Alice groaned in pain. Her writhing movements on Jack's lap rubbed in every which direction over the Mutt, which expanded faster than a string balloon hooked up to a helium tank. Jack covered his face from embarrassment. He knew that Alice could feel his boner. Would she not resent him for receiving pleasure from her pain?

"I don't deserve you. Hit me harder, and treat me like the trash I am," she pleaded as if to answer that last question. But Jack had hit her as hard as he could, and he had lost count as well. Multiple welts had now accumulated on top of her cherry-colored cheeks. Exasperated at the whole spectacle, he dropped the paddle to the floor.

"Why did you stop?"

Jack didn't answer her. Instead, he picked her up and carried her to the bedroom, where he tossed her on the bed. As Alice lay on the sheets, Jack ripped off his shirt, popping all but one of the buttons, and he hurled it to the top of the floor chest, where Alice normally flung her clothes.

"Take your clothes off," he ordered, "and provide me the pleasure I deserve."

Alice complied without one iota of hesitation, and instead of sending her clothes to the top of the floor chest, she dropped them onto the floor. Jack pinned her arms against the sheets and dug his nails into her wrists.

"Take me; use me and possess me," she begged.

Jack took her up on the offer and spared her any offers of tenderness. Instead, he poked, pinched and prodded her in the most sensitive of places. Alice begged for a reprieve, but Jack called her bluff in the pain department and continued the abuse until about half past eleven when an exhausting slumber crept up on them.

"Do this to me again, tomorrow night," Alice said before nodding off.

"No," Jack replied. "I'd prefer that you tie me up with all your fancy knots, and strip me of my dignity rather than go through this again."

"Maybe we can do both!"

"There comes a time when very, very bad goddesses like you deserve absolution. If it is within my power, you are forgiven."

"At last, I am a good girl again."

Alice let out a sigh and drifted into oblivion. Jack kissed her hand and closed his eyes for the nightly ten count.

CHAPTER 46

A Red Herring

Malone looked at the wall map and squinted. A red pin speared New York City. From there, ruled lines fanned out to seven other cities, all of which contained white pins. From these cities, more lines diverged until they landed on ten cities marked with blue pins. The network spread out further into cities marked with yellow pins; however, every so often, the lines would converge in San Francisco, which now merited its own red pin—just like New York.

"What are Tuesday's transactions?" he called to Sparks, who sat at his desk, where he sifted through several dozen reports.

"A certified check from Cleveland surfaced in Cincinnati. Chicago's loot moved to Milwaukee and Minneapolis. After a one day stopover, the St. Louis deposit arrived in Denver plus San Francisco…"

"Damn it, Tom," Malone interrupted, "The way this money is spreading over the map, I'm running out of pin colors. Either these hand offs involve a conspiracy of fifty mugs, or we're chasing Superman."

"There's always the Preston account in San Francisco. It never misses a meal."

"Nah, our man Jones is feeding that account peanuts. He wants to lure us to the back end of the country so he can run the other way."

Sparks approached the map and planted his hand on the Atlantic Ocean. "Then what's the nearest country with John Doe banking in this direction?" he asked.

"Bermuda," Malone replied. Then he hit himself on the head. "Of course! Let's call in our troops, and end this relay."

"It's too late for that," Tanner called out from the doorway. "Washington wants you to shut down the San Francisco drop."

"But that's a red herring," Malone returned. Then he mumbled to himself, "Jones… Jones… such an original name, eh? Somebody is laughing at us."

Tanner shook his head and looked Malone squarely in the eyes. "Listen Mike," he said. "I know you're right, but I had to go to the mats with both the Secretary and the Attorney General to recover our SEC cases from the Bureau. So play by the rules, or you'll be collaring tax dodges until the day you turn in your papers."

"California here I come," Malone replied adding, "Bermuda was an excellent assist, Tommy. You would have been good at tracking Jap Zeros."

CHAPTER 47

The Bum's Rush

By mid July, the heat wave had finally broken, and the firm's attorneys went back to wearing proper business attire. Vacations had already begun in earnest. Mr. Thorpe and his wife had set sail for Europe while many of the lesser luminaries in the partnership circle found refuge in such dependable locales as Newport or the coast of Maine. Even Paul Jeffrey had taken a hiatus to some village east of Poughkeepsie—or so he had told everybody in the firm. Jack figured to push on until late September when he and Alice would finally tie the knot.

The image of a grand hoopla gave him the willies. He wanted to take the vows at City Hall, but Alice preferred a church wedding. As the bride, that was her prerogative. She also confided to him that she was brought up as a Huguenot, which was related to Presbyterianism in a French sort of way. In nearby New Rochelle, Jack had found several Huguenot churches where the ceremony could take place; however, Alice had made her own inquiry at the First Presbyterian Church in the Village, and the good pastor there agreed without hesitation to perform the ceremony. That was better. He would enter the church of his fathers as a lost sheep returning to the fold.

Sticky issues remained. For one, only Oliver knew about the plan. Time would soon grow short if it wasn't short enough already, and invitations had to hit the mailboxes. Jack mused over the situation.

"Yes Mother, I'm getting married tomorrow to that atrocious woman who destroyed my future with Judy. Would you like to come to the wedding?" he imagined asking.

Jack preferred not to muse about Mother's response.

In the meantime, loose ends at the office also needed tying up. For two weeks running, Jack had made it a habit to call San Francisco every other day to check up on the status of his savings account at the Security Pacific Bank. Indeed, Mr. Jones had not been idle with the deposits. Jack couldn't begin to speculate who printed the money.

The wholesale approval of mergers and acquisitions by the SEC had left an unexpected rash of vacancies in his schedule, and rather than fill the slots with assignments from the other legal departments within the firm,

Jack decided to be his own rainmaker and use the time to continue his legal research for the Ambassador. The grandfather clock struck noon, and Thelma appeared at his doorway. Jack handed her his latest scholarly paper, titled *An Impending Reality in Corporate Restructuring: Converting the Holding Company into a Mutual Fund to Maximize the Selling Price.*

"Does this topic have anything to do with transistors?' Thelma inquired.

"Hah! That was last week's report," Jack replied. "But knowing Mr. Kennedy's talent for snatching money out of thin air, I guarantee you that he'll find this paper a profitable read. Regarding transistors, you remind me that business on the West Coast has now commenced."

Thelma departed with the report, and Jack tucked the eraser end of a pencil into the phone to dial 0 for Operator. After making the pertinent request, he waited for the transistor circuits to work their magic, and in the blink of an eye, a hand three thousand miles away picked up the telephone.

"Good morning, Mrs. Garcia," came Jack's melodic greeting. "What's the latest update on the Preston account?"

"Your savings account now totals sixty-two thousand, three hundred and fifty-two dollars."

Jack tapped the pencil on his blotter pad as if to purge nervous energy. Something was not quite right with Mrs. Garcia's intonation, and as for this enormous sum, he vowed to express his concerns to Mr. Hargrave after this call. "Every day, I grow less thrilled at this sudden strike of fortune. Aside from the courier with the mysterious name of Mr. Jones, who is my benefactor?" asked Jack.

"The latest check comes from the Taggart Holding Company. According to Mr. Jones, yesterday's deposit marked the last transaction. Shall I send you your bankbook via certified mail?"

Again, Jack found peculiarity in Mrs. Garcia's voice. It almost sounded as if her flat response came courtesy of a cue card. The intercom then buzzed. "Jack... Jack!" called Thelma, her voice conveying utter panic.

Before Jack could answer, two husky men, each with a prominent bulge under the armpit of his jacket, barged into his office and pushed him against the wall. The phone receiver dropped from his hand and swung around in circles from the back of the desk.

"What is the meaning of this?" Jack protested. One look told him that these two guys were cops, even before the preppy one pulled out the handcuffs.

"Are you John W. Preston?" the grayer-looking version of the preppy one asked.

"Yes, and I demand—"

Demands notwithstanding, the slap of warm steel encircled Jack's wrists behind him. "Mr. Preston," said the senior officer, flashing his badge, "I am Treasury Agent Michael Malone, and my partner is Treasury Agent Thomas Sparks on special assignment for the Securities Exchange Commission. You are under arrest for insider trading and securities fraud."

And, wearing the sour expression of a nauseous child taking out rotten trash, Agents Malone and Sparks escorted Jack past the reception, where Thelma clutched Nora's shoulder to keep from fainting. For her part, Nora screamed and accidentally knocked the Kennedy file off the counter. Papers scattered in every which direction.

"It's a mistake; they must be looking for somebody else," came Jack's parting words as the T-men gave him the bum's rush out the door. From there, they took a short hop to the elevator, then through the lobby past a startled Chester Brown and finally into the back seat of an unmarked car.

CHAPTER 48

Facts and Tidbits

Jack knew the justice system only from law books, which was to say that he possessed enough knowledge to earn the hot seat for a vagrancy charge. Remaining silent throughout the booking procedure, he drew a blank in his mind whenever he reflected upon the charges leveled at him. Following the compulsory mug shot and fingerprinting formalities, he was issued a set of prison grays and led through a series of catacombs deep into the bowels of the Federal Office Building until he was deposited into his own private cage. After slamming the door, the guard retreated back into the subterranean maze, and Jack pondered a limited sensory input comprised of a cot, a sink and the scent of stale urine wafting from a stainless steel toilet with brown streaks caked onto the rim. Jack peered through the bars on either side of him and noted two cells to the left and three cells to the right, all of which were empty. Could it be that federal crime was at an all-time low?

Okay, now what could he do to occupy his mind? Should he measure the cell with his feet and calculate its area? Perhaps he might count the bars on the each cell and add them all up? Surely it would be easier if he counted only the bars on his own cell and multiplied the number by six, but then he would have finished the task in one sixth the time, and what could he possibly do next with nothing but time and more time on his hands?

Think! He had to think.

Jack sat down on the cot, which had all the comfort of a park bench, and for over three hours, he pondered the charges of insider trading and securities fraud; but, in the end as in the beginning and in all that time in between, his mind could not put together any cohesive crime.

Then a door slammed in the distance, and Jack heard footsteps approaching. *Perhaps the guard had come to engage in pleasant repartee, but what would he say?* "Here's your weekly ration of bread, Mr. Preston. Don't let the rats steal it from you." He might even sound a little more upbeat. "Hah-hah! The joke is on you, Jack. You didn't think we were serious, did you?"

Several footsteps later, the guard jangled his keys and opened the cell door for a middle-aged guy with the kind of boxer's physique that planted his shiny head directly onto his torso without any intervening neck to get in the way. Deltoid muscles worthy of Charles Atlas stretched the shoulder seams of his tapered suit, and a ham hock fist carried a worn brief case. The skin-topped fellow seemed at home inside the cell and didn't even blink when the guard slammed the door extra hard.

"Thelma Kane sent out a distress call... Lou Fisher for the defense," he announced in a snappy Bronx timbre, his meaty hand extended.

"Mr. Fish..."

"It's Lou. Mr. Fisher is my father."

Jack laughed. It wasn't just the quick-witted interruption that disarmed him; it was the way Lou held up his hand and shook his head to make the correction. Even without the brassy inflections, he could have delivered that line in a deadpan monologue on a Broadway stage, and the audience would have howled. Obviously, here was an attorney who didn't dicker for a quarter point here or a half a point there in a five-hundred-page contract. No, this guy had come to put on a show.

"Okay, Lou," Jack returned evenly. "Am I missing something here? I'm charged with securities fraud, and I don't even trade baseball cards."

Lou opened his briefcase and handed Jack a short stack of papers. "Here's the indictment from the grand jury. Do any of the companies on page four mean anything to you?"

Jack scanned the list and read the names to himself.

>*Humble Oil*
>*Scully Petroleum*
>*Bethlehem Steel*
>*Birmingham Steel*
>*Great Northern Rail*
>*Burlington Freight*
>*Erie Lackawanna*
>*Allied Piston*
>*Ford Motor Company*

"These are my accounts," Jack admitted. "I worked confidential consolidation or amalgamation agreements on all of them."

"Yes, except somehow and in someway, that confidentiality leaked. The government alleges that you pocketed two and a half million dollars in illegal trades."

Jack's bottom lip disconnected from his top one at about the same blinding speed as the blood draining from the skin of his vampire white face. "If I'm so damn rich, where's the damn money?" he fumed.

"Go get 'em, Jack. You just passed the test!" Lou exclaimed patting him on the shoulder.

"What on earth do you mean?"

"I can't believe it! After more than twenty years defending crooks, I've finally reeled in a boy scout."

Jack covered his lips. Given his limited options, he figured that it just might spare him an episode of spouting vitriol in reply to such a sarcastic remark. The slick delivery coming out the side of Lou's mouth had begun to wear thin, and Jack had second thoughts about his first impression of the man. "Look, I don't expect you to believe me, but—"

"But I do believe you," Lou interrupted. "Trust me... I get it. You've been framed."

Jack wiped his brow in relief. So maybe Lou wasn't such a bad guy after all. "Does your verdict get me a free pass?" Jack inquired.

Lou raised his index finger as if he were making a point with a jury. "I'll tell you what we'll do," he began. "You will make believe I gave you truth serum. I need to know every person you confided in for the last three months. Tell me every juicy tidbit and lurid fact. Getting bail for you might require some magic, so hand me a deck of cards I can work with."

And in that instant, the words, "juicy tidbit" and "lurid fact" hit Jack right in the solar plexus. He recalled revealing the companies named in the indictment to Alice on the night she trussed him to the bedposts like he was Sweet Gwendoline. Talk about juicy! But was this escapade lurid as well?

Aghast, Jack refused to believe that Alice was capable of such a betrayal. You needed money to make money in the stock market, and she couldn't even afford telephone service. Besides if any stock certificates were issued in her name, the SEC would have arrested her days before they raided his office since the stock clearing houses left a convenient paper trail for even the least savvy of compliance trackers. And speaking of paper trails...what about that savings account in San Francisco? That was Paul Jeffrey's doing, and though the indictment never mentioned Paul's name, page fifteen didn't miss one single bank deposit from the shadowy Mr. Jones.

"Well, it all began like this..." Jack began, and for the next two hours when Lou wasn't jotting down all the facts and tidbits, he had Jack write down the chain of events in his own words and handwriting. That last touch might have struck some defense attorneys as redundant, but Lou repeated ad nauseam that you could never have too much overkill. After a final review of Jack's written statement with a red pencil to highlight points of special interest, dinner consisting of fried bologna on a hard roll with a side of peas had arrived. Milk came in a tin cup. As Jack's vacant eyes scanned this repast, Lou left with the guard. Jack heard them talk baseball on the way out.

CHAPTER 49

Horse Trades

Lou Fisher loved Foley Square in the morning. Created like a phoenix from the ashes of the notorious Five-Points tenements of the previous century, it had become a convergence of all levels of government. Squat, box-like offices representing the interests of New York City and New York State guarded the northeast and the northwest corners respectively. At this nine o'clock hour, city and state buildings bustled with human activity coming to obtain business, marriage and driver's licenses, not to mention permits and variances for every manner of human commerce. Lou grabbed a copy of *The New York Times* from a newsboy and then walked south into Thomas Paine Park, where to his left, the Corinthian columns of the New York County Courthouse reminded him of Cicero delivering enlightened oratory to the Roman Senate.

After checking for bird droppings, Lou parked himself on a bench and quickly paged through the newspaper for any mention of Jack Preston. He found nothing, which pleased him. In this line of work, no publicity was good publicity, and the *Times'* top stories instead covered the Indochina conference, which had now partitioned the country into North and South Vietnam. Boring!

Lou knew not to concern himself with any of the tabloids covering Jack's brush with the law. Across the street, the New York County Court-house had five homicide cases in session, which gave the bottom feeding journalists enough fodder to satisfy their blood cravings until Labor Day. By the size of the crowd climbing up the steps, Lou knew that some guilty party would be sentenced to the chair today. What was it about this dark side of human nature? He was ashamed to admit it, but even he wanted to read about the perpetrator's reaction when the judge proclaimed, "You will be taken to Sing Sing, where you will be put to death by electrocution. May God have mercy on your soul."

Lou's eyes shifted to the right, where the Federal Courthouse in all its beaux-arts glory sat alone, seemingly deserted. No spectators would pack this venue to witness arguments over such tedious subjects as inter-state commerce, maritime reinsurance or patent infringement. And that's what Lou loved about practicing in the Federal Court system. Everybody was nameless and faceless, yet the monetary stakes here made the state courts look like five and dime shops.

After dropping the newspaper into an adjacent litter basket, Lou rummaged through his briefcase for Jack's longhand description of the events preceding his arrest. One adventurous passage had even merited encirclement in red.

> *...And I envisioned Alice as a siren perched upon the rocks, where she lured sailors to their doom. I, however, saw myself drowning in a tepid relationship with another woman, and this siren threw me a life preserver.*

Lou scribbled an annotation along the margin. *She screwed you once, and then she screwed you twice. You will never pilot my boat, Professor, but I appreciate you handing me the window to your soul.* Lou blew out a long sigh, and after closing his briefcase he attempted to decipher the passage. Was his client using a Greek classic to elevate horniness into some kind of high art? One trusted that such purple prose never found its way into the corporate contracts.

Lou headed down Pearl Street and entered the courthouse from the side. After bounding two flights of stairs and turning left at the conveniently located men's room, he stopped in front of the door with the inscription:

United States Attorney—Southern District of New York

Lou popped a breath mint. He didn't need to knock. All the secretaries knew him by sight. "Go right on in, Mr. Fisher," said one secretary with a Hell's Kitchen accent. "Mr. Dixon is expecting you."

Lou would have knocked on the door to this private office, but it was open anyway. At a roll top desk in the far corner, Assistant U.S. Attorney Harry Dixon annotated a margin of the grand jury proceedings and balled a fist with his other hand. After simultaneously reaching for a cup of black coffee on his left and a stubby smoke from an ashtray to his right, he took a sip and a drag before returning both articles of dubious nutrition to their former resting spots. As a plume of smoke cleared his yellow teeth, he crushed the butt to an L and left it on top of a pile of deceased pack mates.

Lou made a coughing sound into coiled fingers. Harry swiveled around and looked up over his reading glasses. By Lou's reckoning, Harry's straining eyelids had caused six toes to sprout on his crow's feet. The poor man must have pulled an all-nighter.

"Hey Harry, burn those commies at the stake. That's what I always say," Lou cracked.

But Harry just rubbed his bloodshot eyes. "The public is tired of reading about the red monsters hiding under their beds. It's what rides the sheets that sells copy these days," he said with a gravely rasp.

"So I take it that the government has promoted pimps and prostitutes to the Ten Most Wanted."

"Nah. That's still for the local D.A.'s, the lucky stiffs. Us feds have gone back to what we do best… bore people!"

The sudden commotion coming from outside the window sounded anything but boring. Curious at all the ballyhoo, Lou and Harry looked across the street to the side entrance of the New York County Courthouse, where a battalion of reporters, photographers and ordinary onlookers jockeyed for position around a cordon of police, who cleared a corridor between the doorway and an awaiting black and white. Suddenly, a cuffed prisoner escorted by two detectives emerged into the daylight, and the impromptu mob went bananas.

"Fry slowly, ya bastard!" screamed one voice.

"Say hello to Satan, ya scum!" hollered a second one. Other voices chimed in with insults and epithets that the reporters could never print.

Harry Dixon turned his back to the window. "Do you see what I mean, Lou? The boys over at County get a real lulu, and we get to trade horses over an SEC fiasco that I don't want because even in the best of circumstances the jury never understands the charges."

"So I take it, you pulled the late-late shift to shine a bona-fide turd."

"Here's the lowdown, and don't you tell Nat or Judge Cummings that I—"

"Damn it! We drew Calendar Cummings!" Lou interrupted. From the drawn look on Harry's face, Lou's infallible gut told him that the mighty U.S. of A. had entered the ring against Jack Preston as a ninety-seven-pound weakling. But that was little consolation compared to the reality of facing Judge Harley F. Cummings, whose button-down authority and sense of decorum grated both prosecution and defense attorneys alike. One entered his courtroom with shined shoes and a starched collar, and woe unto those who spoke out of turn. Stern lectures and summary fines followed for the man believed in no-nonsense order.

"Let me break it to you as gently as I can," Harry explained. "His Honor told me personally that he wants this proceeding wrapped up by Labor Day. The constitutional right to a speedy trial keeps his docket clean and my nerves frayed. Can we make this one go away?"

"What have you got?"

"As I was about to say, the SEC really blew this one in spades. First, the legal division decided to go carte blanche with all your client's M&A applications, and then the compliance trackers started hitting flashing reds from six different clearinghouses. Suddenly, the SEC realized that a third of Uncle Sam's agents went fishing for July and that the bow-tied examiners couldn't keep up with the simultaneous flow of certified checks bouncing from holding company to holding company all over the map. I surmise that the operators of this fine scam must have used a private plane to move the dirty paper from shell to shell. They had our boys with the crew cuts running around in circles like Keystone Cops. Are you with me so far?"

Lou scratched his dome. "Classy operation," he said.

"At any rate, sixty thousand and change—coming from nine different sources—hit the Security Pacific Bank in San Francisco and landed in the savings account of you-know-who."

"A beautiful set up. I'm impressed."

"And I'm steamed because while some twenty-odd T-men converged like gangbusters on downtown Frisco, the real money hopped a ride east and touched down unmolested in Bermuda."

"I presume you have a solicitor there."

"To hell with the Bermudan court system. It will take weeks before some white-wigged lord gives us an accounting, and the trail there is already frigid."

"So you lost them."

"The Treasury Department is not without its informants, especially in foreign banks."

"Keep me posted."

Lou turned to leave, partly because he wanted to meet with Jack before the arraignment proceedings, but mostly because he didn't want Harry to see the big grin on his face. He pictured the perpetrators of this crime safely ensconced in their villa overlooking Ipanema Beach, where a bevy of shapely ladies lit their cigars and fed them grapes.

"Lou, please don't go," Harry cried out as if an anvil sat squarely on his big toe. "I've got a deal. It will cost you nothing."

Lou raised one eyebrow. He was skeptical of the nothing part, but he never refused a gift if that's what this really was.

Harry pulled a pack of smokes from his shirt pocket and did the lighting honors for both of them. After a communal drag, he pulled a bunch of mug shots from a desk drawer and arranged them on his desk. Lou gave these well-groomed criminals in two hundred dollar suits a quick once-over. "Such pretty faces," he remarked. "What are you giving me?"

"If your client can identify one of the operators in this enterprise, he gets a free pass on the nine counts of fraud."

"You'd have to scratch those nags anyway," Lou returned. From his perspective this wasn't a free deal at all. Jack would have to jump through at least one hoop by making an ID.

"Okay, then we'll nix the three railroad stocks from the inside trading indictments. Twelve out of eighteen is a nice start, isn't it?" Harry took two puffs on his cigarette.

"What about bail?" Lou asked. The maximum sentence for the six remaining counts amounted to eighteen years. No prosecutor in the country would settle for under five thousand dollars bond. Then again, the way that Harry fiendishly sucked the life out of a cigarette meant that five hundred dollars might represent a more reasonable figure.

"How about personal recognizance? You wouldn't want us to pay him, would you?" Harry offered.

"Sold!"

Harry hit the intercom button. "Betty, please tell the marshal to send in Mr. Preston alone."

"Alone means he'll have to wear handcuffs," the faceless Betty responded.

"Thank you, Betty," Harry replied.

Jack entered in his prison grays, his hands shackled to his waist. A day's worth of stubble covered his face. Lou guided him by the shoulder to the rows of mug shots. "Do you see any friendly faces here?" he inquired.

One by one, Jack studied each face. "They all look like floor traders and clearing house managers to me, but I never met a single one of them," he replied.

"What about these pictures over here?" Harry asked pointing to another group of photos already arranged on top of a second desk at the opposite side of the room.

Jack ambled over and his cuffed hands both pointed to the right. "The third from the end is Dudley! He's the guy who was dining with Alice at Delmonico's before she sat down with me."

"Don't talk about Alice in front of the prosecution," Lou advised.

"Oh, we know all about Alice Mercer," Harry volunteered. "But since no traceable paper headed in her direction, we have nothing to charge her with."

"That's because she's innocent, like me," Jack replied, whereupon Harry broke into a giggle, and Lou bit hard into his right cheek to keep a straight face.

Harry let out a phlegm-rattling wheeze. "Dudley's real name is Terence Dudley Scott. Before we nabbed him for insider trading, Mr. Scott worked as a pension fund broker on the Street. He beat the rap on a technicality and kept his license."

Harry pulled a group of photos from the top drawer of the roll top desk. "What about these gentlemen?" he inquired.

"Objection! That's two IDs!" Lou interrupted. "The deal was for one."

"Another ID gives you a pass on two more counts."

Jack looked over to Lou, who nodded his approval and then turned back to find Harry holding up five photographs, which were spread out poker hand-style between his thumb and forefinger.

On this sighting, Jack's wrists strained and pulled against the handcuffs as if he wanted to strangle one of the pictures. "The guy in the middle is Paul Jeffrey, our summer intern at the firm," Jack huffed. "Why don't you ask *him* about the California savings account?"

"Keep the commentary to yourself," Lou cautioned.

"I have to agree with your defense counsel," Harry said adding, "by the way, you just identified Andrew Scott, the youngest son of the aforementioned Terence Scott."

"But that's impossible," Jack replied, his voice cracking. "Alice told me that Terence Scott was queer. She worked as his beard."

Harry burst into laughter again, and this time even the snug grip of Lou's molars against his right cheek could not keep him from joining in. Regaining his composure, Harry patted Jack on the shoulder and said, "You're a good boy, Jack. I may have promised you two, but I'm dropping four more counts."

"Only two more to go," said Lou, whose face took on a deformed asymmetry due to a sudden swelling of his right cheek.

Jack closed his eyes. "Oh Alice!" he sighed.

"Oh Alice is right," Lou remarked.

CHAPTER 50

Calling Mr. Jones

After parting company with Lou and Jack, Harry Dixon made a beeline next door to his boss's office, that of U.S. Attorney Nat Reiss. As if to convey a sense of magisterial power, parade-sized American and Department of Justice flags drooped from poles situated on each side of the window behind his desk. Two bookshelves loaded down with tomes containing the entire U.S. code from 1789 to the present lined the right and left walls while on the near wall, a smiling headshot of Ike beamed good will to all comers. *Voici le pouvoir de l'état.*

"You know Treasury agents Malone and Sparks," Nat greeted him. Both Malone and Sparks gesticulated with a simple wave of the hand.

"Well," said Harry exhaling a jet trail of smoke through his nostrils, "I left the kid with two counts, and I've still got my shirt, no thanks to you fine T-men."

The remark had the wallop of a Marciano uppercut. Sparks flinched, but Malone blocked his chin with an outstretched finger. "Look, Mr. Dixon—" he returned.

"Let me take over," Nat cut in holding up both palms. "The blame for this disaster goes squarely to our panicky friends in Washington, who called out the dogs. Jack Preston may not have masterminded this project, but he was the only co-conspirator who didn't yet skip out of the country. One had to consider how this affair would have affected the market if it remained a perfect crime."

"So Washington threw the Dow a bone," Harry remarked.

"And so will we," said Nat.

Harry slumped into a seat, and agents Malone and Sparks followed. After an awkward silence, he sucked down a fix of nicotine and looked at Malone. "What about our femme fatale?"

"We have almost nothing on Miss Alice Mercer; no history, no associates and no drivers license. Utilizing a recently installed phone, she made three calls to Hanoi in the People's Republic of North Vietnam," Malone reported.

"Damn it, Mike!" Nat exclaimed. "That kind of talk will have Hoover's troopers storming the Street to look for comrades under the tickertape. As of yesterday, Hanoi still resided in Indochina."

"But we thought the Bureau already invited themselves into this case," Agent Sparks interjected.

Both Nat and Harry gave him a cold stare. "Why weren't we informed?" asked Harry.

"Look," Sparks explained. "We tailed Mr. Preston to the Mercer apartment in the Village. The building faces a narrow street with parking restricted to one side, so with no spots to be had, we pulled up in front of a hydrant, which didn't please the officer of the beat. After identifying ourselves as federal agents, he told us that our colleagues had parked three cars in front of us, and sure enough, two guys with company haircuts kept watch from the front seat of a black Crestliner with a two-way. When I spotted the small brim fedoras on their laps, I knew they were FBI. I followed the training manual to the letter and walked by so I wouldn't blow their cover."

"And to avoid any turf war with Mr. Hoover, we left the scene and killed that line of investigation," Malone added.

"Perhaps our shady lady has diversified herself into other lines of government interest," Nat surmised.

"Did you get her picture?" Harry asked.

"Well," said Sparks, "we tried." Meanwhile, Agent Malone buried his head in his hand.

Nat handed Harry a folder. Harry opened it, and his eyes fell upon the pleasantly rounded derrière of a young woman. The following picture showed her shapely legs, and the picture after that revealed her healthy bosom. Next came the back end of the folder.

"One can presume that her face does the rest of her body justice," Nat joked.

"The agency issued me a camera with a telephoto lens. Every time I took a breath, the image moved ten feet," Sparks said, throwing out his arms as if to make the point.

"Enough!" said Nat, "Mr. Dixon has an announcement to make."

"I do?" Harry returned.

"I presume you buried sixteen charges on Mr. Preston for good cause."

Harry pulled two mug shots from his pocket and handed them to Nat. "Such a beautiful con," said Harry blowing out a smoke ring. "Our patsy in the holding cell should feel honored that he was set up by virtuosos—Terry and Andy Scott."

At that point, the phone rang, and Nat picked up. "Reiss here.... Yes... Yes... Yes! Whatever you pay that man, double it!" he yelled into the receiver and then hung up.

"It's the final destination, boys!" said Nat passing the mug shots to Agent Malone. "The Scotts moved the money into Havana, but there's still one loose end."

"I can take care of her," Sparks volunteered.

"Forget about Miss Mercer," Nat said. "It just occurred to me that this venture required three men to make it work. Who was the third man?"

"My guess is the mysterious Mr. Jones," Malone replied.

"So where, pray tell, is Mr. Jones?" Harry asked. Every man glanced at each other, but nobody answered.

Suddenly Nat grabbed the bottom stripe of the American flag behind him and kissed it. "Mr. Jones," he said with unabashed exuberance "as friend and accomplice to the family Scott is recovering from a rum-soaked night at the Tropicana. You know what that means."

"It means we can't touch them if they made it to Cuba," Malone said.

"Ah, but you can talk to them,' Nat returned. "Compliment them on their little caper, and drink it up with them. Oh yes, offer them complete immunity if they return all the swag, and after they turn blue from laughter, continue to shoot the breeze with them. They'll want to brag about their conquest. I'd lend them my ears and suck in every detail.

"And who is Mr. Jones?" Sparks asked.

"I have a hunch," said Nat, "that Mr. Jones might be one of our own. Find out who at the SEC gave the order to run a fire sale on all those mergers and acquisitions in Jack Preston's dossiers. Methinks Jonesey has taken a permanent vacation."

CHAPTER 51

In Chambers

Nat Reiss's intercom buzzed. "Judge Cummings requests Mr. Dixon's presence in his chambers at once," said Betty.

"Mr. Dixon is tickled pink to oblige," Nat replied.

Just then, another commotion broke out from across the street, and Nat looked out the window behind him to behold Manhattan District Attorney, the Honorable Frank S. Hogan, holding an impromptu press conference on the steps of the County Court. From all sides, cameras flashed in the stark sunlight, and scores of reporters jockeyed into position along the steps to jot down his pronouncements on the latest people's victory.

"Some lucky dogs get it handed to them on platters," Nat commented. When he looked back, Harry had already gone. Obviously, the novelty of witnessing this daily scene unfold upon the county steps for almost thirty years had metamorphosed into a rather monotonous routine for the man.

Harry arrived puffing and wheezing in Judge Cummings' chambers, located on the far side of the courthouse and two flights up. The judge greeted him with a slap on the back and pointed him to Lou, who had already made himself at home by spreading out his case file on one side of a mahogany conference table.

"Sixteen of eighteen charges disposed of! I look forward to working with both you upstanding gentlemen," Judge Cummings said holding up a lit match to the thermometer-like appendage jutting from Harry's lips. Then, the judge shared fire with Lou, and, with cigarettes in motion, all three got down to business.

Lou made the opening gambit. "In review of the grand jury proceedings, let me point out that my client, Jack Preston, had no active part in this conspiracy, *and* as a matter of record, charges of conspiracy were neither contemplated nor entered against him. Here then, the U.S. Attorney charges Mr. Preston with inside trading of common stock when two parties not mentioned in the indictment, but now known to the U.S. Attorney as Messrs Scott and Scott, perpetrated this illegal act unbeknownst to my client. The logic of the indictment rests upon faulty premises."

Judge Cummings nodded in agreement. "A valid point," he said. Then he turned to Harry and asked, "What's your take on this development?"

"The U.S. Attorney appreciates Mr. Preston's cooperation in this investigation and is willing to vacate all charges against him in exchange for the illicit monies on deposit in his name at the Security Pacific Bank in San Francisco and for his testimony against Messrs Scott and Scott—in the event of their arrests—as well as for his testimony against the co-conspirator with the alias of Mr. Jones."

Lou and the judge exchanged curious glances. "Are you saying that the defendant can identify Mr. Jones?" the judge asked.

"Not at all. We suspect alias Jones is a ranking official in the legal division of the SEC. We would merely require Mr. Preston to corroborate future testimony by a witness from San Francisco."

Judge Cummings grabbed a blank piece of legal paper and jotted down a memo. "For the welfare of the securities exchange," he said, "I am issuing a gag order regarding the existence and activity of Mr. Jones until such time that you have discovered his true identity. In addition I find it incumbent upon me to issue a ninety-day injunction against SEC approval of any further consolidations or amalgamations of American corporations."

"And what about Mr. Preston?" Lou asked.

"The defendant shall be held over for trial commencing on the fourth Monday of August."

"But that's my vacation time," Lou returned.

"Mine, too," said Harry.

"Then I trust you two gentleman will have worked out an agreement by then. Let us now formalize these discussions and proceed with the arraignment. The court shall accept the request of personal recognizance in lieu of bond. Any briefs contemplating the dismissal of charges shall be submitted to my clerk no later than Friday next."

Lou and Harry proceeded together to the courtroom. Along the way, Harry hoped agents Malone and Sparks would find out the identity of Mr. Jones before some ear on Wall Street shorted half the American economy based upon this disturbing information. Regardless of the man's real name, the court had no power to keep secret an injunction against all pending mergers and acquisitions. By statute, the court clerk had to publish this information in a journal of public record, and many people in the press and on the Street would want to know the real dirt. A gag order could last only so long.

CHAPTER 52

Almost Clockwork

With ten minutes to go before arraignment, Lou dropped Jack's file on the defendant's table and waited for him to arrive. Since smoking in the courtroom was prohibited, Harry indulged his cravings in the jury room, which was well appointed with ashtrays and water pitchers, both necessities for any dead-locked deliberations in a summer heat wave. The windows in the room, like those of the courtroom and the judge's chambers, faced Duane Street and the solitude of St. Andrew's Church. Unlike the offices on the other side of the building, the street scene below rarely produced anything more boisterous than the occasional toot of a horn aimed at an obstructing motorist who had fallen into a trance-like state when the light at the intersection turned green.

Lou remembered that such quietude was the way that Judge Harley Cummings had decreed his destiny when seniority allowed him to choose a courtroom far from the carnival atmosphere of the steps of the County Court. From this placid dominion, Judge Cummings administered his docket like the Swiss railroad. Justice was swift; justice was sure, and justice never pandered to the gallery. "The federal courts dispense justice, not entertainment," he counseled all newcomers to his chambers. "There will be no bread and circus in my courtroom."

Lou never forgot these words because the judge never stopped reminding him of them. But this didn't mean that Lou questioned the man's judgment. Attorneys of all stripes agreed that when it came to securities laws, no man on the bench understood the esoteric codes and case decisions better than Judge Cummings, who had distinguished himself by serving as judicial advisor to Joseph P. Kennedy back in the early days of the SEC. They had fast become social acquaintances and maintained that relationship even after both had returned to New York from Washington. Lou found it peculiar that given this history, the Judge never again uttered the name, Kennedy, and should casual conversation ever unearth those three syllables, he would adroitly change the topic.

Lou wrote on his legal pad:

> *Thank you Mr. Jones for blowing their case!*
> *Petition the court for discovery and dismissal by*
> *Friday next.*

The clock on the wall now read one minute to nine, and a bailiff and a stenographer entered the courtroom from the judge's chambers. Meanwhile, Harry Dixon dashed in from the other side. *But where was the guest of honor?* Lou looked over to Harry, who looked back to Lou, who then looked at the bailiff, who looked at the stenographer, who looked back over to Harry, thus completing the circle. *How would the judge react if the defendant didn't arrive on time?*

"Hear ye, hear ye! All rise," announced the bailiff in the bombastic timbre of an eighteenth century town crier.

Assuming an upright posture that seemed to add two inches to his height, Judge Cummings took long regal strides to his bench. With everybody up on his feet, Lou looked back across the empty gallery and let out a sigh of relief as a marshal with a linebacker's physique removed the shackle chain beneath Jack's suit jacket. It was the nick of time—or was it?

When the bailiff finished his salutations, all but the marshal took their seats.

"Let the record show," said the judge to the stenographer, "that the marshal and his prisoner arrived late to the venue. A letter of inquiry shall be forwarded to the Regional Director."

With that bump in the road addressed, the rest of the arraignment proceedings, including plea, personal bond and scheduling, lasted about as long as a television commercial. And when the gavel dropped, Jack could once again breathe free air.

"What took you so long to get here?" Lou asked as the two of them proceeded out of the courtroom.

"Forget what you've seen in any noir movie," Jack said. "After I left Mr. Dixon's office, the marshals had me shower and shave. Then I had to wait for my suit to return from overnight service at the cleaners. They had it cleaned and pressed! Did you ever?"

"Uncle Sam always treats my clients well," Lou replied, which was a fish story he seldom told, but one which impressed the average stock swindler so much more than telling him that the deluxe treatment and accommodations came courtesy of Judge Cummings, who had decreed that all courtroom participants should come "dressed in a manner appropriate to the dignity of the proceedings." Had Jack appeared before a more tolerant personality, he might have undergone a real jail time experience at the city's lockup facility, where the federal government leased space for its own prisoners. Within this towering fortress, inhabited the most wicked and depraved criminal minds that only a city of eight million stories could produce. Affectionately, the place was called "the Tombs."

At the courthouse steps, Thelma Kane ran over to Jack and hugged him.

"I told you, we'd get him out," Lou said.

"Oh, Jack!" was all Thelma could say. Using the back of her wrist, she wiped away wet mascara running down her cheeks. Then, she handed him an envelope.

Jack opened it and pulled out a check. "Two weeks severance pay... It's more than I expected."

"If there's anything I can do...." Thelma couldn't finish the sentence.

"You've already done it. You were here for me."

Thelma hugged him again. Meanwhile, a traffic jam had engulfed Foley Square. Angry horns attempted to honk away the obstruction but only succeeded in drowning out the sounds of Thelma sobbing.

CHAPTER 53

Into the Wind

At the second floor landing, Jack rushed past Gus Andersen, who attempted to flag him down from the top of an A-frame ladder. Jack waved back, but didn't stop until he arrived at the fourth floor, where he reached into his pocket for the apartment key. Other than his heavy breathing, the place was dead silent.

Jack turned the key, and when he opened the door, a gentle breeze kicked up the curtains and blew in his face. He grabbed onto the door handle, lest his wobbly knees bring him to the floor, for all of Alice's furniture had vanished into the wind. And in that moment, Jack realized that wherever it had gone, so too went Alice.

Like his arrest, Jack knew that this turn of events was a mistake. Surely the gods had decided that his days of ecstasy and bliss needed a monkey wrench to keep things spicy and interesting. Why not throw a few lightning bolts his way or impose upon him an ordeal to make him prove himself worthy?

Nonsense! Utter Poppycock! Jack didn't have to pinch himself to know that Alice didn't blow town on some winged horse. He knew that to find her, he had to start thinking lawyerly thoughts again. Frantically, he raced from room to room to search for clues, but all he could find were his own clothes in the far bedroom closet and his personal toiletries on one side of the medicine cabinet in the bathroom. Everything else—all of Alice's possessions—had vanished.

After racing around aimlessly for several endless moments in the suddenly cavernous dwelling, Jack retired to the kitchen, where he opened the refrigerator. A half consumed bottle of Chablis sat on the bottom shelf. It called out to him, but now was not the time.

"Excuse me for barging in, but you left the door open," greeted Gus's singsong voice.

"Were you here when she left?" Jack inquired.

"Yesterday evening, two men calling themselves government agents dragged her out of here in handcuffs. I may be wrong, but I suspect they were imposters. Miss Mercer screamed at them in what sounded like French. An hour later, the two same men came back and loaded the furniture into a truck."

"Did you get the license plate number of the truck?"

"The front plate was missing, and a cargo blanket hung off the tailgate just enough to cover the back plate. It didn't seem logical. Why would the government take the furniture?"

"Perhaps they relocated her for reasons known only to them." Jack's throat choked. After gulping down the lump in it, he exhaled in almost a whisper, "Alice is not coming back."

"Well," Gus replied, "The rent is all paid up. Do you want the apartment? Only forty dollars a month."

Jack attempted to reply, but discovered that his mouth had become frozen shut. He nodded yes to the offer, and Gus patted him on the shoulder.

CHAPTER 54

Wandering Aimlessly

Jack sat cross-legged on the kitchen floor of the apartment and rested his back against the wall. He wanted to contemplate his next move, but could only fixate on the curtains flapping in the breeze. Any thinking about Alice produced only chaos. Where was she? And what was the real story behind her discourse in French with the so-called government agents? Surely, the government wasn't in the moving and relocation business. When a G-man collared you, you proceeded to jail, and then you appeared before a federal judge just like he had. Yet as far as he could tell, Alice wasn't within a city mile of the Foley Square courthouse. Nothing made any sense.

Frustrated at his mental ineptitude, Jack ducked out into the fresh air for an afternoon constitutional. On Sixth Avenue, he passed a furniture store, and realizing that he did not want to sleep on a hardwood floor, he doubled back and purchased a queen-sized bed with guaranteed evening delivery. Heading up to West Fourth Street, he came across several candy stores, but could not find any copies of *The Wall Street Journal* on their racks. Instead, *The Daily Worker* proclaimed:

MCCARTHY TO FACE SENATE SCRUTINY

Jack wondered what all the card-carrying reds at that rag might say about his own predicament with the law. Perhaps a cigarette and a blindfold might accompany the appropriate punishment.

Jack strolled toward Washington Square Park and stopped to admire an encaustic on canvas collection of flags, numbers and targets by a fresh-off-the-farm artist, who didn't believe in signing his name on the bottom. A faded likeness of an American flag stirred up nebulous but queasy feelings that Jack considered appropriate for one unjustly accused; however, the nameless man wouldn't budge from his asking price of twenty dollars. Sure, paintings could be had down the lane for the price of a shine, but this one spoke to him. On impulse, Jack emptied his wallet for the framed oeuvre.

Alice... Sweet Alice... Now there was art! Jack's shattered mind couldn't shake her. She was his lodestar, his bearings and his X on the treasure map. But where the hell on the map was the X? Like before, the mush of gray matter within his skull spun in neutral, grinding without traction as he passed the very spot where he and she had batted a Spaldine to each other. There now, a coed duet strummed guitars and sang about life on the chain gang. Jack remembered hearing that same song some years back by a folk group, The Weavers, but it had been many moons since they had received any further radio play. Like Alice, the group had just disappeared into the vapors.

Jack passed under the Washington Square arch and continued on to Fifth Avenue, where the spires and brownstone tower of the First Presbyterian Church saluted the heavens. So this was the hallowed sanctuary where Alice had chosen to exchange vows. Enter it he must....

Such splendor, Jack thought. And what had run through Alice's mind when she had beheld the splashes of color that the stained windows cast upon the carved walnut pews? Did she gasp at the high gothic walls gracefully joining together like prayerful hands in an expanse of groined arches at the pinnacle? This was a far cry from the humble white clapboard of the church he knew.

"I have no business here," Jack muttered to himself, his whisper of a voice carrying under the vaulted ceiling as if it contained transistorized relay circuits.

"Oh, but you do, sir," replied a sexton polishing a distant pew. His steel gray hair and impeccable dress marked him as a church elder. "May I direct you to the church office?"

"Actually," Jack replied, "My fiancée had requested a wedding date here for late September. She said you accepted Huguenots and Congregationalists in your fold."

"Aha! You must be Jack Preston. Your lovely fiancée told me that she couldn't wait until June." The man approached and held out his hand. "So pleased to meet you...I'm Angus Campbell, in service of the Lord."

The heather and thistle in his name didn't match the polish in his diction, which he spiced with just a dash of Fifth Avenue lockjaw that bespoke old money. Beneath the waxy veneer of his grip, Jack felt not only the strength of a person who could polish a hundred pews a day, but the confidence of a retiree, who once commanded a hundred traders on the pits and floors of the Street.

"The beauty of this church overwhelms me. Alice has chosen well," Jack said.

"Beauty inspires the innocent, but it also beguiles the unwary. Do not let it steal your innocence," Mr. Campbell cautioned.

"I'm afraid it already has," Jack confessed. Then he held up his painting. "Today, I bought this image of a faded flag. What does that say about my love of beauty?"

"Only you can speak for yourself. For reasons known only to him, the artist in the park who created your painting recently destroyed all his previous works."

"Perhaps they didn't sell. Even artists have to eat."

"No, he had fallen out of love with beauty. Could it have betrayed him? He won't say."

"Will beauty betray me?" Jack wasn't quite sure if beautiful Alice hadn't already made her final exit. The doubts about her fidelity had gnawed him to the quick ever since Lou revealed the particulars of the grand jury indictment, not to mention that she had also worked with a former securities trader who executed a series of inside trades based upon her extracted information.

"Alice loves you, Jack,'" said Mr. Campbell without a trace of hesitation. "On the day she came to us, her face beamed with joy. Now stop moping around here and go back to her."

If only it were that easy. When Jack returned to his apartment building, Gus stopped him in the lobby. "A messenger from your law firm dropped this off," he said handing Jack his briefcase. "I told him I would give it to you personally."

"Do you remember anything else about the two men who took Miss Mercer with them yesterday?" Jack said.

"I watched their moving truck head straight toward the highway, but I still couldn't get a good look at the license plates."

"That would be the wrong way to go if they wanted to take the Holland Tunnel. Wherever Alice went, she probably remained east of the Hudson River."

"You'll have to do better than that if you want to find her."

"I'll have to do a lot better than that."

Once back inside the apartment, Jack hung his painting on the bedroom wall and waited for his bed to arrive. He remembered the half-consumed bottle of Chablis that Alice had left behind in the refrigerator. A cool glass would hit the spot; however, with no glasses available, he would have to swig it directly from the bottle. Well, nobody was looking. Why not drink like a bum?

As Jack lifted the bottle, he heard a clinking sound, which, upon inspection, resulted from four metal beads resting on the bottom. Jack pulled the cork, and after one whiff of the contents, he swished a somewhat lemony but smooth sip across his palate. He waited a moment, and when he realized that the beads in the bottle didn't produce any poison, he took a hearty gulp. The beads jiggled in unison. What were those damned things, anyway? He'd have to finish the bottle to find out, but not just yet.

Jack opened the refrigerator to return the bottle, and a ticket stub lying on the shelf under where the wine bottle previously sat caught his attention. He knew the stub well from his first outing with Alice.

LOWER Box Seat $3.00
Yankees

The Boston game! That's the ticket! Alice went to Boston. Why? Perhaps the metal beads in the wine bottle might provide a clue. He hastened to the kitchen sink to drain the bottle, but midway through the tilt, his mouth made a diving catch. One swig…two swigs…three swigs…four…. A metal bead landed on his tongue, and he spit it onto his hand, where from his vantage point it had the shape of a shirt stud with three metal prongs sticking out from one side.

Could it be? Yes, it was! The pint-sized thingamajig was a transistor!

And then the phone rang. "Jack, it's Lou… Do you know anybody in Hanoi?"

Jack tried to take it all in—transistors, Boston, Hanoi and a half bottle of wine, the last of which was making him feel warm but stupid at the moment. "Do they make transistors in Hanoi?" he inquired.

"I'll assume that means 'no'. Your fiancée called Hanoi three times."

"Alice might watch the Red Sox play at Fenway this evening. She left town for good. I should go to Boston to find her."

"Forget about Boston, and don't even think about leaving New York unless you want to spend the next six years of your life in stir. She set you up, and then she ditched you…. Have you been drinking?"

"Only a little, and then I almost swallowed a transistor."

"I'll call you back when you're sober, and then you can explain to me what a transistor is. Alice knows your number, so don't leave town, or I'll ditch you too."

"Bye."

Jack returned to the bedroom and picked up his briefcase. He had already accumulated all his citations for his next legal paper on transistors, which he would send off to Joe Kennedy. Now that he had all the free time in the world, he could finish writing the paper by tomorrow afternoon and have it typewritten by a transcription service for the following morning. Wouldn't Joe get a kick when he received a couple of transistors in the special delivery package as a bonus?

Jack squatted and inverted his briefcase causing the smudged baseball to roll onto the floor. He pressed the smudge print to his cheek. *Boston!* He was getting warmer. Now all he had to do was wait for his bed to arrive in this private law office of his.

CHAPTER 55

Ten-Dollar Treats

Nobody went to Havana in August, so why was it so damn crowded? That's what Agent Sparks wanted to know as the taxi navigated along pencil-thin streets overflowing with a mass of humanity that spilled out in droves onto the right of way and caused the traffic to crawl. Sparks loosened his tie. At the SEC briefing, the supervisor had told him that Havana's dog days were no hotter than New York's. If that were the case, why did the seat of his worsted suit stick to his buttocks like wet bubblegum?

Outside the cab, a cavalcade of souls proceeded in tropical glory. Under storefront canopies, gray-haired men in *guayaberas* sat around makeshift tables, where they built bridges of dominoes. Boys played catch with oversized balls better suited for the jai alai fronton, and scattered trios of bare-chested men tattooed rumba beats on their rows of bongos, congas and timbales. The illogical syncopation cast a spell upon the ladies, who swayed their bottoms twofold and threefold for every step and stride. What man could resist such spectacle? Indeed, the expanding girth of so many bellies in pink cotton indicated that a man's night on these shores was far from idle.

The taxi came yet again to a halt. "Hey, Yankee, I have a pretty girl for you. Only two dollars," called a self-proclaimed pimp, who must have slicked his hair with lard or axel grease.

"No quiero," Sparks replied through the open window.

"That's telling him," said Agent Malone, who reclined backward—siesta style—with his fedora tipped over his eyes. "My unofficial source declares that the girls at the hotel still have their own teeth, but it'll cost you ten clams for a clean one."

"And what makes you think I'd pay?"

Malone sat up and flipped his hat onto his head. "Look Tom, it's obvious to me and anybody else with half a cop's nose that you're still a virgin. Pay the ten bucks, and get it out of your system."

"Hey Mister, for ten dollars, I can get you a very beautiful girl," the taxi driver cut in.

"Did you hear that?" Malone cracked. "A ten note gets you a rental in Alice Mercer's class. That's a heck of a lot cheaper than what Jack Preston will pay to get back to square one."

"Leave me alone, Mike. We're on official business here."

"I'm sorry I touched a nerve."

Malone leaned back and tipped his hat back over his face. At the rate the taxi moved, it would take at least a half an hour to get to the hotel.

CHAPTER 56

Exiles

The sedative had worn off, and Alice arose bleary eyed from her bed. Slowly the blurred image of a man reading a newspaper at the foot of her bed came into focus.

"Bonjour Alice… comment ça va?" he asked, his face still buried in the newsprint.

"You are a pig, André. I hate you!" she replied in English, her words slurring.

André tilted his head back and looked down his nose at her. "Why do you refuse to speak to me in your mother tongue?" he said and then turned away.

"Because as you might have learned from that newspaper you hold in your greasy fingers, my mother tongue no longer remains the official language of my mother country. Is it true that the new regime has exiled all colonists?" Alice glared directly at the back of a head of meticulously coiffed, jet-black hair, and she balled her hand into a fist. She wanted to strike the man down, but he would only overpower her and inject more sedatives into her arm. There had to be a better way.

"You can thank your Papa for the new regime. Were it up to me, his head would have landed in a basket on the day after the debacle at Dien Bien Phu," André quipped.

"Ha-ha!" Alice shot back, "the Viet Minh now control the jails in Hanoi. You no longer have Papa in custody."

André put down his paper and faced her again, this time through squinting eyes. "My dear Alice Marie," he said, "we did not train you to become a suburban housewife, nor did we instruct you to consort with stock riggers. Your moonlighting activities with this so-called Dudley character almost brought down our entire operation. Therefore, I ask you this one question, 'Are you willing to gamble on your Papa's life by being careless again?'"

Alice lunged at André with both her fists held high, but he quickly pinned her to the bed. "Go back to Hell, André, and take my drug and whore training with you!" she screamed. *Je te déteste!*

The right side of André's mouth twitched. "I shall leave you by yourself for the next two days, my dear. Please don't gamble with Papa's life by calling New York while I set things up for you here."

"And what if I call Hanoi?" she taunted.

"Please do," André replied. "The Viet Minh have left the telephone system in disarray, and after an illiterate operator connects you to the city dump, rest assured that you will pay the international charges with your own money."

He then released her and shut the door behind him a moment before a pillow slammed into it. Alice dropped back onto the sheets and curled up into a fetal position. She felt too drained to cry, not that it would have helped any. She knew that the moment she walked out the door, the only place she could go would be the first place André would look.

Biting her lip, she picked up the telephone and dialed the operator. "Please operator, this is urgent. You must give me a good connection…"

CHAPTER 57

The Fugitive

Agent Sparks had never seen a palm tree before except in the pages of *Life* magazine, but here at the Hotel Nacional, pots upon pots of every ornamental variety of them stood sentry over the wicker and cane seats that bestowed tropical grace upon the lobby. One particular palm with a cross-hatched trunk topped by spindly fronds that jutted out like Japanese fans from the crown caught his fancy, and he grabbed a wicker chair next to it so that he could rub his fingers along its exotic bark. Sparks was pleased with his pick, for from this vantage point in the corner, he could spy the comings and goings of the prosperous clientele, who darted back and forth through this Sidney Greenstreet movie set as if it were a penny arcade.

Despite the August doldrums, the place did quite well for itself. Gone were the Yankee tourists coming to escape winter's grip, and in their stead, the merchant and professional classes from the occidental provinces came to enjoy a show and wager their pesos on the roulette wheel. With twilight in mid stride, the last of the sun worshippers paraded in already showered, dressed and groomed courtesy of the crack cabana crew, who made sure that no unsightly pot bellies wrapped in towels transgressed the lobby threshold.

This was not to say that bare midriffs were not welcome. To Sparks' left was the entry to the floorshow, whose marquee proclaimed:

MUJERS DEL CARIBE—AIR CONDICIONADO

Alongside the entry, two barely clad ladies in fruit-laden headdresses stretched out their arms and gently tugged feathered boas across the crests of their cleavage. The effect was magnetic—at least to Sparks' wandering eyes, which rebounded toward the casino, where overhead fans slowly churned a sultry haze of cigar smoke and humidity intermingled with scents of vinegar and chlorine to ward off the mildew.

But Sparks could not resist the bosom on display entirely, and as he glanced back to the two ladies in the Carmen Miranda get-ups, his line of sight collided with Agent Malone's belt line. "Jackpot, Tommy!" Malone exclaimed. "I spotted Junior making small talk with one of the Flora Dora girls. Daddy tried to shoo me off, but I convinced him to join us here for Cuba Libres, courtesy of Uncle Sam."

"How'd you know they'd be here?"

Malone tapped his noggin. "Because this place houses the welcoming committee for all fugitives and racketeers with a price on their heads. The rules are simple. Two Gs gets you a yearly pass, and ten Gs buys you lifetime sanctuary with a Cuban passport."

Sparks' eyes widened. A passport meant that the Cuban government knowingly harbored felons, which was a violation of its extradition treaty with the United States. "Which plan did the Scott family choose?" he asked.

"They didn't. The thieves running the immigration ministry spend hurricane season somewhere in the south of Spain. This means that we can still negotiate with the Scotts for return of the loot."

"And what are our chances of success?"

"If we discover the real name of Mr. Jones, then we can consider this wild goose chase a success."

A cigarette girl, two bellhops and a waiter carrying a tray of drinks approached. The bellhops moved a bamboo table in front of Sparks and then arranged two more wicker chairs around the table. Malone took his place, and the waiter dispensed three Cuba Libres from his tray. Meanwhile, the cigarette girl clipped the sucking end of a cigar and handed it to Malone, who sniffed the leaf and then inserted it firmly between his lips. The cigarette girl culminated the ritual with a lighter that could have doubled as a torch, and Malone's cheeks cranked the stogie to life. Finally, he handed the waiter a five-peso note, and the whole entourage darted off with a touch of rumba in their hips.

"Viva los Yankees," the waiter cracked loud enough to be overheard.

"I can't argue with that," said Sparks. "Viva Mantle, Berra and Larson."

Terence Scott strutted toward the impromptu conference table and hailed Malone with a two-fingered salute. He offered Sparks his hand. "Call me Terry," Scott said. "I'll answer your questions out of respect for a fellow human being, but my trail ends here. There will be no deal on return to the USA."

It was a good opening, thought Malone, who appreciated the straight talk, for it would simplify the conversation. If Scott wanted to return to the land of hot dogs and apple pie, he would have had his lawyer directing the conversation. Now with no major stakes on the line, all Malone had to do was get the man to relax and spill his guts until he spit up his rectum. Fortunately, Malone knew he wouldn't have to work too hard in the relaxation department. Four weeks in the tropics with a program of after-noon sun and evening massage had left Scott looking tan and trim. And with over two million dollars in the bank in a country where a man could live in robber baron comfort for ten thousand dollars a year, Malone almost wanted to congratulate him on his victory.

Malone took a long gulp from his drink so that the level in the glass dropped a noticeable amount, and then he held his hand out for Scott to do likewise. "Don't worry about the formulation. If you want to swap drinks with me, feel free."

"Ha, I'll pull the old switcheroo the next time I bump into Alice Mercer," Scott replied. "That dame knew how to serve up a mean cocktail." Scott took a dainty sip from his glass and then swished it over his tongue several times before swallowing it.

Sparks shot Malone a sideways glance. "How did you two meet?" he asked.

Malone nodded his approval at the question. Good interrogation technique in this type of casual setting required the person being interro-gated to lead the conversation. In addition to learning valuable information about Miss Mercer, the identity of Mr. Jones could come from an inadver-tent remark or admission.

"Alice," said Scott pausing after her name, "worked as a Girl Fri-day for the main office of Bell Telephone Laboratories on West Street in Chelsea. From there, she shuttled back and forth to the actual laboratories in Murray Hill and Holmdel in New Jersey."

Scott took a more meaningful sip from his drink and continued. "Back in fifty-one after the U.S. Attorney dropped the charges against me for inside trading, I read about a remarkable invention called the transistor, which would revolutionize electronics. At that time, Bell Telephone used their invention to link telephone exchanges from distant small towns so that their customers could call long distance to each other by direct dialing. The experiment was a success, but the scale-up to involve subscribers in the major cities meant a significant allocation of capital, which the phone com-pany did not possess."

"I presume you stepped in to fill the void," Malone said.

"I contacted their financial officers and offered my services. Given my experience on the Street, they hired me on the spot."

"So that's how you met Alice," said Sparks.

"Actually, Alice didn't show up until last summer. With one year to go before the new system came into operation, business activity accelerated in all departments. I remember escorting a group of investment bankers through our Murray Hill facilities when Alice interrupted the tour to tell me that I had to return to Wall Street to clear a letter of credit that would expire at the clang of the afternoon bell. She picked up where I left off and charmed the briefs off my little entourage with her knowledge of solid-state physics and electrical engineering, although I suspect that those green visor types wouldn't have known a cathode from a capacitor. Be that as it may, they plunked down twenty million dollars on the spot, and so in gratitude and remembrance of our first encounter, I sent Alice a dozen white roses."

"How could a mere Girl Friday know all that science?" Malone asked.

"She typed the technical reports at Bell, so she knew how to talk the talk, but that wasn't the reason I pursued her."

"Aha! You were smitten," Sparks said.

"Oh yeah, I attempted a roll in the hay, but after luring her to a hotel room, she slipped me a Mickey, and I woke up the next morning with the worst hangover of my life. That's when I knew that she played in a bigger league than a gal who just taps on a typewriter. With all those industrial secrets at her fingertips, I figured her to be a plant from another company like GE or IBM."

"Good for her. Industrial espionage is perfectly legal," Malone said.

"And good for me, too. I knew that before the next summer when the new telephone circuits commenced operation and the corporation finance division at the SEC cleared their desks for summer vacation, an industrial spy could work her body magic on a mark contracting mergers and acquisitions. A series of papers in the *Princeton Law Review* put me on the trail of one Jack Preston, and you know the rest."

"How'd you get Alice to go along with your plan?" Sparks asked.

"At first I tried blackmail and threatened to pull the rug out on her little spy game, but she swore she was a Girl Scout, and she called my bluff. Since all I had was a solid hunch to go on, I offered her good ole greenbacks for seducing Jack Preston into revealing the names of his clients, but I did not tell her the utility of the information just in case she felt the urge to blackmail me back."

"And the Girl Scout went for it!" Malone exclaimed.

"After I pointed him out in the lobby of the building where he worked, she said she adored his baby face cheeks, and she accepted the money as a bonus. That's when I planted my son, Andrew, in the firm." Scott slugged down the rest of his drink. "Please do not ask me any questions regarding Andy, or I will terminate this conversation."

"I understand," Malone nodded, "but what about Mr. Jones who made all the transfers and deposits? What were his connections to the SEC?"

"I was Mr. Jones," Scott said. "I filled out the deposit and transfer slips, and with the help of the yellow pages, I hired commercial couriers who made the physical deposits. The transistorized relay circuits allowed me to run the coast-to-coast operations from my office at the phone company effortlessly. As for the SEC, I never could have trusted anybody on the inside. I may take risks, but I'm not crazy."

A surge of acid washed against the lining of Malone's stomach, and he grabbed onto his side. In hindsight he wondered how Nat Reiss could have ever contemplated how an SEC supervisor might dispatch such a tangled web of certified checks all over the map without even arousing one iota of suspicion from his subordinates. The arithmetic was so much easier than that: Terence Scott plus transistorized telephone circuits equaled Mr. Jones. Malone wanted to ask the most obvious question of all, but Sparks spoke first.

"What's a transistor?"

"Gentlemen," Scott said, "the next round of drinks is on me."

Scott spent the next hour rationalizing his crime to Malone and Sparks. The chatter was nothing that Malone hadn't heard before, except that all the previous white-collar criminals had given their spiel under lock and key. Scott told them that he had nothing to apologize for... that what he did wasn't stealing... that nobody got hurt... that any disturbance to the market would soon correct itself... blah, blah, blah. Malone wished he had some chloral hydrate to shut him up. Perhaps Alice Mercer could spare a bottle of the stuff.

CHAPTER 58

A Short Walk

Bronxville life had temporarily faded into a memory, and Jack almost knocked on the front door of his parents' house before entering. Oliver, who sat reading the evening paper in his cozy chair, arose from his place and escorted Jack back out the front door.

"We've got to talk—just you and me," he said, "Let's go for a stroll."

Jack was aghast. Obviously his father knew something was awry.

Father and son made a left at the end of the walk. After rounding the corner, Oliver rested his hand on Jack's shoulder. "Joe Kennedy told me that you now practice law in Greenwich Village. At least that's where your correspondence with him now originates."

"I'm working for myself now. The apartment is my temporary office."

Oliver raised his voice. "Why didn't you ask me for advice before leaving the firm, son? You're too green to strike out on your own."

"I had no choice Dad."

"You mean you were…" Oliver didn't finish the sentence.

"Yes, I was, but having Joseph P. Kennedy as a first client isn't a bad start. Is it?"

Oliver stopped in his tracks and rubbed his forehead. "Alright Jack, you can tell me what happened at work on your own time and your own terms, but please explain to me how on earth you obtained those transistors that you mailed to Joe."

"What's so special about transistors? The Raytheon Corporation now advertises them in the electronics journals. You can buy them commercially."

"Not that kind," Oliver said. "They were NPN transistors, and according to General Sarnoff, that type of transistor doesn't exist yet."

General Sarnoff! The very name gave Jack's palms a shine. The General, nee David Sarnoff, was president of the Radio Corporation of America or RCA for short. Like Joe Kennedy, who was known in most circles as the Ambassador, Mr. Sarnoff carried the legitimate title of General as testimony to his army rank in World War II. Jack remembered that his father and Joe had recently test-marketed those Darwinian ads for RCA Victor, and so it came as no surprise to him that they must have broken bread with the General during the rollout. Indeed, Joe Kennedy's business dealings with the General harkened back to the roaring twenties when movies first talked, and when according to Wall Street lore, they walked away from Hollywood with a bundle after they rigged their theaters with a sound system incompatible with everything but RCA technology.

"I've got two more of those transistors in my apartment," Jack volunteered.

"Then let me delight the General with them. Wouldn't his star be a most welcome account to a fledgling law firm?"

"You read my mind, Dad."

With the wrought iron gates of Crownlands, the former Kennedy estate, looming in front of them, Jack and Oliver doubled back home. Jack appreciated his father not probing into his personal affairs other than to ask him if he was well. The two walked on without exchanging words, and Jack told himself that unless a deal with the U.S. Attorney appeared by Monday, he would have to face a jury of his peers. The government case against him appeared weak, but one never knew for certain about these things, and Lou Fisher had refused to make any promises he couldn't keep.

CHAPTER 59

Fast Eddy

Reina Garcia stepped out of the pew and into the flow of worshipers following the priest and altar boys to the vestibule of the church. Half way there, she traversed a second pew and stopped off at an alcove dedicated to the Virgin Mary, where she dropped a dime in a donation slot and lit a candle. After making the sign of the cross, she raised her black veil, removed from her purse a snapshot of a graying naval officer in dress whites, kissed it and then placed it next to the candle. "I'm sorry Eduardo," she said addressing the picture, "but Eddy likes to sleep on top of your favorite suit. How can I tell your namesake 'no'?"

From over her shoulder, she spotted two clean-cut gentlemen with barely a whisker between them waiting in the vestibule. One of them carried a manila folder. Her eyes then turned back to a marble statue of the Virgin in prayerful reflection, and she said to it in a whisper, "I suppose it would be imposing on you to make them go away."

The recessional continued out the door, and Mrs. Garcia approached the vestibule and its two remaining occupants at a crawling pace. "It's just like government marshals to follow me here on a Sunday." she remarked with a bit of sass.

"Mrs. Garcia... You have barely an hour to go before departure call. Are you packed?" the first marshal said as the second one pulled a subpoena from his folder and placed it in her hand.

She signaled yes with a minute nod and read the subpoena. "So Mr. Harold Dixon again requests my presence for testimony in trial. Who is this man?" she asked.

"His middle name is congeniality. He'll treat you like a queen," the first marshal said.

"You'll like New York," said the second one with radio commercial flair. "The government picks up all travel, lodging and dining expenses... Empire State Building... Broadway... Statue of Liberty..."

Mrs. Garcia feigned enthusiasm at the patronizing travelogue but knew she wasn't fooling anybody as she tuned out the words. At her Nob Hill home, the marshals carried her bags to their car much to the hissing protests of Eddy, her tiger cat, who almost jumped off her lap and out the window as they drove past Golden Gate Avenue.

A half hour later, they arrived at a modest ranch house in San Mateo, and the two marshals accompanied Mrs. Garcia, who carried Eddy to the front door. "I'm glad you could drop by, Mom," her daughter greeted her with a kiss on both cheeks. She took hold of Eddy and added, "Come on in everybody."

"Sorry Mrs. Lupo, but we're on a tight schedule," a marshal replied.

Just then, a boy and a girl stormed out of a bedroom. "Eddy! Eddy!" the two preschoolers shouted with delight causing the startled cat to jump into a shrub from where he dashed across the neighbors' yards and into terra incognita.

Mrs. Garcia froze in terror. "This place is strange to him," she shrieked. "He'll never find his way back!"

"I'll drop the kids off at the neighbors and call for him, Mom."

"Oh Eddy! My sweet Eddy! I'm coming; I'm coming, baby!"

"Please Mrs. Garcia… The airline won't hold the plane for you… You must come with us *now*!"

CHAPTER 60

The Fisherman

Most criminal attorneys would rather represent vagrants and deadbeats than work in the federal court system, but Lou Fisher considered them unworthy for the challenge. In the state courts, the best defensive strategy began with petitions for a series of pretrial hearings that could use up the better part of a year and then follow them up with a marathon request for postponements that burned up another stack of calendar pages. The overworked assistant district attorneys were only too willing to comply with such procrastination, even though it meant that a key witness might die, disappear or develop amnesia. Many of these prosecutors came fresh out of law school and spent their scant free hours cramming for the bar exam when they should have studied up on their inhumane case load. Bleary eyed and raw, they would present a case that they inherited from a colleague now moving up into a private law firm and would proceed to alienate the judge, the jury and everybody else but the defense attorney with their bare knuckled incompetence. Such easy pickings!

Lou leaned in on his swivel chair and pulled a dart from the pencil holder on his desk. With a gentle prick of the point to his forefinger, he exhaled a long breath of satisfaction...and why not? After almost thirty years of practice in the federal courts, he had chalked up a winning average of over eighty percent in a streamlined system where the U.S. Attorneys wrote the rules. These prosecutors had it made...such leisurely schedules—all the better to research a case and finesse the jury with details...such tight deadlines—with memories fresh in the witnesses' minds, it became nearly impossible to bamboozle them with nitpicking and double talk...and such a limited appellate process—meaning that if you lost the case, you might get one chance at appeal with the U.S. Circuit Court or, rarely, a second shot with the U.S. Supreme Court; whereas in the state courts, you had two additional high courts to seek a reversal before you took your case up the same federal ladder.

Lou spun around in his chair, and with nary a glance, threw the dart at a corkboard cut in the shape of a boxer in a pugilistic stance on the far wall. When the dart landed squarely on the trunks of the figure, he let out a war holler. The trial gods had signaled to him that he must fight Jack Preston's battle below the belt. *Oh, the joy!*

It took a moment for Jack to get used to Lou's workplace because it could have doubled as the president's office in a frat house. Sports memorabilia covered each of the walls. Autographed pictures of Mickey Mantle, Joe Louis and Rocky Marciano hung next to a poster of the moon. *The moon? What was that all about?*

"This is my war room," Lou said. "My office is for show, but here is where I gird my loins for battle."

Jack did a second take of the moon poster and realized from its misplaced craters that he was really looking at a picture of the planet Mars, whose name commemorated the Roman god of war. *How fitting!* Jack pointed to the unconventional dartboard staring him down. "Did you ever step into the boxing ring?" he asked.

"I'm merely a spectator to the manly art; however, the participants in the ring inspire me to study my opponents with the same kind of intensity that I devote to the facts and legal issues of a case. When a witness feints a falsehood on the stand, it's my job to beat the truth out of them—figuratively speaking, of course."

Lou pointed to the far wall behind Jack, and Jack turned to behold an oversized sailfish mounted on a walnut plaque. "My passion in life is fishing," Lou continued. "Every weekend from May to October, I cast off from City Island, where I track them; I hook them, and I reel them in. I caught that baby on vacation in Acapulco."

Jack presumed that Lou's tales of adventure conveyed deeper meaning. Among trial lawyers, the term "fishing" meant to ask a witness a question unrelated to the facts concerning the case. Such a query often generated an objection from opposing counsel unless one cleverly buried it in a stream of "camouflage" questions more pertinent to the specifics of the trial.

"So do you fish for the truth?" Jack inquired.

Lou mimed a fisherman casting his line. "The truth may help you, but the lies will set you free," he said. "If I fish long enough, sooner or later a witness will have to cover his tracks with a fib. And when you expose a witness reframing the truth, you have delivered the legal equivalent of a knockout punch. You'll see how it works if we go to trial today."

Trial…Jack dreaded the very word. Today there would be no musings about Alice, Boston or transistors though he watched Lou enter these words on his legal pad. Today Jack would forsake his Greek gods to implore the Roman god of war, and if all went according to Lou's plan, the whole arrest and trial would become a bad memory by Friday…and nobody from Bronxville to Boston would be the wiser.

CHAPTER 61

The Boss

Jack felt out of place in the courtroom. For a lawyer, this was supposed to be home turf, but aside from his own legal proceedings, Jack had not entered this august setting since his second year of law school. The furnishings were all there—just like back then—however, this time, the bench, the witness stand and the jury box reminded him of a sleeping beast, who could awaken at any inopportune moment and devour him piece by bleeding piece.

Jack counted the people in the courtroom. The judge, the bailiff and the stenographer made three, and Lou, Harry Dixon and himself brought the total to six. Behind them, row upon row of oak benches comprised the gallery, and from the look of the spiff and shine on the wood, Jack knew that nobody had occupied those seats since Dutch Dennert bounced a ball for the Original New York Celtics.

After a momentary conference with Harry Dixon, Lou returned to his seat next to Jack. "The offer was for one count of inside trading, and I turned him down flat," Lou said. "Any objections?"

"You're in charge."

Lou patted Jack on the shoulder. "It's good to hear you say that. I've almost always had problems representing lawyers. Most of them think they know my business better than me, but they wind up outsmarting themselves. You'll do fine."

Judge Cummings banged his gavel. "Mr. Fisher, have all discovery items been delivered to you by the prosecution as per my ruling?" he asked.

"We are satisfied to have a complete listing of all witnesses interviewed by treasury agents Malone and Sparks, and it is our understanding that Messrs. Scott and Scott remain unavailable to testify, and that fugitive warrants have been issued in their names," Lou returned.

"Then let us begin with jury selection."

In the state courts it might have taken the better part of two days to impanel a jury, but here in Uncle Sam's domain, the bailiff pulled twelve names from a rotating drum, and—voilà—the occupants of the courtroom increased by a factor of three. The judge asked the group if any of them had served in law enforcement, and when one of the twelve admitted to being a retired truant officer, the judge replaced him with a retired baker, a not-so-noteworthy addition to this assembly of mature white men.

With but a half hour consumed by this proceeding, Harry Dixon asked for a brief recess, and Judge Cummings granted him a five-minute break. Like the federal system itself, Harry was a model of efficiency as he reached into his shirt pocket for his pack of smokes with one hand and into his jacket pocket for the matches with his other hand, all the while hastening toward the back exit.

Lou shook his head and handed Jack a pencil. "Did you ever smoke one of these?" Lou asked.

"What are you talking about?" Jack said briefly wondering about his counselor's mental status.

"When I rub my chin or poke you under the table, you will put the eraser end of the pencil in your mouth, and you will suck in your cheeks as if inhaling smoke. Understand?"

Jack understood all right. Harry Dixon's body needed nicotine as if it were oxygen, and something so trivial as seeing somebody suck on a pencil would trigger this bestial craving into overdrive. What a nasty distraction! Pavlov would have been proud.

Harry returned, and after some opening remarks to the jury about protecting the integrity of the investment banking system from predatory practices, he singled out Jack Preston as one such perpetrator who had "pirated for personal gain the hard earned money of good solid people like you."

Taking his turn, Lou rebutted Harry's statements as fantasy and characterized Jack as the number one victim in this case. "You will see how Jack Preston fell prey to a malicious scheme that tricked even the greatest of minds working to enforce our government's securities laws," he began. Meanwhile, the jury sat bright eyed and hunched forward as if taking in the first night of a Broadway extravaganza.

For his first witness, Harry called one Darryl Hicks, a handwriting expert from the FBI, who testified that the signature on the savings account application from Security Pacific Bank matched Jack's handwriting. When offered his turn at cross-examination, Lou declined.

"That's it! You're letting him go without a challenge," Jack protested.

"If it weren't your signature on the document, I would have called in our own expert to counter his testimony. Otherwise, let's not waste the court's time. These technical guys have a way of spellbinding a jury with gobbledygook until they look like Nobel laureates."

"Oh!"

"Let me say this once," Lou advised. "I'm best at this game when my client doesn't second guess me during the proceedings. We can always recall witnesses, so if you have any questions or comments, you can corner me during the recesses. Okay?"

"Can I suck on my pencil to provoke a recess?"

"Damn it, Jack! That trick is our secret weapon. Wait for me to give you a sign, or we'll lose the element of surprise when we really need it."

"You're the boss."

"Say it again, Jack."

"We wish to call Mrs. Reina Garcia to the witness stand," Harry Dixon called out.

"You're the boss," Jack repeated as a diminutive woman, who could have been anybody's grandmother, took baby steps towards the witness stand.

CHAPTER 62

Breakdown

Harry Dixon didn't believe in Lady Luck. Even with loaded dice in his hand, he expected to roll snake eyes, and so he left nothing to chance in the courtroom. For starters, he always relied upon the federal agents to inspire reverence and awe when they recounted in succinct detail the bird's eye view of the crime. Then, with the jury sufficiently oriented to the mechanics of the caper, he would call to the stand both the citizen and the turncoat witnesses to round out the testimony. Finally, he would summon the forensic experts to cross the T's and dot the I's and otherwise seal a guilty verdict. Only solid cases need apply for this type of treatment. Otherwise, he recommended dismissal, and ninety-nine times out of a hundred, the powers that be complied.

But the decision makers in Washington weren't so benevolent this time, and Harry knew why. For twenty years, the Republican politicos had gnashed their teeth outside the halls of power. Blame it on the Great Depression, or better yet, blame the successive Republican administrations for causing unprecedented economic collapse. In the roaring twenties, America's leaders turned a blind eye to all the stock pools and insider trading that transformed the stock exchange into a rigged casino inflated to the point of explosion. Forget that Democrats like Joe Kennedy put the fix in, or that the hysterical greed of John Q. Public had as much foundation in economic reality as gnomes and goblins. The brutal truth was that the stock market crashed on the Republicans' watch, and all those voters waiting in bread lines and selling apples on street corners never let them forget it on the first Tuesday after the first Monday in November.

But even never had its limits, and so when the Supreme Allied Commander, Dwight D. Eisenhower flashed his victory smile at the end of the second war, the adoring masses wanted those happy lips to become presidential. It wasn't a matter of time or fate; Ike's election was inevitable, and despite wooing from the Democrats, he chose the Republican Party to bear his standard. On January 20th, 1953, he handed them the keys to the White House.

Ike's first order of business was to tell the Street that there was no going back to the old ways, and that it would never again bring down to its knees the Grand Old Party of business. In other words, all riggers and manipulators would face certain justice, which brought up the strange case of one Jack Preston. What was a prosecutor to do when his case was as thin as the skin on a Bermuda onion?

"It's hopeless, Nat," Harry had told his superior barely hours ago. "The boy was framed like the Mona Lisa. Lou Fisher will skewer us like shish kebab on this one."

"Washington won't let it go," Nat Reiss replied. "I suggest that you build your case backwards and give the jury a big finish from Agent Malone. End with a bang."

Harry pressed his trigger finger against his temple. "Yeah, here's where the bang ends up," he said. "Why not use Sparks instead of Malone? We usually spare the senior investigators from testimony. Their time is too valuable."

"Nah, Sparks is still learning. We can't chance it."

"And you don't think Lou Fisher won't see the weakness behind the switch?"

"So what's he going to do? Call in Sparks anyway? No sane defense attorney would ever contemplate putting a second federal agent on the stand. Remember, Sparks is one of our boys."

"Yeah, I guess you're right."

But Harry didn't believe his own words and had merely uttered them to end an argument he knew he could not win. Now, another challenge tore at his wits. On the witness stand, Mrs. Reina Garcia, accounts manager at the Security Pacific Bank in San Francisco, gave a confused story of her business dealings with Jack.

Harry didn't let the white hair pulled back into a bun mislead him. This woman might have doubled for the fragile kind of wilting flower whom boy scouts helped cross the street, but she was no shrinking violet. Those teeth were real, and they snapped like they wanted to bite. After merely a dozen or so questions, Harry wanted to pack her into a crate and ship her back to Frisco on a tramp steamer heading around the Horn.

"Did Mr. Preston ever call you to check on his account?" Harry asked continuing his line of inquiry past a list of boilerplate questions, which had previously asked Mrs. Garcia her name, her age, her occupation, her employer, her employer's address, her years working for her employer, her responsibilities to her employer, etc. etc. etc.

"Somebody calling himself Mr. Preston called me," she replied all spry and crusty. "Since I never met the man, I couldn't confirm his identity. In the banking business, you have to be careful about these matters. That's the way they train us."

And Harry wondered if Lou didn't train Mrs. Garcia to give that very answer. Without so much as one question in cross-examination, she had called into doubt the fact that she ever had contact with the defendant. True, the phone records linked the defendant's common trunk line with the bank's trunk line in San Francisco, but Harry knew that too many people at both the law firm and at the bank had access to those very same lines. Even with Agent Malone's testimony, it would be impossible to pin those calls solely on Jack Preston.

"If Mr. Preston spoke to you now, would you recognize his voice?" Harry asked.

"No," she shot back.

"Obj—" said Lou raising his hand as if to object to the question, but then he segued from that first syllable into a cough. Jack patted him on the back.

Harry's heart, meanwhile, pounded in pile driver strokes. Lou had every right to object to the question, but that would have made it look like he was trying to hide something from the jury. If his impromptu spasm didn't dupe them, then that pat on the back from the defendant certainly did. Why, Harry fumed, did Lady Luck always work for the other side?

Mrs. Garcia continued. "I can't possibly remember the dozens of voices I hear on the phone every day. Besides, the muffled quality of the long distance line makes the East Coast calls all sound the same, and the man who made the actual deposits at the bank called himself Mr. Jones, but I don't suppose he actually was a Mr. Jones, was he?"

Harry couldn't take it anymore. The damn woman was arguing the other side's case, and all he could think of was sucking down thick, velvety smoke. "Take her out of here!" he wanted to say. "What mental midget made her new accounts manager anyway? All women should either work behind the teller's window or type in the secretarial pool."

But Harry bottled his rage and raised the white flag with a whimper. "I have no further questions for now. May we have a five-minute recess?"

"The defense has no objections," Lou agreed. Yet before the judge could declare it official, Harry had already taken his first steps toward the men's room—but not so fast.

"The counsel for the government shall afford all courtesy to the court in matters of adjournment," the judge warned.

"Yes, your Honor," Harry replied. "I beg the court's indulgence but this once."

Lou approached Mrs. Garcia head on and locked eyes with her, but this only made her avert her gaze toward her crossed arms, which she rubbed with her opposing hands as if to ward off a chill. Lou, conversely, dabbed a handkerchief on some beads of sweat dripping down his glossy temples. "Mrs. Garcia, I commend you. You are a very brave woman to take this long journey to New York all by yourself," he said, switching his approach from vinegar to sugar.

"And what choice did I have? A marshal handed me a subpoena and an airplane ticket and told me I had to go."

The timing deserved a rim shot as the jury burst into laughter. Lou knew that if he played the straight man like this for two or three more responses, the jury would be eating out of his hand like it was bone china.

Unfortunately, Judge Cummings stepped in. "I presume that you have questions for the witness, Mr. Fisher," he said.

Lou had to think fast. He wanted Mrs. Garcia to tell the jury that anybody on earth had the power to make a deposit into Jack Preston's account, but he didn't want her to elaborate on the fact that nobody other than a fairy godmother would ever stoop to such generosity. He realized that he had to limit his questions to those that would limit her answers. But was such a feat possible with this spitfire?

"Uh, Mrs. Garcia... were any withdrawals made from the Preston account?"

"No."

"And was a signature required on any of the deposit slips?"

"No."

Lou congratulated himself for the contained responses he had elicited, but he knew better than to push his luck. The bluntness to the one syllable replies almost sounded to him like they had hostile undertones. Yet beneath the tough shell was a woman who wrung her hands as if she were overcome with anxiety. And, what was that? Her eyes had a moistened look of grief.

"Are you all right, Mrs. Garcia?" Lou posed the question with all the gentleness of a family doctor. He reached out his hand, and she grabbed it with both her hands as if it were a life preserver.

"I...I..." she stuttered for something to say, but instead she broke down into a fit of wails and sobs. "Oh my Eddy... my poor lost kitten! Come home, baby... Oh please."

Lou turned to the bench. "I have no further questions, your Honor. I request a recess," he said in a somber tone.

"The court is adjourned until tomorrow at nine A.M.," Judge Cummings returned without even offering Harry the courtesy of an objection. Then he glared at Harry and added, "Light one up for me, counselor."

As the jury filed into the back room, Lou attempted to calm down Mrs. Garcia with a warm hug. Some of the jury looked back at them and stiffened their lips. Others looked back at Harry and just shook their heads.

CHAPTER 63

Contact

The phone rang so many times that Alice just wanted to throw her pillow at it. What imbecile would call at twenty-five minutes after three in the middle of the night? The caller needed a lesson in courtesy.

"Hello," she mumbled her eyes rolling with reverse English into her lids.

"Hello Alice. Guess who's calling?" came the melodic greeting in Parisian French.

"Papa!" she called out as if overcome by smelling salts, "Are you safe?"

"General Giap freed me from jail last week. It took me all the time since then to detour around the minefields to get back to Hanoi. Mama and little Antoinette send you their love, only little Antoinette is not so little anymore."

"I will come to you."

"Listen, my child. The American ambassador has given us resident visas. A military transport will take us to Hona..."

With a click followed by silence the phone line went dead. "Allo!" Alice repeated several times before hanging up the receiver. She waited for the phone to ring again but knew that even in the best of days, the few telephones in Hanoi had minds of their own. It didn't matter. The old regime had fallen, and no colonial court of the Fifth Republic could ever try Papa for treason. Even if he never cleared his name, no gendarmes would ever escort him to the guillotine.

What was the saying in America—*half a loaf?*

Alice turned on the bed light and opened her floor chest from which she withdrew three glass syringes and a bottle of sodium thiopental. Into each syringe, she drew up twenty milliliters. She placed one syringe between the mattress and the box spring. The second syringe along with the bottle of sodium thiopental went into her purse, and the third syringe landed on a high shelf next to the apartment entrance. Finally, she hopped back into bed and fell into a deep slumber that ended when she heard heavy pounding on her apartment door.

Alice opened her eyes again, but this time daylight poured through the windows. "Alice, open the door. I have good news," called André's voice. Alice donned her bathrobe. When she opened the door, André pushed past her and made himself at home on the living room couch. As his back was turned, she grabbed the loaded syringe that she had placed on the shelf next to the door and slipped it into her bathrobe pocket.

"Please tell me that the Republic has released my back pay," she said.

André shook his head. "Please be patient with us. First Indochina erupted, and now Algeria goes up in flames. The Finance Minister tells me that the Republic can barely pay for light bulbs."

Alice wanted to say, "You don't know the finance minister, you lying pig," but instead said, "So that's the good news!"

"Of course not! I came to tell you that I procured for you a secretarial job in the Lincoln Laboratory at MIT. You start tomorrow and may keep the salary you earn."

"You are too generous. I presume you will want me to photograph all the current research in the department."

"That will be the arrangement. In return, the Justice Minister will vacate the charges against your father."

Alice wanted to stab the lying pig in the eye with her loaded syringe, but she just clenched her lips and pretended that André knew the Justice Minister as well. "And with whom do I share my bedroom pillow in this new charade?" she asked.

"Let us find out first who produces the most seminal work. But since you mention it, you'd probably like to know that Bernard and I have already installed the tape recording equipment inside the hidden panel next to your bed. You activate it by opening the teak chest. When you shut the lid, the recorder turns off."

"Just like my old apartment," Alice sighed. She reached into her pocket for the syringe.

"Yes, but this time, you will actually use it to record your bedtime conversations with suitors whose knowledge can serve the Republic."

Alice released her grip on the syringe. Besides being a lying cowardly pig, it suddenly dawned on her that André was also a stupid lying cowardly pig. Did he not read the newspapers? The colonial regime in Indochina was defunct, and the only power its leaders had was to return to Paris in disgrace. True, they could blame Papa for their failure, but soon Papa would come to America, where the current and former military leaders knew him for the hero he really was. Indeed, the lies excreted from the mouths of the pig and his pig collaborators would not stand the light of day here.

Alice patted the outside of her bathrobe pocket and wondered what other lies the pig had promulgated. The sodium thiopental needed to wait for another opportunity. When André departed, she placed the syringe back on the shelf by the door.

CHAPTER 64

Birddog

"The government calls treasury agent Michael Malone to the witness stand," Harry Dixon said, his voice booming so as to impress upon the jury that a real life federal lawman in the mold of a Saturday matinee hero had come to testify. Electrified, the jury stared in eye-popping awe as Agent Malone swaggered to the stand like a John Wayne character coming upon a band of desperados in a backwater saloon.

At the swearing in, he held up his hand rock steady and glared straight into the eyes of the jury as if his steely eyes could x-ray their souls. Then after allowing a moment for the surreal effect to push the "wow!" buttons on their nerves, Harry adjusted his tie and approached the witness stand, where he raced through his boilerplate questions at supersonic speed so that the wow factor would not be lost on them when he hit his stride with the better stuff to come.

"Agent Malone, briefly state your professional experience working for the United States government," came Harry's fifteenth-or-so question delivered in a kind of awestruck wheeze.

"From 1922 to 1933 the Treasury Department assigned me to enforce the prohibition laws," Malone replied in monotone staccato. "Here in New York, where those laws earned little public support, our squads targeted the cut-rate bootleggers whose products blinded and killed. Following the repeal of Prohibition, we processed the applications for liquor manufacture, and near the end of 1935, our law enforcement activities included criminal investigations for the newly created Securities and Exchange Commission. Excluding the war years, I've been active in that role since that time."

"And what about the war years?" Harry said taking the prompt.

"When the war erupted, I was transferred to the Office of Strategic Services—the OSS, which gathered military intelligence, and which became the forerunner to today's spy agencies. I flew missions into Indochina, where I collected information from the resistance. I also utilized distant vantage points to tail Japanese Zeros back to their bases in the Philippines, where I reported on their locations. That activity earned me the flyboy nickname of 'Birddog'."

Lou snuck a peek at the jurors and wanted to gag. As Malone expounded on his "Birddog" derring-do, he bewitched and enchanted them with his manly power. An aura of infallibility had descended upon him, and Harry Dixon buffed it to a lustrous sheen with an added array of puff questions. Lou knew that if he attacked Malone's testimony directly, the jury would resent it. Then he remembered an old sea adage, "You can't sail directly against the wind..." For that, you had to zigzag.

By the time Harry finally arrived at the meat of the case, even Lou needed a boost of nicotine. "Agent Malone," Harry said pointing his finger at Jack, "what activities prompted the SEC to launch an investigation of the defendant?"

"Let me explain that the compliance trackers at the SEC base their investigations upon mathematical probability. The New York regional office houses a staff of forty-two compliance officers, who audit the Wall Street clearing houses for securities transactions on every publicly traded company involved in a recent merger or acquisition."

"Good heavens!" Harry exclaimed, his eyes bulging, "That's some assignment. There must be thousands of daily transactions for each stock."

"Yes there are; however, the trackers limit their inquiries to either stock transactions involving sums greater than ten thousand dollars or options transactions involving sums greater than two thousand dollars. In the case of Jack Preston, the SEC discovered nine such options transactions for companies he represented in either merger or acquisition proceedings. It was a perfect mathematical fit."

Harry nodded. Then he pointed to the jury and asked, "Agent Malone, would you please explain to us what a stock option is?"

"An option is a contract to buy or sell a stock at a specific price at any time within six months of purchase. For example, by putting only ten percent down on a buy transaction, the client has leveraged his money to pick up over ten times as much stock. If the stock climbs ten percent over the negotiated price, the client collects ten times the ten percent, in effect doubling his money. On the other hand if the stock drops ten percent, he loses everything."

"And getting back to the defendant, what amount of money was realized when the options on those nine stocks in question were redeemed?"

"When the options were exercised three weeks later, the net proceeds amounted to over two and a half million dollars."

The jury collectively gasped and then just as collectively turned their eyes toward Jack. "Don't look back at them," Lou advised him quietly. "They don't know if you're a genius or a schmuck. Let's keep them guessing."

"You put it so well."

"I assure you that since the prosecution can't initiate the subject of Alice Mercer on their own, my cross examination will be as easy as sailing on a lake, providing of course that your siren—as you so-called her in your written statement—doesn't lure us onto the shoals. Do you know what I mean?"

"You can scoff at my choice of words, but classic mythology was my favorite undergraduate subject. I believe my professor's recommendation got me into Princeton Law."

Lou hoisted an eyebrow. In all his years of defending the guilty, he had never once run into a true aficionado of the great works. This he attributed to the culture of the Street, where knowledge outside the realm of moneymaking had a value somewhere between a lump of coal and yesterday's trash. "Then I trust that you appreciate how Zeus liked to turn the tables on both mortals and the lesser gods," he remarked. My job here is to think like Zeus."

"Have you gone crackers? That stuff is fantasy; this courtroom is reality."

"Maybe so, but I will turn the tables. This is going to be fun."

"Thank you, Agent Malone. Your witness, Mr. Fisher," Harry said before requesting a brief recess. The judge agreed to a twenty-minute break, and with his hand reaching into his pocket, Harry raced in the direction of the bathroom, presumably to tar his lungs. Lou preferred to light up his filtered brand outside, where the fresh air would invigorate his mind to focus upon tarnishing the luster and sheen that emanated from the aura of Birddog's infallibility.

CHAPTER 65

Sowing Confusion

Lou approached the witness stand with one eye on the judge and the other on the jury. After momentarily making eye contact with Agent Malone, he placed himself to the right side of the stand so that he could look left and observe both Malone and the jurors at the same time. This also had the advantage of making Agent Malone shift his eyes one way to see Lou while he asked him a question and then shift them the other way as he gave his answer to the jury. But Malone wouldn't fall for the shifty eyes trick. He fixed his gaze upon the jurors, and there it remained.

"Agent Malone," Lou began, "I believe Mrs. Garcia previously stated that a Mr. Jones made the deposit transactions to the Preston account in San Francisco. Would you happen to know the identity of this Mr. Jones?"

Malone hesitated before answering. "Mr. Jones is the alias of one Terence Scott."

"And how do you know this information?"

"Mr. Scott told me himself, sir."

"I see," said Lou, rubbing the side of his head as if to convey to the jury that from beneath his shiny top, deep thoughts radiated. Malone took a sip of water, and Lou paid strict attention to the steep rise in his Adam's apple when he gulped it down. Obviously the dry throat betrayed hidden anxiety, which could only come from talking to the fugitive mastermind himself.

"So tell me, Agent Malone," Lou continued, "When and where did Terence Scott reveal his secret identity to you?"

"Last week at the Hotel Nacional in Havana, Cuba."

Lou read confusion on the faces of the jurors, and why not? Harry Dixon's examination of Agent Malone not only left Terence and Andrew Scott totally out of the picture, but also made it look like Jack Preston had cooked up this scheme on a whim. Perhaps the jurors needed a dose of clarity, but now was not the time. More confusion needed to be sown so that at the right moment he could reward those good people with insight.

Lou balled his hands into fists and placed one on top of the other as if he were about to cast a fishing line. "Did the subject of transistors ever come up?" he asked.

Malone broke his line of sight with the jury and almost looked back at Lou but caught himself in mid process. "Mr. Scott told me that transistors allowed him to coordinate coast-to-coast banking transactions via telephone to a network of commercial couriers."

"What, then, is a transistor?"

"It's uh…uh, a device that switches electricity on and off. If you switch on a positive charge, it switches on, and if you switch on a negative charge, it switches off."

"So if I turn on a switch, it turns on a second switch. What's the point, Agent Malone? Why not flip the second switch directly?"

Malone's mouth opened, but no words came out. Lou knew he had him stumped on this one. Several jurors and the judge scratched their heads. Other jurors just gave each other blank stares.

"I believe," Malone finally said, "that the switching function is automatic. It has something to do with the charge or something like that."

"Something like what?"

"Uh… I regret that I can't answer your question. This subject is outside my field of expertise."

"Counselors, please approach the bench," Judge Cummings interrupted.

"Mr. Dixon," said the judge, "I confess complete ignorance regarding these so-called transistors. Did you ever discuss the topic in your debriefing sessions with Agent Malone?"

"Not once," Harry replied. "Perhaps I could call Cooper Union and request their top expert to testify."

"His name is Professor Hermann Strom, and he's currently trout fishing in Vermont. He'll be back a week from Wednesday," Lou volunteered.

"So you already spoke to him," said the judge.

"The twenty-dollar tutorial was well worth it," Lou replied.

"Then I say that you have a problem, Mr. Dixon," the judge said adding, "please move on to your next series of questions, Mr. Fisher, while I try to figure out how to remediate this pocket of ignorance."

Harry reached for the packet of smokes in his shirt pocket. "May we have a five-minute break, judge?" he asked.

"Absolutely not. Mr. Fisher didn't interrupt your examination. I expect you to render him the same courtesy."

At that moment, Lou faced Jack, and he rubbed his chin, causing Jack to suck on the eraser end of a pencil. And before Harry could even blink twice, his forehead took on a clammy twinkle.

Lou picked up where he had almost left off. "Agent Malone, what was the nature of the banking transactions that the transistors had facilitated?"

"The transactions concerned monetary transfers between the accounts of various holding companies owned by Mr. Terence Scott as well as transfers into the Security Pacific account, which was registered solely in Mr. Preston's name."

"And did Mr. Scott—also known as Mr. Jones—transfer funds with the assistance of said transistors into the Security Pacific Bank in San Francisco?"

"Yes."

"And did Mr. Scott—also known as Mr. Jones—ever introduce himself to Mr. Preston?"

"No."

"And at any time did Mr. Preston have any control over the said transfers into the Security Pacific Bank?"

"No."

"So I ask you, what laws did Mr. Preston break, Agent Malone?"

Lou waited for the prosecution to object to such a rhetorical question; however, all he could note was Harry fondling his shirt pocket.

"Please answer the question, Agent Malone," Lou requested, his voice now raised a notch.

"The defendant violated the Kennedy laws against insider trading," Malone replied, at which point the judge slammed his gavel as if it were a sledgehammer.

"You are wrong, sir!" Judge Cummings exclaimed. "There are no Kennedy laws. There are the laws of the Securities Exchange Commission and of the United States of America. Joseph P. Kennedy did not formulate those laws; they were formulated by lawyers and passed by Congress. Are you clear about this?"

Lou rubbed his hands together. Malone had taken the bait, and Harry had missed his chance to stop him. Birddog's lustrous sheen suffered a direct hit, and his aura of infallibility plummeted in flames. The prosecution was in retreat.

CHAPTER 66

Dry Accounts

Clancy's Bar on Fourteenth Street was not a place for dilettantes. Along the walls of this well-lit saloon, scores of placards informed the savvy patrons about the shot price of every brand of whiskey from vintage malt to yesterday's rotgut. Somewhere in between these two extremes, the same three-inch, black-on-white letters advertised bargain deals for the blended scotches and ryes that conditioned livers preferred. Tuesday nights produced the slowest foot traffic for the week, which meant that the bartenders had marching orders to issue buybacks on every third drink. And if you were a regular, you could count on your bonus baby after drink number two.

An ensemble of tabloid reporters occupied the rear table, where they groused that better days at the firm of Dunston, Hargrave and Thorpe had come and gone.

"You'll have to buy the next round. My credit is officially void," said reporter number one.

"Hah! My credit tapped out yesterday. Who's the next sucker?" asked number two.

"This stinks!" said a third reporter while contemplating at eye level the clarity of his empty glass. "Ever since the feds collared that Preston guy for rigging stocks, the court put the kibosh on all mergers and acquisitions. Now we've got to live on what the newspapers pay us."

"The guy deserves a shot in the ticker," said number four, his finger thumping his chest to make the point.

"So get even!" urged number one.

"I'm talking fantasy here, not vendetta," said number four.

But then reporter number five had a brainstorm. "Look, guys... Jack Preston's trial is already underway at the Federal Courthouse. Are we not remiss in checking under the rug for dirt if you know what I mean?"

"Yeah!" his colleagues chorused. Meanwhile, number five slapped a dollar on the table. Now there would be enough in the till for a good luck round for all.

CHAPTER 67

Old Acquaintances

Alice glanced at the clock on the kitchen wall. "Please André, I don't have any coffee. The grocery closes in ten minutes," she begged.

André dismissed her with a wave of the hand, and she scurried down the steps from her Back Bay apartment to the grocery around the corner. When she crossed the street, she looked back at her apartment window and spotted André's shadow against the blinds. *Such a stupid man,* she thought. *Did he not know that the entire block could see his ugly figure?*

Several minutes later, she returned with a bag of freshly roasted beans. She spotted nothing but incandescent light coming from her window. After crossing the deserted street, she strode up alongside a black Crestliner and opened the hood. Next, she removed an insulated wire from her purse and fastened one end of the wire to a blind spot of the cable clamp at the negative terminal of the battery. Then, she taped the free end of the wire to the back of the engine block, where it likewise could not be directly seen, and she closed the hood.

"Your hands are dirty," André noted when she had returned to her apartment.

Alice rubbed her fingers together and sniffed them. "Their idea of French roast in this city is charcoal. I had to settle for a Viennese blend," she said.

"Blame it on the Quebeçois influence here. You should wash your hands before you soil something."

Alice turned on the taps in the bathroom, and as she waited for the hot water to rise up, she remarked, "I have nothing of interest to report. The professors at MIT are all on vacation. Do you have any money for me?"

"I am working my hardest for you, Alice. Do not despair."

Such a lying pig! She wanted to take the wet bar of soap that she rubbed across her palms and wash his filthy pig mouth with it. As gushes of soot-stained water swished along the rim of the drain, Alice's hands took on a more peach-colored hue, and she wished that she could give her soul the same treatment. When she heard the front door slam, she knew that the pig did not want to hear any more complaints about money. *Good!*

Alice raced to the door and then down the stairwell, but instead of following André out the front door, she detoured out a side door, which led to a side alley, where under the cover of shadows she observed him look back toward her apartment window. Then, he lit up a smoke, took several drags and proceeded to his car, where he flicked the lit butt into the gutter. Once inside the car, he gave the starter button a soft tickle, but the engine responded only with a slow grind that descended into a full silence, which could only mean a dead battery. A good pounding of his fist against the steering wheel did not bring it back to life, and Alice wondered how his porcine mind in its frustrated state of rage could comprehend why such a mere basin of lead and acid might conk out in the summer heat, especially since the car was only nine months old.

André stepped out of his lifeless car and headed around the corner. Alice, meanwhile, followed as far as the corner building, where she tucked herself snugly against its vertical edifice. She counted to three in French and then peeked around the side to find him passing the grocery, which had just turned its lights out. When he reached the next corner, he looked up at the street signs and then ducked into a phone booth underneath a street lamp. Minutes later, a twin Crestliner pulled up next to the booth, and its driver called out to him.

"André san, why are you always getting yourself into these predicaments?"

André waved to the driver, opened the car door and settled himself into the passenger's seat. The car barreled away, and Alice stepped out of a shadow, where she clutched her chest as if she were having a heart attack. "Colonel Nishimura!" she gasped. "Has the Vichy pig come to lick your boots again?"

Before returning to her apartment, Alice stopped off at André's car to remove her wire from the battery cable. For good measure, she let out the air in the rear passenger tire before heading back to her bathroom to wash the engine soot off her hands again.

CHAPTER 68

Vultures

Lou couldn't keep a poker face. He turned away from the prosecution's table and clasped his hands in front of one shoulder. "We did it!" he exclaimed patting Jack on the back. "You plead guilty to misdemeanor misconduct, and you walk away with a hundred dollar fine plus a letter of reprimand from the State Bar. It's a good deal. Take it."

"But my reputation still leaves here tarnished. You know I'm an innocent man." Jack returned.

"Look, Jack... you're finished on Wall Street. Clean record or not, you'll have to learn to grease the palms of ambulance drivers like the rest of us shysters. I urge you... let it all end here and now."

"And what about the jury?"

Lou bit into his bottom lip and looked over to the twelve empty seats in the jury box. "The jury is confused, and that's good," he explained, "but they could still go either way. I wish I could get them to hear how Terence Scott's son, alias Paul Jeffrey, bamboozled you into opening that Frisco savings account, but that would require putting you on the stand."

"Do it. I'm game."

"And so is Harry Dixon. When he cross-examines you, he'll go straight to a jugular vein named Alice Mercer."

"Then let him give it all he's got. I'm not pleading to a crime I didn't commit."

Lou wished that the wall were within reach so that he could punch it cold, and he vowed to himself that he would never defend another lawyer for as long as he lived. Any other professional would have jumped on the opportunity.

Meanwhile, the bailiff and the stenographer took their assigned places, and a somewhat boisterous party of gaunt individuals in threadbare suits caught Lou's eye as they paraded into the back of the courtroom. "Reporters!" he exclaimed. "Shall I inform them that the county courthouse is across the street?"

Jack turned around, and one member of the group waved to him. "I know those guys; they're my friends," Jack said.

"They're vultures, and don't you ever forget it," Lou returned.

At this point, the jury filed toward their seats. Harry waved at Lou and threw out his hands. "Deal?" he asked silently mouthing the word. Lou merely shook his head and shrugged his shoulders.

"All rise," said the bailiff. Judge Cummings made his entrance, and Lou shut his eyelids so hard that they turned white.

CHAPTER 69

Betrayed

Harry Dixon had rested his case, and all eyes turned to Lou. He attempted to think nice thoughts such as marlin fishing off the Florida Keys, but reality intruded. "We're waiting, counselor," said the judge, adding, "and so too are the members of the Fourth Estate."

"I call as my first witness, Jack Preston," Lou blurted out, his voice strong and commanding. Harry smacked himself on the cheek as if to convey that Lou had lost his mind.

Surprisingly, Jack's testimony prompted silent nods and tilted heads from the jury. "...I considered Paul Jeffrey an outstanding assistant. I would have given him my highest recommendation. How was I to know that the San Francisco bank account was a setup?" Jack stared into space as if in cardiac shock.

"And how did that make you feel?" asked Lou.

"I felt utterly betrayed when I found out that he was Terence Scott's son. I may have been tricked, but so was everybody else in the law firm."

"And did Paul Jeffrey have access to your sensitive files?"

"No. I locked them away in my safe whenever I left the office."

"What kind of safe is in your office?"

"It's a Mosler four by three. I don't know the exact model number, but I can tell you that the firm purchased it new in 1935 when the SEC laws against insider trading went into effect."

Judge Cummings nodded his approval at Jack's response, which made no mention of the Kennedy Laws. Several jurors nodded in return as if to state that that the defendant's testimony had received a judicial seal of approval. Harry's sour apple puss, meanwhile, could have signified that he wanted to kick a curb, a tire or even Mrs. Garcia's lost cat.

"Didn't Willy Sutton once say that cracking a four by three safe was easier than squirting mustard on a hot dog?" Lou said, the last words coming out the side of his mouth.

"Objection," Harry said.

"Sustained," said the judge.

"Your witness," Lou said to Harry.

Harry jumped out of his seat. "Your Honor, may we have a five-minute recess?"

"I thought you'd never ask," the judge replied.

Five minutes later, Harry returned with Agent Malone by his side. "Forget about Malone," Lou advised Jack. "He's here to throw you off your stride. If your mind goes blank or if you start to stutter, reach for a glass of water, and take a long sip. After you swallow, suck in your cheeks, and ask the prosecutor to repeat the question."

"So we're back to one of your smoking tricks."

"Be prepared to hear bad things said about Alice. I would have told you them myself, but it'll be better if the jury sees your gut reaction first-hand... Now go break a leg!"

CHAPTER 70

Tethered

Lou knew that all the objections in the world would not keep Harry from zeroing in on Alice Mercer, and he surmised that if Jack had even a half an ounce of crooked blood in him, he would deny ever telling Alice the names of all those companies in his trust. Let the jury deliberate on the theory that alias Paul Jeffrey really did crack Jack's safe for Daddy's retirement fund, and Jack could keep his innocent victim image intact. But that was precisely the problem. Jack wasn't a hard-boiled swindler of widows and orphans, who could woo a jury with pathological lies delivered with brazen sincerity. Instead, he would tell the truth, the whole truth and nothing but the truth as well as defend his lady's honor even if it meant a ride on a rope hanging from the beam of a gallows.

Lou needed to calm his mind. He closed his eyes and imagined the wind at his back in the Gulf of California. But ahead of him loomed the shoals, and what was this? Jack had taken the wheel, and high on the Rock of Cabo San Lucas, sirens called to him.

"No, you idiot! Come about to port!" Lou screamed.

Lou last remembered a great white leering at him off the starboard bow before he snapped out of his daze. Then, a shark in Harry's clothing bared mud-covered teeth at him and proceeded to the far side of the witness stand where Lou had previously stood when he cross-examined Agent Malone.

"Mr. Preston," Harry began, "You told the court that you did not know that the man who called himself Paul Jeffrey was actually the son of Terence Scott."

Jack turned his head around to answer. "That is correct, sir," he said.

"Did you also know that you were acquainted with Terence Scott's office assistant?"

Jack creased his brow. "Who do you mean?"

Lou scribbled gibberish on his legal pad and pretended that his pencil was a razor blade and that the pad was Jack's tongue. By answering a question with a question, he had allowed the prosecution to enter into the record the name of any person it wanted without any recourse to objection from the defense. Certainly, the defense could challenge the veracity of the prosecution's response, but the name remained—there and forevermore—part of the record. *And what was that name?* Lou gave himself one guess.

"Alice Mercer," Harry answered.

Lou could predict the prosecution's strategy from this point to the end: *Don't ask the defendant point blank about his bedroom revelations. First, confuse him with what you know and with what he doesn't know, and then hit him with a series of emotional challenges that wear down his delusions of love and fidelity from his partner. Finally, get him to inadvertently reveal the truth about his seduction by allowing him to believe that it validated the said love and fidelity that never existed in the first place.* This was a tall order to fill, but despite the prospect of many objections and cigarette breaks to come, Lou knew that Harry Dixon could deliver it gift-wrapped.

The cross examination continued into the late afternoon at which time Harry had exhausted every conceivable question regarding Jack's day-to-day transactions with clients and the SEC. As Harry wound down from this line of inquiry, he threw in a question here and a comment there about Jack's relationship with Alice. Lou objected at almost every turn but was usually overruled when Harry cited Alice as "the crucial link between Mr. Preston and Mr. Terrence Scott." With this change in subject matter, Jack's answers had become accompanied by telltale twitches and blinks, which Harry construed as demons of doubt riding roughshod over a crumbling fantasy world. Harry felt confident he could break the man. *She left you cold at the station, counselor. It's all over but the crying!*

Harry pressed on. "So why won't you admit, Mr. Preston, that Alice Mercer deserted you on the day that you were arrested for insider trading?" he teased.

"Deserted implies that she left me for good. She had to go to Boston."

"Did she leave you a note on where to find her?"

"Not exactly…she left a ticket stub from a Yankees-Red Sox game underneath a bottle of wine in the refrigerator. She was playing a game."

"I see…sort of like playing baseball in the park or one of those games you played in the bedroom?"

"Objection," Lou called out.

"Sustained," said the judge.

"You would never understand," Jack said. "Alice even apologized for one of those games she played when I had passed out from too much wine."

"Your Honor," Lou called out again. "Please instruct Mr. Preston that he does not have to respond to taunts."

"I can not stop the defendant from volunteering information after I sustain your objection. I dare say that Mr. Preston is an officer of the court. He should understand the rules of procedure."

The rhythmic back and forth chatter under the restrictions of courtroom protocol had produced a sense of tedium in the jury. While one juror checked his wristwatch, another one's head bobbed into a sinking nod. Even a couple of reporters could no longer take the monotony; however, when they attempted to leave, their colleagues held up their hands to urge them to persevere. Lou, meanwhile, tapped his pencil against his pad. Despite repeated attempts to conjure up Harry's tobacco cravings, the man pushed on with his grilling. And then Lou noticed a lump in Harry's cheek and remembered that the man had displayed mud-covered teeth when he had commenced the cross-examination. It all made sense now. Lou observed Harry's jaw, and, sure enough, it moved side to side at irregular intervals.

Could it be? Yes it could…the sly devil had immunized himself in the tradition of a starting pitcher on game day.

With Jack's admission of bedroom play, Harry saw his opening. "*In vino veritas*," he said. "Is that not so, Mr. Preston? Alice Mercer gave you wine; you gave her truth, and then after you incoherently mumbled your inside secrets to her, she deserted you."

"Stop saying that she deserted me," Jack protested. "I could have followed her to Boston except that it would have been against advise of counsel."

"Assuming that that's where she went, why hasn't she contacted you yet?"

"She must have her reasons. I refuse to believe that she deserted me."

The stupid fool… The poor-pathetic-stupid-fool… Harry wanted to grab Jack by the shoulders and shake some sense into his thick head, but this kid was beyond all reason, and Harry had lost the urge to bring him down from his castle in the air while Messrs. Scott and Scott danced in a conga line at the Hotel Nacional. *Such a miserable tragedy…* If the boys in Washington had given him the leeway, Harry would have marched the kid into his office and let Agent Malone deliver the unvarnished truth about how Terence Scott had laughed it up over Cuba Libres while dishing the dirt about the real Alice. But Harry didn't have this option, and what's more, he didn't want to burden his conscience if the trauma of this revelation made the kid dive deep into the bottle—or worse yet, dive deep off the Brooklyn

Bridge. Harry decided he would do the next best thing; he would take a dive, himself.

In every cross examination of a defendant, Harry took it as his sworn duty to garner as much testimony as it would take so that any professed or potential alibis became untenable when he snared the guilty party with his ultimate question, which in tribute to all those boxing enthusiasts in the legal profession he called the kayo. The defendants never saw it coming.

"Come now Mr. Preston," Harry said throwing back his shoulder as if to pull a punch, "Miss Mercer's supervisor at the phone company optioned only the corporations that you represented before the SEC. The chain of information about these clients clearly backtracked from him to Miss Mercer to you. So I ask you; was it the wine that made you talk when you woke up?"

Harry expected Jack to say, "But counselor, what about my assistant, Paul Jeffrey nee Andrew Scott? Wouldn't this fugitive son present a more direct link to his fugitive father?"

And Harry would have stammered like a palooka reciting Shakespeare—were that the case. But in this real world of hopeless hope, Jack's eyes had the faraway look of a lovesick teenager, which as far as Harry could tell, had become blind to anybody but sweet Alice.

"I was perfectly coherent when I woke up," Jack replied. "It's just that when I came to, she had me tethered."

Harry glanced sideways to find Lou shading his eyes with one hand and holding his pencil between his teeth with the other. He then looked directly at the bobbing and nodding heads of the jury, and he cracked his knuckles. *Tethered! Does not this assembly of twelve know the titillating significance of the word? Let me make it easy for them.*

"Mr. Preston, please explain to the court what you mean by tethered," Harry inquired.

"You know…she had tied my arms and legs to the bedposts."

The revelation hit the room like a bucket of ice water. Suddenly, the jury snapped out of its collective fatigue, and the members of the press mumbled to one another. Lou maintained a straight face, but Harry knew a bluff when he saw one.

"Were you naked?" Harry asked.

"Objection! Irrelevant!" Lou cried out.

"I'll decide what's irrelevant," the judge returned. "Overruled!"

"While I was unconscious, she removed my clothes," Jack said, his face ashen.

As the jurors and reporters all gasped in unison, Judge Cummings' put on a satanic scowl. Harry turned back again to look at Lou, who bit down on his pencil until it snapped apart in his mouth. After spitting out the pieces, he poured himself a glass of water, but instead of swallowing a mouthful, he regurgitated it back into the glass.

Harry glanced at the wall clock, which read five minutes to five. "At this time, I would like to request an adjournment until tomorrow morning."

"The defense has no objections," Lou said, "however, I would request that Agent Malone, who is still seated in the courtroom, avail himself for further testimony." Lou then handed Harry and the judge an identical list of names. "And I wish to subpoena these witnesses for further testimony," he added.

"So moved," said the judge. "The witness may step down. The courtroom is adjourned until tomorrow at nine A.M."

Harry returned to his table and pulled a sheet of wax paper from his briefcase. After folding the paper down the middle, he spat a wad of fecal-brown crud into the crease and folded it over again before dumping it into an adjacent wastebasket.

"Harry, you ought to see a doctor," Agent Malone said as Jack and Lou made a beeline for the hallway.

Harry waved a pouch of chewing tobacco and said, "My perfect health aside, I plan to keep the kid on the stand all day tomorrow, so don't worry about your availability until Friday."

"It's good you say that because the kid confirmed what I already suspected. Some of my former OSS buddies picked up telephone calls from Boston to Hanoi and back again. Our femme fatale has nested in an apartment near Copley Square."

"Damn it, Mike! You shouldn't be working with spooks. The law says you can't cross pollinate with the CIA in a domestic investigation."

Malone crossed his heart. "CIA! What CIA? My buddies are so top secret, they don't even exist."

"Then make sure they don't get declassified in this courtroom. And good luck in Boston if that's where you're heading tomorrow."

"Would you be kind enough to cadge me a subpoena for the little lady?"

"Not on your dog's life! I don't want this curvaceous pro turning the trial into any more of the farce it's been, and besides, you crossed the line when you went cloak and dagger on me. Just keep your nose clean in Beantown."

"I'm taking Sparks with me."

"Then for his sake, go easy on the tail flippers when you reach cruising altitude. The war ended nine years ago."

By this time, Jack and Lou had just exited the courthouse when a flashbulb lit up their faces. "This isn't a good sign," Lou said. "The last thing we want is visibility."

"I have nothing to hide," Jack said taking the smudged baseball out of his pocket and kissing it. "These people know I'm innocent."

And "pop" went another flashbulb. To Lou, however, the sound reminded him of a boat hitting the rocks. The vultures would have a feast.

CHAPTER 71

Extra Extra

The tabloids made quite a splash Thursday morning; so much so that Harry Dixon bought three copies of each, yet little did he know that Nat Reiss had the very same idea. When Harry arrived at Nat's office, his arms straining from newsprint, Nat ushered him inside, where stacks of each paper already bore down on his desk. The headlines said it all:

> *I WAS HER LOVE SLAVE* read *The Daily News.*
> *SHE STRIPPED ME AND TIED ME UP*
> proclaimed *The Mirror.*

And below each headline was a similar picture of Jack kissing a baseball. Harry put down his papers on the floor, and Nat greeted him with a double-handed shake. "Harry, Harry, Harry! It's a royal flush of head-lines. Dinner for two at the Stork is on me," he gushed.

"Too bad the real crooks are laughing over their rum and Cohibas right now," Harry returned.

Nat wagged his finger. "Misgivings? Do I hear misgivings? Did you not offer the store to the man?"

"You forget about the farm and the firstborn, too," Harry joked.

Nat placed his arm around Harry's shoulder and said ever so softly, "Then listen to reason. You represent the *people* of the United States of America. If Judge Cummings wishes to save the kid's soul with a slap on the wrist, who are we to object? Your job is to get him to stick his foot in deeper and deeper. Think of the fun you'll have reading about yourself in the cover story."

"Lou Fisher keeps wearing me down by playing upon my one and only vice. Would you like to continue the cross-examination?"

Nat broke into a hideous grin, but then he covered his open mouth with a fist. "I wouldn't dream of pulling rank," he said.

"It would give me supreme pleasure to watch an artist such as you play with his food before he devours it. Please, grant me this pleasure?"

Nat rubbed his palms together. "This act of generosity does not go unnoticed, my devious friend. Let us then share your pleasure with the world."

But if the world included Bronxville, one could argue about the pleasures obtained. No sooner had Emily Preston picked up her morning paper than she fainted into the arms of Oliver and Will. Denise picked up the pages scattered across the floor, and when she spotted the front page, she hung her head.

Meanwhile, over at the Faraday household, Judy threw her newspaper on the floor and stomped on it. "Deviant!" she shrieked, realizing that the man in the picture had actually once kissed her.

Back in the city as a crowd of people mobbed the newsstand inside 24 Broadway, Chester Brown nonchalantly grabbed one of few remaining papers to see what the fuss was all about. "Oh, sweet Jesus!" he cried out when he beheld the less than flattering picture of Jack. "Has the world gone crazy?"

CHAPTER 72

Banned in Boston

Agent Malone inserted his penknife into the door lock of apartment 4B and after applying a gentle clockwise twist, he jiggled the key pins with an uncoiled paper clip. Sparks stood in back of him and looked down the stairwell. "Completely deserted," he said.

"Wait until the cartoon shows end at nine, and you'll have dozens of snot nose kids running down the halls playing Cowboys and Indians. With all those Irish names on the mailboxes, I'd say we've got an average of seven people crammed into each apartment."

"And what if Alice shows?"

"No daytime message units have been charged to her telephone since Monday. I believe she has found a regular job."

The last of the pins clicked free, and Malone turned his knife as if it were the key. "The good stuff is always in the bedroom," he said leading the way. "Just remember to leave everything exactly where you found it."

The teak floor chest drew Sparks toward it like a homing beacon. *What impeccable craftsmanship,* he thought as he ran his fingers across the bas relief figures carved into the ivory inlays. "Hey Mike, look at all the naked people on this chest," he said. "They're all twisted and tangled together in some pretty uncomfortable positions."

Malone gave the chest a cursory once over. "That's the Kama Sutra. It comes from an Asian manual on making whoopee."

Sparks opened the chest and memorized the relative positions of the contents before diving in. "I didn't think one needed instructions for that... Oh, look at this... she's got training manuals all right, but they're written in Chinese." He picked up the top book and thumbed through page after page of intertwined lovers in positions requiring flexible bones and rubber joints.

Malone peered over Sparks' shoulder. "That's a Japanese Shunga book. I believe this one is called *Temple of the White Tigress.* It's not for novices," he said.

Sparks sat down on the bed and flipped through more pages. "So where can I buy this book in English?"

"Sorry, but it's banned in Boston. Try one of those leftist stores that the Bureau fronts in the Village."

Malone's eyes drifted toward the far wall, where Alice's painting of the old quarter in Hanoi hung. "Such a worldly girl," he remarked before proceeding to rummage in a stepwise fashion through her top drawer.

"Bingo! We've come to the right place!" he exclaimed as he handed Sparks a strip of vending booth photographs showing Alice and Jack posed together with a baseball bat. But Sparks had become obsessed with the contents of the floor chest, which included a paddle, a bottle of hot-sauce, a loaded syringe, plenty of rope and finally a strange looking dildo with a ribbed shaft. Attached to the blunt end was a chain from which hung several barbell weights.

"What the hell is this?" he said showing his find to Malone.

"Hah! That's a Bangkok Banger, a Shanghai Slugger, a Yokohama Yoyo!"

"Thanks for the geography lesson.... what does it do?"

Malone stroked the shaft and sniffed his fingers. "First, a girl puts weights on the end of the chain, and then she shoves the hot end between her pearly gates. Finally, she does knee bends, hip gyrations and pelvic thrusts, and when she can dead lift twenty pounds with her slot machine, she's ready to turn your sausage into a string bean."

Sparks curled the device with one arm. "Damn!" he gasped. "She's got at least thirty on this contraption. What does that tell you?"

"Only kryptonite can stop her!"

Malone glanced at the clock on the dresser, which read five minutes to nine, and he placed the photograph of Jack and Alice back inside the drawer. "C'mon, Tom, We've seen enough. Time to snow-job some judge into signing a search warrant."

"But what's the point?" Sparks countered. "Harry Dixon doesn't want the lady's testimony, and you and I both agree that Jack Preston is a poor consolation prize in this whole investigation. Can't we just loosen her tongue with a few Cuba Libres?"

"When a flesh dancer with the moves of a trained spy lands in your lap, you know she's the perfect bait to hook bigger fish. We've got to stake first claim on Miss Mercer before that queer, J. Edgar Hoover, gets his hooks into her."

Sparks shut the lid to the teak chest. "If you keep calling the director that name, we're both going to wind up guarding exotic dignitaries who smell like Bowery bums in July. Cut it out!"

Malone pointed toward the door, and he and Sparks bounded out of the apartment. When the two reached the ground floor lobby, the sound of doors opening and noisy kids coming out for high jinks put a smirk on Malone's face. "Perfect timing," he remarked.

CHAPTER 73

The Circus Comes to Town

The bailiff opened the courtroom doors, and the huddled masses stampeded in like cattle. A marshal stood guard over the first two rows and allowed only members of the press access to those choicest of seats. Meanwhile, the *hoi polloi* scrambled for seats in what might have been called the hottest ticket in town. The weatherman had predicted a scorcher for the day, and yet willing spectators one and all crammed into the seats, a veritable carnival of misbegotten souls including a couple of prostitutes in fishnet stockings, some pock-faced johns with oily hair and beanpole physiques, a jowly fat man with a silly grin that came and went, a craggy-cheeked reverend with a Bible in his hand, some elderly ladies armed with their needlepoint and twelve-inch needles and everybody else, minus the jugglers and clowns. When the bailiff realized that a sardine tin might offer better refuge for space, he closed the courtroom doors, much to the groans of disappointment of the hundreds of folks outside who had not made the cut.

The temperature in the courtroom climbed from tolerable to intense, and Jack started to loosen his tie. Lou pushed Jack's hand down and shook his head. Appearances would count in Judge Cummings' courtroom, but apparently nobody in back of the bar ever received that instruction. As Jack scanned the cacophonous gallery behind him, a hundred hands waving the morning dailies against the soggy air resembled a flock of motley butterflies from an island of giants. A reporter in the front row flashed him a circled thumb and forefinger, and Jack returned the salutation with a lopsided smirk.

"Hear ye... hear ye... All rise... The court of the United States of America in the southern district of New York is now in session. The United States of America verses Jack Preston. Judge Harley Cummings presiding," the bailiff shouted, but amidst the din, nobody heard a word.

Judge Cummings took his place and went right to business with his gavel. "Order! Order in the court!"

So as to impress upon everybody the meaning of those words, marshals paced the gallery and shouted, "Quiet!" Those who didn't comply received a swift escort out the back doors. At last, the courtroom took on a more suitable decorum.

"Does the U.S. Attorney offer to redirect?" the judge asked.

"No, your Honor," Harry replied. "We wish to continue cross-examination. I request to bring in special counsel, Nathan Reiss."

"Uh oh... here comes the Hiroshima wrecking crew!" Lou whispered to Jack.

"I can handle him. Remember... I'm an attorney, too."

"Stop thinking logically. This isn't finance; it's theater! So far, your reporter friends have you pegged as a sex fiend. Redeem yourself!"

"I'll show 'em!"

When Jack took the witness stand, the clock on the wall read nine-thirty, and the bulb sign on the Chemical Bank down the block read eighty-one degrees. Both readings were destined to change.

CHAPTER 74

Sunny Jim

Agent Malone handed his affidavit in cursive script to the secretary, who according to the nameplate on her desk was one Agnes Murphy, and who, according to the family pictures next to her typewriter, was a mother of six and a grandmother of four. As he and Sparks retreated to the water cooler for respite from the Havana-like weather, Mrs. Murphy's fingers rattled across the keyboard of her mechanical Underwood at such blinding speed that she had finished the transcript before the two agents had taken their second gulp. When Sparks retrieved the typed copy, he noted that it had neither legal headings nor signature lines at the bottom.

"Does the First District here use a different protocol for this document than what we use in New York?" he asked.

"Let's leave out the legal niceties for now. Judge Curran will insist on making stylistic changes so that the warrant doesn't get suppressed in any future proceedings."

Murphy...Curran.... Such fine Hibernian names, thought Malone. He knew that if he picked up the Boston phone book, it would read like one from Dublin or Galway with a few stray names like Bernstein or Lombardo tossed in for good measure. God bless this place! Yes, this would be an easy sell. First, tell Judge Curran a few anecdotes about the most recent stock swindle on the Street and then mention a few colorful characters in the mix, especially those with Irish surnames. For courtesy's sake, let the man chat about his beloved Red Sox, and while he makes whatever corrections to the affidavit he deems necessary, secure his goodwill by telling him that the great Ted Williams will go to the Hall of Fame on the first ballot. Finally, let Mrs. Murphy attack the typewriter with her knobby fingers, and walk out of here with an instant search warrant, not to mention the extremely talented Alice Mercer firmly ensconced in the back pocket of Uncle Sam's treasury cops.

The intercom buzzed. "It's a glorious day when we have two fine agents from New York come to visit our little city. Send them right in, Agnes," said the voice with a brogue as thick as shepherd's pie.

Mrs. Murphy led Malone and Sparks down the hall, and Judge Curran defied all formalities by waiting for them outside the doorway to his chambers. "Do come in, Michael and Thomas," he said greeting them with sturdy slaps on the backs; his elfin face alight, his eyes sparkling. "Judge James Patrick Curran at your service."

James... Malone considered the name for a moment but refused to believe that anybody so animated would remain attached to an appellation equivalent to a slice of white bread. Sure, the 1926 Boston College and 1929 Harvard Law degrees on the walls said "James", but this guy had to be a Jim or better yet a Jimmy. Malone's experience taught him that trophies and plaques of appreciation given at moments of light-hearted celebration often revealed the true name earned by years of enduring friendship, and so his eyes gravitated to the proclamation hanging beneath the picture of Senator John F. Kennedy on the right hand wall.

> *...And in appreciation for his twenty years service*
> *on the Boston City Council, The Governor and Legislature*
> *of the COMMONWEALTH OF MASSACHUSETTS*
> *declare this day*
> *James - Sunny Jim - Curran Day.*

Now then, Sunny Jim was more like it! Malone pictured the man smooching babies in the election campaign and belting out a sudsy rendition of *Sweet Adeline* for his constituents in the taverns and chowder houses. He'd regale them with a joke and warm the cockles of their hearts with stories of the old sod even though his youthful mop of black hair and the dates on his diplomas gave fair indication that he had emigrated with his parents from the Emerald Isle in his early teenage years.

Mrs. Murphy laid the draft of the affidavit and a small train of yellow papers with perforations on both sides on Sunny Jim's blotter pad. "Service for three, Agnes," Sunny Jim requested, and she scooted out the door, leaving it open.

Malone made an attempt to close it, but Sunny Jim cut him off. "That's all right, Michael. Mrs. Murphy will return with our lemonade. Besides, nobody is here but us mice. The whole kit and caboodle of government employees packed their bags for either the Cape, the mountains or the rocky shore. Even the post office downstairs is working with a skeleton crew, minus a few bones of course."

Malone offered a feeble nod. Already Sunny Jim was on a first name basis with him, and he liked to talk, which shouldn't have come as a surprise given his credentials of Boston Irish politician. "Uh, the reason we brought this matter to your attention, sir—" Malone said, but he went no further because Sunny Jim waved his hand.

"—Oh Michael, do I detect a trace of South Boston in your voice?"

"I'm originally from Roxbury, sir." Malone replied now resigned to the fact that Sunny Jim was a raconteur, who would steer the conversation where he willed, and only a fool would dare wrest the tiller from him.

"You sly devil! And what's your middle name?"

"It's Timothy, sir, but I would prefer that you didn't address me as Michael Timothy."

"Ah, but did the good Sisters at St. Patrick's call you that?"

"Only when they were about to caress my knuckles with the brass ruler."

Sunny Jim slapped his desk and let out a guffaw that echoed down the hallway and registered somewhere on the Richter scale. "Hah… such wit Michael! The saints be praised!"

Sunny Jim first looked over the writings on the perforated paper, which Malone now recognized as the product spun out from a Teletype machine. Then he gave the affidavit a once-over just in time for Mrs. Murphy to bring in a tray carrying three iced glasses of lemonade plus another train of Teletype paper. When she left this time, she closed the door behind her.

"To the gallant guardians of Wall Street," toasted Sunny Jim to clinked glasses.

A silence followed, and Malone used it to get back on track. "So what do you think of the affidavit, Judge?" he asked.

"It's a fine piece of writing. You have the knack of a bard…. Yes you do, Michael. Did your father's family come from County Westmeath?"

Malone knew it was hopeless. With nobody to talk to but Mrs. Murphy and the janitors, this former politician was starved for an audience and would even make small talk with a scarecrow until real people arrived back for work after the Labor Day weekend. "Yes sir, Westmeath is the ancestral home of the Malones. My mother, however, is a McCarthy—"

"—Of course she is!" Sunny Jim interrupted. "I had a sixth sense that you might have a tinge of County Cork in you. Did you ever kiss the Blarney Stone there, Michael?"

Malone's own sixth sense told him that Sunny Jim was playing him like a Sligo fiddle. "I've never been to Ireland, sir… Perhaps in retirement," he replied.

A brief silence returned as Sunny Jim dug into the second ream of Teletype. Malone opened his mouth to interject a word or two about the real business at hand, but then took another sip of lemonade.

"It's heavenly lemonade, isn't it, Michael? Mrs. Murphy won't reveal her secret formula, but I have my spies at work." Sunny Jim poured over the Teletype pages and flipped them back and forth as if they were study material. Malone, meanwhile, wished that he would stop saying "Michael" at every turn of address.

Sparks craned his neck at the Teletype paper. "Is there something hot off the wire, sir?" he asked.

Sunny Jim dropped the ream into a wastebasket. "It goes like this, Tommy," he replied. "The AP and Reuters Teletype machines down the hall keep chattering back and forth like two biddies at an afternoon tea. What concerns me is that according to the wire services, this Alice Mercer, whom you wish to serve, features very prominently in the testimony at a Foley Square trial that you never mentioned in your affidavit. I presume that you can pull a subpoena signed by Judge Cummings out of your back pocket."

"Heck, Judge, we left without thinking about—"

"—You can dispense with the royal 'we', Tommy," the judge interrupted, his sunny temperament now becoming a wee bit dark and stormy. "You left without thinking, but your mentor here should have known better, especially since this case will assuredly grace the front pages of every evening daily in Boston by rush hour."

"Look, Judge," Malone said, "We don't want to arrest Miss Mercer, and we don't even need her testimony for trial."

"Then what do you plan to do? Drag her to confession, and tell her to say three Hail Marys!"

"We want to question her and find out her relationship with the stock swindlers, Terence and Andrew Scott."

"And for that you need a warrant? Something tells me that you already searched her place, but I won't ask. As for the affidavit, I find it quite creative. You should publish it in *True Crime*. You truly do have the knack of a bard, Michael Timothy."

Sunny Jim handed Malone his affidavit back, and Malone in turn pitched it into the litter basket when he and Sparks reached the pavement. They wandered around downtown for a while without saying a word, and then Sparks pointed in the general direction of Alice's apartment.

"Let's go stake her place out," he said.

But Malone preferred to ruminate. "I blew this operation, and the judge rubbed my nose in it. Let's just find a seafood shanty and order up clams and lobsters."

"A blown warrant can't stop public surveillance. I say that after lunch, we wait outside the door for our little princess."

"And I say you set your snare on your own time. Either we go through channels or we just go. I'm not risking my pension on this one."

"Then I'll see her alone. What will you do?"

"My eighty-year-old mother awaits on her rocking chair. Just make sure that you're back at the airport by seven, or you'll have to hitch a ride home on a mail carrier."

The two walked over to the Quincy Market and found a mom and pop establishment to their liking. When a dozen cherry stones landed on the table, Malone splashed on the hot-sauce.

"Look, only two peppers on the label," Sparks said pointing to the bottle. "I found a four-pepper brew inside Miss Mercer's hope chest. Why would she store it in the bedroom instead of the kitchen?"

"Because Indochinese courtesans rub the four-alarm stuff on their nipples to make them puff up and tingle," Malone replied in a disinterested drone. He held a clam to his lips and sucked the meat right off the shell. His taste buds ignited with pleasure.

"But wouldn't the sauce burn the lips if a man were to... you know... place his mouth on her... on her... you know..."

Malone pounded his hand broadside against the table. "Damn it Tommy! I believe the word you want is 'breast'!" he said almost spitting out the clam. "Are you sure you can handle Miss Mercer without choking on your tongue first?"

"I'll let her do the talking. Besides, I know that she hides her knockout drops in a syringe next to the hot-sauce. I'll have the upper hand as long as I keep her away from that toy box."

"Then stay out of the bedroom too!"

Back in the courthouse, Mrs. Murphy fished Agent Malone's original hand-written affidavit out of her wastebasket and picked up the telephone. "Hello, Bernadette, this is Agnes at the Post Office Court House," she said. "Please connect me to Chief Superintendent Fallon. I have an item of interest to the vice squad."

She reached across her desk for a telephone directory, but instead, she beheld Sunny Jim rubbing his forefingers together. "Shame on you, Agnes Elizabeth," he said adding, "and tell that piker, Fallon, that your item of interest merits *two* wallet size engravings of Old Hickory."

Sunny Jim raised a glass of lemonade in a mock toast and departed. As Mrs. Murphy waited with her shoulder wedging the phone to her ear, she paged through the directory until her index finger came to rest at the direct number to the city desk of the *Boston Post*. It had been previously circled in pencil. This time, she added a star.

CHAPTER 75

Panties

The bulb sign at the downtown Chemical Bank read ninety-two degrees; however, with all of the warm bodies crammed together in the courtroom, the temperature made it into triple digits in the shade. Judge Cummings, however, appeared cool and crisp in billowy robes made all the more puffy by a floor fan blowing a stiff breeze up his legs. For the prosecution, pitchers of ice water and tissue paper for the sweaty brow provided a modicum of relief while for Lou Fisher, mere ice water sufficed. Pity then all those sweaty souls in the gallery, who made do with paddling the air and panting like canines. Would they have traded places with the hundreds of folk waiting outside for a vacant seat? How about this—the courtroom clock now read two-thirty, and not one derrière had voluntarily vacated a seat except to sprint the short round trip to the bathroom.

The newspaper people, who had witnessed many a star trial at the county courthouse over the years, kept the heat in check by utilizing a relay system in which they pooled their stenographers. At every third page of shorthand, either a stenographer or a reporter would rush the transcript to an air conditioned office across Foley Square, where AP and Reuters Teletype operators would wire the copy to Teletype machines all over the world. After several minutes of rest and recuperation via ice-cold drinks, the newspaper employees returned to their reserved seats in the courtroom to wait their turn to become messengers again.

If only Jack Preston were so lucky. For the trial, he had planned on wearing a cotton suit, but Lou warned him that such wrinkly threads ran counter to Judge Cummings' sense of decorum, meaning that one had to dress in more appropriate attire. This Jack did, and after his worsted suit absorbed every ounce of perspiration secreted from his neck on down, his body heat became trapped in an impermeable wrap. Effectively, the only locations where he could radiate his excess energy were from his head and palms, which both looked like they had bathed in an oil slick.

Now, with four hours of testimony and a one-hour lunch break under his belt, Jack had the seedy and worn out look of a two-bit punk. He wished he could tear off his itchy suit and frolic in front of a gushing hydrant. Instead, he had to repeatedly endure questions and badgering about that night... that night! Jack felt queasy. *Why didn't the U.S. attorney pursue this line of questioning in the morning when the room was merely hot? It wasn't fair.*

"You have me confused, Mr. Preston," Nat said. "You could have screamed for help at any time, but you didn't. Did Miss Mercer gag you?"

"No," Jack returned.

"Of course not... you merely thought your fiancée was still playing games. You liked being tied up."

"Objection!" Lou called out.

"Sustained! Strike that last remark from the record," the judge ordered.

"So was it the ice torture that made you reveal the confidential information?" Nat said.

"No, it wasn't the ice."

"So you just spilled your guts without any prodding at all."

"The ice weakened me. It threw me off."

"You're evading the question, Mr. Preston! Did Alice Mercer do something further or nothing further to extract confidential information from you?"

Jack took a sip of water, and he realized that in his exhausted state he had indirectly affirmed to the court that he had broken client confidentiality and the law to boot. This revelation must have occurred to the jury as well because they leaned forward with such perfect synchrony that they could have sculled a boat. Jack's eyes wandered around the room, and he spotted Nat winking to Harry with the one eye that the jury couldn't see. In reply, Harry mouthed the word, "Knockdown." Jack then turned to Lou, who closed his eyes and fiddled with his pencil while from the third row, a prostitute blew a kiss. As Jack established eye contact with her, she held up a pair of handcuffs and fondled them. Jack gulped down his water and looked away.

"Please answer the question, Mr. Preston," Nat said. "Shall I repeat it?"

"Alice did something further," Jack replied.

"And what was that?"

"Kayo," Jack read from Harry's lips, but the only sound anybody could hear was the hum of the fan blowing air up the judge's robe. White knuckles clenched the edges of the seats, and Jack beheld every eye in the room riveted squarely upon the taut line between his lips.

"She uh... she uh..." Jack couldn't get the words out.

"Yes, Mr. Preston." Nat said.

"Alice rubbed her panties in my face."

The entire room gasped in one synchronized breath. An elderly woman held her hand to her gaping mouth. The fat guy grinned, and one of the johns started rubbing himself on the leg. Meanwhile, Lou pushed his pencil into his pad, where it promptly snapped. Adding to the din, side conversations between the spectators in the gallery could have made the place match decibel readings with Grand Central Station during rush hour.

"Order!!! Order in the court!!!" the judge screamed, but with all the clamor, his voice barely carried to the third row.

Then, the reverend arose and with outstretched hand, he waved his bible. "Verily, it is written… the wages of sin are death!!!" he cried out to high, holy heaven.

"Cast that miscreant out onto the streets!" the judge ordered, and two marshals seized him in a double hammerlock.

But he did not go quietly. "Behold! The weapons of our warfare are not carnal, but are mighty through God—*Corinthians Two, chapter ten, verse four*!" he screamed.

When the threesome reached the hallway, flashbulbs went off like Chinese New Year. Meanwhile back in the courtroom, Judge Cummings kept banging his gavel until it popped out of his limp hand. Such was the majesty of the District Court for the United States of America.

CHAPTER 76

The Black Market

Alice had never seen anything like it before. When she emerged from the subway, a mob of people crowded around the newsstand but could not gain access to the papers because a human chain comprised of a priest, a vicar, and several gray haired women in black dresses from a prior century blocked the way. From all directions, church bells pealed in groups of three and police sirens blared. Alice attempted to avoid the newsstand by walking in back of it, but this put her on the blacktop just as a police cruiser pulled up. A sergeant stepped out of the passenger side and blew his police whistle in three short blasts at which point the newsvendor tossed his afternoon dailies into the back seat. The sergeant shook the vendor's hand, and Alice spotted a greenback passing from cop to citizen. What was this she wondered…reverse bribery? Then she caught a glimpse of the banner headline.

ALICE RUBBED HER PANTIES IN MY FACE

Alice had a bad sense of déjà vu about this, and she wanted one of the newspapers, but the reaction of the crowd told her that none could be had. "Damn Sin Squad," taunted one onlooker. "There they go again, crushing the free press."

"We are saving your souls from eternal damnation," replied the vicar. "One day, you will thank us in glory."

Who was this Alice in the headline? Alice had to know, and only that newspaper could tell her. But how could she get a copy? Perhaps a time-tested technique might work. Alice pulled a five-dollar bill out of her purse and offered it to the young officer in the driver's seat. "Not here, miss," he said. "Go to Public Alley 439 near Copley Square, and pay with one single exactly, or you won't get change."

Alice soon discovered what the man had meant. A cop stood sentry at a service ramp in the middle of the alley, where pedestrian traffic rivaled that of Commonwealth Avenue on Patriots' Day. At the blind end of the ramp, people lined up behind a locked box, and each person deposited a dollar in the top slot before proceeding to several stacks of newspapers, which were placed headline side down on the pavement. After making the deposit, the "customer" would then pick up a newspaper and fold it under the arm so that the headline could not be seen.

One bow-tied gent in a chauffeur's cap held up two singles, but a voice from a shadow gave a stern reprimand. "Only one to a customer, Mac! Keep the line moving."

Alice cast her eyes toward the shadowy figure and noted that he wore his fedora tipped almost completely over his forehead. Oversized sunglasses blocked out his eyes, and a toothpick shifting to and fro across his incisors kept his mouth moving in a nibbling fashion, which made the bottom of his face hard to discern. A snub-nosed thirty-eight packed into a shoulder holster meant that this fellow could have been either a cop or a hood; however, when Alice spotted white socks gleaming beneath shrunken trousers, she knew he was one of the good guys.

The alley had its own ground rules, and Alice realized that nobody in the line talked to each other, nor did they establish any kind of eye contact. After picking up your newspaper, you were expected to leave as anonymously as you had entered. The whole ritual reminded her of the black market in Hanoi, where you could buy smuggled jade and rubies as well as a ten-gram slab of opium—all under police protection of course.

Alice tucked her newspaper away in appropriate fashion and trotted in double time to her apartment, where she fully expected to read about some bored couple, who had decided to spice up their lives with unconventional playtime, only to get collared by the local vice squad. What she got, however, when she settled into her living room couch and read the details, was a blow-by-blow description of her affair with Jack topped off by a nutshell description of his arrest and trial for inside trading of companies, the names of which she had extracted from him in the bedroom.

"Oh my God, what have I done?" she shrieked and then ran to the toilet to empty herself of her lunch. She looked in the bathroom mirror and threw a hairbrush at it, shattering the glass to pieces. "Pig! Tramp! Whore!" she screamed in English, French, Vietnamese and Japanese, all the while smacking herself in the face with both hands.

Finally composing herself, she said to herself, "Think, Alice, think. Do not let the crisis overwhelm you." And then she ran to the kitchen, where she pulled a working bottle of Chablis from the refrigerator and guzzled hard causing bubbles to rise up the glass.

With bottle in hand, she proceeded to the bedroom, where her bedspread displayed a prominent indentation on the side over by her floor chest. Close inspection revealed that somebody had poked around inside the chest. *But who could that somebody be?* Alice pushed against the adjacent wall, and a hidden panel swung open to reveal a tape recorder in which the counter had advanced to a reading of "zero-two-eight." Alice hit the rewind button, and when the counter reached triple zeros, she hit stop, then play and took another swig of Chablis.

Meanwhile, the bow-tied chauffeur had pulled up to the curb in front of the New England Telephone Building and awaited his passenger. Moments later, the back door opened, and Joe Kennedy took his seat next to the evening newspaper. "Where to, sir?" asked the driver with a pleasant Dublin Brogue.

"Home, Eamon," Joe responded, adding, "I see that you placed my newspaper face down. What lovely headline does that portend?"

CHAPTER 77

Tartar Sauce

The day's courtroom proceedings could at last be put to rest as an unpleasant memory, and Jack and Lou exited the courthouse through a gauntlet of reporters and popping flashbulbs. The reporters had only one thing on their mind.

"Jack…Jack…did Alice make you wear her panties?" screamed one faceless voice coming from behind a battalion of photographers.

"Jack! Jack! What did her panties taste like?" asked a front and center reporter with a press card jutting out of his hatband.

"They could have used some tartar sauce!" Jack replied.

Jack and Lou descended into the back seat of an awaiting car, and Lou closed the door to blissful silence. "That was smart!" he said as the car pulled away.

Jack's lips curled upward on one side. "I had to answer him with something so absurd that nobody would dare print it."

Lou turned away. He detested that half smile worse than running aground on a sand bar with the tide going down.

CHAPTER 78

Back Bay Bedlam

Sparks had second thoughts. This wasn't official business. It was voyeuristic curiosity at best and official misconduct at worst. He turned to leave but then reconsidered his reconsideration with the understanding that he had admired her from the distance during his stakeout detail in the Village. So why not get an up-close glimpse and maybe some useful information to boot, especially since he was already standing in front of her doorway?

Sparks knocked, and Alice opened the door at a turtle's pace, revealing herself bit by luscious bit from behind the receding door. Sparks' eyes moved up and down in elevator fashion to behold everything from her buffed toenails to her mane of auburn hair draped over a luxurious kimono, which revealed only so much leg and so much bosom as to make a man want to beg, roll over and play dead for just an itty bitty peek at some more.

Sparks held up his badge. "Alice Mercer, or whatever your name really is, I'm Agent Thomas Sparks of the U.S. Treasury."

Alice licked her top lip and then puckered both of them. "And such a handsome devil you are, Agent Tom! What are you? Twenty-three? Twenty-four? And where's your wedding ring? I bet you're still a virgin."

Sparks took a half step back, but Alice grabbed him by the tie and put her face to his. The flicker... the whip action... and the reptilian flutter stormed into his mouth like Sherman's army, and before he could even catch a second breath, Alice spun him around into her apartment and slammed the door behind them.

"You can't seduce me!" Sparks said.

Like hell she couldn't! Alice ran the dagger edges of her nails up and down his back, his neck and his arms, and he felt nibbling pinches on his exposed flesh.

"I'm not one of those lead-lipped icebergs that teased you in college or a birthday bash stripper with limp loins that move like a squid. My body is alive, Tom,'" she taunted. Sparks backed away until his back was to the door.

Alice fondled her breast and moved in for the kill. "I won't bite you, Tom. I'm the dream girl who is about to give you the joyride of a lifetime... You want me Tom, and don't say you don't."

Did he ever!

Alice thrust her torso into his arms, and Sparks made a feeble attempt to push her away, but she nimbly moved his hands onto her breasts and commenced lashing and stabbing his neck with her tongue, which caused his manhood to swell into a log. Her pinching fingernails dispensed morsels of pain; however, this pain only added to the pleasure…that is until a particularly sharp jab caught Sparks in the back of the neck.

"Ouch! Your nails should be registered as weapons," he said.

"Step into my lair, Agent Tom, and you will discover the first two rooms in the temple of the white tigress."

Ah yes, the white tigress! On this very day, Sparks had become aware of the niceties of the white tigress and that peculiar device called a Yokohama Yo-Yo, which fortified the palace walls. And now this luscious beauty had offered him a guided tour. Could he resist the invitation?

Alice led Sparks into her bedroom, and he removed his suit jacket and shoulder holster. For added protection, he spun the bullets out of the cylinder and dropped them into the jacket pocket. Then he placed the jacket on top of the floor chest, where it would hinder any attempt to retrieve the contents inside. Alice did the rest, slowly unfastening his tie, his shirt and his trousers while softly caressing the most sensitive parts of his neck, his underarms and his loins.

"So where is the first room in the temple?" he asked with one eye glancing at the floor chest.

Alice laughed, but it seemed to Sparks that her laugh wasn't synchronized with her lips. And then her face became blurry… and then everything went black…

Sparks woke up nude to find every major joint in his supine body bound within a latticework of intricate rope patterns meandering across the entire bed frame from bedpost to bedpost. Still wearing her kimono, Alice brandished a steak knife in her right hand. "Scream for help, and I'll feed you your testicles. Kryptonite won't save you now," she said.

Sparks struggled against the ropes but only succeeded in chafing his wrists. And then he remembered that kryptonite was a word first uttered in this room by Malone. "Kryptonite! You wired this place!"

Alice held the knife up, but with the blade pointing down. "Shut up!" she said. "And don't move unless you want to explain to your superiors how you got rope burns."

Sparks settled down, and Alice lowered the knife. "You couldn't possibly understand how much I want to plunge this blade into your heart, assuming you have one. Jack Preston is a good man, a decent man, and you people are trying to destroy his life."

"I treated him square... ask him! It's those damn reporters who blew this nightmare out of proportion, but look in a mirror to see who set him up."

Tears rained down Alice's cheeks. "We made love, and you people turned it into a sick joke. I hate you! All of you!" she sobbed.

Sparks was unmoved. "The room wire makes sense to me now," he said. "What regime trained you in industrial espionage and the bedroom hula?"

"Let's just say my country is a proud but bankrupt NATO ally and that my civil servant's salary lasts three weeks of the month here. A girl has to moonlight if she wants to eat... Right, Mr. Underpaid-Government-Official?"

"I will still track you down..." And then Sparks added for emphasis, "...mademoiselle."

"Oh, really?" Alice dropped her kimono to reveal her black brassiere and panties. Next, she pulled a tripod-mounted camera with a shutter wire from out of her closet and then removed the belt from Sparks' trousers. After coiling the belt so that it resembled a whip, she sat on top of Sparks' spread eagle body and held the belt to his face. She assumed a menacing grimace and then clicked off a quick succession of humiliating snapshots with the shutter wire. For the finale, she rubbed lace panties in his face and tickled him until he burst out laughing. Three clicks of the shutter followed, and that was it for the thirty-two-frame roll.

"If you ever come after me," she threatened, "I swear you'll find these pictures on the front page of every tabloid in New York. Know too that after I ruin you, your State Department will send me home with a first class ticket." Alice pulled a loaded syringe from her floor chest and squirted a short stream straight up.

"What the hell is that?" Sparks shrieked.

Alice plunged the syringe into Sparks' outstretched arm. "Bon soir, Tom!" she said, and then she rummaged around the room to pack up her belongings into two suitcases even as he still lay there conscious.

Both suitcases sat squat on the floor, their sides bulging from an overstuffed inventory of clothes, toiletries, the camera, two paper bags of transistors and an eclectic collection of papers including a passport, reams of modeling photos and assorted reports on transistor doping. That accounted for everything worth taking, but Alice just knew she had forgotten something of equal worth. Sparks had finally drifted into oblivion, and Alice untied the master knot, which released an interlocking series of loops harnessing his upper body to the bed. After taking a quick hit from the bottle of Chablis, she hastened toward the door only to find that most detestable of swine species blocking her path.

"Who is that man there?" André demanded, pointing to Sparks.

"He's an American agent, and he knows all about your dealings with Hiroshi Nishimura."

"Lies!" André slapped her across the face and jammed the headlines of the evening paper into her eyes. "Your escapades with the Wall Street crowd have captured the nation. Congratulations, my little whore!"

Alice grabbed the newspaper, and pretending that she hadn't read it before, buried her eyes in the copy. Slowly, she worked her way toward the floor chest, and when she reached it, she pulled out a loaded syringe, but André saw it coming.

"I know your tricks, whore!" he said, grabbing the syringe.

"Ah, but do you know them all?" she said as she slammed the bottle of Chablis against his temple. André bounced unconscious off the bedspread and hit the floor.

For road insurance, Alice jammed the syringe of thiopental into André's neck. She then grabbed a length of rope from the bed and hogtied him. Suddenly realizing what she had forgotten, she reopened the hidden compartment housing the reel-to-reel recorder. She rewound the tape until it spun free and shoehorned it into her suitcase.

"Mr. Pig, you owe me two-thousand dollars. I shall take my first down payment today," she said to André's limp frame. She picked through his wallet and found a cool six hundred and forty dollars in the billfold. "Lies! Who tells the biggest ones now?" she asked, neither expecting nor wishing an answer.

The street beckoned, and this time Alice made it. "Logan airport...take me to Eastern Airlines and step on it!" she said to a passing cabby. Screeching rubber met the road.

The percussive thump of a ransacked drawer hitting the floor rousted Agent Sparks from his unplanned nap, and before he could shake the drug effects from his cranium, he covered his eyes with a pillow to shield them from a harsh glare filling the room. Voices hollered from all directions.

"Where'd she go?" asked one.

"Who are these two creeps?" asked another.

"Hah, the rope lady strikes again!" said a third.

Sparks' eyes adjusted to the ambient light, and the cold reality dawned on him that these dozen or so guys crashing the bedroom were Boston police. "What in blazes are you guys up to?" he said.

"We've got a search warrant, Bub. Is this your revolver?" asked a uniformed cop with captain's bars on each shoulder.

Sparks looked toward the window, which faced the street. Klieg lights shining from the street below cast everybody's shadows onto the ceiling, and judging by the commotion coming through the screens, there could have been twenty, fifty or even a hundred cops outside. "I'm a federal agent," he said. "Who were you expecting up here—Cagney and Bogart?"

André began to stir. "My head, my head... I'm in pain... Where am I?" he groaned.

"Hah! The old amnesia game, huh? Do you expect me to buy that?" the captain asked.

"No, Skipper, this guy is legitimate. Somebody cracked his skull. He needs stitches," replied a plainclothesman with fresh blood on his fingers.

"Then untie him, and get the first aid kit. Call Doc Fleming, and have him meet us at the precinct. Nobody leaves my sight."

Meanwhile, at Logan Airport, Agent Malone checked his watch. He had waited an extra half hour for his partner as a courtesy, and that was all he would get. The daylight was gone, and all Malone could think of when he hit the magneto switches on his aircraft was how Lou Fisher might pummel him again on the witness stand tomorrow.

On the opposite side of the tarmac, Alice buckled her seatbelt inside a spanking new L-1049 Super Constellation. "Welcome to Eastern Airlines Flight Four to New York's LaGuardia Airport," greeted the captain on the intercom.

Since leaving the apartment, Alice had an uncertain feeling that she had forgotten something else, but what could it be?

"Look at this, captain," said a plainclothesman back in her apartment. He held up the picture of Alice and Jack in the Coney Island photo booth. "I believe we have a face to go with the name."

"That's her, alright," André said, slowly coming around. "But the black and white picture doesn't do her auburn hair justice. You can pick out that head in a crowd of thousands."

After Sparks put his clothes back on, the police led him through a hallway teeming with onlookers and curiosity seekers. The street outside was even worse. Beyond the searchlights and scores of cops standing around a dozen or so black and whites, hundreds of ordinary citizens pressed elbow-to-elbow against police barricades while reporters and trigger happy photographers in the police zone called out to anybody who left the building, "Where's Alice? Have you seen Alice? Show us Alice..."

A commercial radio station blared through an apartment screen. "…And according to Chief Superintendent Edward W. Fallon of the Boston Police Department, Alice Mercer is believed to be living in the Back Bay area on…"

When Sparks finally reached his ride in the captain's car, his flash-bulb-strained eyes could barely make out the door handle, and he grabbed the coiled mounting of the police antenna by mistake. Recognizing it for what it was, he groped his way forward to the back door and fumbled for the latch.

CHAPTER 79

A Call for Help

While Oliver read the cover story so many times he could almost recite it verbatim, Emily paced the length of the living room. Neither one said a word. Then, Emily hid her eyes in her hand as if to blot out the world, and with two steps too many, she walked into a breakfront filled with crystal. The sound of glass knocking against glass filled the room.

Oliver jumped out of his seat. "Are you alright?"

Emily examined her hand. There was no blood. "Forget about me," she replied. "I insist we go to the courthouse tomorrow. Jack needs us."

"What Jack really needs is an acquittal. We must be sure that our presence at his trial doesn't backfire in the dailies." Oliver made steps towards the kitchen.

"Don't walk away from me!" Emily cried out.

"I admire your concern, my dear, but we need counsel from a cooler head." Oliver reached for the phone. "Hello operator... Long Distance Hyannis Port, Massachusetts..."

And as soon as Oliver had dictated Joe Kennedy's telephone number, Emily snatched the phone from his hand. They locked eyes for a moment, and Oliver would have sworn that she had glowered with the fierce passion that a mother bear reserves for any creature threatening her cub.

But would that not be Darwin's cant on the situation?

Baloney! In all the years of their marriage, Oliver knew that Emily was as proper as proper could get...

...Or was she?

When the phone rang, Senator Jack Kennedy stared at the wheelchair and thought nothing but bad things about it. The pain had gotten so bad that a mere half step with his weight borne on crutches generated agonizing bolts of electricity reverberating back and forth from his spine to his heel. And if morphine could not tame this souvenir of a Japanese torpedo finding its mark on his PT boat, then all that remained for him in this life was that wheelchair.

He hobbled to the phone. He would master the pain, lest he become its slave. "Hello... No Mrs. Preston, it's Jack... Everybody outside of New

England makes that mistake, but I don't think I sound anything like Bobby... Dad went to Boston, but he knew you would call... Yes, I understand... He was quite emphatic that you and Mr. Preston should remain away from the courthouse while he attends the trial... I see... You know Dad; he doesn't make promises, but he always seems to find the solution... Yes, bless you too... Everything is wonderful here; I'm feeling fine... Jackie, Mom and the whole clan send you their love... Goodbye."

The couch appeared a mile away, yet the wheelchair was within reach...

...But the senator refused to let it own him.

CHAPTER 80

The Third Degree

Sparks didn't like the blunt hospitality dished out by the Boston Police. Captain Paddy Doyle of the Back Bay precinct had escorted him to an interrogation room with chipped paint and flaking plaster, and an hour and a half later—in spite of repeated requests for a courtesy ride to the airport—two nameless detectives sat him down in front of an obnoxiously powerful light to "ask a few simple questions." All the standard items were in place. Both dicks had rolled up their sleeves, loosened their ties and unbuttoned their collar buttons. On a table across the room, a freshly placed pack of cigarettes and a blackjack represented the police version of carrot and stick. The pen and paper off to the side meant that by whatever means necessary, a signed confession would be had.

One of the cops lit up a smoke and held out the pack for Sparks to take one, but Sparks declined. "Actually, I'd prefer a beer," he said.

"Not when we're on the job. I mean, you are on the job right now, aren't you?"

Sparks attempted to look the interrogator in the eyes, but his whole face had disappeared into darkness behind the bright interrogation light. Sparks knew from memory that this so-called brother in law enforcement had the tough kind of mug that came with a name like Clooney or O'Hara as did every other cop in the station house. He wondered if the entire Boston police force marched with bagpipes on St. Patrick's Day; but with further scrutiny, Sparks figured that such an ethnic monopoly resulted from a migratory accident of history, and that it merited no further interest.

An offer of a cigarette struck Sparks as a friendly opening gesture, and so he decided to reciprocate with a tidbit of information. "I believe I previously spotted the hogtied fellow at a stakeout in Greenwich Village. At the time, my partner and I believed him to be from the Bureau."

"He tells us he's from the French Justice Ministry. He's got an ID issued from their overseas bureau in Indochina."

Sparks rubbed his eyes. "That's interesting. Could you please shut off that light?"

"It's standard procedure."

"I said please."

"And I said standard."

"Standard for muggers and thieves. Is that what you take me for?"

"Is that what you are?"

Sparks looked around the room for the silent partner, but the hot light obscured everything and anything except a giant sun surrounded by a black void. He decided that he would not play the foil anymore. "Look, gentlemen. I am in the midst of a federal investigation of illegal stock trading that concerns neither the City of Boston nor the State of Massachusetts—"

"—It's the Commonwealth of Massachusetts, not the State."

Sparks resented the interruption over something he deemed so trivial. "Ah yes, Commonwealth," he cracked. "That sounds British to me. Do you curtsey to the Queen around here?"

"I'll curtsey to you, you queen!" a threatening brogue called out. At last the silent partner had spoken. But what exactly did he mean?

"We have sodomy laws here in the Commonwealth of Massachusetts," his talkative partner explained. "Do you have a fondness for nude rope play with Frenchmen?"

Sparks threw out his hands. "Fellows, judging by the multitude of spectators in front of that apartment, I presume you heard about a certain rope wielding vixen named Alice Mercer, who according to Judge Curran should have made the local headlines despite the fact that I find it impossible to find an evening newspaper in this town."

"So maybe you had a threesome with the Frenchman and her?"

Sparks curled his lip. The shamus sounded serious. "Are you calling me a fairy?"

From out of the black void, a syringe hit Sparks and landed in his lap. "We also found loaded needles in every nook and cranny. Maybe you're a hop fiend fairy."

Sparks pointed his finger at the invisible voice. "Get this straight, Sherlock," he thundered, "it wasn't my apartment. Alice Mercer knocked me out with one of those syringes. You won't find any track marks on my arms, and I ain't no fairy!"

"Oh yeah, then what do you call this?" A hand shoved Alice's exercise device in Sparks' face.

"It's… it's… it's a Yoko-homo Yo-Yo," Sparks stuttered.

"Yeah, it's homo, sweetie. What does it do?"

"After my nude ass sits on it, you pick it up with your teeth."

Sparks heard a collective gagging sound just as two hands grabbed him by the collar. "You people make me sick!" the detached voice exclaimed.

But Sparks had taken enough of these insults to his manhood. He kicked the light over, shattering the bulb. The room went black, and as his eyes adjusted to the sudden darkness, the hands forced him to the ground, while a third hand reached for the blackjack.

"This is a federal government matter, you retards! You'll be turning tricks in Alcatraz for obstruction of justice!" Sparks screamed.

While one cop pinned Sparks by the shoulders, the other took a stretched wind up and sent the blackjack flying toward an exposed groin. Fortunately, however, Captain Doyle's hand blocked the blow inches before it would have relayed unimaginable agony into every conscious fiber of Sparks' collective soul.

"Boys! Boys! His ID checks out. He's one of us," the captain announced.

"Gee, Tom, I'm sorry," said the talkative detective who had pinned Sparks to the floor. "Let me help you up. No hard feelings, right? Detective Sergeant Ed Quinn at your service."

Sparks knew that he had to handle the turnabout with a stock reply. "You fellows were just doing your jobs," he said.

"So let Detective Finn Sweeney here buy you a beer," said the detective with the brogue.

"Later for that," the captain said handing Sparks his badge, wallet and gun. "A baggage clerk at Eastern Airlines identified Miss Mercer from her picture, but her plane had already landed in New York."

"And what about Frenchy?" Sweeney asked.

"Doc Fleming took him to the Brigham for overnight observation. His billfold had stretch marks, but we found nothing inside. Obviously, Miss Mercer rolled him; however, he never uttered one word of protest. I have a tail on him if he decides to make a move."

"Gentlemen, it's been wonderful," Sparks said. "But I've been subpoenaed for tomorrow's trial in New York, and I missed my ride home. Could one of you give me a lift to the airport?"

"The airport closed at nine," Quinn said, "but I can drive you to South Station."

Sparks dreaded the idea of traveling by rail, but what choice did he have? After a three-hour wait, the milk train departed Boston, only to stop in every city, village and cowshed in Massachusetts, Rhode Island and Connecticut. When the train finally pulled into Grand Central Station, dawn had already broken, and back cramps brought on by a night of restless sleep in a coach seat forced him to walk at a cantilevered angle. If only his wrists and ankles could have stopped itching from all the damn rope abrasions, Sparks might have chalked up his Boston sojourn to a character-building exercise.

CHAPTER 81

Wakeup

The courtroom took on a dark hue. Jack looked at the jury but could not see their faces. Likewise, the judge had disappeared into a black shadow, and only the shifting eyes of the Kit-Cat clock on the wall had any semblance of clarity.

"The defendant will rise," came the command from the bench, and Jack did as so ordered.

"What say you, the jury?

The jury foreman stood and read from a list that unrolled like toilet paper from his hands. "As to count one of insider trading, we find the defendant guilty...'

Jack held onto his head as the words of the Jury Foreman pounded his brain.

"...As to count two, we find the defendant so guilty you wouldn't believe it."

Then a light shining from beneath the bench revealed a contorted sneer within a hooded robe, and the judge issued forth. "Jack Preston, you have betrayed your clients, your firm and our respected profession. You are part and parcel of the creeping filth and moral turpitude that has come to infect our books, our movies and our music. Your degenerate and perverted acts shall not serve to inspire our youth, and as such I sentence you to six years confinement at the maximum-security prison in Fort Leavenworth... Guards, you may escort the prisoner to his cell."

A phalanx of marshals surrounded Jack, and Lou called out to him. "Don't worry, stupid. You'll be out in five."

Meanwhile, the judge mumbled under his breath, "I'll give you tarter sauce!"

The afternoon rays shone through the bars as a guard lead Jack past cages filled to the brim with half humans, some snarling and others groaning. Coming from the distance, he heard a radio announcer. "...And it's all over for the New York Yankees as the Cleveland Indians clinch the American League pennant..."

The guard opened a cell door and called to its plug-ugly occupant, whose muscle bound torso served as a canvas for skulls, serpents and daggers with blood dripping from their blades. "I've got a new playmate for you, Duke."

The guard pushed Jack into Duke's arms and slammed the bars behind him. Duke puckered his lips. "Hey cutey, where ya been all my life?" He smiled to reveal a mouth full of decay.

Jack grabbed onto the bars. "Alice! Alice!!!" he screamed, and the inmates one and all returned her name in snarls and groans until it became an abomination to his ears.

Jack awoke in a lather of sweat and realized that he should have taken Lou's advice from day one. A smarter man would have jumped on the deal for misdemeanor misconduct rather than face a probable trip to the penitentiary, and a wiser man would have banished Alice from his memory…

…But Jack felt neither smart nor wise this morning—only scared.

CHAPTER 82

A Breakfast Summit

Lou lit everybody up with one match and took a gentle puff. Nat inhaled deeply, and Harry nearly retired his stick with a single drag, but then everybody exhaled together in a sign of universal bonhomie. The takeout coffee and Danish from Ratner's Cafeteria stood half consumed on Nat's conference table, and that's how they would stay. The thermometer again threatened to blow its top, and thick coffee and overly sweet treats didn't seem too appetizing in the heat. Moreover, tar and nicotine always represented a good substitute for nutrition in the morning. Lou said it kept him sharp; Nat complained about dragging around a full stomach, and Harry didn't need to rationalize. He was beyond help.

Lou pulled the morning edition of the *Daily News* from his briefcase and plopped it on the table. The headline was an instant classic.

PRESTON: HER PANTIES TASTED LIKE FISH

Lou buried his eyes in his hand. "As you see, my client has lost his marbles. I throw myself upon the mercy of the court."

"Perhaps he suffers from the quaint notion that prosecutors have to prove him guilty. He should have cut those classes in law school," Nat opined.

"If it's any consolation, we're going to wrap things up today. We figure that if we drill him any more, the jury might start to feel sympathy," Harry said.

Lou crossed his fingers. "Any chance of a plea?"

Nat threw up his hands. "Why waste your time? This guy wouldn't plead *no contest* to a parking ticket. Let's play this one out. If it's thumbs down, we'll ask for six months at Danbury."

"It's a nice place with tennis courts and steam rooms," Harry added exhaling a donut-sized smoke ring. "Your client will come out a new man."

"By the way," Nat said. "What's up with all the subpoenas? If you delay the case without merit past the weekend, Judge Cummings just might throw a book named Leavenworth at your client."

"What does that mean? You get to call your witnesses, and I can't call mine?"

"Hold your water, my friend. If the need arises, I'll plead your case for leniency… Now if you could only deliver us Terence Scott, we'd not only cut your patsy loose, but we'd also toss in a dungeon party with the hookers of his choice."

"He's not the rope buff you make him out to be."

"Oh, we know that," Harry said, "but just to make him feel snug and warm, we'll tell the guards to treat him to an extra helping of leg irons and body shackles."

Everybody let out a hearty chuckle over that remark, and Harry laughed so hard that he hacked up something green and putrid. Always prepared, he pulled out a handkerchief to hide the gaffe.

CHAPTER 83

A Face in the Crowd

Joe Kennedy didn't know what to make of all the madness. Traffic into Foley Square had come to a dead halt from a crush of pedestrians spilling down the Federal Courthouse steps and out onto Pearl Street, where the police erected barriers to turn it into a paradoxical one way dead end. A mounted policeman approached all motorists, and when he reached Joe's limousine, Eamon, the chauffeur, dutifully lowered the window.

"Turn around. You can't pass through Foley Square," the officer said.

Joe let down his window, and the officer's horse took a liking to the cool air coming from the door vent. Joe stroked his intruding muzzle. "How do I get inside the Federal Courthouse?" he asked. "I have government identification."

The officer pointed to a doorway behind them. "According to the marshals, only courthouse workers and those people with subpoenas or on official business may pass through that entrance."

"I have diplomatic papers."

"All I can say is give it a try."

The mounted cop moved on to the next driver in line, and Joe stepped out of the car. "Mr. Kennedy, Mr. Kennedy... what brings you here?" Chester Brown called out from the crowded end of the block.

Through thick eyeglasses, Joe spotted a suit and derby clad figure hurrying toward him and wondered how the man's eyesight kept improving with age. "I should ask you that very question," he remarked. "Jack Preston is working on a project for me now, and if he goes to jail, I may take a bad hit. Besides, I always liked the boy. You know that."

"Indeed I do...the funny thing is I got served with a subpoena yesterday. Why on earth would these legal folk want to talk to a shoeshine man?"

"Because you're observant, and because you never miss a detail. So let's see what your impeccable vision picks out of the mob."

Joe led Chester past the police barricades, where the two dissolved into a sea of humanity. "Your attention, please," a marshal on the courthouse steps announced. A bullhorn amplified his voice but made it barely intelligible. "Due to increased demand for seats by members of the press, only forty admission tickets to courtroom nine will be made available to the general public. The rest of you may go about your business."

Moans, groans and boos erupted spontaneously. "Incredible, isn't it?" Joe remarked. "What switch in what dark room inside our minds turns us into cattle ready to stampede?"

"I have to be going, sir. The subpoena says I have to be in the courtroom by nine."

"You've got plenty of time, besides—"

Joe didn't finish his sentence because Chester did a double take. "Excuse me, Miss; Hello, Missy in the scarf..." he called out to a kerchief-bedecked woman about two dozen bodies in front of him.

Out of the several thousand people in the square, the woman never noticed Chester, and so he pushed his way in her direction. Joe followed along.

"Hello, Miss Alice," Chester said extending one hand and holding his derby over his heart with the other. "I've seen you on TV. You sat next to Mr. Preston at the Yankee–Red Sox game and at the Marciano–Charles fight back in June. You sure did the right thing coming back to him."

Chester turned on his high beam incisors to reveal a tangle of congeniality lines encircling his mouth, and Alice reciprocated with partially raised lips. "But how could you have possibly remembered my face from a TV screen?" she asked.

"Chester has a photographic memory. That's one of the reasons why he works for me," Joe said tipping his Panama hat.

Alice took a step backwards as if to flee but only succeeded in bumping into a wall of flesh. "I can save Jack from all the lies they say about us," she volunteered, her eyes darting back and forth, her voice jittery. "The treasury agents broke into my apartment without a warrant, and they searched it. I have photographs; I have a tape recording, and I have these." She reached into her purse and pulled out a handful of metal beads.

Joe's eyes lit up. "So you're the source of those NPN transistors that Jack sent me!" he exclaimed. "I had a hunch he..."

"Mr. Kennedy," Chester interrupted, his hands fidgeting. "I do have to go inside, or I'll be pounding rocks for Uncle Sam. Please excuse me."

Joe brushed the lapel on Chester's Savile Row suit and straightened his tie. "Before you enter the courthouse," he instructed, "look for my car at the end of the block, and ask Eamon for my morning newspaper. Read it, but don't let anybody else look at it until you are seated on the witness stand. I'll see you later."

Chester retreated to the sparse side of the police barricades, and a crush of humanity pushed Alice into Joe. He waltzed her around with a half turn so as to take the brunt of this sudden onslaught.

"I'm impressed with your knowledge of transistors Mr. Kennedy, but they have little to do with Jack and much to do with me," she said.

"Then why did you show them?"

"Because the newspapers in Boston said they bewildered Agent Michael T. Malone's testimony. I shall go into that courtroom and mystify him."

Joe tightened his lips. "Think before you jump, young lady. The transistors are good for a sideshow, but they won't get your testimony past first base on an inside trading rap. Where are the photographs and the tape you just mentioned?"

"I left them in my hotel room. They are of no use at the moment because the film needs development, and the tape needs a playback device."

"Those are easy enough tasks. I know just the expert to give us prompt service."

Alice pressed her fingers to her forehead. "And why should I trust you?"

Joe gently pushed her hand aside and held up her chin. "Because my dear Alice, you have run out of options to right your wrong, and come this evening, you will have run out of time."

And Alice blinked.

Joe and Alice headed back down Pearl Street, where his car squatted beside a hydrant. He rapped on the side window, and Eamon stepped out to open and close the back door for Alice, whose eyes momentarily lingered on his features. "Do I know you, Miss?" he inquired.

"Public Alley 439 near Copley Square... The policeman in the shadow refused your gesture for two newspapers."

"Excellent recall, young lady!" Joe interjected stepping into the back seat from the opposite door. "I shall inform Chester that you offer him competition."

Eamon bore down on the accelerator. "Where to, sir?" he inquired.

"The Chelsea Hotel," Alice answered in Joe's stead.

"And after Miss Mercer returns from her hotel room, let us swing by the RCA Building. I have need of the General's expertise," Joe added.

Alice arched her eyebrows. "Do you mean General David Sarnoff?" she asked.

"He's quite a storyteller. Please don't get him started. I don't want him rambling on about our life history together."

Eamon turned on the radio and tuned it to a classical music station. He then slid shut a glass partition between the front and back seats, and as quickly as a cacophonous symphony of brass and kettledrums sounded, the partition silenced it. "Is your chauffeur trying to tell me that our talk is privileged?" Alice asked.

"I'm not the one who tape records conversations, young lady," Joe said with a trace of scorn in his voice. "Now assuming I've finally earned your trust, tell me who the heck you are."

Alice's looked away for a prolonged moment, and when she turned back, Joe held out his hand as if to say, "Whenever you're ready."

"I grew up in a château outside Hanoi," she began, her voice hushed. "My father served as a logistics instructor for the French Military Academy. We had many servants, and life was good."

"But then the Japanese Imperial Army invaded your country." Joe interrupted.

"Please, Mr. Kennedy. You are an impatient man, and I would rather forget those years," Alice returned, her voice stronger.

But Joe persisted. "How did your family deal with the invaders?"

"On the first day of the invasion, one of our groundskeepers told my mother that Papa had died as a hero in battle. The truth is that he had faked his death and hid out in the jungle, where he trained Indochinese partisans in guerrilla warfare tactics."

Joe nodded his approval. "Given the dense terrain, your father made a wise choice. May I presume that the accord between Vichy France and Nazi Germany gave the rest of your family political protection against Japanese harassment, seeing that Germany and Japan were allies?"

"Yes." Alice replied, hissing the S to the point of insolence.

"And what would have happened if the Japanese had found out that your father was not only alive, but was also training an effective guerilla resistance?" Joe asked.

"They would have killed my entire family by utilizing the slowest and most hideous methods imaginable," she returned, the whites of her eyes engulfing her irises. "Shall I go into detail?"

"Spare yourself the pain."

Alice kicked the floor. "And what kind of pain did the war dole out to you, Mr. Kennedy?" she ranted. "Did the newsreels at the cinema spawn nightmares of enemy atrocity in your safe and secure bed?"

"My dear Alice," Joe replied, knowing from her challenging tone that he had touched a raw nerve. "People I don't know call me 'the Ambassador'—and I never quite fathom if that salutation comes out of respect or mockery for the only job I ever failed at. Back in the waning days of peace, I served as the American envoy to Britain, where I worked tirelessly to avert a war that would call my eldest boys by name. Unfortunately, however, I had dismissed the darkness of that time as a passing squall, and for that mistake, I paid the ultimate price as a parent." Joe pulled a hanky from his top pocket and wiped the corners of his eyes.

Alice measured her words slowly. "Mr. Kennedy, it's been a rough week for me. I had no idea that..."

But before she could finish her thought, Eamon had slid open the partition. "Chelsea Hotel," he announced.

Alice grabbed Joe by the hand. "Please come to my room, and help me bring along everything we need," she requested.

"I don't escort pretty ladies to their hotel rooms, especially ones who could knock me out and tie me to the bedposts."

"But I have the latest Bell Lab papers on transistor doping. Wouldn't that interest you... or perhaps even the General?"

"Then no funny stuff! Last year, I officially became a senior citizen."

Despite Joe's plea of advancing age, Alice set a quick pace up the hotel stairwell; however, this former captain of the Boston Latin high school baseball team matched her step for step all the way to the third floor. Neither one broke a sweat—despite the record heat.

CHAPTER 84

The General's Lair

The car cruised down Forty-Eighth Street, and Alice craned her neck at the Rockefeller Center skyscrapers as if she were a tourist just off the farm. Joe cradled a 1912 vintage briefcase on his lap and stroked the belt straps. Eamon made a hard left, and the car descended into a tunnel, which led to a gated booth. He flashed a red card at the parking attendant, who then waved him through to a special lane privy only to oversized luxury vehicles, which were parked on either side. With plenty of spots to be had, Eamon pulled up next to a walkway and provided doorman courtesy for his passengers.

"It's a great day. I can just feel it," Joe said rubbing the briefcase. The two followed the walkway, which by Alice's reckoning took them under Forty-Ninth Street. At the far end, they passed though a doorway labeled "30 ROCKEFELLER PLAZA" and arrived at an elevator bank. Rather than push a service button, Joe inserted a key into a wall slot on the far elevator. With a flick of the wrist, the doors opened.

"I see you're a big shot," Alice commented.

"There are no big shots," Joe said, "only pathetic souls craving recognition for their power, money or luck."

"Well, I presume you have all three."

"Very true, but I'm not yet pathetic. Please shoot me if I become so."

The elevator rocketed to ear popping speed, and when it hit the fifty-third floor, the doors opened directly to the executive offices. "Mr. Kennedy!" the youthful receptionist exclaimed, her index finger zigzagging down a calendar book. "I never put your name down for an appointment. How could I have missed you?"

"Relax, Suzy. I never called. Where is he?"

"The General has a conference in the boardroom until noon—wait a minute, Mr. Kennedy, sir, you can't go in there—"

"Gee that's a swell entrance, Joe," greeted the General, who sat at the far end of a bowling-alley-sized conference table hosting his senior executives. "Did Gloria May teach you that one?"

"Who is Gloria May?" Alice asked, two steps behind Joe.

"She's the actress, Gloria Swanson. I used to manage her business affairs. Our names frequently intertwined in the Hollywood gossip sheets," Joe replied.

"But you didn't fall out of the sky to reminisce about our Hollywood days, did you, bubeleh?" the General remarked.

Joe strode to the head of the conference table and opened his briefcase. He pulled out a paper bag and spilled its contents of several hundred transistors onto the table. The General was speechless. Joe's mouth filled the void. "My lady friend and I have another bag of these goodies for you as well as the formulary that tells you how to dope them. What do you say to my lady friend?"

"Meeting adjourned!" The General called out adding more sedately, "Hello lady friend. Will you be my lady friend too?"

"Only if you do everything Mr. Kennedy asks you," Alice replied.

The room cleared, and the General closed the door behind the exiting gray suits. He flicked a switch on the wall, and as the lights slowly dimmed, floor to ceiling drapes retracted to reveal the spires of the Chrysler and Empire State Buildings gleaming in the morning sun. Tall buildings of lesser stature rose up from all sides to pay them homage.

"And to whom do I have the pleasure?" the General said holding out his hand.

"I'm the infamous Alice Mercer. Do you still want me to be your friend?"

Again, the General was mute, and Joe took over. "Listen, David, don't believe what you've read in the newspapers about this woman. The government is going after the wrong guy downtown, and Alice has the pictures and a sound tape to prove an illegal search. We need expedited service on the film and a conversion of that tape to forty-fives. I'll also need to use a phone. When Alice enters that courthouse, I want one of my lawyers walking by her side and holding the evidence. I'll also need a record player that doesn't weigh more than twenty pounds."

"What about the transistors and the doping formulary?"

"They're yours for a price. You and Miss Mercer can work out the details later."

The General hit the intercom button and marshaled his troops. "General alert... General alert... Hello, Laboratory, Suzy has a roll of film for you.... I need the prints yesterday.... Hello, Studio A, this is your General requesting you to make a wax copy in the time it takes Roger Bannister to run a mile...please see Suzy.... Hello, Suzy, please report for duty... Hello workshop... Please stand by."

Suzy stormed into the room, and Joe relayed her the film and audiotape from his briefcase in Olympic time. "Make some insurance copies," the General called out to her vapor trail. "If the judge excludes this evidence, we can always broadcast it on NBC for the jury's further enlightenment."

A slammed door followed Suzy's departure, and the General held a transistor up to the sunlight. "I'm curious Alice," he said. "How did you ever get your pretty hands on so much vanguard technology?"

"Do you promise you won't interrupt me?"

"Do you take us for philistines?" the General retorted flashing a sour glare directly at Joe.

"Well..." Alice began, "two years ago, I graduated from UC-Berkeley with an MS in electrical engineering. When I returned home to Hanoi, Indochinese resentment against the colonists and especially the Vichy collaborators for their actions during the war had boiled over to the point of bloodshed. My family was safe because my father had utilized American aid and weaponry to train the resistance in the war against Japan. But by this time, those former comrades in arms effectively used the very same weapons and tactics against the colonial government, and the ministry officials blamed my father for their own ineptitude in dealing with the situation. To cover their stupidity, they had him arrested and charged him with treason. A midlevel functionary in the justice ministry and former Vichy collaborator by the name of André Grignard promised to dispose of the charges if I passed him trade secrets in the doping of transistors. Ostensibly, this information would be forwarded to the French government; however, I recently discovered this traitor enjoying the company of a certain Colonel Hiroshi Nishimura, who had quartered his officers in my family's estate during the war. This connection has convinced me that I have been working for the Japanese all along."

"That's not a bad thing," the General said in the most soothing of tones. "The Japanese have become our friends, and Hiro Nishimura heads their trade delegation, which showcases their discount tchotchkes at the Coliseum tomorrow. How much did he pay for the trade secrets you borrowed?"

"I have no idea because other than a few hundred dollars, my salary from André the collaborator pig has been my father's neck. Papa is safe now. The Viet Minh liberated him, and the American ambassador has offered him sanctuary here, but can he ever clear his name?"

"First let's concentrate on clearing Jack Preston's name," the General said.

"Amen," said Joe.

The threesome stepped out of the boardroom, and Joe laid claim to Suzy's telephone. The General excused himself to make calls of his own, which left Alice to look out the windows and count the tallest buildings in the midtown skyline. When she reached thirty, she pointed to building thirty-one, which caused refracted sunlight from her engagement ring to race along the ceiling and dazzle her eyes with a flash of colors. She stared at the ring for the briefest of moments and broke down in a convulsion of sobs. Suzy offered her a friendly shoulder, and Alice didn't hold back.

"I may be just a fragile woman," she said choking on her words, "but I will scratch out the eyes of any person doing wrong against the only man who has ever worshipped me like a goddess."

Alice then looked Suzy straight in the eyes and added, "So help me God."

CHAPTER 85

The Sublime and the Ridiculous

With Harry Dixon back at the prosecutorial helm, Thelma Kane took the stand, and Lou knew he had found his perfect witness. Her gray dress was understated but not drab. Her perfectly coiffed hair whispered success without ostentation, and her open posture boldly told the jury that she didn't pussyfoot around with small talk, meaning that she told the truth without unsolicited commentary. For an attorney, she was not the type of witness you wanted if your client was guilty; however, in the singular case of a bum rap, she became the legal equivalent of a knight in shining armor.

Before going into his opening round of questions, all Lou wanted from this woman and for all of the subsequent witnesses he had called for the day was a delay to send the trial past the Labor Day weekend. The whole bondage bit had caused the trial to careen out of control, and Lou knew that he needed to bore all of the voyeurs in the courtroom with legalistic tedium until the unwanted spectacle of Alice's rope trick had become a distant memory. Lou realized that Nat and Harry were on to his strategy and had even warned him that the Judge would not take kindly to such delaying tactics; however, the more Lou questioned Thelma, the more he realized that she spouted an unadulterated testimony that came across as scripture. This was a treasure not to be wasted.

"So tell me, Mrs. Kane," Lou said in mid-examination. "In your capacity as office manager, what were your duties to the defendant, Jack Preston?"

"I scheduled his appointments, and I attended to his general welfare," Thelma said quick and straight.

"That last part sounds rather vague."

"I advise young attorneys such as Jack of the pitfalls in their day-to-day meetings with clients. I give them business sense to supplement their legal talents."

"And how would you characterize Jack?"

"His work was daring, innovative and brilliant; but socially, he was naïve and immature. He had a need to impress people and hear their praise. That made him susceptible."

With his hand held against his cheek, Jack winced. Lou, however, latched onto Thelma's final word, which gave him the impression of bait dangling from a hook. "Susceptible… susceptible to what? Dishonesty?" he asked trusting his gut.

"You've got the wrong number there, sir. I've seen enough unscrupulous lawyers come and go in my career to know that you couldn't buy Jack at any price."

"Then susceptible to what?" Lou repeated.

"Jack needed a sycophant, and Paul Jeffrey filled that roll. When Paul wasn't buttering Jack up, he was sneaking around the firm and not minding his own business. Jack was blind to all that, and I regret that I never found the words to bring all of this to Jack's attention without insulting him. I attempted to have Paul fired, but my request was turned down by Mr. Hargrave, the senior partner in the firm."

"And Paul Jeffrey, whose real name is Andrew Scott, now lives in Havana in luxury for assisting his father with this caper."

"Then I presume that he won't be coming back for his paycheck."

Spontaneous laughter erupted, and rather than bang his gavel, Judge Cummings laughed along with them. "I have no further questions," Lou said.

As he returned to his seat, Lou held two fingers to his lips to signal Harry to take a cigarette break, but Harry shook him off. After spitting out a cheek load of chaw into folded paper, he approached the witness stand.

"Counselor, please wipe your mouth," the judge said, his gaze fixed upon a juice trail dripping from the corner of Harry's lips down to his collar. Harry pulled out a used handkerchief and wiped away the goop, much to the dismay of several jurists.

"Mrs. Kane," he asked, "can you tell me what you know about Mr. Preston's relationship with Alice Mercer?"

"I was not aware of such a relationship until I read about it in yesterday's newspaper. Jack never mentioned her."

"I have no further questions."

Lou had to hand it to Harry for simultaneously reminding the jury of Alice Mercer while using up as little of the clock as possible. Lou knew that he could have pelted Mrs. Kane with dozens of more questions to waste time, but that would have detracted from a sincere testimony that affirmed Jack's honesty while pointing out relatively minor character flaws that gave credence to her statements.

Harry reached into his pouch for a pinch of tobacco, but then the judge called out in a booming voice. "Mr. Dixon, You may take a five-minute break, and—if I may suggest—you should save the chaw for your next campfire in the woods."

"Yes, your Honor," Harry replied before scrambling past the gallery of reporters and to a location, which in Lou's mind had begun to smell less and less of sanitary cleanser, and more and more of the befouled odors that spoke of flatulence and poor aim at the urinals. Once back in the courtroom, Harry caught his breath just as the judge lay the hammer down.

"I wish to call Miss Nora Kincaid to the witness stand," Lou said, and up strode Nora, wearing enough mascara, eyeliner and shadow to color a Pontiac. Lou figured that if he could keep her talking until noon, he could have the shoeshine man take over after lunchtime for another couple of hours, and then he could finish up with either Sparks or Malone, leaving the other one to testify on Tuesday. By then, the city editors might relegate Alice Mercer to the pages just shy of the sports section.

For openers, Lou wanted to ask the Alice question, which would preempt Harry's pat counterattack. "Miss Kincaid, did Mr. Preston ever talk to you about Alice Mercer?"

"No... she was as top secret as Mata Hari," Nora replied, her nasal voice jarring everybody like nails on a blackboard.

Lou scratched his chin. He could only infer what she meant. *Mata Hari was a real life spy who seduced men to betray their country during World War I. So too had Alice seduced Jack. This wasn't exactly a flattering comparison.* Lou decided to move on.

"What about Paul Jeffrey? Did you have any impression of him?"

"He was a real asp."

"I beg your pardon, young lady," Judge Cummings cut in. "We'll have none of that language in this courtroom."

"But, Judge," Nora explained, "it's a three-letter-word ending in P. It means snake."

"Now I've got you," the judge smiled.

But Lou wasn't smiling. The lady's characterization of Paul certainly deserved repetition, but she had the diction and face paint of a stripper, which meant that unless she could explain Einstein's theory of general relativity, the jury would cast her off as an adolescent bimbo. It seemed so unfair and yet so natural. Underneath all the five and dime varnish, Lou spotted a striving ingénue, who needed a crash course in cosmetology before running through the gauntlet of shutterbugs posted outside the courtroom. Yet a girl wanted to look glamorous for all the cameras, and what better way was there to look like your favorite starlet than to go whole hog with all the pigments on the bottom shelf of the medicine cabinet?

Lou decided that this witness would be more helpful if he could elicit quick answers fueled by emotion. "Miss Kincaid, did Paul Jeffrey ever do anything or act in any way to arouse your suspicion that he was a liar and a thief?"

"I never knew any liars or thieves, so how could I tell? At worst, I mistook him for a heel."

"Thank you, Miss Kincaid." As much as Lou wanted to burn up the clock, he knew that the jury couldn't take any more of "I nevanu-eny-loyas-awthieves" with the word "liar" sounding more like "lawyer."

Perhaps the shoeshine man might keep everybody entertained for as long as necessity required it. According to Jack's jailhouse notes, the man had the gift of gab and could spot a needle in a hundred haystacks. That certainly trumped a crossword puzzle maven, especially one from whom Harry Dixon declined any cross-examination.

CHAPTER 86

Revelations

With a newspaper tucked under his left arm, Chester Brown raised his right hand and swore, "I do." For Lou now, the trick was to show the jury that this colored bootblack was no cotton-picking simpleton endowed with natural rhythm and a taste for muscatel. If the courtroom were situated somewhere south of Baltimore, Lou might have led off with a patronizing question such as, "Now you know what the truth is, don't you Mr. Brown?" But Lou couldn't sink to that level for this respectful man clothed in his Sunday best. Instead, he would go directly to the mother lode.

"Mr. Brown, as far as you can recall, you have never seen nor met Alice Mercer? Is that correct, sir?"

"Oh no, sir," Chester replied, his pearly teeth on full display. "I spoke with Miss Mercer earlier this morning. She's a very charming lady, and she's in good hands with Mr. Kennedy."

The response generated mumbling in the gallery, and Judge Cummings smacked his gavel down. "Need I remind you that you're under oath, Mr. Brown?" he warned. "And how would you know this woman if you saw her?"

Chester held up his newspaper and pointed to the picture on the front page. "Look, judge… here she is sitting next to Mr. Preston. It looks like they got their picture taken at the batting cages in Coney Island. That's the woman I spoke to this morning."

"Please pass me your newspaper, Mr. Brown," the judge said now accompanied by more grumbling from the gallery than before. "Members of the press," he ordered, "do not tempt me to throw the whole lot of you out of here. Take this as your second warning. You will not get a third."

Chester handed his newspaper to Lou, who then handed it over to the judge. "Mr. Brown," said the judge, his eyes widening, "this is the morning edition of the *Boston Post*! Please state the full name of the person who gave this to you."

"Mr. Joseph Patrick Kennedy Senior… sir."

"Thank you, Mr. Brown," the judge said adding, "You may continue with your examination, Mr. Fisher."

Lou faced the witness stand and said, "I take it, sir, that you read that Boston newspaper cover to cover."

"You're right this time," Chester chuckled tapping his noggin. "I've got all the pictures up here."

"And is there anything of significance that you'd like to tell us from up there?"

Chester pointed to the first row on the prosecution side of the gallery and said, "Do you see that man who keeps on rubbing his wrists? He and three police officers walked out of Miss Mercer's apartment building in Boston yesterday. You'll find them all in the middle picture on page three."

Judge Cummings flipped the front page and put on a dog-faced scowl. "Young-man-in-the-first-row, please state your name and occupation."

"Your Honor, I am Thomas J. Sparks, treasury agent assigned to criminal investigations for the SEC."

"I see your name on the list of witnesses. Are you with the Boston office?"

"No sir, my assignment is southern New York."

The judge cast a wicked glance toward Harry, who upended his palms as if he had no idea of what was happening. "Counsels, approach the bench," the judge ordered.

Harry reached into his pocket and pulled out a broken cigarette. When he came within earshot of the judge, he whispered, "Hey Lou, can you fix me up with a couple of sticks for the morning proceedings?"

Lou pulled out a pack of smokes, but Judge Cummings held out his arm and shook his head. "You know, Harry," he whispered, "I've reached my limit with this dog-and-pony show. Let's see how long you can survive breathing room air."

"Listen, judge," Harry replied, "I never sanctioned those two cowboys heading up to Boston. I flat out refused them a subpoena."

"Gee thanks, Harry," said Lou pocketing his cigarettes. "If I knew they were on Alice Mercer's trail, I would have demanded a subpoena. She's the one person who can vouch for Jack."

"I don't buy it," Harry returned. "You managed to keep the lady off the transcript until your client's big mouth intervened."

"Enough gentlemen," the judge said. "Join me in chambers. It's time to investigate the investigators, and if I don't get some satisfactory answers, I'll recess the trial until Tuesday."

"Bailiff," the judge then ordered, "Make sure that Mr. Brown remains on the witness stand, and that he communicates with nobody except you while I adjourn the trial."

Lou crossed his fingers. He couldn't imagine what had transpired in Boston, but he knew for certain that Sparks and Malone had struck out on their own without either agency or court approval. Lou could only guess at their motive. Whatever it was, it didn't matter, for when he, Harry and the judge arrived in chambers, a foursome awaited them at the conference table… and the lone woman of the group had flaming auburn hair.

CHAPTER 87

The Smoke-Filled Room

Given his seniority on the bench, Judge Cummings kept the most spacious chambers in the courthouse, which came in handy when he mentored Columbia Law students. For trial proceedings, however, he preferred a more intimate setting in which he could look the participants close in the eyes and decide which ones had those telltale twitches or blinks. With seven people seated around the conference table, the judge now believed that the taxpayers had finally received some practicality from this cavernous room. To ensure comfort, he flicked the air conditioning unit in his wall to its maximum setting and sat down at the table directly across from Alice. He recognized Joe Kennedy to her left and David Sarnoff to Joe's left. On her right sat Huntington Collins, a tax attorney who usually represented corporations in his court; however, on this occasion, the folder on the table meant that he had taken on a more famous client.

After Judge Cummings had taken his place, Lou sat to his right facing Joe, and Harry sat to his left facing Mr. Collins. As introductions were made, the judge broke out the smokes, and Harry did the honors for everybody but Joe and Alice, who preferred the taste of fresh air. They wouldn't get any at this meeting.

Joe broke the ice. "I presume that you're not thrilled to see me, Harley," he said.

"Your personal business is of no concern here," Judge Cummings returned.

But Joe persisted. "Let's see... it was back in '37 when I chaired the Maritime Commission. Our paths crossed outside the Shubert Theater. Remember?"

"My wife and I had just exited from the show, *Babes in Arms,* when we caught you escorting Miss Gloria Swanson. All I remember during the drive home were words like 'cheat' and 'philanderer'. We thought better of you before that incident."

"Nothing happened between us, and here are the facts: Gloria kissed my cheek, and then she stepped into a taxi for a ride to the Waldorf; I returned to Bronxville."

"You should have explained this to me back then."

"I never explain myself except when others might get hurt, so let's move on with our lives, and drop all these nonsensical charges against Jack Preston."

"Sorry Mr. Kennedy, but that's my department," Harry said blowing out a cloud of smoke worthy of a steam locomotive.

"I knew you'd say that. Hit it, professor," Joe returned, at which point the General placed a compact record player on top of the table.

"Gee, that's the smallest Victrola I've ever seen," Lou remarked.

"Behold the miracle of transistors," the General replied, his voice taking on the energetic hustle of a barker at a medicine show. He lowered the needle onto a spinning forty-five.

The sound coming out of the three-inch speaker had the clarity of a loge box at Carnegie Hall, and amid the clatter of Alice's bedroom getting tossed by skilled professionals, the voices of Agents Sparks and Malone came through with sparkling clarity, especially the last three lines of the play through.

> *"C'mon Tom, we've seen enough. Time to snow-job some judge into signing a search warrant."*
>
> *"But what's the point? Harry Dixon doesn't want the lady's testimony, and you and I both agree that Jack Preston is a poor consolation prize in this whole investigation. Can't we just loosen her tongue with a few Cuba Libres?"*
>
> *"When a flesh dancer with the moves of a trained spy lands in your lap, you know she's the perfect bait to hook bigger fish. We've got to stake first claim on Miss Mercer before that queer, J. Edgar Hoover gets his hooks into her."*

Judge Cummings hit the intercom button. "Bailiff," he ordered, "send in Agents Sparks and Malone."

The judge headed over to a roll top desk and removed a legal form. After scribbling in the blank spaces, he returned to the table and handed Mr. Collins the form. "Behold Huntington. I am giving your client blanket immunity. Now please allow me to inspect your client's folder."

Mr. Collins pushed the folder across the table, and the judge nonchalantly opened it... But then he pounded the table. "Jumping Jehoshaphat! I'll have those two hotshots boiled in oil!" he exclaimed at the sight of a succession of eight by twelve photos exhibiting Alice's bedroom encounter with Agent Sparks. He slammed the folder shut and looked directly at the General.

"David, my dear friend," he said, "I trust you would have the good taste not to broadcast these photos. I believe that given the nudity, the FCC would have valid grounds for censorship."

Huntington Collins answered for the General. "Judge, we would remit to your office all originals and duplicates of this material if the government dropped all charges against Jack Preston."

"I don't think the big shots in Washington will deal," Harry interjected, and then came a knock on the chamber door.

"Take another drag, counselor," said the judge rising to his feet, "and don't you dare look inside that folder."

Outside the threshold waited Agents Sparks and Malone. "Oh, do come in, boys," the judge said, his voice bubbly. He draped an arm over each of their shoulders and escorted them to the conference table. When Sparks beheld Alice tactfully waving to him, he stepped on his shoelace and almost tripped.

"Agent Sparks, I believe you already know the little lady here," Judge Cummings remarked. He retreated once again to his roll top desk, where he filled out two more forms. When he rejoined the group, Harry had already bummed a second smoke from Lou, who lit not only him up but Sparks and Malone too. Sparks, however, wound up hacking out half his lungs on the first drag. Meanwhile, Alice twitched her nose at the gray haze drifting in her direction, and Joe fanned it back with one of Huntington Collins's legal folders.

"By the way, Agent Malone," the judge asked, "is Mrs. Murphy's lemonade as good as my colleagues claim it is up there in Red Sox country?"

"Wow, that lady sure is famous," Malone replied, his teeth clenched.

But then the judge slapped writs of immunity in front of both him and Sparks. "Against my better judgment, I'm letting you and your partner keep your jobs. Now tell me truly, Agent Malone, before I call Boston myself. From which judge did you attempt to finagle a search warrant?"

"James Curran, sir!" Malone barked out the name as if he were addressing a drill sergeant from boot camp.

"Ah yes, Sunny Jim... A veritable salt of the earth," Joe cut in adding, "and you can keep half my oil portfolio if you snookered him."

"Actually, he told me to publish my affidavit in *True Crime*," Malone admitted.

"And may I see a copy of the affidavit?" the Judge asked.

"You'll have to call Mrs. Murphy, sir. I threw my copy in a litter basket."

"I presume you were attempting to give garbage a bad name."

Another knocking sound came from the chamber door, and this time, Harry opened it to behold the golden shield of a police chief hovering two inches in front of his blinking eyes. "Good morning, sir," said the square-jawed cop pocketing the badge in his civilian suit and brushing back his crew cut. "I am Edward W. Fallon, Superintendent-in-Chief of the Boston Police Department."

"Hello, Ed," Joe called out. "What gifts do you bear?"

"I carry a fugitive warrant for Alice Mercer. Is that her on the far side of the table?"

"Sorry, Chief, but you're five minutes late," the judge said, "I already immunized her. What did she do?"

"Miss Mercer is wanted for violations of the Comstock act. We found a banned edition of the *Boston Post* and a banned book by the title of *Temple of the White Tigress* in her apartment."

"You can't be serious," Alice protested. "I bought that newspaper from an undercover cop, and the book qualifies as a work of literary art. I want it back."

"I'm curious, Chief," the judge said. "The *Boston Post* stated that your department served a search warrant on Miss Mercer's premises. From what investigation did your detectives gather enough information to author an affidavit for this warrant?"

"You'd have to ask the detectives, sir."

Judge Cummings nodded politely and motioned for the chief to take a seat at the table. Lou offered the chief a cigarette, and the two of them shared a match. Meanwhile, the judge returned yet again to his roll top desk to fill out yet another writ of immunity, which he slammed on the table in front of the chief.

Let's get this straight," the judge said with a contrived grin. "I don't care if you think I'm an easy mark, and I don't give a hoot about the shell game which your department works with banned newspapers. But you know, Chief... It would bother me if a federal judge rejected an affidavit for a search warrant from a federal agent, and then the very same information from that affidavit mysteriously wound up in a second affidavit before a state judge, who approved the warrant. Now I do know that there is nothing illegal about levels of government sharing investigative information, but I do wonder about the validity of a once rejected search warrant. So, given your writ of immunity, sir, I ask you...whose idea was it for the second search warrant?"

The chief stared at his writ of immunity and gulped. "It was mine, sir."

"And whose idea was it for the number two man in the Boston Police Department to come to New York on account of a couple of petty violations?"

"Again sir, I took the initiative."

"And like a number of professionals who have appeared in my court this past week, you couldn't resist all that free publicity out there, could you?"

"Guilty as charged, sir."

Judge Cummings looked around the table and noted expressions of relative calm coming from everybody except Harry Dixon, whose stiff lips and wrinkled cheeks radiated distress. "Does all this immunity disturb you, counselor?" he inquired with a sideways glance.

"You're turning your chambers into a grand jury proceeding with biased interlopers working for the defense," Harry replied. "I question the appropriateness of your method."

"And would you question the truth wherever she may lie?"

"Let us let the jury decide what the truth is."

Expecting that answer, the judge fingered the dossier containing the sordid photographs of Alice and Sparks. Neither Harry nor Lou had yet seen the pictures, and the judge knew that both of them had every right under the law to examine them. What if the trial proceeded? The judge held his fist to his stomach as if he were holding a Japanese sword. He knew that given all the immunity handed out in his chambers, the recipients could now bear witness to illegal and unsavory acts by government agents that would harm the good name of the government in front of the national press...and those damned photographs! Did this jasmine-scented woman batting her eyes from across the table realize what kind of scandal would explode in the media on account of her actions? Of course she did. And nobody short of a hired gun could stop her.

"Miss Mercer," the judge asked, "why did you agree to assist Mr. Terrence Scott with his insider trading scheme?"

Alice looked at Mr. Collins, who in turn handed her the writ of immunity and said, "Tell him everything, and don't hold back."

"Actually," Alice began, "I never had any concept of insider trading. Dudley—Mr. Scott always preferred me to address him by his middle name—told me that his mother suffered from breast cancer, and that scientists working for a small technology company had discovered a cure. As a result of this, the company found itself subject to hostile takeovers from larger corporations, which profited from the disease, and which would do anything to squelch a cure. Dudley said that only Jack Preston had the legal wherewithal to put such an acquisition together, and that in the name of humanity, I should find out the names of all the companies he represented to prevent this."

"Did Mr. Scott ever tell you the name of the company with the supposed cure?"

"He refused to divulge the name of such a potentially valuable stock to anybody, including me. When I expressed outward skepticism, he showed me over a dozen research papers by a Doctor Ernst T. Krebs regarding a curative called Laetrile. I mentioned the findings to my gynecologist, but he told me that I needed to confer with a cancer specialist... If only I had the courage to enter that dreary world..."

"I see..."

Another knock on the chamber door meant yet another visitor, and this time, Lou performed the doorman duties. "Leave the door ajar," Judge Cummings called out. "My air conditioner must be choking on the fog in here."

At the threshold, a Japanese gentleman bowed halfway to the floor and then handed Lou his business card. "Good morning, esteemed sir," he said with superlative politeness. "I am Hiroshi Nishimura. Mr. Sarnoff requested my presence here, and the office of Senator John Fitzgerald Kennedy vouchsafed my entry into the courthouse."

Alice jumped back from her seat at the table and turned her head so as not to gaze upon Mr. Nishimura. "Why did you invite that man here, General!" she shrieked. "He used to beat me with a bamboo cane!"

"Only when you disrespected your teachers, young Alice," Mr. Nishimura replied. My soldiers taught you our customs, our culture and the art of tying knots for which you seem to have excelled."

"I did not ask to be your student."

"True, but your mother requested it in the memory of your father, who died a warrior's death on the battlefield."

"She deceived us. My father led the resistance even though you and I believed he had joined his ancestors.

The General cleared his throat with a flamboyant thrust of air, and as a collective reflex of heads whipped in his direction, he rose from his chair. "Welcome, Mr. Nishimura," he said bowing ten degrees. "I believe Mr. Kennedy here can provide the financing for a transistor factory in Tokyo if you can lock in labor costs at the current rates."

"Gentlemen!" the judge interrupted. "My chambers are not a board room. Save the business conversation for lunch."

Mr. Nishimura bowed to the judge and slowly kowtowed backward toward the still open door. When he reached the threshold, his derrière bumped into the French cut suits of yet two more arriving visitors.

"Please stay, Mr. Nishimura," the judge called out. "I find your conversation pertinent to this case."

Then the Judge turned his attention to the two men standing in the doorway. "And who might you gentlemen be?" he said.

Alice bolted from her seat and raced into the arms of the gentleman on the right, whose graying hair left traces of auburn on the top and back. "Papa!" she shrieked, plowing full speed into his arms, "I am so happy to see you safe."

But Papa looked less than delighted to see his little girl. "Alice!" he barked. "You shame me with all this trouble you cause. Go stand in a corner, and face the wall."

And a tearful daughter complied.

"Good people," announced Papa's distinguished companion. "With gratitude to General Sarnoff for this invitation and to Senator John F. Kennedy for gaining us entry into this courthouse, I greet you on behalf of the citizens of the Republic of France. I am Henri Hoppenot, the Ambassador to the United Nations, and I accompany Monsieur Jules Mercier. The Republic regrets any embarrassment caused to the American people by M. Mercier's daughter, Alice."

Agent Malone offered a firm hand to M. Mercier. "I am honored to make your acquaintance, sir," he said, "The military intelligence that your Indochinese partisans provided us during the war saved the lives of thousands of American soldiers."

"Well, you can thank Alice for that," M. Mercier replied. "While she entertained the Japanese command with ritual and recitals, they discussed their plans in front of her."

"But how was it possible for her to understand us?" asked Mr. Nishimura pulling out a pack of Cavaliers. "We never taught her a word of conversational Japanese."

"A sister at the Couvent de Sainte Marie tutored me," Alice said from the back corner. "She gave special emphasis to military terms and logistics. Whatever items your officers discussed, I told Mama verbatim.

"And from there, Alice's Mama forwarded that information to me via the only telephone line in Hanoi that consistently worked," M. Mercier added.

After inserting a cigarette into the corner of his mouth, Mr. Nishimura offered smokes to M. Mercier and Ambassador Hoppenot. Alice peeked at them out of the corner of one eye and remarked, "How could you share fire with Mr. Nishimura, Papa? The pig collaborator, André Grignard, sold him all the doping procedures for transistors that I procured from Bell Labs. Those trade secrets were meant for the citizens of the Republic."

"And do you still have copies of those procedures?" Ambassador Hoppenot asked.

"Of course I do."

"You realize, Miss Mercer or Mercier," said Chief Fallon, "that André Grignard won't be leaving the hospital until tomorrow. Somebody bopped his skull with a bottle of Chablis. He won't name names, but I have my suspicions."

"The Republic would be most interested in extraditing M. Grignard to French soil," Ambassador Hoppenot said. "According to today's accounting, his embezzlement of postwar funds for reconstruction in Indochina exacerbated an already tense relationship with the people. Unfortunately, the Republic's treasury does not possess the assets to institute legal proceedings against him in this country."

"I'll take your case pro bono," Lou volunteered. "I'm always willing to help an ally who produces outstanding vintage."

"Actually," said the chief, "I believe that in Boston, Mr. Grignard would voluntarily hand himself over to French authorities. Just leave everything to me."

"And make sure you don't violate any federal laws in the process," the judge cautioned.

A knock on the open door announced two more visitors. This time Nat Reiss came with an escort. "I was wondering when you'd pay us a visit, Nat," the judge called out. " I believe I recognize your friend, but his name escapes me."

"Deputy Attorney General Walter Haskell, sir. We met at a reception for Ike."

"I wish I could introduce you to everybody in the room, but I'm beginning to forget some of the names already. Gosh, there must be a dozen of us here."

"Fifteen to be exact, including just two nonsmokers," Joe said.

"Well," said the judge, "we have all the makings of a fine luncheon here; however, I do have a trial to attend to. I invite all counsels present to gather behind my shoulders. That would include Harry, Lou, Nat and Walter. In addition, I would request that Mr. Nishimura provide expert testimony for what I'm about to unveil."

The judge waited for the chosen names to line up behind him, and when that subgroup settled into place, he held up the first picture of Agent Sparks, resplendent in his birthday suit and stitched into the bed while Alice lorded over him with a leather belt. Nat and Harry cast shocked eyes upon the picture and then evil eyes upon Agent Sparks. As Sparks swallowed hard, Lou slapped himself on the cheek, where his hand remained as if glued.

"Of course you realize that these pictures can never be shown in my courtroom," the judge said flashing one revealing photo after the next. "Please explain to me, Mr. Nishimura, what kind of knots these are?"

Mr. Nishimura studied the picture for a moment and remarked, "This is so beautiful! The cocoon of the silk worm embraces the legs and ankles. From there, the web of the tortoise shell binds the abdomen and chest to the side frame. Finally, a slave's harness immobilizes the arms to the top posts. These last knots are difficult to position; however, young Alice has tied them perfectly. The harder you pull on them, the tighter they become, and if you pull too hard, your hands become blue."

Mr. Nishimura pointed at one object lying on the floor next to the bed. "*Aso!*" he exclaimed. "That is the lost teak chest of the Bagan Temple. I have long vowed to return it to its rightful place in Burma. The spirit of the Temple is troubled without it."

"Then you'll have to go back to Boston to get it," Alice said, her face still facing the far corner. "Just don't say anything you might regret after you open the lid. The chest remembers every word you say."

"Who is that woman?" Nat asked.

"She's a disobedient daughter," the judge replied, "and she's being punished by her father for her transgressions, so let's put this case to pasture. Lou Fisher here wants you to drop the charges against Mr. Preston, and you will agree. Otherwise, I will dismiss the charges without your assent and wait for you and the entire government to commit public suicide on any appeals process."

"Can I call Washington for approval?" Mr. Haskell asked. "I believe I could use a cigarette."

CHAPTER 88

A Touch of Pork

Deputy Attorney General Haskell placed his hand over the mouthpiece of the phone. "Mr. Kennedy," he called out. "The publicity on this case has placed the Justice Department in an awkward position. I believe that your son, the senator, could provide my staff with a fig leaf if a medevac brought him to Washington on Tuesday to vote on the farm bill that was tabled in May. Ike needs his support on this one."

"And what makes you think that the senator would listen to me?" Joe replied.

Laughter broke out from all sides of the room as if to say that Joe wasn't thinking clearly. "Please don't insult our intelligence," Judge Cummings said. "Without your guidance and wisdom, your fine son would be lost in the woods at midnight. He'll do whatever you tell him."

Joe rubbed his chin and mulled it over for a moment. "I suppose the senator would be happy to oblige the President, but what about Chief Fallon here? Does he get a fig leaf for his journey here?"

"Actually," the chief said, "our harbor unit has need of two launches to patrol Boston's international harbor. If Washington pays the bill, we would be happy to assist the Coast Guard and Customs in patrolling the ports of entry."

After speaking briefly into the phone, Mr. Haskell turned his attention back to Joe and said, "We're agreed. Boston gets two boats added to the farm bill, and Jack Preston gets a free pass."

"Isn't pork barrel politics wonderful?" the judge remarked. With applause ringing out from all directions, he added, "All right, counselors, let's go back into the courtroom and put this case to rest. Your settlement will certainly upset the press. Please be discreet when offering commentary."

For Lou, the judge's words really meant, "Keep your mouth shut," since the temptation always existed for the victorious counsel to crow about his achievement to any available microphone or note pad. And the more Lou thought about it, the more he liked the idea. He imagined that as the years rolled by, the mystique of the Preston case would grow into mythic status.

Clients would beat a path to his door to see if he might reveal anecdotes and unpublished insights, and Jack Preston's law practice would benefit from the same notoriety as well. Indeed, instead of ostracism from proper society, Jack might find himself invited to escort Alice to every cotillion and ball sponsored by his blue blooded peers and their svelte wives with the long gloves and the big hats. Yes, Lou saw it all, and he would say nothing of any meaning about this case to anybody at any time, now and forever.

CHAPTER 89

Reunion

When Lou, Harry, and Judge Cummings returned to their places in the courtroom, the members of the press had become restless children from the long recess. But with one smack of the gavel, they settled in like obedient second graders lest they receive an eviction notice from a trial that could easily push the circulation past two million for each of the major dailies. And when the only sound heard was the whirr of the judge's floor fan, Lou Fisher stood up and said, "Your Honor, the defense requests the court to dismiss all charges against Jack Preston in these proceedings."

The reporters cast sideways smirks to each other in recognition of this feeble plea that would go nowhere. "Mr. Dixon, how do you respond?" asked the judge.

"The United States has no objection, your Honor," said Harry in a low enough voice so that the back of the room could not hear him.

"Very well." said the Judge, "the court dismisses all charges against Jack Preston, and it personally thanks the jury for its service... Mr. Brown... You may step down from the witness stand."

As soon as the gavel dropped, the judge scooted back into his chambers. Meanwhile, the reporters stared blankly at each other, and nobody said a word. This was not how the story was supposed to turn out. In a fishnet stocking trial like this one, every ink-stained veteran expected the prosecution to deliver unprintable testimony of bedroom exploits, followed by a summation of the scandalous details and concluding with the silent drum roll that accompanied the reading of the guilty verdict. There would be drama, anticipation and suspense. But instead of a finale laden with bombs and fireworks, all that these gentlemen of the press got was the dull thump of a worn pillow hitting a soft carpet. And to each and every one of them, the long session in the Judge's chambers prior to the dismissal could only mean that the case against Jack Preston hit quicksand by way of some kind of legal technicality.

The readers would not be amused. Technicalities did not sell newspapers. Only hot dirty sex did. And now there was no more sex to sell. So with their heads hung low, reporters from over twenty states and three different continents mumbled to themselves in soft monotones as they shuffled out of the courtroom and watched their meal tickets sprout wings and fly away.

Only Chester Brown had any zing in his step. "Yes sir, Mr. Preston," he said greeting Jack with a bear hug, "I knew you were innocent all along. Even the United States government can't make these kind of charges stick against a good man."

Like the reporters, Jack too wore a dumbstruck expression. "How'd you do it, Lou?" he asked. "What was it Chester's testimony or the Boston newspaper that dropped a bomb on the case?"

"You were innocent, my friend, and sometimes that's all that counts," Lou said adding, "the judge requests that you join him in chambers. He has dozens of questions about transistors and I told him that you were the legal expert on this topic."

"You teach him well," Chester said waving adieu, but then Jack grabbed him by the hand.

"Alice! You said you met Alice! Where is she?" Jack asked.

"Trust me; she'll find you," Lou cut in adding. "Let's not keep the judge waiting."

Lou led Jack to the hallway entrance to the chambers, and after Jack knocked on the door, Lou wandered away. "We'll talk," came his parting words, and when he reached the stairwell, he looked back but did not linger.

The door to the chambers opened, and Jack beheld the vision of a siren with auburn hair, and he longed to go crashing against her rocks. "Jack, I hurt you, and I'm sorry," Alice said. "I should have called you, but—"

And before Alice could finish what she had to say, a baseball pressed against her lips muffled any remaining words that might have been. "The only thing we should be sorry for," Jack said, "is that as a result of coming to testify at my trial, a nice woman from San Francisco lost her cat. And for that, I am wracked with guilt."

"Is there anything we can do?"

"Let me handle this," Judge Cummings called from his roll top desk, where he paged through a stack of briefs. "And I promise you that the United States government will leave no stone unturned in the search for Mrs. Garcia's cat."

True to his word, the judge called the marshals' agency in San Francisco, which agreed to track down the missing tomcat. Indeed, the judge offered the services of two T-men from New York but reconsidered the idea when told of the extra expenses that the journey might entail. For one intoxicating moment, a scheme to send Agents Sparks and Malone clear across the country on a cat chase sent the judge into rapture and ecstasy... but rapture and ecstasy had no proper place in the sober thinking of a United States judge.

CHAPTER 90

A Short Ride

Halfway down Pearl Street, Joe Kennedy spotted his chauffeur waving at him, and the General, Mr. Nishimura, and he hastened to their air-conditioned ride. "I tell you, you're a cheapskate, David!" Joe exclaimed stepping into the car. "You should have paid Alice a hefty bonus for all the swag she brought you."

"I offered her a top managerial position with matching benefits, and she accepted. Doesn't that count for something?" the General returned. "Besides, an electrical engineer, who speaks Japanese, doesn't walk in your door every day. Isn't that right, Hiro?"

"Despite the tragedies of a difficult time, I believe that Alice is the perfect liaison in our enterprise," Mr. Nishimura said.

"Where to, sir?" Eamon asked.

"Just drop us off on the corner of Wall and Broadway, and we'll take it from there. I like barging in on people unannounced," Joe replied.

"Is that a fact?" the General quipped.

The car swung down Broadway, and Joe spotted a lone derby wending its way downtown against a tide of fedoras. "There's Chester. Let's pick him up," he said.

The car pulled over to the curb, and with the window rolled down, Joe and Chester exchanged toothy smiles. Chester claimed the front seat.

Joe patted Chester on the shoulder. "In celebration of our silver anniversary, I traded out your utility stocks for twenty thousand shares of RCA."

"You know best, Mr. Kennedy. I just shine shoes."

"Twenty thousand shares for a man who shines shoes!" Mr. Nishimura exclaimed. "America truly is a rich country. Why, you even celebrate anniversaries with silver."

"Actually, the twenty-fifth anniversary that Joe refers to happened on this very day in 1929," the General said. "Back then everybody played the market."

"That's a fact, sir," Chester added. "And when Mr. Kennedy sat in my chair for his morning shine, I asked him what stocks were good picks for the day."

Joe picked up from there. "Chester's question made me realize that if a bootblack had put down his hard-earned money into the market, then everybody from busboys to bellhops had done the same. This could only mean that the market had reached its peak with sucker money coming from an uninformed public. I made a few inquiries, and soon discovered that over ninety percent of the stock purchases came from borrowed money, and that with each flurry of purchases, the stock equity increased—only to be used as collateral to buy yet more stock with only ten percent down. The purchase cycles kept feeding upon themselves until blinding psychology alone floated the stock prices."

"And that's the gospel truth, too," Chester said. "The next week, Mr. Kennedy came to me with wild eyes, and he thanked me for opening them. He said, 'Sell it all! The market is a house of cards about to collapse. From now on, I'm managing your portfolio with mine, and we're investing in gold-backed greenbacks.' Heck, I figured he was crazy, but something in my bones told me he was right. So when all the aces to the deuces came crashing down in October, we walked away with our shirts still on our backs."

"So to celebrate that wondrous occasion, let's commence our foray onto the Street at your chair. Let's show Mr. Nishimura here what a first rate shine looks like."

"It would be my pleasure, sir. I'll give the man a shine to be proud of."

CHAPTER 91

The Stowaway

The attendant pushed the wheelchair past the hospital reception, and once out the door André Grignard pushed off the seat and took a deep breath of the crisp September air. Vengeance weighed heavily on his mind, and he vowed that Alice would pay dearly for the stitches sewn into his scalp. Yes, he would track her down, and when she least expected it, he would pop out of her bedroom closet and give her a monster dose of her own medicine. Just thinking about tying her to the bedposts and taping her mouth shut made his pulse race, but that would be just the beginning of the fun. After stropping a straight razor, he would disarticulate one hemline after the other from her body and pause between garments so that he might inscribe cursive epithets into the newly revealed flesh. For extra excitement, he would load a revolver with a blank shot and spin the cylinder so that every now and then between the cigarette burns and electric shocks, he might aim the barrel straight into her mouth and pull the trigger just like the Japanese soldiers had done to their prisoners during the occupation...

Except they used real bullets!

André waved to a taxi discharging a hospital visitor and had hastened toward it when Detective Finn Sweeney and Detective Sergeant Ed Quinn jumped out of an unmarked car and slapped handcuffs on him. "André Grignard, you are under arrest for the murder of Hiroshi Nishimura," said Sergeant Quinn.

"But that's not possible," André protested. I helped Hiro prepare for a New York trade show not even an hour before I arrived at Alice's place. He was alive!"

"So how come the fingerprints on the syringe that poisoned him match the fingerprints we took from you when you were out cold?" Detective Sweeney asked.

"It's a lie! Alice must have done it. On the night you found me, she tried to inject me with thiopental, but I snatched the syringe away. That's why my prints are on it!"

Detective Quinn palmed André's head into the back of the unmarked car, and the three sped off past downtown, eventually winding up at the docks, where they drove onto a pier. On one side of the pier, stevedores had just finished loading spools of electric cable onto a freighter and now strolled toward the street while on the other side, customs agents and brokers passed in and out of the customs house.

"Why have you taken me here?" said André.

Sergeant Quinn removed the handcuffs and pointed to the end of the pier. "An alert customs agent spotted the body floating over there."

Then, Detective Sweeney pointed to brown spots beneath André's feet. "But that's where Mr. Nishimura met his setting sun. We have a witness who can place you here."

"You're crazy!" André exclaimed momentarily eyeing the crew of the adjacent ship casting off her lines. "Why would I want to kill Hiro? We had a profitable relationship together."

Just then, a customs agent approached the three and said, "I see you got your man, detectives. We saw him mucking around at the far end of the dock last night."

The customs agent headed into the customs house, and Detective Sweeney shook his head and clicked his tongue. "We've never fried a Frenchman before," he cracked. "Do we serve you up with a glass of white or red?"

Suddenly shots rang out from the street end of the pier, and while André froze, the detectives hit the ground.

"Cop shot! Cop shot!" a stevedore screamed, and the two detectives raced toward the street. At this point, the freighter blasted its horn twice, and as a stevedore throttled in the gangplank, André took a flying leap from the retreating end to land safely on the deck.

The ship's engines roared to life, and as she angled away from the pier, Quinn and Sweeney arrived dockside just in time to receive a salute from the ship's captain. After returning the farewell gesture, the two detectives fixated on her stern, which said:

BOIS DE VINCENNES
MARSEILLES

The customs agent returned with a clipboard and said, "We've got a full plate of Bordeaux in Superintendent Fallon's name. Can one of you guys sign for it?"

Sergeant Quinn put down his John Hancock. "The chief is throwing a party tonight on account of his cadging two new launches for the department from Uncle Sam. He told us to invite Customs and Coast Guard. Do you want to come?" he asked.

The customs agent tore off a carbon copy of the bill of lading and handed it to Quinn. "You may not realize it," the agent said, "but you just signed for the preeminent vintage of France. We wouldn't miss this bash if we had to sail back there again for World War III."

CHAPTER 92

Operation Felix

The word came down from the top. A joint training exercise would involve multiple departments at the federal, state and local levels.

The scenario was this: A communist infiltrator had stolen several tomes of top-secret information, which revealed the names and addresses of all allied intelligence agents and their informants behind the iron curtain. The information was encrypted with an unbreakable code; however, a second infiltrator in San Francisco had already stolen the code and had tattooed it on his landlady's cat. As an FBI dragnet closed in on him, he fled with the cat to a house on Tenth Avenue in San Mateo. There, the infiltrator went down in a hail of bullets, but not before the spooked cat jumped out the window and fled in panic.

The mission: find the landlady's cat before the communist infiltrators got to him and skinned him alive!

At 09:15, FBI agents knocked on the door of Mrs. Reina Garcia, a resident of Hyde Street in San Francisco. At their request, Mrs. Garcia provided several black and white snapshots and matching negatives of a tomcat responding to the name of "Eddy."

At 09:42, photography technicians at the federal crime laboratory in San Francisco enlarged the photographs to eight-by-twelves and cropped out the extraneous background.

At 10:41, the technicians had finished replicating one hundred copies of each photograph for joint distribution to the FBI, the U.S. Marshals' Agency, the Metropolitan San Mateo Police Department, the San Mateo County Sheriff's Department, the San Mateo Animal Control Department, the California Highway Patrol and elements of the National Guard at Fort Ord. At this same time, FBI agents interviewed Dr. Eric Landers, a zoologist and feline specialist at the San Francisco Zoo, who stated that uprooted tomcats in strange environments could become disoriented to their new home if they immediately chased after a female in heat once they ran from the premises. Dr. Landers also said that feral cats often frequented the porches and garages of lonely widows, who left food out for them. These cats often made their homes underneath the porches.

At 11:33, the Department of Motor Vehicles issued a list of all women sixty years of age or older, who lived in San Mateo.

At 12:17, the combined taskforce fanned out over the greater San Mateo area and focused their greatest attention upon the homes listed by the DMV.

By 14:26, the task force had encountered their tenth feral cat living under the porch of a LOL (little old lady). So far, no cat matched the photograph of Eddy.

At 17:21, county deputies made tentative identification of Eddy lolling in the bushes of the home of one Edith Morrison of Edinburgh Street. The deputies radioed Animal Control units for backup and opened a can of tuna fish, which they placed on the front steps of the residence to keep the animal occupied.

At 17:25, the Animal Control unit captured the animal unharmed with a spray net.

At 18:21 after positive identification, the mission was declared a success, and the animal was reunited with its tearful owner.

Utilizing a combined manpower of one hundred and twelve public employees, the entire operation took nine hours and six minutes at a cost of $3,525!

CHAPTER 93

Sacred Vows

Beneath a veil of white lace, Alice's eyes cast a spell upon Jack, and he never heard a word the pastor said, not that it would have mattered much. The pastor's homily began with tributes to marital love, parental love and God's eternal love with quotes from scripture tying them all together. Yet with their eyes still locked in upon each other, Alice leaned in on Jack and whispered, "The vows are insufficient. I find them too pedestrian."

"The Church will not let us write individual vows," Jack whispered back. "Vow to me here and now, and I will vow to you in return. In this sanctuary, all that we promise shall be held sacred."

"Very well, my love...I vow that I shall never turn you away from our bed, but if I ever catch your idolatrous dog poking around in another gal's shed, I vow that you will wake up with your four limbs tied to the bed-posts, and you will watch in horror and agony as I slowly hack him off with a serrated knife."

Alice batted her eyes, and Jack knew that she meant business, but he too had business of his own to declare. "And I vow to you, my sweet, that you may tie me up and tease me with as many naughty games as your mischievous heart desires, but if you ever again attempt to extract privileged information from me, I vow that I will lace your Chablis with strychnine, and you will wait until your retching and convulsions blow out matching hernias before I call for an ambulance."

Jack held out his hand and said, "Do we have a deal?"

"Deal!" Alice said shaking on it.

The pastor descended from his pulpit to administer the marital vows on top of the more binding declarations that the handsome couple had already exchanged. And with ritual and formality remaining intact, Jack and Alice did promise to love and honor each other, and when asked if they took each other to have and to hold until death do they part, they each replied in succession, "I do."

"I now pronounce you man and wife."

At about that same time, Mickey Mantle hit a grand slam into the upper right field deck of Yankee Stadium. When news of this reached the wedding reception, Jack knew that pleasures greater than ever before awaited him from Alice that night.

Indeed, in the nine celibate months before the wedding when Mama Mercier chaperoned all their dates, some anonymous soul had mailed Alice back her White Tigress Book. This allowed her substantial time to master the difficult exercises in the final three chapters...

...And the thought of turning Jack into a quivering pile of mush made her tingle with pleasure.

EPILOGUE – VIGNETTES OF 1959

CHAPTER 94

Cuba Si—Yanqui No

The New Year came to Havana with a seismic jolt. Shortly after the stroke of midnight, the events manager of the Hotel Nacional interrupted the orchestra in the Grand Ballroom and played a radio news bulletin over the PA system to the rum-soaked revelers. President Battista had fled the country, and in his stead, an advance party of the Orthodoxo Revolutionary Guard had moved in to take over the administrative buildings of government. After several jokes circulated about the questionable hygiene of these unshaven comrades and their hirsute leader, Fidel Castro, the band pumped the dance floor with pulsating mambo rhythms, and the well-heeled patricians partied until dawn, around which time Andy Scott and his date disappeared into a room upstairs for a bit of sunrise romance.

Nothing had changed in Havana... or so it seemed.

As the January sun beat down upon the bougainvilleas and poinsettias, and tropical birds chirped and cawed in the back garden of his walled hacienda, Terry Scott sucked deeply on his Cuba Libre and dialed from channel to channel on his TV set only to find Generalissimo Fidel's cigar chomping puss on display at each station. Terry put down his glass and listened. So this was the man who toppled that son-of-a-bitch Battista, whose minions couldn't pause for a moment to keep their hands out of a rich fugitive's pocket. Let's see what the new kid in town wanted.

"...Yes, my fellow countrymen... Throwing out the corrupt guard was the easy part. Now comes the hard work. The revolution must continue, and together we will create a new paradise of empowered citizens, each equal to the other. Your people's army succeeded not just because their revolutionary training brought down a rotting system destined to fail, but also because these former peasants learned to read and write. Yes, my countrymen, with true revolutionary fervor, they read the great works of the scholars of history such as..."

Terry dozed off into the land of Nod, and when he woke up, the television had walked away along with the china, the silverware, and the entire collection of cellared wine. A receipt left on the kitchen table and signed by one Captain Juan Sanchez revealed that this booty had been confiscated for the benefit of the revolution.

So the new kid wanted to play hardball! Terry gave long odds that the bearded one wouldn't survive two months in office.

But two months came and went, and the situation went from bad to desperate. The Generalissimo, meanwhile, had become bolder by the moment, and each night he donned his fatigue cap and lit up a presidential-size Cohiba before his beaming mug addressed the adoring masses out there in television and radio land, where he supplied them with the latest update in revolutionary progress. Sure, he could brag about the revolution producing new childcare clinics and discounted prices for bread and tobacco, but what in blazes was revolutionary in taking at gunpoint a thriving whorehouse and turning it into a clinic? And did anybody ever tell His Excellency that those ridiculously low prices on bread caused long lines and shortages?

An official-sounding knock pounded on Terry's door, and the local block captain of the revolution handed him a signed ultimatum. All homeowners in the Varadero Beach area had to share their dwelling with a second family henceforth, and they could not charge them rent.

This became the final straw; Terry knew that it wouldn't be long before the revolution confiscated the deed to his property outright, and better judgment told him that he dare not complain to anybody for fear that one of the ubiquitous informants new to the neighborhood might tattle on him to some revolutionary this-or-that and accuse him of counterrevolutionary activity. The consequences here were thus; he would wind up with his back to a wall taking lead in the chest like the numerous high-ranking acquaintances he used to know, and who had simply disappeared.

Terry realized that he had to leave Cuba, but because of his fugitive status, he knew he had limited options on where to go. Brazil had no extradition treaty with the United States, but it also had a notorious reputation for bleeding embezzlers dry. He wasn't going to chance getting squeezed by any muggers with badges. Switzerland represented a more viable option, and although it extradited murderers and rapists back to the United States, his recent research had shown him that it had no laws on its books for the return of inside traders. Yes, the logic of Switzerland was compelling: over three quarters of his assets resided in a bank in Zurich; Swissair flew there nonstop from Havana; and because his American passport didn't expire until May, he reasoned that he would have no problem leaving Cuba unmolested.

Unfortunately, the revolution refused to pay a gargantuan bill for aviation fuel, which was racked up by the previous administration, and so in true counterrevolutionary fashion, the oil companies cut off their fuel supplies to the Havana airport. This meant that all transatlantic flights had to stop in Miami for refueling, and Terry couldn't risk any spot checks there by the American authorities. He needed an alternate route.

After downing a half-liter of rum for inspiration, Terry called his son Andy and invited him to his hacienda for dinner. Andy owned a fishing boat, whose name, "Papa Hemingway," evoked images of deep-sea adventure and marathon battles reeling in airborne marlin. Andy had built up a respectable business with the boat, which the tourists chartered with cash, and which the occasional showgirl hired with her other assets. As of late, however, Andy had complained that the tourists had to contract him through a central agency, which collected the payment in dollars and then paid him in revolutionary pesos. Obviously, the revolution got the better part of the deal, but like his father, Andy knew better than to tread down the path of counterrevolutionary commentary in public. As a consolation, the revolution provided him with all his marine fuel plus a free slip in a marina, where a garrison of revolutionary guard kept his craft from getting hot-wired by anybody looking to joyride into Key West. Andy appreciated this in spite of the fact that he couldn't put his pesos down on any more cock fights because they were, well, counterrevolutionary.

Terry failed to convince his son that night to beach the boat somewhere in the Bahamas, where they could charter a jet to Geneva or Zurich. Andy had his reasons; he liked the tropics and didn't want to learn yet another language, and besides, Switzerland didn't have a coastline. Then again, a cute trainee in the revolutionary maritime guard had made goo-goo eyes at him, and she had the finest set of knockers he had ever wanted to sink his face into. Andy kissed his father goodbye and told him to write when he reached his new address.

The next day, Terry flashed his American passport to board a plane for an expedient detour to Mexico City, and the revolutionary guard let him pass without incident. Two hours later, he presented the same passport to curious federales in the Mexico City transit lounge but found himself surrounded by armed officers. To appease them, he ripped open a seam in his jacket and pulled out a hundred dollar bill, but they wouldn't accept the money.

"I am sorry, sir, but this matter is beyond my control," the jefe said. "You are one of the most wanted fugitives to fly out of Cuba to date. I advise you to go with the American authorities when they come for you. You will not like our jails here."

Terry wrote to his son from his new address at the Tombs.

Later that night, Harry Dixon and Nat Reiss toasted their overdue case by clinking Cuba Libres at Manhattan's version of the Copa Cabana.

CHAPTER 95

A Day's Work

Agent Sparks and his men pulled off to the side of the road and stared straight up. A trail of smoke drifting over the cliff told them that they were downwind of both the fire and any hound dog's nose. Sparks looked toward the gully and noted the bullet holes on the yellow curve sign just before the road veered left. Three miles back, a local marksman had shot out the inside of the O in the stop sign, and for good measure, had shot off its octagonal corners. By Sparks' reckoning, only a nine-year-old would have had the irresponsibility to waste all of that precious ammo. Daddy must have put a switch real hard to him for not bringing back any food for his efforts.

The pop of a rifle shot echoed off the cliffs, and the men hit the ground like marines on the last day of boot camp. False alarm...

The stoker had fed the fire with green pine cured in gasoline, which cracked like a Winchester when it landed in the hearth. Sparks knew the sound, but he also knew that real Winchesters as well as cocked Brownings and Remingtons awaited them just over the rise. He motioned to his men, and they checked their weapons, all of them vintage Thompson automatics with drum clips. Sparks remembered how Mike Malone used to romanticize about bootleggers surrendering en masse at the very sight of a Tommy gun. That might have been true back on Long Island, but here in the Great Smoky Mountains, Tommy had to talk as well.

The men draped camouflage netting over their Jeeps and trekked up the mountainside. Ahead of them, a curious pile of leaves stayed intact where the prevailing westerlies would have blown them further. One man gently swept the leaves with a bamboo rake, only to uncover three bear traps, each one ready to bite a leg off.

The men sidestepped around the traps and kept a lookout for any stray snares or booby traps. Slowly and methodically they advanced until they came in sight of the operation, and what a beauty she was! Two neatly stacked piles of cinder blocks provided the necessary support for a pair of railroad irons upon which a three hundred gallon cauldron fashioned from welded oil drums sat, the butt end getting roasted by a roaring fire from below. The top of the cauldron tapered into a vertical tower, which assured that all the water vapors and heavy oils dripped back into the boiling mash while only the most volatile of spirits rose up into the copper condensing coil, where they cascaded into a sawed off garden hose that the tiller directed over a row of milk bottles.

Sparks timed the tiller and noted that roughly forty seconds passed for him to change bottles. A driver then crated the merchandise and loaded it into the back of his pickup. Meanwhile, two sentries wheeled out a dolly holding a bathtub full of mash.

Sparks couldn't believe his good fortune. While the sentries were preoccupied with housekeeping, nobody was watching out for the revenuers. But then the pungent wind shifted, and a gray pile of wrinkles lying in the only patch of sun that the tall pines allowed let out a hound dog howl.

"Federal agents! Everybody freeze!" Sparks hollered though a bullhorn, whereupon two of his men ventilated the boiling cauldron with their Tommy guns.

Mash gushed out the bullet holes and doused the fire below. All was safe. With raised arms, the bootleggers came quietly, and as a reward, Sparks allowed them to take a gallon of the good stuff along for the ride. Those hillbilly grins would have made a jack-o-lantern feel in good company.

For Sparks, this kind of work beat the heck out of working on Wall Street. Sure, the bigwigs in Washington took it upon themselves to banish him to the hills for his indiscretion with Alice, but all that did was cast him into his element. Back in New York, the crooks made ten times his salary, but here in his not so newfound home, the earning ratios had become reversed. Asheville, North Carolina may not have been paradise, but Sparks saw it as a good place, where a man earning a government wage could raise his family in comfort. And the booze wasn't too bad either.

CHAPTER 96

Dodger Blue

Opening day brought a full house to the Los Angeles Memorial Coliseum, and Chester Brown loaded up his carry tray with wieners to serve them. In his mind, the Brooklyn Dodgers had passed into ancient history even though they had played in California for only one year. But back in their Crow Hill brownstone, the year dragged for Chester and his wife, Miriam. Their youngest daughter had walked down the aisle in January, and, come spring training time, the baby of the family shoved off on the SS Saratoga for the Canal Zone. Along with the Dodgers, the Giants also headed out to the Golden State, and New York City suddenly found itself without a National League team. As Chester saw it, if a man had to drive all the way to Philly to see the Dodgers play, then a move to the fault line never looked better.

Following their westward trek, Chester and Miriam settled into a Baldwin Hills Mediterranean, where after two months of working at absolutely nothing, an old craving grabbed Chester by the buffing hand. On impulse, he called the Statler Hotel to apply for a bootblack position because that morning, *The Los Angeles Times* had reported that Walter O'Malley, the owner of the Dodgers, always stayed there whenever he came to town.

Mr. O'Malley may not have remembered, but Chester intended to remind him that he used to polish his wingtips back in the 1930s when Mr. O'Malley had an office in the Lincoln Building across from Grand Central Station. This was no coincidence. In those hardest of times, Mr. O'Malley had established himself as such a successful bankruptcy lawyer that Mr. Kennedy drooled at the very prospect of discovering his client list, so that he could short their stocks. Given his singular talent, Chester's marching orders were simple. He had to memorize the pictures of hundreds of corporate executives and report back which ones took an elevator ride to the "grave dancer's" floor. To accomplish this, Mr. Kennedy acquired concession space in the lobby of the Lincoln Building, where even Mr. O'Malley's shoes felt Chester's skilled touch.

After the war, Mr. Kennedy had the opportunity to buy a one-quarter interest in the Dodgers, but he eventually declined the offer by stating that if he and O'Malley locked horns, the newspapers just might rename the team the Fighting Irish. Chester wasn't amused; neither were the folks in South Bend, Indiana.

Chester never did get that job at the Statler Hotel, so he did what Mr. Kennedy might have done; he leased concession space in the lobby, where his business sign proclaimed, "Get That New York Shine." The hustle worked with the bankers and brokers visiting downtown L.A., and Chester's customer flow exceeded his best days on Broadway. For the hotel, however, the in-house shoeshine business dropped substantially, and so the management approached Chester with a buyout offer. Thinking again like Mr. Kennedy, Chester told them that he would accept the deal, but only if they could deliver Mr. O'Malley for personal service. The next day, the two men renewed old ties, and Mr. O'Malley offered Chester a job of his choice at the Coliseum if he would shine the shoes of all the ballplayers including those of the now retired Jackie Robinson. Chester didn't have to say a word; the tears running down his cheeks said it for him.

"Red-hots! Get your red-hots!" Chester hollered, much to the puzzlement of the spectators in the field level seats.

"Uh, mister... what's a red-hot?" asked a freckle-faced boy.

"It's a hot dog," his father answered. "That's what we used to call them back in Brooklyn."

"Your dad sure got that right," Chester chuckled.

"We'll take two red-hots with mustard, sir... and welcome to California."

Chester moved on with his wares, and a thunderous crack of the bat electrified the fans. "...And it's a moon shot for Wally Moon!" shouted the radio announcer's voice coming from the transistor radio of a nearby fan.

Chester watched the ball sail over the right field fence. He just knew the Dodgers would take the World Series this year.

CHAPTER 97

Family Business

Emily never thought business or money were proper subjects for dinner-time conversation, but what choice did she have? Barely a month after receiving his masters degree in psychology, Will had joined Denise in Oliver's behavioral research firm, and to hear the three of them talk, it seemed like only one client really mattered. Denise stretched her arm over a serving platter of carved roast beef and handed Oliver an eight-by-ten glossy. She then waited for him to don his reading glasses and study the photo's framing and composition.

"The picture of Big Jack at the helm of his sailboat resonates on all the right emotional levels with our subjects," she said. "His steady hand on the wheel shows resolution in the face of a stiff wind tousling his hair. The image certainly evokes a presidential persona."

"I would add," said Will, "that all the maritime shots of Big Jack that we tested on our subjects scored exceptionally well. I believe that at this point we should move past the images and onto the political issues."

"That's not our purview," Oliver replied. "Our job is to motivate the customer—or in this case the voter—visually, by using the proper imagery. Let's leave the politics to the politicians."

"If you ask me," Emily interjected, "the senator could always use a little more meat on his bones. Besides, he hasn't even declared his intention to run for the office let alone receive the nomination from his party. That's why I'm rather puzzled why Joe Kennedy would call upon you to sell his son to the voters as if he were a bar of soap."

Oliver liked the comparison between a political candidate and a bar of soap, and he wondered if Emily realized how much truth she had uttered in that statement. "Jack Kennedy will become our next president. Joe Kennedy has decreed it, and we are fulfilling that destiny," he returned. "Please pass the gravy, Denise."

CHAPTER 98

Soft Time

With bowed head and stooped posture, Terrence Scott faced the judge. As a show of support, Lou Fisher placed his arm on his client's shoulder. At the prosecution table, a somewhat chubbier Harry Dixon drew an oversized V for victory sign on the first page of his trial notes. Meanwhile, the judge motioned to the defendant. "Mr. Scott, do you have anything to say before I pass sentence?"

"Only that I will do whatever is humanly possible to convince my son, Andrew, to return to these shores to accept American justice. He is politically naïve and has become seduced by that freebooter, Castro."

"I wish you success in that endeavor. The court now finds that because of your cooperation with the U.S. Attorney's Office for full restitution of funds, you shall serve six months at the Federal Prison in Danbury, Connecticut. The said sentence is to commence on the first day of September."

The judge tapped his gavel to close the proceedings and departed. Lou and Harry shook hands, and after popping a stick of chewing gum into his mouth, Harry followed the bailiff and the stenographer out the door, which left Lou and Terry by themselves. For Lou, an opportunity to broach a secretive subject had arrived. "Reliable sources at the Tropicana tell me that you and your buddies ran a stock pool on the Havana exchange. Come March the first, exactly how much legal tender awaits you in your alpine piggy bank?" he asked.

"Well," Terry said, his hand momentarily covering the side of his mouth, "my accountant in Zurich tells me that three and a half million dollars in untaxed funds await me next spring. Dare I say that if our good friends at the IRS think they can charge me ninety cents on the dollar for money earned outside the country, they are whistling Dixie."

Lou always appreciated honesty from a crook, and so he had some free words of wisdom to offer. "And I say, you won't break the law as long as you don't repatriate your money for the next eighteen months. Assuming the statutes don't change, I'll refer you to a tax lawyer, who can legally import your funds for two cents tax on the dollar. Does that change the picture?"

"Damn it, Lou, I love this country!"

Lou placed his hand back on Terry's shoulder. "And does that love extend to setting me up with Captain Andy for a little Marlin fishing?"

"For as long as the revolution allows, you've got a second home in Havana."

Lou winced at the very mention of the revolution. The way things stood, Cuba was becoming redder than a ripe tomato. Within a year, maybe two years tops, he foresaw the American government breaking relations with the country. Still, that gave him plenty of time to hook the big one.

"Set me up for January," Lou said adding, "and by that, I mean the entire month. I'll tip your boy real money on the side."

Terry shook on it. "For real money, Andy might even throw in a girlfriend," he remarked.

CHAPTER 99

Saturday Morning

Jack placed JP on the baby swing and lowered the safety bar. With a gentle shove, he pushed the swing and sent the boy on a pendulum's journey. Alice watched from her park bench roost and rubbed her belly. Baby number two would be making his or her debut in a matter of weeks, and Alice remembered that she had once promised to give Jack a dozen of them. Ever since her return from the infamous Back Bay apartment, Jack had never reminded her of those loose words, and she silently thanked him for his selective memory.

Alice told herself that she would only think of the present moment even though she had a laundry list of errands to run before Mama and Papa came down from West Point. There, Papa carried the bloated title of Civilian Academic Adviser for Guerilla Warfare Training at the Military Academy, and Mama grew somewhat sugary viniferous grapes on their ten-acre farm near the river. Always the cutest one, little sister Antoinette taught second grade in the village, where her off limits status broke many a cadet's heart.

Alice looked toward the street and admired all the stately oaks. After only one season of living in Bronxville, she had developed an arborist's love of the suburbs despite the fact that all the ladies donned in pearl necklaces and clip-on earrings insisted upon practicing their fractured French with her. For his part, Jack avoided any gaze toward the thoroughfare. Moments before, Roy and Judy Tucker had escorted their two girls past the park, and only the air raid siren would have drowned out the young ones' squeals of protest about having to come back later to use the swings when three safety seats hung empty and waiting. Jack might have used this opportunity to square things with Judy, but Alice had noted her standoffish demeanor on a previous near encounter and had advised him from a woman's point of view to respect Judy's distance.

Jack also wanted to settle with Roy. After marrying Judy back in '56, Roy must have hit the jackpot on their wedding night because Judy delivered twins nine months later, at which time the neighbors spotted a delivery of separate beds to their household. Jack considered telling Roy about the pregnancy preventing pills that Alice had received from Dr. John Rock up in Boston; however, Roy would have to make the first move in any rapprochement before Jack would reveal this greatest of secrets. Otherwise, Judy would never consent to the possibility of bearing an accident, and Roy's only bedroom companion would be his hand.

"Push me higher, Daddy!" JP squealed, and Jack gave a little extra *oomph* in his push.

Both the big kid and the little kid giggled in harmony, and with a few pushes more, Jack felt a tap on the back of his shoulder. When he turned around, Alice nailed him on the kisser.

"Mommy, are you kissing Daddy again?" JP asked.

"You'll get your turn, sweetheart," Alice replied.

She never could resist that little face.

CHAPTER 100

Temple Rites

The evening sun cast long shadows from the spires of the Thatbyinnyu Temple in Bagan, and Hiroshi Nishimura covered his eyes to better plead for absolution from the spirits keeping watch over this house of weathered stones. Hiro had taken possession of the teak chest right after Jack's trial and had always intended to return it to its rightful place here, but due to a hectic schedule working for the Ministry of International Trade and Industry, an opportunity in the form of free time had not presented itself. Nevertheless, the past five years of unprecedented success at the ministry deserved recognition beyond money and praise, and so in gratitude for outstanding work, the government awarded him and his associates a two-week furlough. Hiro vowed to use that time to clear his conscience.

And here he was in Burma at last. Upon removing his hands from his eyes, he bowed once to the temple and then once to the teak chest. Finally, he bowed once more to a Shinto priest, who held a cylinder of burning incense. The priest then bowed in return and led the way into the temple, where Hiro placed the chest between the two life-size statues of the Buddha. In unison this time, he and the priest bowed once to each statue and then to the teak chest. As the priest chanted, Hiro opened the chest and placed a single pearl inside. So that all could see it shine in the faint light, he left the lid open.

Hiro took a deep breath and as he exhaled slowly, his mind wandered to another time. *Straighten the sash on your kimono and gently remove the tea service from the chest, young Alice. Remember all that I teach you and learn from my soldiers as well.*

For Hiro, the incense had never smelled so sweet as it did at that moment's recollection. This was a good omen, for the spirits were pleased.